LITTLE SISTER LOST

A POWERFUL STORY OF THE SEARCH FOR
ANNA LIEBER, HER HUSBAND, AND CHILDREN:
CASUALTIES OF THE COLD WAR

By:

Anthony Joseph Sacco Sr.

WESTBOW
PRESS
A DIVISION OF THOMAS NELSON

As previously mentioned, this book is a work of fact-based fiction. Several names have been changed to protect the privacy of some of the people involved, who may or may not be public figures.

Occasionally, characters, places and incidents have been created and inserted into events that actually happened. In those instances, dialogue is the result of fictional interpretation by the author of certain events — what might have been said or done — thus giving each event a plausible explanation or meaning. Where this occurs, the interpretation is the product of the author's sometimes fertile, sometimes not so fertile imagination.

If you're reading this, you're probably reading a re-write of Little Sister Lost, which was originally published in 2004 by iUniverse.com, but has now been re-published by WestBow Press, a division of the Thomas Nelson publishing house. I'm hoping that the changes, corrections, and revisions to this edition will make the book a stronger, more interesting, and more rewarding read for all you Matt Dawson fans.

WestBow Press books may be ordered through booksellers or by contacting:

WestBow Press
A Division of Thomas Nelson
1663 Liberty Drive
Bloomington, IN 47403
www.westbowpress.com
1-(866) 928-1240

Anthony Joseph Sacco, Sr.
2812 Foothills Road
Cheyenne, WY 82009-4538
Tel: 307-638-9338
Fax: 307-638-9338

Because of the dynamic nature of the Internet, any web addresses or links contained in this book may have changed since publication and may no longer be valid. The views expressed in this work are solely those of the author and do not necessarily reflect the views of the publisher, and the publisher hereby disclaims any responsibility for them.

Any people depicted in stock imagery provided by Thinkstock are models, and such images are being used for illustrative purposes only.

Certain stock imagery © Thinkstock.

ISBN: 978-1-4497-7836-1 (e)
ISBN: 978-1-4497-7837-8 (sc)
ISBN: 978-1-4497-7838-5 (hc)

Library of Congress Control Number: 2012923042

Printed in the United States of America

WestBow Press rev. date: 2/25/2013

This book is dedicated to my children: Sue Ellen,
Mary Catherine, Tony, Jr.,
and Lee Anne. May God bless you, always!

"Run the straight race

through God's good grace,

Lift up thine eyes

and seek His face;

Life with its way before us lies

Christ is the path

and Christ is the prize."

John Mansell, Poet

Acknowledgements:

THE FEDERAL GOVERNMENT REPOSITORY AT Johns Hopkins University, where I reviewed transcripts of House Un-American Activities Committee (HUAC) hearings that took place in 1948, 1949 and 1950.

The Francis X. Archibald Collection at Loyola University Maryland, where I found additional corroborative documents dealing with HUAC and the Senate Internal Security Subcommittee during that same period.

In Book 2, Chapter 10, the reminiscences of Richard M. Nixon about his marriage to Thelma Catherine "Pat" Ryan Nixon, known to her friends and the rest of the word as "Patricia," or simply "Pat," and their honeymoon trip, were based upon a book whose title and author I cannot now recall. I apologize for not being able to give complete credit to a fine author.

THANKS:

To Karen Christianson, Vice-Consul, US Embassy, Warsaw, Poland, and Francisco J. Hernandez, Vice-Consul, US Embassy, Mexico City, Mexico.

To L. Eugene Towner, Esquire (who passed away on April 10. 2007), a Towson lawyer and as close a friend as I've ever had, who referred me to Janet Gaines, a resident of Branford, Connecticut.

To Janet Gaines, a fine lady possessed of an inquiring mind, for assistance in running down leads and obtaining records. She discovered Rhoda Loeb and put me in touch with her.

To Jean W. Larch and her son, Richard, the former and present owners of Riptide Cottage respectively, who provided vital information.

To Rhoda Loeb, without whose concern and help the final piece of the puzzle might never have been put into place.

To George Brendan Dowell, another friend, a former Hollywood scriptwriter, author of several plays and former teacher at Vassar and Goucher Colleges. George, who passed away on January 7, 1997, was a truly cosmopolitan man who grew old gracefully. More importantly, during his final years he was a holy man whose life became a model of spirituality for those who knew him.

To Joan Henley, a former English teacher in the Graduate Division of the University of Baltimore, now retired, for her suggestions regarding clarity, punctuation and detail.

To Dr. Charles J. Scheve, of Towson, Maryland, now also deceased, for his fine job of proofreading, once again. Charles had worked on *The China Connection,* earlier.

To Eric B. and Eric S. Bettelheim, Esquire, Ralph W. Bettelheim, Jim Haynes, Esquire, Howard Keller, Richard La Course, Mary Mc Garvey, Jennifer and Marcella Walton and all of Alvin Zelinka's friends, co-workers and acquaintances who took the time to talk to me. Alvin was truly blessed to have had such fine people around him during his life.

To Dr. Kevin Hula, associate professor of Political Science at Loyola College, Baltimore, MD, for his comments regarding Book Two.

Author's Note:

LITTLE SISTER LOST IS THE first of the Matt Dawson adventures. In this book, I introduce Dawson and chronicle his initial venture into the investigative field. It's a work of fact-based fiction, the emphasis being on "fact-based." Events described here occurred before those recorded in *The China Connection*, so if you have *that* kind of orderly mind, you might want to read this book first.

I was pleased to play a part in the attempt, by another good friend and fine attorney, Robert N. Winkler, to deliver the assets of Alvin Zelinka's estate to his deceased client's heir. Bob's diligence, his willingness to go the extra mile for his clients, and his cooperation during the investigation were extremely helpful. Bob Winkler likes people and enjoys the practice of law. These attitudes show in the way he deals with his clients. Seeing Bob at work, one is tempted to say, "Now that's the way all lawyers should be." His actions were in the finest tradition of the Bar. Many lawyers would have done no less. Many do less.

This was the first investigation to locate a missing person that I ever did after entering the business in 1990. I'm grateful to Bob for giving me the opportunity to test my skills in this type of work. I also thank him for his thoughtful critique of the manuscript.

BOOK ONE

"The United States has become great and rich under the power of an economic system that has set no limits on the free pursuit of the individual, and has thereby made room for the development of the country's productive power. America's unprecedented economic prosperity is not merely the result of the richness of the American land, but rather of the economic policy that understood how best to take advantage of the opportunities that the land offers. American economic policy has always rejected, and still rejects today, any protection for inferiority and uncompetitiveness over efficiency and competitiveness. The success of this policy has been so great that one would believe the Americans would never change it."

> — "Changes in American Economic Policy," by Austrian economist, Ludwig von Mises, in a talk delivered to the Vienna Industrial Club in 1926, upon his return from a year of traveling in the United States.

> *"We hold these truths to be self-evident, that all Men are created equal, that they are endowed by their Creator with certain inalienable Rights, that among these are Life, Liberty and the Pursuit of Happiness —That to secure these rights, governments are instituted among Men, deriving their just powers from the consent of the governed ... "*

> — The Declaration of Independence, United States Constitution, July 1776.

PROLOGUE

Saturday, March 3, 1990
Cuernavaca, Morelos, Mexico
The American Community
4:50 p.m. Mexico Central Time (MCT)

CAMINO REAL, A TREE-SHADED SIDE street just off the main drag, was only two blocks long. No one was around as Matt Dawson turned the nose of his rented car into it. This place had been nicknamed "The City of Eternal Spring," by the German explorer - naturalist, Alexander von Humboldt, in the Nineteenth Century.

The warm Cuernavacan day was coming to an end. As the late afternoon sun descended toward the western horizon, cooler air had already begun flowing down to the city from the higher elevations in the nearby Sierra de Chichinautzen Mountains.

Like all the houses here, George Cohan's modest adobe hacienda was old, rambling and all on one floor. The vegetation surrounding it included thick *dama de la noche* bushes, which partially screened the abode from its neighbors. The front yard, lacking a young, energetic *jardinero*, a gardener, to tend it, presented a neglected look to its occasional visitors. Out back, a shallow *arroyo* carrying just a trickle of water, ran behind the houses.

Matt pulled into the driveway, and cut the ignition. The air-conditioning shut down with a whine, like the sound WWII prop-driven, piston-engine fighter planes used to make. Opening the car door, he heard a dog barking from somewhere down the street and stopped for a moment to listen, before approaching Cohan's front entrance. Much of the paint on the old wooden door had long ago peeled away. Years of strong sunlight had faded the rest. A rusted wind chime of black, metal horse figures stood guard on the wall next to the door.

Matt pushed the bell but heard no sound. *Doorbell's not working,* he thought. He pressed an ear against the door and tried the bell again. The unmistakable odor of propane gas, like the kind used for cooking, reached him.

"George? George!" He called loudly. There was no response.

Alarmed now, Matt tried the door. It opened easily, and he pushed it wide. Gas poured out, driving him back a step. *If Cohan's in there he's gonna need help,* he thought. Glancing around quickly, he spotted a dirty red cloth in the flower bed next to the porch, grabbed it, and wrapped it so that it covered his nose and mouth.

Inside, he headed for where he thought he'd find the kitchen. Cohan was sitting on the floor in front of the stove, arms resting on the open oven door, head inside. Matt moved quickly to turn off the gas burners. That done, he pulled the cloth from his face, leaned over and felt the side of Cohan's neck. No pulse. He was in that position when he heard a voice behind him.

"Police! Place your hands on top of your head, señior. Other than that, do not make any sudden moves, por favor."

CHAPTER 1

Thursday, February 15, 1990
Timonium, Maryland
Padonia Village Apartments
2312 Chetwood Circle
10:00 a.m. Eastern Standard Time (EST)

THE SOUND OF THE WALL-MOUNTED phone in his kitchen broke Matt's somber mood. He listened to its insistent clamor for a few moments. Realizing it was going to keep ringing unless he did something, he cleared his throat and picked it up.

The Padonia Village Apartments, where he lived, had been built on a sun-drenched hillside at the eastern end of a densely populated valley in Baltimore County. They provided housing for four hundred families. The development's wide streets were canopied with tall oaks and maples, now bereft of leaves because of winter, but promising to burst into bloom at the first sign of spring.

The place Matt Dawson called home was a ground floor unit on Chetwood Circle. The area was pleasant enough. But two years before, when he had first moved in, he had been so deep in his private well of despair that he had paid scant attention to the azaleas, boxwoods, spreading yews and privets that graced each building. Nor had he noticed until weeks later that many tenants had decorated their patios with stylish furniture, and red and pink geraniums in green flower boxes and hanging clay pots. To him the apartment was simply a semi-safe haven in his temporarily tempest-tossed world.

"Matt? Robert Winkler. How are ya?"

"Hi, Bob." Dawson forced a light-hearted tone. "I'm good. It's been a while."

"I understand you're doing investigative work now. Searching for missing people?"

"Yeah. Needed *something* to put bread on the table. The real estate business is the pits what with the recession and all. Sales are way off."

"So I hear. Can you come to my office this afternoon? I need to have somebody found."

"Hold on. I'll check my calendar." Matt covered the receiver with a hand. Several days ago, his savings account scraping bottom and his prospects for work dim, he had put out the word among a few local lawyers that he was available to do investigative work and process serving. This was the first response about an investigation. He didn't want to sound too anxious. After what seemed a suitable pause, he removed his hand. "Yeah. That'll work."

"Terrific. Say about twelve thirty?"

Praise God, he thought, as he hung up. He had cut his discretionary spending to the bone, but the ordinary expenses — rent, food, electricity, gasoline and auto insurance — kept recurring with soul deadening regularity. His rent was a month behind and he didn't know where he'd get the money to pay it. He had no choice. Either he took whatever he could get or he'd be on the street in a month. He shrugged. *Who knows? Maybe the work Winkler's offering will turn out to be interesting.*

Thursday, February 15, 1990
Timonium, Maryland
Padonia Village Apartments
2312 Chetwood Circle
10:00 a.m. EST

Before moving to the Padonia Village Apartments, Matt had spent ten years on a thirty-five acre farm in northern Baltimore County, just a stone's throw from the Mason-Dixon Line. The house, built in 1820, had needed work when he and his ex-wife, Miriam, their four kids in tow, had moved in. Realtors call places like that "handy man's specials." What handy man skills he did not have, Matt speedily acquired as he and Miriam painstakingly restored the old home. After doing all they could themselves, a builder was hired to construct an addition, so their kids could have the space and privacy that separate bedrooms would provide.

Then, too, there had been Miriam's mother to consider. A widow, she was not doing well after her husband's death, so they thought it best for her to come and live with them. Busy as parents of four, neither he nor Miriam had been terribly religious back then, but they had absorbed at least one truth taught by their Roman Catholicism — honor your father and mother — and another more secular one: parents are seldom around for as long as we'd like them.

But after his family split apart, it seemed to him that shimmering ghosts of their abruptly terminated family life haunted the fields, paddocks and woods, flitting from tree to tree and rock to rock, ethereal shadows of what used to be. After eight months of hanging on there alone, he decided that the memories were too painful. So, even though he preferred life on the farm to living in suburbia, he had leased this apartment, and with the help of his brother-in-law, an old friend, and one of his daughters, loaded the things Miriam hadn't taken with *her* onto his blue Ford pickup, and headed for the suburbs.

Thursday, February 15, 1990
Towson, Maryland
The 606 Baltimore Avenue Building
12:30 p.m. EST

Bob Winkler shared office space with another lawyer in a four-story office building on Baltimore Avenue, in Towson. A few hundred feet north, the Immaculate Conception Church crowned a grass covered hill, its Gothic spire reaching for heavy clouds that threatened snow at any moment.

Matt, wearing jeans and a long-sleeved blue shirt open at the collar under a tan car coat, pulled his white Buick Skyhawk into the first empty space he saw, locked it and fed some quarters into the parking meter. The Skyhawk's rear window was missing, grim affirmation that often, when life's important issues are going badly, maddening minor problems will often occur as well. A few weeks earlier, a person or persons unknown had thrown a brick through it. He had no cash to repair it, so he had taped a clear plastic trash bag over the gaping hole that had once been the window, and convinced himself that the temporary repair would have to do for a while.

Putting his concern about someone breaking into the car out of his mind, Matt turned his back on it, and strode to the building's glass doors. *Actually, if someone steals it they'll be doing me a favor,* he thought. *They'll get a huge surprise when they find out the passenger door won't open and the driver's side window won't roll down.* He entered the building, crossed a lobby flanked by faux potted palms, and pushed a button to summon an elevator.

He was no longer a young man, but his brown hair had not yet turned gray, and his body was still trim . In his socks, he stood five feet ten inches tall and weighed a hundred and seventy pounds, only five more than the day he had left nearby Waterford University clutching a Bachelor of Science degree in his twenty-one year old hands.

Two secretaries were tucked into one end of the pleasant front office, staring at computer screens as Matt entered. A dozen file cabinets stood along one wall. Several chairs completed the furniture. Poster art of hungry wolves cavorting in snow graced the walls. The symbolism, unfortunate in a lawyer's office, was lost on whoever had hung this artwork.

"Is he in?" Matt addressed Deenie and Pat, both competent secretaries, and without waiting for an answer, headed for Winkler's office.

He paused on the way and thought about the fact that he was up to his ears in financial problems. He also thought about the fact that he really didn't want too many people to know about it. He paused. *I need a facial expression,* he thought. *I know. Upbeat. Happy to be here.* Once he had the expression just right, he continued on back to Winkler's office.

His friendship with Bob went back more than twenty years. Matt, in law practice for two years by then, had learned where the courthouse was, and that he was expected to show up there on time to try his cases. Actually, the local Bench thought of him as a hard working practitioner who displayed genuine concern for his clients and always tried to be thoroughly prepared. He was capable of emerging from a courtroom with good results more often than not.

Shortly after Bob hung out his shingle, Matt had invited him to lunch and explained that lawyers in solo practice lacked an advantage that associates in the firms had; access to older, experienced attorneys to whom they could turn for advice. Tired of that situation, he was forming a luncheon group of half a dozen sole practitioners who would be accessible to each other as resource persons, to kick around common problems and exchange advice. Bob eagerly jumped at the chance to join.

The group had met weekly. But a few years ago, Matt had dropped out because of marital difficulties and financial problems. By working hard, he had achieved a high standard of living for his wife and family. Sobered as he peered down the road at the need to maintain it while raising and educating four children, he'd conceived the idea of developing their recently-purchased farm into a horse breeding business. After studying everything he could lay his hands on and consulting with others in the business, he had jumped in with both feet.

No one was more surprised – and pleased – when his early efforts met with success. Encouraged, he had tried to move forward too quickly by borrowing excessively to make improvements to the farm. He was not being greedy. Improvements seemed necessary if his new venture was to grow and accomplish what he needed it to do.

But the borrowing had led to too much debt. He could not handle it on the income of a sole-practitioner, while paying all the other expenses of supporting a family of six. Then the bottom fell out of the horse breeding market before he had understood that such a thing was possible. While battling to work his way out of financial trouble, his mother, mother-in-law, two close friends and an aunt with whom he'd been close, died within a short time span, triggering a depression that sapped his energy. High blood pressure and a potentially dangerous stomach ulcer hadn't helped at all, and the effects of these conditions plus the side effects of medicines he was taking, had turned him into a surly, ill-tempered husband and father, unable to manage his emotions and prone to angry outbursts.

Besides impeding his ability to function, these things had wreaked havoc on his relationships. Soon, noting how distracted he was, clients began to leave him. Overextended, problems with creditors followed. Soon, the Bar Association took notice and the life he'd so painstakingly built collapsed around him like a house of cards in a stiff breeze.

"How ya doin', Matt?" Bob Winkler stood as Matt entered his office. Six feet one inches tall, he had sandy hair and a long, thin face that made people think of Abe Lincoln. Married, with two children, at that stage in his life he was attracted to loud ties with floral patterns, which he wore with otherwise ordinary business suits.

"Hangin' in there, Bob. " Matt shook Winkler's extended hand, parked himself in the only chair and crossed one ankle over the other knee. "*You* look good."

Coffee was offered and accepted. As he and Bob made small talk, Matt's mind toyed with the thought that he badly needed this work. Finally, Winkler moved some of the clutter on his desk with a forearm, picked up a thick manila file and pulled at a string that tied it closed. Half a dozen beige folders tumbled onto his already chaotic desk. He pointed to it.

"This is why I called you. It's the estate of a guy named Alvin Zelinka. He died three years ago here in Towson. I inherited the file two and a half years ago from John Harris, a friend of Al's. John's a lawyer, but he had never done any estate work. Took it on because he was the only friend of Al's who had the slightest idea what to do. But he couldn't close it. Went to work for the State Accident Fund shortly after that, and turned the file over to me."

"What's the problem?"

"We haven't been able to locate the missing heir. Zelinka had a sister who will inherit everything. *If* she's still *alive*, that is. She had two kids. They'll inherit if their mother's dead."

"What's been done so far to find them?"

"Harris did some things. I did a few things. No luck. And now the Orphan's Court is beatin' on me to close this file and turn the money over to the State of Maryland."

"Is there anything to go on?"

"A few letters written by Alvin's sister, Anna Lieber. That's her married name."

"Where was she living when she wrote them?"

"In Cuern - ahh - vaca, May - hee - co," Winkler said, dragging the words out for maximum effect.

Matt brightened. "Do I get to go to Mexico?" He didn't volunteer that this would be his first investigation.

Winkler shrugged. "Harris flew down there and poked around a bit. But he took his girlfriend with him, so I don't know how much time they actually spent hunting for Anna Lieber. If you think it's necessary, go ahead. But keep the expenses down. The Orphan's Court will be lookin' over my shoulder on this one."

Matt made a nondescript hand gesture. "Of course."

A broad grin appeared on Winkler's face. "By the way. Alvin died on April 15th. Tax time. Went out as the taxman was coming in. Didn't have to pay his income taxes that year." He leaned back in his chair, clasped his hands behind his head and chortled.

Matt rolled his eyes. "Harris didn't find out anything down there, huh?"

"Nothing. No one had heard of the Liebers."

"That's kinda strange. How long ago were those letters written?"

"A while ago," Winkler hedged. He lowered his head and fidgeted with the folder.

"How long, Bob?"

"Um ... in 1951."

As this reluctant disclosure registered, Matt's face fell apart with surprise. But he recovered quickly. "Okay," he said, summing up. "Lemme see if I've got this straight. This estate's been open for almost three years. You want me to find the decedent's sister, but all we've got are some old letters she wrote when she was living in Mexico thirty-nine years ago."

"That's about the size of it. What d'ya think?"

Matt rose to his feet. Panic was gnawing around the edges of his battered self-esteem, but there was no time to acknowledge it. Winkler was waiting for an answer. Matt's eyes met Bob's. "Piece a cake," he said. He glanced at his cheap wristwatch. "You still drink manhattans for lunch?"

CHAPTER 2

Thursday, February 15, 1990
New Haven, Connecticut
The New York-New Haven Commuter Express
3:00 p.m. Eastern Standard Time (EST)

THE ATTRACTIVE WOMAN WHO OCCUPIED a seat in the third car from the front of the afternoon's early Commuter Express extracted a pack of Virginia Slim Ultra-Light 100s from her purse, nervously tapped one out, lit up and placed it between her lips. Leaning slightly to her right, she examined her tired face in the train's window, and watched the reflected smoke as it curled above her head.

From her window, Ann Kelly gazed at the white blanket of snow covering the Connecticut countryside through which the train was quickly passing. *Smashing,* she thought, irritably. *Three inches of the evil stuff will make it terribly difficult to get around while I'm here.*

The car was almost empty. Racing over the rails east of Bridgeport, her train was devouring the snow-covered ground, like a giant worm on the desert planet Arrakis in Frank Herbert's novel, *Dune.* Bound for New Haven's Union Station, the noisy mass of metal had quickly covered the distance from Chappaqua, thirty miles north of the Big Apple in northern Westchester County, New York, to this mid-sized city in Connecticut.

Ann was a tall, sophisticated woman with long red hair, a waist still slender at forty-five, shapely legs that were envied by women ten years younger, and full lips that could become petulant or sensual at a moment's notice.

She had grown up in the smoggy city of Birmingham, England, a hundred miles northwest of London, in Warwickshire. The surrogates filling in for her real parents from the time she turned seven, were hesitant to take complete charge of her, as they would have had she been their own child. And because they were atheists who thought that belief in God was based on irrational, immature needs and wishes, whereas atheism flowed from a rational, self-reliant view of things as they *really* were, they had not exposed Ann to any religious instruction, as religious parents would have. Consequently, she had never been taught the life-sustaining precepts of conventional morality, based squarely on a belief in a Creator; God as a loving, kind, benevolent Father who had set down rules for his human creation to follow.

As she began to assert her independence from her stand-in parents, never having learned that sex before marriage was wrong because, in addition to the diseases one might contract, it could cloud a young girl's mind to the faults of immature, selfish boys, she had done many of the usual appalling things that some teen-agers do. An amoral girl eager to be accepted by her peers, she had flung her virginity away at an early age. Not surprisingly, the recipients of her sexual favors had simply used her and moved on.

Later, having run squarely into the problems of meaninglessness and alienation felt by so many who reject or never begin a relationship with God, she tried filling her emptiness with all the worldly things: job, career, relationships with men, travel, and acquisition of material goods. She thought she was pursuing happiness. What she was *really* seeking was something else: meaning and purpose to her life.

In her teens, Ann had lacked a strong sense of self-worth. Often, she had entertained childish fantasies of her future marriage to a handsome young man. She visualized her husband arriving home from work after a busy day. They would eat a delicious dinner and retire early to their room where, after showers and some quiet time together, they would make love and she would lie peacefully in his arms. At first, there would be a red sports car in their driveway. Later, when they had two dark-haired children with *his* skin and coloring and *her* cheekbones, they'd buy a station wagon.

But the years had flown. Suddenly she was twenty-five and *Mister Right* had not made his appearance. As the days flew by, she was besieged by the feeling that "Fate" had deemed her somehow unworthy; that she did not deserve or merit happiness. Her dreams of marriage, of white dresses and pearls, of gentle mornings awakening to the scent of blossoming lilacs outside their windows, had flown with the years. Panicking then, she had, for six rowdy years, thrown herself into Birmingham's singles lifestyle; smoky pubs, loud bands and dense crowds, the smell of booze and sweat, and the sickly sweet reek of marijuana smoke, frantically looking for the happiness that always seemed just out of reach. As she traveled that road, she carefully secreted her dreams in the attic of her mind, like a young wife carefully packs away her wedding dress for the future daughter who might someday joyfully wear it.

Bright and quick-witted, Ann was also contrary, abrasive, cynical, and intensely socialist. The oldest child as well as daughter, she had been close to her communist father during the brief time she had lived with her parents. Later, her only male role model had been the husband of the socialist couple who had taken her in. Socialism being part of the *zeitgeist*, the spirit of her time in England and in most of Europe for that matter, he had neither hidden nor soft-pedaled his radical views. She emulated him in this regard. But, because he spent his time working at the business he'd built, and because he was retiring and distant around females, she had never been emotionally close to him.

The qualities Ann possessed, softened neither by tact nor diplomacy, were hardly a recipe for attracting a husband. Not surprisingly, the young men who entered her life quickly made their exits, relieved. Defiantly, she continued as before, untamed, thumbing her nose at conventional morality and those around her who practiced it. She ignored the fact that it was *their* lives not hers that seemed happiest, more orderly, less stressful. *They can take me as I am, thank you very much,* she thought. Until … Sean.

Ann was dressed in a navy blue pantsuit bought at Macy's Herald Square, on 151st Street. Under her jacket, she had on a white blouse, and a sage green, cashmere V-neck sweater, vintage Oleg Cassini. A bright red cravat at her neck provided a splash of color, matching her hair, which, today, she was wearing in a ponytail, with bangs that made her look years younger than she actually was. Her lipstick harmonized with hair and cravat, and she had applied dark eye shadow around her green eyes, forcing a contrast with the white skin of her face. She wore no coat, but she had packed a dark green, heavily lined raincoat in her garment bag, in case the weather turned nasty. *At least I did that right,* she thought as she peered out the train's window again, at the snow-covered ground.

Her thoughts went back to the night she and Sean Kelly had first met. She had been excessively tired and in a decidedly out-of-the-ordinary mood. For weeks, she had been wrestling with serious questions; *what's the meaning of life? Where is the meaning in mine? Is there any purpose to it all? If so, what is it?* Her feelings were not so much hopeful as they were bitter.

When, earlier that evening, the couple with whom she had lived, Barkley and Agnes Weatherall, now elderly with the passage of years but perhaps sensing her emotional struggles, had invited her to dinner at their country club, the Edgbaston Golf Club, one of the oldest and best in England, her reaction had been mild annoyance. *It had been years since I'd spent any time with them, much less let them into my life for an entire evening,* she thought. *To admit them then was unthinkable. But, that's what I did.* Dreading a long evening alone, but too drained of energy to dress for a night at a local pub, she had mumbled her acceptance. *What on earth possessed me to go with them that night?* She wondered. *Ordinarily, I wouldn't have been seen dead in such a bourgeois place. Was it because I had nothing better to do? Or was I meant to be there so Sean and I would meet?*

The Club, located just two miles from the center of Birmingham, was noted for its fine food. But that night, the dining room had quickly grown oppressive with the smell of prime rib, the smoke of countless cigarettes and cigars, and the funereal music to which these older people danced. Just when she had begun to look wildly about for some means of escape, she saw *him.* A tall man, he seemed to glide easily through the clusters of people at the edge of the dance floor. Instantly, because of his clothing, she pegged him as an American. *Whatever is he doing here?* She wondered. Opposite her table, he stopped to light a cigarette, a quirky grin playing around the edges of his mouth. Their eyes met. I do *not know what he saw in me at that moment, but in my barmy mood, I knew him immediately as the one I'd been looking for; the man straight from my schoolgirl dreams.*

No clever pick up line sprang to her mind in the few seconds it took to close the distance between them, so she used the only thing she could think of. "You look *so* familiar. Have we met before?"

"I really doubt that," he said, smiling graciously. "But, you look like someone I'd want to know." He stuck out his hand and introduced himself.

She learned that he was a lawyer, in Birmingham to try a copyright infringement case, assisted by a firm of London barristers. Despite his workload, they had seen each other almost every evening. At the conclusion of his case, believing they were compatible, she had packed her bags, said goodbye to the Weatheralls, and followed him to New York. They had married a few months later. He *had* been her strength and her safety for the next almost thirteen years. But not her joy. Those years had been good, but they weren't quite like the life she had conjured up in her childhood fantasy.

Now, Sean Cornelius Kelly was dead! During their courtship and twelve-year marriage, he had been a man who worked too hard, lived too heartily and enjoyed life too much. Although his income permitted them to live a lifestyle free of financial concerns, the stress and tension under which he labored daily was a crushing burden for any man. Life, for Sean Kelly, was too good to last. Before he died, she had not known how much she could cry. Afterward, she had found out. Oh, how she *had* cried. Not because she had loved him, but because, despite her good intentions, she could not love him at all. *What had he been to me? An answer to a prayer? No, not that. I've never prayed. He had simply been a safe haven in a stormy sea. After he died I felt incredibly guilty.*

And incredibly angry. *What terribly bad timing,* she thought selfishly. *To die on Christmas Day is in such poor taste. But, that's what he did. Not that Christmas day actually meant anything to me. It was a day just like any other day. Still …*

It had happened as they exchanged gifts next to the garishly decorated tree he insisted on putting up every year, against her wishes. She was from a family of Austrian Jews who did not practice a religion because they did not believe in God. Her parents, lacking faith in anything but the power of government, had not celebrated either Christmas or Hanukkah. And the family friends who had raised her, the Weatheralls, had never put up a tree. During her marriage, she had reluctantly acquiesced each year to please Sean, who was a big, sentimental Irish Catholic.

On that Christmas Eve, unaware that it would be their last, Sean had insisted that they attend Midnight Mass at Saint Patrick's Cathedral in midtown Manhattan. Afterward, they were invited to the residence of John Cardinal O'Connor, for drinks. Her husband was a corporate lawyer who regularly made seven figures, and the Diocese of New York was his firm's most important client. Cardinal O'Connor liked him and relied heavily on him. In the rectory, surrounded by dark paneling and oil paintings of long-dead pontiffs, they talked corporate structure for a new charitable venture the Cardinal was hatching, which would raise funds to assist the poor and needy of the Diocese, smoked their foul smelling Havana cigars, and sipped Cognac until three-thirty in the morning. She had helped them liberally with the Cognac. It was five a.m. before she and Sean, thoroughly inebriated and equally exhausted, had finally settled into bed at their Chappaqua home.

But that morning Sean was up before noon. He was fifty-two years old, forty pounds overweight, with a body suffering from years of stress and a sedentary life behind a desk, punctuated by stress-filled weeks at a time in a courtroom in front of a jury. He grinned, reached over and picked up a package containing one of her gifts, handed her the box, and had a coronary so severe that when the paramedics arrived a few minutes later, there was nothing for them to do except transport his lifeless body.

Sean had been the *only* man in her life who had not simply used her and discarded her afterwards. They had had a comfortable, if not a loving, relationship throughout their marriage. But having spent a substantial amount of her early life living to excess, she had developed a selfish concern for personal freedom; a freedom *from* everything, not a freedom *for* anything. By her late teens, her concern had evolved into a freedom that meant license to do as she damn well pleased, and throughout the years before Sean, she had vigorously embraced her passions and desires, seeking to eliminate every obstacle to their fulfillment. Sean, a disciplined and somewhat moral individual, had proven an unforeseen impediment to her pleasures *and* her freedom.

And so, had I thought about it at all, that sordid affair with Marvin Jonathan Freedlander had been predictable. For a while, cheating on Sean had been worth it to me because the sex, romance, and excitement had been better than at home. But as excitingly erotic as it had been, the affair had soon become terribly tedious. We were both very nervous about being caught, so we were forced to avoid places where we might be seen, recognized, and exposed. For that reason, she had ended the relationship with the tall, handsome son of one of her father's old friends before she was ready, not because of fidelity to her husband, whose ideas about marriage were, she thought … archaic at best. True, he had always been good to her. But perhaps sensing that she did not love him, he had never been terribly considerate and had proven it again at the last, dying on Christmas day. *I'll never forgive him for that,* she thought.

But her husband was gone and she was filled with a dull anger. *I planned and executed his funeral flawlessly, she though. I spared no expense. Afterwards, Sean's poor excuse for a mother and his hideous siblings, with whom I never could get along, had returned to Chicago where Sean had grown up, and the life to which I had become accustomed had been dramatically altered. I spent six boring weeks alone, waiting for Sean's Will to be probated, bouncing around in our huge colonial home on five wooded acres. And I had to tolerate maddeningly tedious sympathy visits from well-meaning friends, until I was thoroughly vexed.*

Sean, lawyer to the end, had provided well for her. *That Will he drew up was thirty pages long,* she thought. The trust created for her was funded by a hefty life insurance policy. There was also a substantial outright bequest. To say she would have no financial worries for the rest of her life was a glorious understatement.

So she had decided to travel: to spend some of her inherited wealth lavishly on herself. Why not? She certainly had the time. But, she was not bound for the casinos at Cable Beach outside Nassau, or the sultry sands on the French Riviera. There would be time, later, to lose fifty or sixty grand playing Blackjack, or to bake, topless, on the hot sand of a magnificent Mediterranean beach, her skin glistening with suntan oil applied by some nameless European playboy. Just now, she had something else in mind.

The sparse blue sky had given way to heavy gray clouds that threatened more snow as Ann glanced out the window of the almost empty coach again a few minutes later. She shivered. It was not snow that she recalled from her summers as a five and six-year old in the nearby town of Branford. It was fog. Wet, leaden fog that moved in quietly, blotting out the summer sun and cutting off her view of the blue waters of Long Island Sound. What the locals jokingly referred to as 'pea soup' would quickly turn her pretty jumpers soggy, drenching her to the bone as she obstinately tried to finish a game of hopscotch or hide-and-seek with her friends before being forced inside.

CHAPTER 3

Thursday, February 15, 1990
Timonium, Maryland
Padonia Village Apartments
2312 Chetwood Circle
3:30 p.m. Eastern Standard Time (EST)

THE WINTER SUN WAS RAPIDLY fading in the western sky. Matt Dawson, back from a late lunch with Bob Winkler, stood in his apartment kitchen, thinking about the dinner he was going to cook for himself and a few friends that evening.

I've got the menu firmed up, he thought. *Sirloin steaks marinated in red wine, garlic and mushrooms, baked jumbo Idaho potatoes, a salad with tarragon vinegar and olive oil dressing. Simple to fix, but with the right touches, delicious. I should be able to get it ready in a couple hours.*

For years sampling food in elegant restaurants had been one of his favorite pastimes —until his deteriorating financial situation had forced him to give it up. Necessity is the mother of invention. Single again and short of money, Matt had decided he needed to learn to cook. When friends complimented his early efforts, he actually began to enjoy his forays into the culinary art. Quickly, he mastered a few simple-to-make meals like the one he would prepare this night.

Some introspection is good for a man. But for Matt, it had become a habit. Again and again he had reexamined the last six years of his life. In rapid succession, he'd been forced to terminate the horse breeding business, sell the farm and all the horses, file bankruptcy and watch his marriage go down in flames. To finance farm improvements, he had borrowed excessively from the guardianship estate of a client. The Bar Association did not approve. Eventually, after a four-year investigation, during which time Matt had almost convinced himself that the Ethics Committee would dismiss the matter, that group had determined that even though the personal representative had had knowledge of the loans and Matt had signed promissory notes and given a second mortgage on the farm as security, this was an unethical practice. When they finally made their decision, a sorrowful, weary, and depressed Matt Dawson signed a consent disbarment agreement and said goodbye to the profession he'd worked so hard to enter.

Interspersed among these events, death had reared its ugly head. His mother, mother-in-law, two close friends and an aunt had died in rapid succession. Then, just when he thought he'd seen an end to life-changing events, his brother had suffered a fatal heart attack, and a year later, his sister was killed in an automobile accident. For months afterwards, thoughts of his own death and the impermanence of life had intruded on his consciousness, bringing a black depression that rolled over him, just as a rain cloud driven by the wind will obscure the sun.

Guilt, grief, lack of work, bills he could not pay, memories of beautiful family life as it had once been, feelings of loss, rejection and loneliness. Any one of these could motivate a man. All of them, together, could destroy him. They had dogged Matt until he felt like he was drowning in a deep, black pool. Grief had grown like a cancer, driving out the healthy tissue of hope for the future. And as hope had drained away, his courage and self-confidence had drained away with it. Finally, in the wee hours of a night like the one John of the Cross wrote about in *"The Dark Night,"* filled with emotional pain so intense that he was almost breathless, and so empty of any comfort that he felt totally abandoned by God and man, Matt had dropped to his knees and cried out for help. And God had heard his cry!

At dawn the morning after this experience, exhausted by his nocturnal ordeal, Matt had become dimly aware that something wonderful had happened. He had passed through a spiritual purging, a purification of the senses, which is the necessary first stage in an intense relationship with God.

> O guiding night!
> O night more lovely than the dawn!
> O night that has united
> the lover with his beloved ...
> The Dark Night, John of the
> Cross, 5th Stanza.

Having survived his night of purifying contemplation, with the help of the Holy Spirit he had begun the demanding task of putting his life back together again.

First, he had enrolled in a real estate course at his alma mater, Waterford University, reasoning that with his experience in real estate law, it shouldn't be hard to make a living selling residential, commercial and farm real estate while searching for the great job that he believed would come; the one that would restore him financially and permit him to resume his role as provider for his family, or for his kids, at least. A few months later, he had taken the brokers' exam, passed it, and opened a real estate business. But having dumped all his assets into the bankruptcy to satisfy creditors, the new venture was without start-up capital. Still, he had decided to risk it. *What's life without a gamble now and then?* He had reflected, unaware that this kind of thinking was a chunk of dangerous flotsam left over from his former lifestyle.

However, no sooner had he invested the last of his cash in office furniture, signs, checks, stationery, and membership in the multiple-listing service that was so essential to realtors, the storm clouds of a nationwide economic downturn gathered. Real estate sales, one of the leading indicators of both recession and recovery, declined sharply. When the recession hit soon after, he found himself in hot water, without reserve funds to tide him over this bump in the economy. For a while, eating had become … iffy. Weeks ago he had realized that his fledgling business was not going to make it. And, he was also forced to admit that despite over a hundred resumes and a dozen interviews, the dream job he had thought possible was not going to materialize. And there was no one to whom he could turn for help!

Failure is like that. During those times, the instinct of the pack is to turn away from the person in trouble. So for him it was panic time!

He had prayed then, as he'd never prayed before. And out of his newly discovered understanding of how dependent he was on God, his practice of daily prayer had been born. That's when the idea had come to try investigative work and process serving.

Soon, his developing relationship with God through Jesus had taken shape, until it was more important to him than anything else. As a kid, Matt had been given the gift of faith. But by the time he'd reached college, he'd thrust it aside in favor of the modernist view that we are material machines living in a purely physical world; that nothing exists beyond what our senses perceive; that we are self-governing and free to choose our own direction; that we should be rationalistic optimists who depend only on the data of our senses and reason; and we are progressing quite nicely toward a glorious future by relying on science and reason alone.

Later, he reached law school and was exposed to postmodernism, the philosophical reaction against the excesses of modernism. He had not *directly* bought into postmodernism because of its glaring rejection of the enlightenment project, an important part of which was the idea that people *can* be reasonable and objective, and its insistence upon casting everything in terms of a struggle for power between groups. Still, like so many others, he'd unconsciously absorbed many of its beliefs. Because of that and his education and training, he had not thought a return to a faith-based life, a theistic worldview, possible.

Now, however, he was pleased to admit that his relationship with Jesus had grown until it overshadowed his problems. *Surprise, surprise!* He had thought, the day he realized that he was experiencing a sense of contentment that he'd never known before; a feeling of peace amid his cares, the peace promised by Saint Paul that few could understand. *The prospect of another failure isn't quite so unsettling now,* he thought. *If I have to, I'll simply try something else.* With God's help, both his self-esteem and self-confidence were slowly returning. That passage from Saint Paul's Letter to the Philippians had taken on real meaning;

> "… I have learned to be content in whatever circumstances
> I am. I know how to get along with humble means, and
> I also know how to live in prosperity; in any and every
> circumstance I have learned the secret of being filled and
> going hungry, both of having abundance and suffering
> need, and I can do all things through Him who strengthens
> me."

CHAPTER 4

Thursday, February 15, 1990
New York City, New York
Daniel Patrick Moynihan US Courthouse
500 Pearl Street, Lower Manhattan
4:45 p.m. Eastern Standard Time (EST)

MARVIN JONATHAN FREEDLANDER, UNITED STATES District Attorney for the Southern District of New York, was grinning from ear to ear as he walked down the wide second floor corridor, accompanied by his staff and members of the press corps. The group came to a halt in front of the double glass doors leading to his office. This building also housed the federal courts on the floors above, and in one of those courtrooms, he had just scored another big win. A jury had returned with a guilty verdict in the case of the *United States of America v. Albertson,* a high profile murder-kidnapping in the course of a bank robbery. District Attorneys everywhere refer to cases of this type as "heater cases" because of the inflamed emotions that always accompany them.

"Mr. Freedlander?" A reporter from *The New York Times* asked. "Will you be requesting the death penalty at Albertson's sentencing hearing?" The case had garnered more than its share of attention in this "city that never sleeps," because of the mainstream media's bias against inherited wealth, an offense which, in their opinion, Albertson's parents had been guilty of, and by association, their son, too.

Freedlander turned and gazed at the reporter as if he had just climbed out from under a damp rock. "This was a particularly heinous crime. I'll do what I think is in the best interests of the people of New York. And as always, in accordance with the mandated guidelines of federal law." He held up a hand. "Just one more question, gentlemen."

"Is it true that you'll soon announce your candidacy for mayor, Mr. Freedlander?" This one came from a staff reporter for the *New York Daily News.*

Surprised, Freedlander's brow wrinkled, but he instantly replaced the frown with a paternal smile that spread gently over his face. "I've always been willing to answer the call to serve," he said gravely.

Stepping into the suite, he walked across the waiting room without further comment, entered his own office and started to close the door behind him. That would have effectively shut out Assistant US Attorney John Walter Foreman, who had helped try the case, Special Agent Kenneth Andrew Starling of the Federal

Bureau of Investigation, who had been the prosecution's star witness, Assistant US Attorney William "Willie" Preston, Freedlander's fetch-and-carry man, Daphne, his secretary, and Peter and Sam, his law clerks. Also to be cut off were numerous members of the wire services and local press, the latter of which Freedlander often referred to as his "fan club."

Following his boss into the inner office, Foreman turned. "Run along, guys," he said. "That's it for today. Mr. Freedlander isn't going to confirm or deny a rumor you picked up somewhere." He shut the door without waiting for their response.

An excellent prosecutor, Freedlander had done a good job since becoming the DA. Lately, however, he had become bored with prosecuting cases, and had begun to slough off the unglamorous grunt work of preparation and trial onto Foreman, his loyal subordinate, who was quite willing to spend seventy hours a week in a stuffy office preparing cases. Foreman had done exactly that with the *Albertson case*, handling the direct examination of the police officers, bank guard, the tellers, and then cross-examining several witnesses for the defense. But the high-profile sections, cross-examining the defendant's most important witness, and, of course the defendant, Freedlander handled himself.

Politics was now one of Marvin Jonathan Freedlander's passions. His years of glad-handing, backslapping and carefully nuanced responses to the press, to judges, to FBI agents, and others had led to the discovery that, for him, being charming was instinctive. That had helped morph him into the consummate politician; a man who sought always to be the center of attention and the one in charge. Now, he wanted to run for mayor of New York so badly he could taste it.

Freedlander slipped into a chair behind the desk and breathed a sigh of relief. Foreman flung himself into the one in front of it and shrugged. "How did that reporter get wind of it, anyway?" He asked. "You haven't announced your intentions, yet." He gestured with a thumb toward the outer office. "And none of *us* have told anybody, either."

"I don't know," Freedlander said. "But, I've spent months testing the local political waters; assessing how much support I can count on within the party once I throw my hat in the ring. I don't want some nosy reporter messing things up with a premature announcement."

"You're gonna make an announcement soon, right?

"Yes. Soon."

Freedlander rose and removed his double-breasted jacket, loosened his expensive blue and red paisley print tie, and unbuttoned the collar of his Brooks Brothers shirt. The pleasant fragrance of Nicotianas, tobacco plants with long white flowers, drifted to him from half a dozen window boxes and several pots scattered throughout his office. These were his *other* passion. He assiduously cultivated them, not only because he enjoyed the rainbow of colors the eighteen-inch tall plants produced, but because he was a smoker, and their leaves, organically grown, were free of the tar and other chemicals contained in commercially purchased cigarettes.

"Think you can expect any financial support from your grandfather's firm?" Foreman asked.

"I don't know. Marvin Jesse Freedlander was a well-known corporate lawyer here in the 'Big Apple' for years. Graduated from Columbia University Law School. Then, he started his own law firm, focusing on corporate and securities law. Only took him five years to build it into the biggest and best in the state. Had well over two hundred lawyers. The old man made millions, and along the way, he'd become well connected. Knew everybody who was anybody. Mayors and governors all sought him out for his political wisdom. And his campaign contributions."

Freedlander paused, thinking back. Marvin Jesse had yearned for the day his son would follow him into the law and eventually take over the firm that he had built. However, Marvin Jesse Junior had had other ideas. Pliant at first, the boy had attended his father's alma maters, as the elder Freedlander had insisted. But unlike when Marvin Jesse had gone there, both of those schools had morphed into bastions of ultra-liberalism. Many of the professors there championed socialism and espoused a hatred of capitalism and private enterprise, while showing their contempt for the United States, the idea of American Exceptionalism, and the moral values that had made America great.

By the time Marvin Jesse Junior had reached his senior year in college, he had become a flaming liberal. In law school, he had honed his socialist beliefs to a fine edge. It was no surprise to anyone when young Freedlander rejected his father's offer to join the firm and began representing socialists, communists, and communist sympathizers throughout the area. The Communist Party of New York soon sought him out, and since his services did not come cheap and he did not discount his fees for anyone, not even his ideologically compatible clients, life actually became pleasant for Marvin Jesse Junior, his wife, and their young son, Marvin Jonathan.

But in the early '50s, something horrible had happened. Marvin Jesse Junior had returned from one of his trips to Mexico, where he often went to visit a friend, in a state of extreme agitation. For the next several weeks, hushed conversations ensued between Marvin Jonathan's parents. Each usually ended in a violent argument. His grandfather was called in. More volatile arguments ensued. A few months later, just before Marvin Jonathan's ninth birthday, his mother moved out, taking him with her. He seldom saw his father again.

Whatever had occurred south of the border was an event of such magnitude, and possessed such potential for embarrassment to the entire Freedlander family that it was never spoken of again. But Marvin Jesse Senior re-wrote his Will and disinherited his son, thereby confirming the seriousness of the rift between them.

It did not matter to Marvin Jesse Junior. By the time he and his wife were divorced, he was well on his way to substantial wealth of his own. And during the fourteen years he practiced law before his death from a heart attack while in the US District Court defending the socialist head of a labor union who had been charged by the government with converting to his own use several hundred thousand dollars of union funds, Marvin Jesse Junior had acquired his own fortune.

From a very young age, Marvin Jonathan grew up practically fatherless. For years, he spent time and energy trying, first, to understand why his parents had divorced, and later, because no other reason became obvious to his child's mind, blaming himself.

"Did you know your grandfather well?" Foreman interrupted his thoughts.

"No.." He shrugged. "I tried. With no father around to be a role model, I tried to cultivate him as a surrogate for a while. It didn't work. Marvin Jesse Senior was the founding partner of a multimillion-dollar law firm. I think he loved me dearly, but he had no time for me."

"Didn't he croak when you were in high school?"

"When I was finishing high school. My senior year. He became seriously ill." Marvin Jonathan got up, walked to the window, and stood there staring out. "They called me to the old man's bedside. He told me several secrets. I told you all this before. The first was that my father was a murderer. The second, the fact that my dad had been unfaithful to my mother with a Mexican woman who he later killed. That's what caused the separation and divorce of my parents. Not me, as I'd always thought."

"You didn't know that, before?"

"No. And I later learned that I had been well provided for in my granddad's Will; with a trust fund that would pay for my college and graduate school and provide me with an income while I concentrated on my studies."

Foreman rose. "I'll go make sure the press has left," he said.

Alone, Marvin Jonathan continued his brief journey into his past. Although stunned by this shocking bit of family history, and mortified by the notoriety his father continually received while representing high profile communists and socialists in New York, he had nevertheless acquired his father's and his grandfather's fascination for and love of the law. However, after his grandfathers' death and still during his senior year of high school, not wanting to be connected in anyone's mind or memory to his infamous father, he applied to Harvard instead of Columbia to do his undergraduate work, so that he could remove himself from New York City. But he had shrewdly recognized that it might take his father's clout to get him onto Harvard's campus. Expedient to the core, he contacted his father, and shortly thereafter, was provided the kind of help that only the well-connected can give their children. One phone call from Marvin Jesse Junior, and the doors to that Cambridge campus outside Boston swung wide.

Even though Marvin Jonathan had solicited his fathers' efforts, he continued to have nothing to do with him up until the man's death just after Marvin Jonathan entered Yale Law School. By the time he graduated from Yale Law, third in his class, the cataclysmic event in his fathers' past had been forgotten. Certainly, no one connected *him* to the infamous Marvin Jesse Freedlander, Junior, the former Communist Party lawyer from New York.

That was good, he thought, *because by that time, I had become seriously image conscious, and my dead father's past could have been a huge impediment to my securing the job I coveted; Assistant US Attorney right here in the Southern District of New York.*

As he grew older, expediency combined with moral relativism, an unhealthy belief that truth did not exist, or if it did, it was whatever one wanted it to be at any given moment, were two qualities that Marvin Jonathan cultivated intensely. His expediency came to the fore when he discovered that the daughter of one of the States' two senators lived in the same apartment building that he did, and belonged to the same expensive fitness center at the Regent Wall Street Hotel. He speedily contrived a meeting, found that Marta was reasonably attractive, and set about the business of convincing her that she should become Mrs. Marvin Freedlander.

Shortly after the happy couple announced their engagement, he learned that he was one of two finalists for an opening as an Assistant in the US Attorney's office. He persuaded his fiancée to pump her father for the identity of the other candidate. She was able to glean the young man's name. Marvin Jonathan was not surprised to learn that his competition had been at Yale Law with him. His disregard for the truth was useful at that point. He simply planted stories with Marta about the "disreputable activities" allegedly engaged in by the unfortunate young man while at Yale, including cheating on examinations and making a local girl pregnant and refusing to stand by her. Neither allegation was true, but Marta, unaware, innocently communicated the tales to her father. The conscientious Senator passed them along to the US Attorney. The job went to Marvin Jonathan.

Not that I was unqualified, he thought. *I graduated from Yale with a 3.75 grade point average and I had been an assistant editor of the Law Review. To hold that position, you had to publish at least six articles on various criminal law topics of wide interest. I did that. I may well have won the spot on my own merit. It was just that, well ... I always felt the need for some extra help, that little something more to give me a competitive edge. Most people simply suck it up and worked harder. That was not my style.*

But he *had* done an excellent job in his seven years as an Assistant US Attorney. The fact that he won more than his share of criminal cases earned for him the respect and trust of his boss. He had also become active in his political party and very selective with his monetary support of certain candidates backed by the party.

There was one thing more. Marvin Jonathan's life in New York City was lived at a brisk pace. He had a gift for doing everything on a grand scale, whether it was a birthday party for one of Marta's nieces, or a cocktail party for a few hundred notables. These gatherings always included dozens of his fellow Assistant DA's and representatives of the local press. By the time Marvin Jonathan was selected for the top job, he had become well-known among the latter group. Admiring his style and flair, they touted his fearlessness in confronting criminals, his unfailing support of victims and his brilliance of mind to the entire world locally, gradually building a public perception of him that was embellished, to say the least.

Freedlander slipped his six foot two inch frame behind his massive desk again and examined his impeccably manicured fingernails for a moment before picking up the phone. Glancing at a beautifully framed color photograph of Marta on the console behind his desk, he suffered a momentary twinge of conscience, but dialed a number anyway.

"Kelly residence," a maid spoke softly from a designer phone in an expensive home situated on a large, tree-shaded lot in Chappaqua, thirty some miles north.

"Mrs. Kelly, please." As always when he called there, he attempted to disguise his voice slightly.

"I'm sorry. Missus Kelly's not home. She left yesterday on a trip."

Freedlander's face fell. He was emotionally and sexually charged, as he always was at the conclusion of an important case. He needed a woman to help relieve that feeling. Someone sexy and wild. Not Marta, who had proven dull and unimaginative in the bedroom. Ann Kelly filled the bill. When breaking off their affair the year before, she had told him that, in the future, she would be available to him only the night after one of those trials, because she enjoyed the passion and creativity he brought to their lovemaking on those occasions. He was aware that she was using him for her own pleasure, but since she was allowing him to use her for his, he had no complaints.

He ran a hand through his coal black hair. "Did she say when she'd be back?"

"No, she didn't. Just that she'd be away for a while. Is there a message?"

"No. No message," Freedlander said and hung up. He glanced at his expensive Seiko wristwatch. His Kiwanis Club speaking engagement in the Bronx was not until eight o'clock. Impulsively, he leaned forward and flipped the switch on his intercom.

"Yes, sir," his secretary said.

"Tell Willie to bring the Buick around front. I'll meet him downstairs in five minutes," he said brusquely. There would be just enough time to slip over to the South Street Seaport area, pick up one of the expensive hookers who plied their trade along Maiden Lane at night, and take her to the nearby So Ho Grand Hotel for a quickie.

CHAPTER 5

Thursday, February 15, 1990
Timonium, Maryland
Padonia Village Apartments
2312 Chetwood Circle
7:00 p.m. Eastern Standard Time (EST)

MATT'S DINNER GUESTS ARRIVED A few minutes after seven; "fashionably late." He was not offended because he knew that was the okay thing to do in what passed as polite society these days. Amid noisy good-natured banter, they shed coats and gloves, and deposited themselves into chairs in his eclectic living room. Along with Livingston Cellars rosé, a tasty California wine, Matt served Coke and Pepsi, brought out some sharp Cheddar cheese, added Wheat Thins and an onion dip, which he had quickly thrown together by combining a package of onion soup mix with a container of sour cream, and the evening got underway.

Daniel and Barbara Davis were evangelical followers of Jesus, who strongly believed that the Bible was the inspired word of God. Dan and Matt had attended high school together, but after graduation their paths had diverged. Dan had gone into the Marines Corps, while Matt had entered Waterford University.

A year before, while eating breakfast at a local Friendly's, Matt and Dan had met again, and Matt had impulsively poured out his troubles. After listening, Dan had said, "Matt, I know you're hurting. Would it be all right if we prayed together about these things?" Surprised, Matt nodded. They had prayed quietly for a few minutes. A bond, formed in prayer and sealed by the grace of God, had existed between them since that morning.

Jim and Denise Crowley were Roman Catholics. Denise, short and tending toward heavy, battled a weight problem without complaint. She was wearing a white rayon blouse, tan slacks and brown pumps. Her dark hair was pulled back and tied with a white ribbon. Bright lipstick, but only a touch of eye shadow adorned her face. The gift of faith had been given to her early but she had not tended it. Faith, to remain strong, must be nurtured by prayer, bible reading, occasional fasting, regular almsgiving and other types of religious reading. Inspired by her new friends, Denise was now beginning to do these things.

Jim was Matt's height but on the heavy side, with a high forehead and large ears. An intelligent man, he was the owner of a small, successful insurance agency. For years Jim had been very self-assured, almost cocky; confident that he could handle anything sent his way. Until that day two years ago when his brother had been killed in an auto accident. Since then he had been struggling with an emotional issue. Grieving at this tragic loss, he had blamed God for what he viewed as a senseless act. Not well grounded in either the Bible or his Church's theology, he was unable to understand why it had happened. Consequently, he was having doubts about God's existence. His was a complaint voiced by many in times of adversity; if God exists, why does He cause bad things to happen? But although Jim was wrong headed in this regard, he and his wife had good hearts. They seldom let an opportunity pass to help someone in need. Recently, that someone had been Matt.

The common bond of their Christian faith joined these friends. Understanding that everyone experiences pain and suffering, they believed that people should be there for each other. Matt, his emotional defenses battered, had been drawn to them out of his need. He was grateful for their support.

The talk was about the lop-sided results of Super Bowl XXIV, in which the San Francisco Forty-niners had routed the Denver Broncos, fifty-five to ten.

"I told you the Forty-niners would make short work of Denver," Jim gloated.

"It would've been different if the Broncos hadn't had so many injuries," Matt answered.

"Football, football," Denise said. "Isn't there anything else you guys can talk about?"

Jim made a show of thinking. "There's baseball!" He exclaimed brightly.

"Basketball, too," Dan added. "College basketball's in full swing, right now."

Barbara mimed surprise. "I didn't *know* that."

This elicited a contemptuous snort from Denise. "I didn't, either. But it wouldn't have made much difference, even if I had."

Matt, having played some football, and a lot of baseball and soccer in his youth, was an avid sports fan. But sensing that it was probably best to talk about something in which the women could be included, he changed the subject —to what had been uppermost in his mind since returning from his visit to Bob Winkler's office. "Good news," he said. "I was hired by a Towson lawyer today, to find someone."

"Your first investigation, Matt? Congrats!" Jim and Dan offered closed fists in high fives, after which Matt quickly filled them in.

"But, no one's heard from this woman *or* her kids in thirty-nine years?" Dan was incredulous. "Sounds like a great way to get your feet wet."

"If *I* only had one sister," Barbara said, "I sure as heck would wanna stay in touch."

"From the male point of view, I think it's the same," Jim said, thinking of how much he missed his deceased brother. "Wonder why the guy didn't make the effort?"

Denise folded her arms. "Something must've happened. Maybe they didn't get along. Or maybe she died. Otherwise, *she* surely would've stayed in touch. That's the way sisters are."

"Whatever," Jim remarked cynically. "Now, it's too late."

As Dan Davis listened, his mind was elsewhere. In his mid-fifties, tall and wiry, his full head of sandy hair beginning to gray, he still had the build and bearing of a former marine, but his manner was that of a gentle and patient man. He knew that Matt's sister had been killed two years before, and his brother had died the year before that. He also knew that because of Matt's reborn faith in God, he had handled both deaths well, combining faith and reason as he grappled with the problem of why death, pain, and suffering existed. Recently, Dan had been wondering if Matt could help Jim. Now, he decided to take a risk. As they moved to the dining room, he steered the conversation to that subject.

"Matt, isn't this week the anniversary of your sister's death?" He asked as they took their places around the table.

"Yeah. Two years ago tomorrow," Matt said. He served the sizzling steaks, placed a large salad bowl in the middle of the oak pedestal table, and sat down.

Denise took the bait. "How did she die, Matt?"

"Automobile accident," Matt said. "Coming home after a visit with her daughter." He passed the baked potatoes and the salad. Then, reaching for the bottle of Livingston Cellars, he poured the wine until each crystal goblet was almost full.

They began to eat. Jim, whose eyes had clouded, spoke up. "My *brother* was killed in a car accident. Three years ago." He glanced over at Matt and raised his wine goblet. "It kind of makes you wonder how God could have done that, doesn't it Matt?"

"I don't believe God did it, Jim," Matt said quietly.

"Well, it happened. Everything that happens is God's will, right?"

Matt's jaw tightened slightly. He put down his fork and looked at Jim. "No. Tragedies are not God's will."

"Evil is not God's will, either," Dan chimed in. "That idea is called Fatalism. It's not Christianity."

"Well, if God didn't will it then how did it happen?" Jim asked.

Matt gathered his thoughts. "When my sister was killed, I was upset," he began. "My brother had died the year before, so I was the only member of my primary family left. Thought about it a lot. Finally, I realized what should have been obvious. God is *not* the source of evil. He doesn't *cause* pain, suffering or any of the evils that exist in the world. Then I understood that this didn't come from Him. That was a starting point. If a person doesn't understand *that*, he can blame God for things He doesn't have anything to do with."

"But even if God didn't *do* it, He *allowed* it, right?"

"Yeah. He allowed it."

" That doesn't make any sense," Jim responded derisively. "Why would a kind, compassionate, loving God allow such a senseless act to happen?"

Reaching for the wine bottle, Matt topped off their goblets. "Let's back up a minute. I said these things were evil. *I didn't* say they were senseless."

"What do you mean?" Jim's chin jutted aggressively.

Matt tried a smile. "When I was going through that series of losses a while back, I realized I didn't understand why pain and suffering exist. So I started reading, trying to make sense out of it." He paused and sipped some wine. "My conclusion was that it has to do with free will. That's not an original idea. Lots of others have come to the same opinion over the past two thousand years. But, this is the second part to understanding the problem. As Christians, we believe God created us with free will, and although it's been drastically diminished by the fall from grace, people are still responsible for the use of their remaining free will. We don't hold the modernist view that humans are self-governing and free to choose their own direction autonomously, and we don't hold the post-modernist view that people are products of their culture and only imagine they have free will. Right?" That brought nods of agreement from Dan and Barbara, but Jim's eyes remained fixed on Matt, his face a mask.

Denise had a question. "What's wrong with the idea that we're self-governing and free to choose our own direction?"

"We're not biological machines, Denise," Matt said. "We were created to ultimately depend on God, not on ourselves, so that we'd develop a closer relationship with Him."

"Oh, I see," she said.

"Well, because God created Man with free will," Matt continued, "He had to allow for us to exercise that free will; to permit us to make choices. I think *that's* why He allows evil to exist. If He had created us with free will and we had nothing to choose but *Him*, to choose good, His gift would have been meaningless. And if He'd created us *without* free will, or *without* the power of choice, then love, devotion, caring and all those things that make life worth living would have also been meaningless. They only have meaning when freely given."

"So we have the ability to choose between God and something else," Dan interjected. "That something else is evil. I think God rejoices every time we exercise our free will to choose Him. And He rewards us with His grace."

Barbara put down her knife and fork carefully and leaned forward. "Death, suffering, pain; those *are* evil things, aren't they?" She asked.

"Most people would say so," her husband answered. "They all entered the world because of sin."

"Right," Matt sipped some more wine. "The sin of Eve was a choice. Adam's sin was also a choice. God had given them free will and the chance to exercise it every day."

Jim shook his head. "I'm not following. How did He do *that?*"

"According to the Bible, the tree of the knowledge of good and evil had been in the Garden from the beginning," Dan said, trying to keep it basic. "In the Book of Genesis, God told them they could have and use everything except that. But Eve, tempted by the serpent, made a choice; to eat the fruit from that tree."

Picking up his napkin, Jim swathed his lips. "Don't read the Bible much," he mumbled.

"Oh," Barbara said. "She exercised her free will and chose not to obey God. She did an evil thing."

"And," Dan added, "sin entered the world. That was spiritual death for us, because God hates sin and this sin separated us from His love."

Jim's face reddened. He pointed a finger at Matt. "I thought you were smarter than that, Matt. I stopped believing in all that God and angels and saints business years ago."

"Why, Jim?"

"Because it's all superstition," Jim shot back. "Only real dumb people still believe it." He would have continued on in this vein, but it dawned on him that smiles had frozen in place as the others stared. "It is, isn't it?"

"That seems to be a common view just now in some circles" Matt responded. "But, no, it isn't superstition. Some of the best minds of the past two thousand years have been believers."

Jim decided on a different tack. "Are you saying my brother was exercising a choice for evil? He wasn't. A drunk driver hit him. And your sister? Was she exercising a choice for evil? You said she was just driving home after visiting her daughter."

"Well," Matt held his ground, "that depends on the facts. In your brothers' case, it sounds like the driver of that other *car* made an evil choice. He chose to drive while drunk. His choice produced evil consequences."

"What about your sister?" Jim was somewhat mollified.

"In my sisters' case, she made a wrong choice. Wrong, like getting the wrong answer to a math problem. But not evil. She hadn't slept much the night before, but she climbed behind the wheel of her van dead tired. She could've waited until the next day, or asked her husband to drive her. On her way home, she fell asleep at the wheel and hit a tree. Didn't kill or injure anyone *else*, but her death was a tragic loss for her husband, her kids and for me, too, because our relationship had been strained for several years. But after my wife left, my sister found out about our separation and contacted me. We'd been close ever since."

"Why did it have to be my brother?" Jim asked rhetorically, his voice cracking. "We were more than just brothers. We were friends, too. I loved him very much. There isn't a day goes by that I don't miss him."

Denise placed a comforting hand on her husband's arm.

"I miss my brother and sister, too," Matt said, shaking his head. "There's one thing I know for sure though," he said, looking directly at Jim.

"What's that?" Jim asked.

"When you decide to love, you need to accept the pain that's bound to follow."

CHAPTER 6

Friday, February 16, 1990
Towson, Maryland
Immaculate Conception Church
200 Ware Avenue
8:00 a.m. Eastern Standard Time (EST)

THE GOTHIC SPIRE OF THE one hundred-year-old Immaculate Conception Church pierced gray clouds that threatened snow, as a group of Roman Catholics braved the bone-chilling cold to attend morning Mass. Matt Dawson was one of them.

For Matt, sleep had been elusive. Much of the night his mind had turned the events of the last several years over, like the pages in a picture album. He had resolved that he'd not dwell on the events of the past, but the thoughts had come, roaring out of the darkness like a speeding freight train. Hoping to ward off another sleepless night, he had resorted to prayer, chiding and cajoling, opening his heart and mind to God and asking for a restful sleep. But at dawn, he understood that he had slept only fitfully throughout the night, although with the realization that nights like this were becoming fewer and farther between. To him, that was a sign that he was making progress in his efforts to forgive his ex-wife, his kids *and* himself, and move on.

It occurred to him now that he, Jim Crowley and Alvin Zelinka had something in common. Each had suffered a painful loss. For himself, first his family had been split apart by divorce, and then several family members and two close friends had been taken by death within a short time span. Jim? His only brother had been brutally wrenched from him, causing a gap in his life impossible to fill. And Alvin? His sister had, for some reason yet unknown to Matt, been lost to him forever. Estrangement? Distance? Either, like death, meant a serious loss.

Had Al Zelinka been overwhelmed with feelings of anger, injustice, and sadness once he realized that he might never see his sister again? Had Jim wrestled with these emotions after leaving the site of his brother's grave and returning to the solitude of his own home? He knew that he himself had experienced those feelings when Miriam walked out.

Matt thought back to that bleak April day four years ago. For months afterward his heart had ached like an open wound. In the woods behind the farmhouse one Sunday morning, he'd brought it up to God. *What's going on? I've worked hard for my wife and kids. But I've lost her and I seem to be losing them. How could this happen?*

As the months had passed, his relationship with Jesus became strong and he began to place God at the center of his life. And as he did so, his power of discernment, one of the fruits of the gifts of the Holy Spirit, had been sharpened and he'd begun to comprehend. Yes, he *had* worked hard for his wife and children. But, because of the long hours he had put in at the office, he had probably damaged them by his remoteness, had not taught his kids well and had probably failed to bond with and pass his values on to them. During his marriage, he *had* worked hard to attain financial security and a high standard of living. And for a time, success had been his. But, burdened by the responsibilities and trappings of that lifestyle, he had not always been what a good husband and father should be; loving, attentive, receptive, appreciative, encouraging and kind. For years his wife had put up with his detachment, indifference and occasional rudeness without complaint.

Still, he *had* felt pride in what he'd achieved. But that pride of accomplishment was now muted by the knowledge that Miriam was gone, and he, himself, had been at least partially responsible for destroying their marriage. And there was something else. It seemed that they had not, as he had once thought, shared a common vision. She possessed neither his love of the land nor his desire to pass the farm on to their children as a legacy.

At seven o'clock, knowing that sleep was impossible, Matt dragged himself into the shower. Finished, he quickly shaved and dressed in khaki slacks and a tartan plaid wool shirt. He felt the need to go to Mass, to lay his hurt and rejection at the feet of his friend, Jesus.

Inside the church, Matt rose stiffly with the other parishioners as a tall, thin priest he'd never seen before entered the Sanctuary. During the first part of the Mass, Matt's mind was unfocused. He was so weary! His gaze drifted from the altar to the crucifix and back. *Was what I told Jim Crowley really true?* He wondered. *Was there actually a purpose to it all?* Christianity, especially Roman Catholicism, taught that there was value in suffering. Pain of loss, either from the death of a loved one or divorce by a spouse, and even the suffering caused by a serious illness, could be offered up to God as an expiatory act in reparation for prior sins. *Is it true? I don't know. It's something that has to be accepted on faith, if at all.* He shrugged and said the offering words silently. *It can't hurt,* he thought.

"My brothers and sisters, the Lord be with you," the priest began as he adjusted the microphone in preparation for his homily. Perhaps seventy or more, his face was lined but serene and peaceful, and a friendly array of crows-feet graced the corners of his blue eyes.

"And with your spirit," came the response from those in attendance.

"St. Francis of Assisi said, 'God alone is our salvation. Apart from the Lord, all is lost in darkness.' In St. Paul's letter to the Ephesians, he tells us we are chosen by God and sealed by His grace through the redemption. No one is excluded from His presence. You need only to choose Him." He paused and leaned forward on the podium, intently scanning the church. "Someone among you has come here this morning badly hurting, and burdened by rejection."

Matt's head snapped up. The old priest seemed to be talking directly to him.

"Rejection comes to each of us in many forms," the priest continued. "Was it a parent who walked away when you were young? A wife who lost interest? Or was it that she wouldn't stay and see you through a time of adversity? Or your kids, who've made it plain they've lost all respect for you? These things can bring a deep emotional pain that can keep you bound up in anger, fear and depression."

The elderly priest paused again. "Whatever the problems are, I can tell you this; these difficulties carry a great opportunity for spiritual growth and freedom. I know you're trying, despite all the problems you've experienced, to grow closer to God through your relationship with Jesus. That's the right way. Jesus said, 'No one comes to the Father except through me'. You're doing fine. You've made real spiritual progress. Remember, when you feel that impulse toward Jesus, it's God Himself who is drawing you. So keep going. Don't allow yourself to become bitter and angry. Resist those things. In their place, substitute love, kindness, gentleness and forgiveness." The church was now so still that Matt could almost hear the altar candles burning.

"Just one other thing," the priest continued. "There is a freedom that comes from being loved and accepted by another. But in order for that to take place you must *first* have an understanding of just how much God loves *you*. One of the most profound and life-changing truths is that God *does* love you. *Unconditionally.* Despite what you've done or been through, despite how desolate you feel about the past or about your future, and regardless of what *others* may think of you. To *believe* that God loves you is the first step in experiencing His love in your life in everyday, practical ways. I think you're in the process of accepting that truth, or you wouldn't be here.

"When you leave after Mass this morning, remember this. Even though you're facing seemingly insurmountable trials and you feel broken in spirit, no one is excluded. Anyone who seeks eternal salvation will find his needs met here at God's altar. Those who long for a sense of *belonging to* and of *being loved by* those they love, instead of indifference, will discover, *here*, at the foot of this cross, the love of the One who can reshape your life into something joyous and wonderful."

The old priest clambered down from the podium and returned to the altar. His sermon had been brief but effective. As Matt left the church after Mass had ended, he was both relieved and thankful; relieved of the burden that he'd carried in, and thankful that God had sent just the right person to do His bidding that day. With a lighter heart, he walked to his Skyhawk, eager to return home and begin work on the Zelinka case.

BOOK TWO

"Communists believe they have a destiny. Their destiny is to create a New World and regenerate mankind. To do this, they must conquer the world, shatter the Capitalist system and, by Communist dictatorship, establish (what they believed to be) the regenerative environment of Socialism."

"You Can Trust the Communists
(To Be Communists)" by Dr. Fred Schwartz,
Prentice-Hall, Inc., Englewood Cliffs, N.J. 1960

CHAPTER 7

Tuesday, February 3, 1948
Washington, DC
Old House Office Building
6:15 a.m. Eastern Standard Time (EST)

EARLY MORNING DARKNESS CLOAKED THE streets of the nation's capital as Richard Milhous Nixon (R-CA), the collar of his navy blue topcoat turned up against the penetrating cold, pushed his way through the heavy revolving doors of the Old House Office Building.

The cavernous lobby was empty except for two uniformed guards sipping early morning coffee behind the security desk just inside the glass doors. Nixon waved in their direction and strode briskly to the elevators.

His office was on the fifth floor. That entire level, known as "the attic," was reserved for freshmen Congressmen. Although he'd won the right to represent California's 12th Election District in the election of November 1946, and had assumed his seat in the House in January 1947, he had not, at the end of his first year, been able to relocate his offices to the newer Congressional Office Building, as many second year Congressmen did. Space in that building was at a premium. Absent its competing noises, the old, ornate elevator with dark wood paneling and polished brass fixtures seemed louder than usual.

Dick had been working long hours for the past few weeks. Leaving his office well after nine o'clock and arriving home, which was a suite of rooms he and Pat had taken at the Mayflower Hotel, close to ten, he'd sleep for six or seven hours and return to the office the following morning as dawn broke over the Potomac.

Emerging from the elevator, he moved rapidly down the long corridor, his mind mulling news of the assassination of Mohandes Gandhi, Indian political and spiritual leader, by a Hindu radical just a few days before. The clatter of his black shoes on the cold marble floor echoed the length of the empty hall. Unlocking the outer office door, he flipped the light switch and walked through to his office. His aide and secretary would not be in for an hour and a half.

Hanging his topcoat, scarf, and suit coat on a hook, he retraced his steps to the outer office, where he ran cold water into the percolator, spooned in fresh coffee and flipped a switch under the gas burner. He washed and rinsed his carafe, cleaned the white porcelain cream pitcher and set them both on a silver tray on the corner of his desk. These preliminaries finished, he slipped his wiry frame into the padded leather chair behind his large executive desk, opened a desk drawer and pulled out a yellow pad filled with writing.

This sure is gonna be an eventful day, he told himself. The House Un-American Activities Committee (HUAC) was beginning its second round of hearings of the 80th Congress. HUAC had been created by Congress on January 3, 1945. Edward J. Hart (D-NJ) was its first Chairman. House Resolution 5 of the 79th Congress authorized it "to make investigations into the extent, character, and objects of un-American activities" in the United States, and to assess the "diffusion of subversive and un-American propaganda." Essentially, it would continue the work of the older Dies Committee, which had been operating since 1937, under the direction of Congressman Martin Dies (D-TX), investigating activities of the American Communist Party (CPUSA) and its connection to the Soviet Union. Dick was a key member of that Committee.

A few weeks ago, Committee Chairman, J. Parnell Thomas (R-NJ), and Karl E. Mundt (R-SD), the second ranking Republican member, had decided that a subcommittee would conduct this hearing dealing with legislation to curb the increasing power and influence of the American Communist Party. But Mundt was extremely busy and Thomas's health was failing. Neither wanted to chair another sub-committee. So Dick, young, energetic and ambitious, had asked for the job. Knowing these hearings would be well-publicized; he had shrewdly seen another opportunity to get his name in front of voters across the country, as had been the case with his Education and Labor Committee assignment when he first came to Congress. News that he was chairing this sub-committee had leaked, and the press was already referring to the upcoming hearings as "the Nixon subcommittee hearings." Dick was pleased about that.

But what if the damn hearing turns out badly? Well, I was right about Taft-Hartley and I'm probably right about this. Back in early 1947, after just a few months in the House, he'd become a leading supporter of the Taft-Hartley Labor bill. Although his work had put him at odds with President Truman, who opposed its passage, it had brought him favorable national publicity, as he and a few others led the Republican Congress in its fight to override Mr. Truman's veto. Would this be the same? Or would he wind up embarrassing himself? *If it's a wrong move, I'll deal with it later,* he thought. *In politics, the only thing worse than being wrong is being dull. I've been wrong a couple of times in my career. But, I think most people would agree I've never been dull.*

To prepare for this assignment, he had reviewed some Committee history. Its early work was catalogued in a House Report of the Special Committee on UnAmerican Activities, 76th Congress. The first Special Committee on Un-American Activities had been set up in 1937, initially to investigate the German-American Volksbund, a fascist organization with ties to Hitler's National Socialist government. That was followed by an investigation into the threat of subversion by the Communist Party of the United States (CPUSA), which, it was feared, had turned its autonomy over to Moscow. He shook his head. *This thing with the communists is scary,* he thought. *It's as if we're at war but the public is only vaguely aware of it, and the government agencies that are supposed to be conducting the war have never been told, officially or otherwise, that what's happening is, in fact, a war directed against this country.*

The rich aroma of freshly brewed coffee flooded the office. He grabbed the carafe, walked to the outer office and filled it. Back at his desk, he poured a steaming cup, savoring the smell of the black liquid. He added sugar and cream, sipped from the cup and sat back.

In 1920, the Communist International (Comintern) had been created in Soviet Russia.

That summer, the Comintern had issued a list of twenty-one conditions for the admission of any national party to the Communist International, thus ensuring that Moscow would control all the parties. Condition three had become a source of unease internationally. It said that all national parties:

> *"should create a parallel illegal apparatus which at the decisive moment should do its duty by the Party and in every possible way assist the revolution [by a] combination of lawful and illegal work."*

Because of this and the language of several other conditions, concern quickly spread throughout the United States of America that the Soviet Union, through the international communist movement, might be attempting to overthrow the government of the United States and other countries by force. But, the American public, going about its business of living, was not taking it seriously, even though that view had been reinforced in 1935, when Earl Browder, general secretary of CPUS from 1932 to 1945, had read a membership pledge to a group of new Party members in New York:

> *"I now take my place in the ranks of the Communist Party, The Party of the working class. I take this solemn oath to give the best that is in me to the service of my class...pledge myself to remain at all times a vigilant and firm defender of The Leninist line of the Party, the only line that insures the triumph of Soviet Power in the United States."*

Browder's speech had set off alarm bells everywhere except in socialist quarters. Curious, the House Committee subpoenaed him in 1939. Under intense questioning, he stated that members could be expelled from the Communist Party for refusing to carry out Party decisions. He also revealed that if someone's views differed from the party line, by expressing them, he was separating himself from the Party. When asked if a Party member's disagreement with Stalin's pact with Nazi Germany would result in expulsion, Browder had answered, "Yes."

With the entry of the United States into World War II, concern quickly developed about possible guerrilla activities within US borders. The existence of a "fifth column" in America was discussed often. The Nation's bridges, railroads, highways, tunnels, oil tanks, shipyards, power plants, dams and reservoirs, all unprotected, provided targets of opportunity for bands of guerrillas, trained by and dedicated to a foreign power. The Committee soon began holding hearings on German-American and Japanese-American activities.

During the early years of the war, Dick and his wife had read newspaper reports describing sightings of Japanese submarines in West Coast waters. California newspapers pointed out that the Japanese were located in strategic areas, that they operated fishing boats up and down the coast, and, if they had not already done so, they could easily make contact with the Japanese submarine fleet. Those articles generated fear in the minds of many Californians.

California's Attorney General, Earl Warren, a liberal Republican known in the Republican Party as a RINO (Republican in name, only) who later would oust Governor Culbert Olson from Sacramento, acting on the premise that war with Japan was inevitable, had, for a year prior to December 1941, actively called for the evacuation of all Japanese, whether aliens or citizens. On January 30, 1942, Warren publicly declared:

> "I have come to the conclusion that the Japanese
> situation as it exists today in California may well be the
> Achilles heel of the entire civilian defense effort. Unless
> something is done, it may bring about a repetition of
> Pearl Harbor."

Two weeks later, in February 1942, President Roosevelt, following recommendation of the commander of the Western Defense Command, Lieutenant General John L. DeWitt, that all people of Japanese ancestry should be removed from the Coast due to military necessity, created the Wartime Civil Control Administration (WCCA). Under its direction, people of Japanese ancestry living in the three Pacific coast states were rounded up and placed into detention camps.

In agreement with DeWitt's proposal, Warren watched as between one hundred twelve thousand and one hundred twenty thousand residents of his state were removed to camps, their homes and businesses confiscated and their lives suspended indefinitely.

Dick Nixon had had mixed emotions about that policy. He knew that some recent immigrants were not yet eligible for citizenship, so the Constitution did not apply to them. But it seemed to him a blatant violation of the constitutional rights of those Japanese who had become citizens. And as to their children born in the United States, the Constitution clearly stated that they were American citizens by birth. However, like many Americans, Dick had conceded that it was probably a wise, protective step. After all, there was a war going on. But in 1944, when the US Supreme Court decided that this practice was unconstitutional and ordered a halt to it, Dick had not been unhappy.

In addition, serious concerns were developing about Soviet communism. The American Communist Party, active in the United States since at least 1919 under various innocuous names designed to hide its real purpose, such as the Workers

Party of America, had captured the hearts and minds of leftists, radical liberals, communists and socialists. Many of them, aware of the power of indoctrinating young minds, had infiltrated the campuses of American colleges and universities as teachers. Some had become members of the media and film industry. Indeed, the zeitgeist, the prevailing mind-set of philosophers and social scientists of that period of the 20th Century was the socialist ideology. Supported by supposedly objective studies such as 'theoretical welfare economics,' the failures of free market systems to meet certain idealized political standards were spotlighted. Set against these alleged 'failures,' the 'ideal' economic system envisioned by the materialistic Marxist ideology held strong appeal. In Communism, preceded by an evolutionary period of Socialism, they saw an economic system they believed would be more just than Capitalism. On the surface, for some who had experienced it first hand, the depression, instead of being seen as only a temporary blip on an otherwise successful Capitalist scene, seemed to confirm this. They sought a way to end poverty on earth and thought communism would achieve that goal. They did not foresee the loss of individual freedoms and the deadening effect upon the human spirit necessarily involved in such a system.

As the anti-American activities of CPUSA accelerated and public perception of where Party sympathies actually lay became widespread, some members of the Roosevelt Administration had been accused of being communists. It was proven that some were. Because CPUS began to sound more and more like an arm of the Soviet government, the American people became alarmed.

Then, in the early 1940s the US Army's Signals Intelligence Service, a predecessor to the National Security Agency (NSA), deciphered the first of many Soviet cables sent from Moscow to its intelligence stations in the West between 1940 and 1948. A crack team of American code breakers, working secretly and using the latest in signals intelligence (SIGINT) technology, which allowed America to eavesdrop on the commanders of foreign military forces and foreign embassies, discovered that a previously unsuspected yet vast network of at least two hundred agents were engaged in spying for the Soviet Union inside the United States. Many had penetrated to the highest levels of government and were stealing and passing on to Moscow information on America's military capability: our Armed Forces readiness levels, our jet aircraft project, and secrets involving radar and rocket development. Of special interest to the Soviet Union and the Germans was US atomic energy research, specifically the status of our efforts to develop an atomic bomb.

During that period, information about codes was tightly guarded by all intelligence agencies. This code-breaking project was assigned the name Venona; a code word for secret Soviet spy communications, as distinguished from the name Ultra, which was the name given to secret German spy messages. 'Venona' was a program designed to intercept and eventually decrypt stacks of secret Soviet cable traffic; coded and enciphered messages sent over commercial telegraph lines. The existence of Venona was not made public. President Roosevelt, his wife, Eleanor, herself suspected for a time of being a Communist, and a few senators and congressmen on the Senate and House Foreign Relations Committees knew of it. The Federal Bureau of Investigation (FBI) was also apprised, so that counter-espionage actions could be developed. A fellow Republican representative who sat on the House Foreign Relations Committee had made Dick aware of it a few weeks after he had first come to Congress.

Through his work on the Education and Labor Committee in early '47, Dick had met Father John Cronin, a Maryknoll priest and teacher at Saint Mary's Seminary on Roland Avenue in Baltimore. Father Cronin, who at the time was the Assistant Director of the National Catholic Welfare Conference and a social activist, had served as a labor organizer in the early 1940s. His CIO experience had shown him the attempted communist takeover of the Labor movement. Concerned, he began collecting information on communist involvement in Labor. While doing so he exchanged information with Bill Sullivan, a former Assistant FBI Director.

In 1944, Father Cronin sent a report of his findings to his bishops. Impressed, they gave him a sabbatical year off to prepare a study of communism in America. By the end of '45 he'd finished his work. Entitled, "The Problem of American Communism," it revealed communist infiltration tactics in labor and government, and brought him to the attention of the House Labor Committee, which invited him to Washington to testify in 1947.

Some of Father Cronin's materials were provided by the FBI from information supplied by David Whittaker Chambers, with whom the FBI had been talking for several years. Chambers, himself a member of a Communist Party cell, had described the existence of another communist cell, this one within the government, that included Alger Hiss among its members, and had vowed to expose Hiss if Hiss were named Secretary General of the United Nations founding convention.

The United States government had, early on, developed the view that American Communists, because of their loyalty to the Soviet Union, would spy on their own government. But, not enough was known about just how they'd go about it. Venona and several other sources made it clear that American Communists with access to sensitive information were expected by the Party to turn it over to the Soviets. It also became clear that the American Communist Party leadership sought out these people and turned them over to work for the Soviet Union. Earl Browder, head of the American Communist Party, was deeply involved in recruiting Party members and vetting them for espionage activities.

When rumors began circulating that several communist cells such as the Ware Group were operating in Washington, DC to target the federal government, HUAC began holding hearings on the influence of Communism in the government, in the media, and in Hollywood.

Dick had asked to be assigned to HUAC because he knew that the conservative 80th Congress was committed to rooting out communists and communist sympathizers from within the government. So strong was the congressional commitment to this effort that it would soon vote on an appropriations bill allotting two hundred thousand dollars, the largest appropriation ever, for its work.

The 80th Congress had developed plans to hold three sets of hearings during '48. The first, focusing on communist espionage in the United States, had already been concluded. The second, set to begin today, involved proposed legislation to curb or control the US Communist Party. The third, scheduled for November, would examine communist efforts to ferret out secrets of America's atomic bomb project.

Dick poured himself another cup of coffee. In his opinion, the hearing would help make this nation of a hundred and forty-seven million people aware of the extent of communist efforts to infiltrate their government. In addition, because the sessions would command wide media attention, they would have the attention of many voters.

Am I prepared for these hearings? Dick asked himself. *I want them to be thorough and tough, but I also need them to be perceived by the media and the public as fair and impartial.* To accomplish those goals, he needed to create a judicial atmosphere. No bullying of witnesses, no running roughshod over their rights, no speeches or tirades by anyone on either side of the ideological fence. He didn't want the Committee subjected to charges that it had embarked on a "witch-hunt" for communists.

Picking up his phone, Dick buzzed Robert Stripling, Chief Counsel for HUAC, whose office was three floors below. Stripling would be handling questioning of witnesses at this session.

"Bob Stripling," a high-pitched male voice answered.

"Bob? Dick Nixon. You ready?"

"Yes. I was just going over my notes."

"After you finish your questions, I'm gonna allow five minutes for each committee member who wants to ask his own questions. We'll alternate: Republican, Democrat, Republican and Democrat, until everyone's finished."

"Good. That way, no one can claim that the hearing was not a bi-partisan effort and that we didn't conduct this hearing impartially."

"The Administration leaked word that if Truman's re-elected in November he'll try to abolish the Committee. Have ya heard that?"

"Heard it from Karl Mundt over breakfast in the cafeteria this morning," Stripling said. "Since then, in the short time I've been in my office, I've read it in *The Washington Post*, digested it over coffee with my clerk, and been bludgeoned with it from several other sources. Sorta puts some pressure on us, doesn't it?"

"Sure does. Truman's dug in his heels on this one. The radical liberal end of his support base wants our collective scalp, and he'll be happy to hand it to them. See you in the hearing room in a few minutes."

Replacing the receiver, Dick rolled down the French-cuffed sleeves of his white dress-shirt, removed two black onyx cuff links from his jacket pocket and inserted one into each cuff. Fastening the sleeves, he reached for his suit coat. Because of his preference for quiet, three-piece suits, what he wore today gave him the appearance of a successful young lawyer in any city in the country, on his way to court.

Over the past three months, several bills dealing with controlling the Communist Party had been introduced. Their thrust was to simply outlaw it. But he and Karl Mundt had authored the MundtNixon Bill, which would require the Party and its front groups to register as subversive organizations attempting to overthrow the government. *With any luck,* Dick thought, *our bill will be the one approved by the Committee and brought to the floor for a vote.*

CHAPTER 8

Tuesday, February 3, 1948
Washington, DC
The Capitol Building
House Caucus Room
10:01 a.m. Eastern Standard Time (EST)

"THE HEARING WILL COME TO order," Representative Dick Nixon announced, rapping his gavel sharply on a wooden block in front of him on the committee table. He tested his microphone with a fingernail, causing the hot mike to emit a rasping sound, which reverberated throughout the room. The startled crowd of reporters, staff members and spectators looked up, like a herd of deer caught in the headlights of an oncoming car, and scrambled to their seats. A hush settled over the pale green Caucus Room.

"This is a session of a subcommittee of the House UnAmerican Activities Committee," Dick began. He glanced toward the stenographer to make sure she was transcribing his remarks. "For the record, my name is Richard M. Nixon and I'll be acting as Chairman for this hearing." Placing his notes squarely on the table, he steepled his fingers at eye level in front of his face and continued gravely. "We are seeking answers and we hope to obtain answers to three basic questions. First, we should like to know whether the Communist Party, the American Communists, constitute at the present time a real danger to national security. Second, if they do, are our present laws adequate to cope with that danger, and if not, what new laws are necessary to meet it? Third, is there a substantial risk that adoption of any proposed legislation will impair any fundamental constitutional rights?"

Representative Nixon's eyes roved over the spectators. *I was right. The hearing room is packed.* He smiled a satisfied smile. "Robert Stripling, Counsel for the Committee, will conduct the questioning at this morning's session. Are you ready, Mr. Stripling?"

"I am, Mr. Chairman," Stripling answered in his characteristically high-pitched voice.

"Then you may proceed. Call the first witness."

Dick leaned back and took a long look at the Committee's counsel seated at the table to his right. Stripling was tall and lean, with a sallow complexion, a thin, drawn face and slicked-down black hair. A stylish dresser, he wore a gray, three-piece pinstriped suit, a white dress shirt and a silver and black striped tie. He had attended both Texas A. & M. College and the University of Texas, but bored as a student, he had not earned a degree at either one before leaving for Washington in 1932. Beginning in a low paying patronage job, he had risen through the ranks until becoming counsel to the House Committee. After a stint in the Army, he returned to the Committee in 1946, after which HUAC's productivity had immediately improved. His talent as an interrogator was recognized by just about everyone. But having been Counsel for eleven years, Stripling planned to retire from that post in August.

As testimony began, Nixon relaxed. He knew the hearing would go well. Stripling was one of the best informed men in the country on the tactics and objectives of the communist conspiracy.

In a few days, another subcommittee composed of John Ralph McDowell (R-PA), and himself was going to take testimony from Arthur Garfield Hayes regarding Hayes's opposition to laws banning CPUSA. Hayes, a Democrat, was a lawyer who practiced Constitutional Law and Commercial Law in New York. Some considered him to be the leading Constitutional lawyer in the country.

Although Dick opposed outlawing CPUSA, he did favor registration of it. At the end of the session, the Committee would deliver a bill to the full House for its consideration. Since a majority of the Committee did not favor outlawing CPUSA, he was almost certain that the Mundt-Nixon Bill would be the one approved and sent to the House floor. If passed by the House and Senate and signed by the President, it would replace the Alien Registration Act of 1940. That law, known as the Smith Act, was weak and had been ignored for years. The Mundt-Nixon Bill specified that all members of CPUSA must register or face criminal penalties. Its sponsors had worked hard to produce a bill that would withstand a constitutional challenge. Dick, anticipating being named floor manager when it reached the House floor, had taken an informal poll. The votes for passage were there.

‡ ‡ ‡ ‡ ‡

Friday, April 2, 1948
Washington, DC
Old House Office Building
Office of Representative Richard M. Nixon (R-CA)
8:30 a.m. EST

Dick Nixon, seated behind his desk piled high with files and papers, was in a pensive mood. But that was an improvement over the foul frame of mind he'd been battling since the Nixon Sub-Committee hearing had come to an end after seven chaotic days in early February.

Because he'd worked to establish a judicial atmosphere in that hearing room, the first few sessions had gone well. On February eleventh, however, that had changed.

A drizzling rain had fallen the night before. The temperature hovered just above freezing until close to dawn, when it dropped sharply, ushering in a biting wind that carried the hint of snow. At daybreak, the streets and sidewalks had been transformed into sheets of ice, a commuter's nightmare.

As usual, Dick had left his car in a nearby parking garage and walked to the Old House Office Building. Rounding the last corner, he was appalled to see that the front of the building was crawling with reporters and photographers. Resolutely, he moved forward. They descended upon him from all sides, shouting questions. Two security guards pushed through the melee, but just before they reached him, distracted by a reporter who thrust a microphone in his face and yelled a question, he had slipped and sprawled full-length on the ice. A *Washington Post* photographer had caught him on film in an undignified position as he struggled to regain his feet. At the flash of the camera, Dick's face had turned crimson.

One of the security guard rushed out and helped Dick to his feet. With his briefcase in his left hand, he had tried to break his fall with his right. Serious pain was building in his right wrist. Believing that he had broken it and in too much pain to attend the session, he requested that he be driven to the nearest hospital. That evening's edition of the *Post* had carried a very unflattering picture on its front page. AP and UP picked it up and, their somewhat misguided ideas regarding what constitutes news being similar, published it in newspapers across the nation.

In Dick's absence, John McDowell had presided as Acting Chairman. Testimony was taken from Adolph A. Berle, a former Assistant Secretary of State for Latin American Affairs from 1938 through 1944, in whose department many communist sympathizers were known to be working. Berle, a thin man with a high forehead, receding hairline and a hooked nose, appeared uncomfortable as he answered Stripling's questions.

Why was Berle of interest to HUAC? It seems that after the Hitler-Stalin Pact of August 1939, Whittaker Chambers and Isaac Don Levine paid him a visit on September 1st, the day the Germans invaded Poland. At that meeting, Chambers told Berle of the existence of many "underground espionage agents" operating within the government. These included Lee Pressman, John Abt, Charles Kravitsky, Lawrence Duggan, Julian Wadleigh, Eleanor Nelson, and Donald and Alger Hiss. Later, Levine had contacted Chambers and reported that Berle had given the information to President Roosevelt, who simply laughed. Apparently, HUAC wanted to explore this meeting of Chambers, Levine, and Berle, place the names of these alleged spies on the public record, and make the public aware that this information had reached the ears of the President, Franklin Delano Roosevelt.

Representative John Elliott Rankin (D-MS), a member of HUAC and this subcommittee, supported racial segregation. A wispy little man who represented Mississippi's 1st Congressional District, he looked as if he'd blow away in the next strong wind. He had chosen this session for some theatrics. Rankin, lacking in both tact and sound judgment, often spouted racist views from the House floor about Blacks, Jews, and Japanese. He was known to have been jealous of Berle, who at twenty-one had been the youngest graduate in the history of Harvard Law. Trying to embarrass Berle, Rankin made a circus of the session.

The press had had a field day with the story. Even though Dick, his wrist in a plaster cast, had returned the following morning and quickly restored order, it was the Committee, not Berle, which had been embarrassed. Dick sighed. He was beginning to think that at times his life had a life of its own.

But from Representative Nixon's point of view, that was not the worst of it. Since that hearing had become known in the press as the Nixon Sub-Committee hearing, heads soon were turning toward him in the corridors and tongues began wagging as people connected him to a hearing in which incidents embarrassing to HUAC had occurred. *I need to find something to take public attention off the Rankin-Berle debacle,* he thought. He had been mulling this over, on and off, for several weeks.

His desk intercom broke into his thoughts. "Yes," he said quietly. The last thing he wanted just now was an interruption.

"The paperhanger has arrived, Mr. Nixon," his secretary said briskly.

"What?"

"The paperhanger," she snapped. "You put in a work order three months ago." Her voice was at once accusatory and defensive. "She's here. Now."

Dick's eyes roved the office as if looking for a place to hide. He sighed. "Okay. Let her come in." Seconds later the door opened and a sturdy-looking woman dressed in gray coveralls backed in, her arms full of rolls of wallpaper, a large, metal tray and several wide brushes with natural wood handles and nylon bristles. His phone rang.

"Nixon," he said, his voice betraying his irritation.

"Dick? Lou Russell. I wanted to talk with ya. That Federal Grand Jury in New York? You been followin' it?"

The paperhanger let fall to the floor everything she was carrying. Dick was visibly startled by the clamor, but stifled his annoyance and nodded pleasantly at her. She acknowledged his nod with a smile, turned and left for more supplies.

"What about it, Lou?"

"Well, the talk is they're close to indictin' a bunch a people up there. Under the Smith Act. They've been workin' on this fer over a year."

"Who are they gonna indict?"

The woman returned carrying a five-gallon drum of wallpaper glue, a yardstick and a wooden level. She glanced at Dick, frowned and quickly left again.

"About a dozen officers of CPUS. Gus Hall's one a them."

"Under the Smith Act? You think a Grand Jury will finally have balls enough to bring an indictment under the Smith Act?" At that moment the paperhanger returned carrying an aluminum stepladder. She kept her eyes fixed on a spot near the window, but two small red splotches appeared on her cheeks. Dick watched her absently. An idea was forming.

"It might. But I doubt if the District Attorney'll be able to get a conviction even if the Grand Jury *does* return an indictment. It'll probably wind up just like all the other investigations up there in the last couple a years. Lots a talk. No real substance." The paperhanger walked back into the outer office.

"This sounds like something our Committee should look into," Dick said. "Possible subversive activities threatening our American institutions. It has a nice ring to it, doesn't it?"

"What're you thinking, Dick?"

"I'm thinking about us maybe holding a public hearing. Advertise it. Hype it big. We can fit it into our schedule. Possibly at the end of July or early August."

The paperhanger returned carrying a folding wooden rule. Avoiding Dick's gaze, she set her ladder in the corner near the door, mounted it and busied herself with measuring. Dick's eyes followed her movements but he was not actually seeing her.

"You're right," Russell responded. "It *could* be done. And it *is* within our jurisdiction."

"Do you know who the Grand Jury's been taking testimony from?"

"Yeah. A lady from Connecticut name of Elizabeth Bentley. She was a KGB agent. Says she worked as an auxiliary agent handler and courier for a Soviet spy network. She joined the Communist Party in New York in 1935. She became involved in Soviet intelligence activity in 1938. Worked for Jacob Golos, who was her lover and boss. Left in 1945. She gave a statement to the FBI. Named lots a people who've been secretly supplying information to the KGB. Also, another guy, a senior editor for *Time* and *Life* Magazines named David Whittaker Chambers. He broke with the Communist Party in '38 or '39 and has been writin' articles in *Time* warning against the Soviet Union and Joe Stalin's regime. Chambers has been talkin' to the FBI and he's named several people, including Donald and Alger Hiss, as communists."

Dick frowned. He was interested. "I'll talk to Parnell about this," he said. "His health the way it is, he may not want to take on anything else for a while. But if he gives the okay, you and Ben Mandell can get the ball rolling. Take statements from Bentley and Chambers first. If there's any substance there, Stripling can set a date on our calendar and issue subpoenas."

Hanging up the phone, he settled back in his chair and began to massage his temples with his open palms. The paperhanger applied glue to the paper like an artist coating a canvas. To Dick, this idea seemed perfect; just the thing to take everyone's mind off the recent hearing and his embarrassing connection to it.

He watched the paperhanger set the first strip in place, and then remove a folded wooden rule from a pocket of her bulky coveralls, unfold it and measure the corner again. Dick reached for his phone and dialed Parnell Thomas's number. Busy. *If, say by the end of the year, HUAC could call a press conference and reveal findings that spies had penetrated to the very heart of the government, its reputation would soar in the public mind. It would be a positive piece of public relations, and a feather in my cap, too.* He replaced the phone. The woman wheeled around and approached his desk.

"Hi," she said. "I'm Iris." She extended a hand sticky with glue, and before he could protest, grabbed his right hand and shook it vigorously. "I've worked exclusively on Capitol Hill since the war, hanging paper in the offices of senators and representatives."

"You have?"

"Yes, sir. And this paper *you* selected is the absolute best. It should last a long time."

"Good," he said, without much enthusiasm.

"Goes well with your rug and furniture, too." Finally, she returned to her work, mumbling things that Dick could not quite hear.

He was finding it difficult to concentrate. Wiping glue residue from his hand, he reached for his suit coat and walked into the outer office.

"I'll be back shortly," he told his secretary. Strolling into the hall, he stopped at the elevators and lit a cigarette. He wasn't overly concerned about his campaign for re-election to the House in the fall. He had cross-filed in the primaries of both parties and was confident that he'd win in both. He'd already begun thinking about a Senatorial campaign down the road. Sheridan Downey, the Democrat who held one of California's senate seats, did not look well. *He hasn't yet said anything, but rumors are flying that his health is failing. Maybe he'll announce his retirement next year,* Dick thought. He took a last drag on his cigarette, dropped the butt, crushed it under a foot and strolled back to his office.

"Karl Mundt calling," his secretary said as soon as he walked through the door. With a strained glance in the direction of his office, she hesitated. "Rosie the Riveter's still back there," she said, and handed him the phone.

"Nixon."

"Dick? Karl." The voice of the senior House Member from South Dakota, always unflappably calm, came over the line. "Just wanted to let you know the Mundt-Nixon Bill will be introduced into the full House on Monday."

"Really? That's great news." Dick allowed himself a brief smile.

"Your work in steering it through the subcommittee was very helpful."

"Thanks, Karl."

Mundt was silent for a moment. Then, "The floor fight on this one's gonna be rough."

"Yeah. Swing and Sway with Sammy Kaye."

Mundt laughed. "Seriously. Blood's gonna flow. Have you done any planning for how you're gonna manage it on the House floor?"

"Am *I* gonna manage it?"

"Um - hmm. You're the logical one for the job. I talked it over with the Speaker and the Majority Leader. They agree. Told me to let you know today."

"Well, I've given it *some* thought," Dick admitted. "Opponents will probably concentrate on unconstitutionality; they'll say it's a violation of civil liberties. We might counter with fairness; too many groups have been unfairly labeled communist fronts, and this bill will spike all those loose charges. If your group is not on the Attorney General's list you're home free."

"Sounds good. We can talk more about it tomorrow."

Elated, Dick hung up. Newspaper editors, like politicians, were aware that assignment as the floor manager for an important bill was a sign of growing recognition within his Party, of the talents of a young congressman. They were also aware that along with that recognition came an increase in power. So they watched for any important assignment, ready to herald the person receiving it as a new player of significance. *This development, together with the idea I just came up with is all I need. Not only will I save face, but also the daily media reporting of the House floor fight will give me name recognition nationally. That won't hurt me in California either, if I decide to announce for the Senate next year.*

CHAPTER 9

Monday, May 17, 1948
Washington, DC
Old House Office Building
Office of Representative J. Parnell Thomas (R-NJ)
2:30 p.m. Eastern Standard Time (EST)

"So," LOUIS RUSSELL WAS SAYING, "I tried to get copies of the transcripts of testimony Bentley and Chambers gave before the Grand Jury in New York ..."

It was midafternoon on a warm but pleasant day in the District. The Japanese cherry trees blossoming along the Tidal Basin's rim had given way to the bright yellow forsythia and vivid pink and white dogwoods set further back. Tourists, making the most of the nice weather, had flocked to Washington, creating a mosaic of humanity in the area that day.

But in the Middle East, weekend news had been bad. The British had withdrawn from Palestine on Friday, May 14th. The Jewish National Council had immediately proclaimed the state of Israel and the Truman Administration had extended recognition hours later. That Saturday, Arab forces from Egypt, Jordan, Syria, Lebanon and Iraq had invaded the fledgling nation, intent upon driving the Jews from their new homeland.

Dick Nixon sat in the conference room in Representative Parnell Thomas's office listening to Russell. Thomas was there, looking pale and distracted. Dick, Representatives John McDowell of Pennsylvania, and John Wood of Georgia sat on one side of the table. Representative Karl Mundt of South Dakota, Representative John Rankin of Mississippi and Committee Counsel Bob Stripling occupied the other. Thomas's secretary, a young government girl with silky black hair, wearing glasses and a harried expression, was perched in a chair directly behind her boss, taking shorthand notes. Representative Fred Busby and Researcher Ben Mandel stood along one wall smoking and shifting their weight from one foot to the other. Cigarette smoke hung like a filmy cobweb above their heads.

"... but I was unsuccessful," Russell continued. "The DA won't release copies without a subpoena. So Don Appell and I tracked both witnesses down. They're being kept under wraps, with FBI agents acting as bodyguards 'round the clock. It seems there's some fear for their safety." He paused to let the significance of this information sink in.

"Elizabeth Bentley lives in West Hartford, Connecticut. Chambers lives on a farm near Westminster, Maryland." He paused again, enjoying the suspense his words were creating.

"Bentley said she'd been involved since the 1930s in an espionage ring run by one J. Peters, alias Alexander Stevens. She claims he heads up the underground section of the US Communist Party." There were a few gasps from the men in the room. Russell paused again to let them digest the fact that CPUSA, following the directive of the Comintern of 1920, was now operating an underground unit in the United States.

"Do you believe her, Lou?" Thomas asked.

Russell took a long drag on his cigarette and held the smoke for a few moments before exhaling. "Yeah. Don and I both think she'll make a believable witness. She went through several days of questioning in front of that New York grand jury and wasn't intimidated. And don't forget, the DA's office up there has evaluated her, too. She obviously impressed them or they wouldn't have gone forward."

There were a few murmurs of assent from the listeners.

"When we visited Chambers," Russell continued, "he told us he was reluctant to testify because he might lose his job or worse. But he's doing it because he wants the world to understand why people like himself and Alger Hiss would, and I quote, 'heed the destructive call of communism.' During the interview, we got what we were looking for —corroboration of Bentley's testimony. And we got a lot more." He made eye contact with Thomas. "Chambers can confirm some of what Bentley says. But he has more *important* information. Dynamite!"

The people in the room grew quiet. Through the partially opened windows, muted traffic noise floated up to them from the street below.

"Whittaker Chambers is a former Soviet spy," Russell said. "Been talking to the FBI since 1940. His activities in the '30s as a member of the Soviet Communist Party underground can shed light on those rumors about a Party cell called the Ware group, which apparently began functioning in Washington in the mid-thirties."

"Really?" Dick Nixon murmured.

"In fact," Russell went on, "even though the Soviet Union has an elaborate spy network functioning in the United States, and even though they attempt to protect the identities of their agents, he can finger people like Witt, Abt, Perlo, Pressman and both Alger and Donald Hiss as Communist Party members and as members of that group."

The small conference room came alive with excited voices. These names had surfaced regularly in HUAC hearings. Alger Hiss was the best known. Dick exchanged a meaningful glance with Thomas.

"Also," Russell went on, "he told us these guys and others were recruited for the purpose of infiltrating the government and working their way up to positions of influence. Once they were established, their mission was to mess up policy wherever possible."

"*My God!*" John Wood muttered under his breath.

Ruddy-cheeked John McDowell glanced at Nixon. "This is certainly interesting."

"He *also* has information about the activities of Maxim Lieber, John Loomis Sherman and others whose names have been popping up in testimony recently," Russell said.

The air in the room was now thick with cigarette smoke. Thomas began to cough. Mundt shot a concerned glance in his direction, went to one of the windows, and threw it open wider.

"Should we schedule a hearing and take testimony from these people?" Dick asked.

"We've been learning bits and pieces about this Ware Group for over a year," Thomas said. "This'll be our first opportunity to develop concrete evidence about it." He glanced at Lou Russell. "Lou? Keep trying to get copies of their grand jury testimony. Stripling can issue subpoenas for it, if that's the only way. Also, see if you can find out what the FBI knows about these two."

People began to rise from their seats. By mute consensus, the meeting was over. Turning to Bob Stripling, Thomas barked, "Stripling, set it on the calendar right away and make up subpoenas for both Bentley and Chambers."

As the men filed from his office, Thomas, catching the eyes of Nixon, Mundt, Wood and Stripling, gestured for each to stay. When the room had emptied, he shut the door firmly.

"Heard from the White House this morning, gentlemen." He grinned impishly. "The President's not happy. He's shown nuthin' but contempt for our efforts up to now. Now? He doesn't like our attempt to focus the attention of this Congress on communist infiltration into the government. Mr. Truman thinks our findings might embarrass his Administration. Is that an accurate assessment, John?"

John Wood nodded. "That's a faih assessment, Pawnell." Wood, the ranking Democrat on the Committee, was a conservative from a conservative southern state. He didn't like the President's policies and did not always vote with the Administration, as his Party's leaders thought he should. Crushing his cigarette in the ashtray on Thomas's desk, Wood continued. "Algah Heiss, huh? Russell's raht. This *is* dahnamaht. These hearings could be the most impo'tant we've evah held."

"And the most controversial," Parnell Thomas said. "Alger Hiss has become a poster boy for liberalism over the years. I think the entire Washington Press Corps will take his side."

"I can see it now," Nixon chimed in. "Bureau chiefs, columnists and commentators ready to go to bat for him the first time HUAC even looks cross-eyed at him. During Hiss's years in public life, the media has called him" - he struck a pose – "'one of America's ablest public servants ... a man with a wide-reaching and perceptive approach to governmental problems ... someone with a solid liberal mind...'" The others laughed.

Thomas turned to Stripling. "Bob, I know you want to leave Washington as soon as possible, but if we schedule this hearing for late July or early August we're going to need you."

Stripling grinned a toothy grin that turned his face into a facsimile of a skull. "I was thinking the same thing."

"Yeah, Bob," Dick Nixon said. "It'll be awkward breaking in a new Counsel while hearings as important as these are going on. Maybe you could postpone your retirement until the end of the year."

‡ ‡ ‡ ‡ ‡

Tuesday, August 3, 1948
Washington, DC
The Capitol Building
10:04 a.m. EST

J. Parnell Thomas, out of breath, entered the hearing room at a trot. He had been delayed by a phone call from syndicated columnist and radio broadcaster Drew Pearson's office. The call would change his life forever.

Congressman Thomas had listened as a Pearson associate informed him that on the following day, Pearson intended to go public with charges that Thomas may have been demanding a portion of the pay of his staff members as kickbacks for keeping their jobs.

He had been tipped off earlier in the year that Pearson was investigating him. His health, bad due to his age and the crushing workload he carried, had worsened under the strain of waiting for possible exposure. HUAC's activities were unpopular with the Truman Administration, and Thomas had become a lightning rod for objections from its opponents. The opposition party had been digging. Liberals on that side of the isle were leaving no stone unturned, hunting for anything that might embarrass him, hoping to delay or even shipwreck any further hearings of the 80th Congress into communist activities within the government. This was something they could use. It would probably trigger a Justice Department investigation. He might be forced to resign. Worse, he could be indicted. He might need to defend himself against criminal charges.

"Let the record show," the white-topped Republican began as he tapped his gavel lightly on the table, "that the full Committee is convened to take testimony from Whittaker Chambers dealing with acts of espionage of the US Communist Party and the International Communist Party." Members of the press sprinted for their seats and the room quieted down.

Thomas removed his glasses and peered at the witness who had just entered the hearing room. His vision blurred, a sign that his blood pressure was elevated and approaching dangerously high levels. He forced himself to concentrate. Russell and Appell had already taken a statement from Chambers. Thomas had read it and knew the general nature of his testimony. But this was his first opportunity to actually *see* the man who was creating such a stir among Committee members and staff.

David Whittaker Chambers was five feet eight inches tall, stocky, with a high forehead. His fleshy face rose above a prominent double chin. He wore a wrinkled, out-of-style, light blue suit. Ill at ease and obviously intimidated by his surroundings, he was sweating profusely even though all the windows were open.

"Please take your seat, sir," Representative Thomas said gently. "It's hot, gentlemen. Anyone who wishes to do so may remove his coat and tie. I'm going to do that myself. Mr. Clerk, will you kindly swear the witness?" After the clerk had performed this function, Thomas nodded to Stripling, seated at the Committee table immediately to his right. "You may proceed, Mr. Counsel."

"Please state your full name for the record," Stripling began.

"My name is David Whittaker Chambers," the witness said, his voice almost inaudible.

Chambers sounds tired and possibly depressed, Thomas thought. *Wonder if I should appoint a psychiatrist to examine him? After his testimony becomes public later today, Hiss's sympathizers will likely mount a smear campaign against him, using anything they can find or conjure up to discredit him. Will he be able to hold up under the stress and pressure of the next several months?* Then, as the irony of his concern for Chambers in view of his own situation occurred to him, he chuckled. *Will I myself be able to bear up under the strain of what's coming?*

Seated at Thomas's left, Dick Nixon heard him chuckle. Turning slightly, he noted that Thomas's face was chalky and he seemed extremely agitated. "Are you okay?" He whispered.

"Yes. I'm fine, just fine," Thomas muttered.

The hearing room was crowded, its benches filled with representatives of the wire services, local press and spectators. In addition, several members of the House had drifted in to stand along the walls and listen. That often happened during House Committee hearings, but this was the first time a HUAC hearing had enjoyed such popularity. After Mrs. Bentley had testified the week before, word had spread that something significant was brewing.

With Bob Stripling asking questions, Chambers explained that his affiliation with the Communist Party had begun in 1922. He described how he broke with the Party forty-eight hours after publication of the Russo-German pact of August 23, 1939, to express his complete disagreement with that move. Fearing for his life, he and his family went into hiding. He had then tried, unsuccessfully, to see the President. After that, in the company of Isaac Don Levine, a columnist for the *New York Journal-American*, he'd gone to see Assistant Secretary of State Adolph A. Berle, at his home overlooking Woodley Park in Washington. After a brief discussion of the German invasion of Poland and its implications for the Soviet Union, which was then an ally of the Nazis, for the next one and one-half hours Chambers had outlined his activities as a communist operative, naming nearly thirty secret agents active in the US Departments of the Treasury, Interior and State, including Alger and Donald Hiss. Shortly thereafter, he had approached the FBI and had been giving information for several years. Recently, he'd testified before a grand jury in New York City.

The Committee wanted to learn if Chambers could corroborate Elizabeth Bentley's testimony regarding the operation of a Soviet espionage ring within the U.S. She had testified that she'd been a courier for that spy ring, and had revealed the names of other members. But because she had no documentation, much of her testimony was hearsay, inadmissible in a court of law. And because of the conspiratorial nature of the communists, she knew very little about the espionage activities in which her spy ring had been involved.

"During your involvement with the Communist Party, did you become aware of an organization known as the Ware Group, Mr. Chambers?" Stripling asked.

"Yes, sir. While I was living in Baltimore prior to 1935. I attended several meetings of that group over the course of a year or more."

"Can you tell us who was in charge of it?" Stripling asked.

Chambers cleared his throat, began to speak, stopped and cleared it again. "The group was formed by a man named Harold Ware. He's now deceased. Later, it was run by Nathan Witt. But it continued to be known as the Ware group."

"And if you know, sir, tell us the purpose for which that group was formed."

"Well, it was made clear to me that the purpose was not primarily for espionage, but to infiltrate the government with men who were sympathetic to the communist cause. They were to find jobs in one department or other of the federal government, remain in those jobs and then move up in the normal course of things, until they were in positions to influence policy." Chambers was beginning to relax now.

Dick leaned into his microphone. "Did I hear you right? The purpose of the group was *not* to perform acts of espionage?"

"That's correct. When it was formed it was simply meant to place people in positions within the federal government," Chambers quickly responded. "Later, they were to try to influence policy, to sow confusion and so forth." Chambers sipped from his water glass. "This may not sound like much, but it really was. Influencing policy was an important but dangerous activity for a spy. If he intervened actively in policy decisions, he might call attention to himself, reveal his hand, and be exposed. But that kind of intervention is worth the risk if the agent is placed high enough to have a reasonable chance of success."

Frowning, Dick sat back and continued to listen.

"Please tell the Committee the names of some of the members."

"In addition to Harold Ware and Nathan Witt, there was John Abt and Lee Pressman. Also Alger Hiss, who at *that* time was an assistant to the political advisor for the Far Eastern Division of the State Department, and his younger brother, Donald, who was an aide to Dean Acheson, an Assistant Secretary of State."

At mention of Alger Hiss, the chamber became still, as if reporters, spectators, and staff had ceased to breathe. Then gasps of surprise erupted. The audience began babbling excitedly while members of the press scribbled furiously on their pads and photographers, pushing and shoving, moved forward to get better angles for taking photographs of the witness.

Alger Hiss was well known. He had been an official in the State Department, had been to Yalta with Roosevelt, and as a high-ranking diplomat, had helped found the United Nations. With his good looks, crisply tailored suits, and Harvard law degree, he was the exact opposite of this man in the witness chair. Thomas used his gavel to call for silence.

When quiet had been restored, Stripling continued. "Can you describe how the Ware Group accomplished its mission?"

"Yes. We can see how it worked by following the career of Alger Hiss. He wasn't the only one, but he's a good example. When I first knew him he was employed in the Department of Agriculture under Henry Wallace. He held a position in the Agricultural Adjustment Administration. But he —"

"Under who, sir?" Representative Fred Busby, one of the members of the Committee who was attending this session, spoke up.

"Henry Wallace, the former Vice President under Mr. Roosevelt, and recent Secretary of Agriculture. That department is where Pressman and Abt began their government careers."

"Mr. Chairman," Busby said in his slow, deliberate manner, "it's a curious thing to see that so many people who have been linked to the Communist Party began by securing positions in the Department of Agriculture."

"Yes, I agree," Representative Thomas responded.

"And I also think," Busby continued with an ironic smile, "that the Civil Service Commission has failed in its responsibility to root out communists from government employment." He paused. "However, I'm most concerned with the Department of Agriculture under our esteemed former Secretary, Mr. Wallace. It seems his department was the spawning ground for almost all communists in the government. They came in there and then fanned out into other branches. If Mr. Truman hadn't sacked him in '47 for bein' soft on communists, that'd still be goin' on. I think we've barely scratched the surface there. I suggest that we subpoena Mr. Wallace, to inquire into why that might have been and to look at the implications of that."

"The Chair will take your suggestion under advisement, sir," Thomas said.

"I do have one or two questions for the witness, Mr. Chairman." Busby continued.

"Proceed, sir," Thomas responded.

"Mr. Chambers, you mentioned a meeting with Assistant Secretary of State, Adolph Berle. If you know, sir, what, if anything came of that?" Busby asked.

"I understand that Berle was, at first, inclined to discount my whole story. But after thinking it over, he approached President Roosevelt with it, and was rebuffed in no uncertain terms. Mr. Roosevelt ordered him to drop the matter." More murmurings from among the spectators. Tension was beginning to mount now in the hearing room.

Parnell Thomas jotted a note on his yellow pad. "You may continue, Mr. Stripling."

"You were describing the career of Alger Hiss, Mr. Chambers," Stripling prompted.

"Yes. After his service in AAA, Alger was offered a position in the Solicitor General's office. Stanley Reed was the Director at the time. Reed is now in line for an appointment to the Supreme Court. But Alger didn't remain there for long. It was thought that he could be more useful elsewhere. So when he came to the attention of Francis Sayre, an Assistant Secretary of State, and he moved to the State Department to become Sayre's assistant, the Party was very happy with that, because *that* opened the possibility of widening the Party apparatus within the State Department. He quickly became Chief of the Office of Special Political Affairs, I believe."

"Did the Communist Party make any attempt to exploit this opening?" Nixon asked.

"Yes, sir. In that post, Alger saw numerous important documents. *That* soon became his underground activity. Over the next year or so, Alger passed along *many* documents to be sent to the Soviet Union. Also, he met several liberals in the Department whom he thought he might possibly recruit. People like Noel Field, for instance."

"Who is Noel Field?" Dick asked.

"He's an official in the State Department, currently serving in the West European Division," Chambers answered. "Alger Hiss was given the assignment of recruiting him. But Alger found out from Field that he was already working for Hede Massing's apparatus."

"Anyone else?" Stripling asked.

"Lawrence Duggan, who had been Chief of the Latin American Division in the State Department. A rumor was floating around that had Roosevelt died in '44 instead of '45, Duggan would have been appointed Secretary of State. He's no longer with the government, but works in New York City."

"Were you acquainted with Alger Hiss?" Stripling asked.

"I was," Chambers replied. Members of the press corps were listening intently.

Representative Karl Mundt was also present at this hearing. Mundt had been elected to Congress in 1938 from South Dakota, where he had been a schoolteacher, a magazine editor and a writer. He had business interests in real estate, insurance and farming. He became one of HUAC's charter members when it was first formed, and seemed to enjoy his assignment.

"Mr. Chambers," Mundt said, "I've been following the career of Alger Hiss. As a member of the House Foreign Affairs Committee, the personnel committee, I've had occasion to check on his activities while he was in the State Department. There's reason to believe that he organized within that Department one of the communist cells which tried to influence our Chinese policy and bring about condemnation of Chiang Kai Shek. I think it's important to know what happens to these people after they leave the Government. Do you know where Mr. Hiss is now employed?"

"Alger Hiss now heads up the Carnegie Foundation for World Peace," Chambers said.

"That's the same information that came to me and I am happy to have it confirmed," Mundt responded. "Certainly there is no hope for world peace under the leadership of men like Hiss," he concluded somewhat triumphantly. He knew that this statement was the stuff of which newspapers from Maine to Oregon selected headlines for their next morning's editions, and he smiled as several reporters immediately raced from the room to send out their leads.

"Mr. Chambers," Bob Stripling resumed, "how close a friendship did you have with Alger Hiss, and over what period of time did it evolve?"

"Our relationship was close and personal. Our wives were close. We spent time at each other's homes. In April 1935, my wife and I gave up our apartment at 1010 Saint Paul Street in Baltimore and moved to the apartment which Alger and his wife vacated when they left for Washington. That was on 28th Street. We stayed there a few weeks until moving to a house." Raising his water glass to his lips, he drained it.

"We had mutual friends," he continued. "Harry Dexter White was one of them. He was considered a world-class economist. Maybe not on the level of the Brit, John Maynard Keynes, or the German, Hjalmar Schact, but close. He has played a major role in planning our postwar economic strategies."

"Let's talk about your relationship with Alger Hiss, Mr. Chambers," Stripling prompted.

"Oh. Yes. He sold me an old car that he owned. During the late summer and fall of 1935, my wife, myself and a mutual friend, Max Lieber, who had been divorced, rented a cottage in Smithton, New Jersey. Smithton is south of Frenchtown. We rented this house from a man named Boucot. It's on the Delaware River. We stayed there two or three months. Priscilla Hiss spent a week or ten days with us. We enjoyed it immensely."

"Who is Maxim Lieber, Mr. Chambers," Stripling asked.

"Maxim Lieber was my closest friend in the movement. He's an Austrian Jew, a literary agent with an office in New York City. He represented many international literary figures, and as such, was able to travel extensively abroad. He'd been recruited by a Russian named Boris Bykov, who was head of Soviet Communist Party activities in America at different times. In 1936, I was assigned to work for Bykov, too. He was the one who first suggested paying the underground members for supplying information."

"What did you think of that idea?" Stripling asked.

"I was against it. In my view, the underground was made up of and should continue to be made up of dedicated Communists who helped the Soviet Union out of loyalty, not for money, like mercenaries."

"Why did Boris Bykov recruit Maxim Lieber?" Stripling asked.

"Bykov wanted to use Lieber's business as a cover in England and Japan. They had, of course, already been doing that here."

"In what way did they use this man's business as a cover?"

"Well, in 1935 there was a proposal that I would go to England as Max Lieber's representative. I was to open a literary agency using *his* name and *his* line of credit, obtain one or two British writers, and represent them while recruiting people to help the Party."

"Did you ever actually do this?' Stripling asked.

"No. I *did* go so far as to obtain a passport. I used the name David Breen, and it was planned that when I arrived in London, I'd use a religious cover and attend a church so as to conceal my real activities. But the trip never materialized."

"You stated that you and this Lieber rented the house in Delaware. Could you explain how and why you did that?' Dick asked.

"Yes. The summer of 1935 ... we were meeting at Lieber's apartment, putting together plans for the London operation, which was to take place in the fall. Because of the heat and noise, Max Lieber decided to move to the country for the summer. His agency was doing well. He was financially well off. He kept his New York apartment, and my wife and I decided to give up our rented house and move in with him. That had a practical purpose; we could use the name David Breen and establish a record that Lieber had spent a summer in the country with the future manager of his London office."

"Did Maxim Lieber know Alger Hiss?" Karl Mundt wanted to know.

"He did."

"Was Maxim Lieber present at this cottage during the week or ten days you said Priscilla Hiss stayed there with you?" Dick Nixon joined in.

"Yes, he was."

"Did Alger Hiss visit you at the Smithton cottage?" Parnell Thomas asked.

"Yes. During the ten days his wife stayed with us, Alger came up from Washington twice, and stayed overnight each time."

"Was Lieber there when Alger Hiss stayed overnight?" Dick asked.

"Yes, he was."

Dick, Mundt and Thomas exchanged glances. This was better than expected. Clearly, the information could be used to establish the Communist Party's subversive intent. Further, Chambers's evidence indicated that a former State Department employee active in the Roosevelt Administration, and an Assistant Secretary of the Treasury, Harry Dexter White, had been Soviet spies. And here was proof that these matters had been brought to the attention of the State Department and the FBI, but neither the Roosevelt nor Truman Administrations had taken any action. Also, Chambers's testimony proved the existence of the communist cell known as the Ware Group and pointed to criminal laxity in security procedures within the government. If made public on the eve of the election, it would embarrass the Administration, enhancing chances of Republican candidates. It might even help to relieve the pressure the White House had been recently exerting on HUAC.

CHAPTER 10

Tuesday, August 3, 1948
Washington, DC
Old House Office Building
Office of Representative Richard M. Nixon (R-CA)
11:00 p.m. Eastern Standard Time (EST)

REPRESENTATIVE DICK NIXON'S TELEPHONE WAS ringing. But except for that and the sound of his light snoring, his office in the deserted building was silent. Dick's feet were up on the desk, crossed at the ankles, his body reclining in the leather executive chair, head back, mouth open. Transcripts of witness testimony obscured the green blotter on his desktop. Others were piled on the floor next to the desk. One was clasped in his hands, resting on his stomach.

He had been burning the midnight oil this past week, preparing for both the Bentley and Chambers hearings. Now, exhausted after the first day of Chambers's testimony, he had given in to his need for sleep.

It took ten rings before Dick sensed the noise of the phone. Finally, he was able to rouse himself sufficiently to reach over and pick it up. It was his wife.

"Why haven't you called?" Pat asked coolly yet with a touch of concern in her voice.

"I'm sorry, sweetheart. I must have fallen asleep." He stifled a yawn with the back of his hand. "What time is it?"

"Eleven. I wish you had called. I had a great meal prepared for us."

He rubbed his right temple with an open palm. "I'm sorry," he said again, a bit sharply.

There was a long silence. "Are you coming home?"

Dick thought of the preparation still needed if he were to be ready for tomorrow. "No. I need to work all night."

"All night? You *can't* work all night, Dick."

"Of *course* I can work all night. We're taking testimony from a very important witness. This hearing is extremely significant. For the Committee and for me … for us."

"Does Mr. Chambers really have a history of mental illness?"

Dick was startled. "Where did you hear that?"

"On the television. This evening's news broadcast reported on the hearing. Made him sound like a horrible person. They said he's envious of Hiss and wants to destroy him."

He frowned. "Sounds like Alger Hiss's supporters are already hard at work."

"You mean character assassination?"

"Yep."

She changed the subject. "I expected you home. The least you could have done was call me. Dinner is still on the stove."

"Pat, I'll make it up to you, honey. I'm up to my ears. I apologize."

There was another long silence as she considered his apology. "When do you think you might be home?"

He rubbed his hand over the stubble on his chin. "I'll come in for a shower and a shave around seven."

"I see. If I'm asleep, don't wake me," she said icily and hung up.

He examined the receiver as if it were something from another planet before putting it down carefully. He could tell she was upset. She'd given birth to Julie on July 5th, and, even though his mother had come to help for two weeks, Pat was temporarily overwhelmed by the added burden of caring for their new baby. Their eldest, Tricia, who had been born on February 21, 1946, was only a bit over two. His absence from home many evenings this past month had not helped; it had definitely not improved her frame of mind.

Staring at the transcripts on his desk, he considered. *Should I go home now? Take a hot shower and get a good night's sleep?* He picked up a transcript of testimony from the last day of the Bentley hearing. He needed to read it. This was important. He'd smooth things over with Pat later, with a weekend at the Robert Morris Inn, that historic, very popular vacation spot in Oxford, on Maryland's Eastern Shore. She'd like that.

Wednesday, August 4, 1948
Washington, DC
Mayflower Hotel
The Apartment Suite of Richard and Pat Nixon
6:30 a.m. EST

Thelma Catherine "Pat" Ryan Nixon, known to her friends and the rest of the word as "Patricia," or simply "Pat," sat at her kitchen table as the yellow orb that was the morning sun climbed over the Potomac River and became visible beyond the glass doors of their balcony. Although the day promised to be another scorcher, she was sipping steaming coffee, having just finished reading *The Washington Post's* account of the new South Korean assembly's adoption of a republican constitution and its election of Syngman Rhee as the country's first president. Turning back to page one, she scanned the *Post's* account of yesterday's session of the Chambers hearing. Tricia was not stirring yet. Julie had been breast-fed and put back in her crib. She noted that the *Post's* article described Whittaker Chambers as an alcoholic. *Hmmm. Last night, ABC News said he has a history of mental illness. This morning, the Post says he's an alcoholic. The man's got real problems. If those things are true, that is.*

She yawned. For her, sleep had been elusive. During a warm shower, she had tried to pep-talk herself out from under the cloud of melancholy she'd been feeling ever since the baby had been born. *Is it post-partum depression?* She wondered. She was wearing a white velour robe and matching white slippers. Her hair, damp from the shower, was swept back in a ponytail.

She listened to the sound of gears, wheels and cables as the elevator stopped at their floor. Moments later, she heard it leave again, and Dick unlocked the door. Placing his coat on the baby grand piano that he sometimes played for relaxation, he approached her, his eyes dark with fatigue.

"Good morning," he said. Pecking her cheek, he took his place across from her. His breath was heavy and he badly needed a shave.

"Good morning to *you*," she said, flashing a fake smile.

"You're up early." She understood that he was trying to be cordial, but she wasn't buying it. Instead, she shrugged and sipped her coffee.

Dick inhaled deeply, exhaled loudly, and let his gaze wander around the room. "Still mad about last night, I see."

"Not really. I don't stay mad for long."

She watched him drum his fingers on the table. Then, "Pat, I said I was sorry and I meant it. It won't happen again. Believe me. You're right. I should have called. From now on, I'll call you if I'm gonna be late."

Pat knew full well that it would happen again. But she had wanted him to show her some consideration — an apology and a promise to do what she'd asked — that was a good start. He'd always kept his promises to her. She felt that she'd gotten what she needed. She managed a real smile. "You look terrible."

"What's under your bathrobe?"

"Just me. Absolutely nothing else."

"Let's see."

"Why don't you take a nap first? You look like you wouldn't be able to do anything."

"Let's go take a shower together."

"I've already had one."

"Naked?"

"Of course."

"Describe it to me. Every little detail."

She blushed. "If you'd come home in the evenings at a reasonable time you wouldn't need to feel depraved. Or deprived, either."

Dick took another deep breath. "There'll be many nights when I'll need to work late, Pat. There were lots of all-nighters when I was campaigning. You never complained *then*. Why now?"

With an impatient gesture, she rose from the table. "I put up with it then. Now you're an elected congressman. I thought that after you won the election, things would be different. We'd be able to spend time together. Nights. Weekends. Like other families. Instead, since we came to Washington, I feel a distance between us that I never felt before."

He stood, walked around the table and took her in his arms. "But this hearing is really important. Truman put out the word that he wants to disband HUAC. The next few days will make or break it. I need to be well prepared for every session."

"*That's* what worries me," she said into his shoulder. "This isn't the *only* important committee hearing. They're *all* important. Will it get worse?"

"Maybe it will. Politics is a rough business. Underneath all the backslapping and the flag-waving speeches it can be cruel. People play for keeps. The weak don't survive and the strong go on to bigger and better things. Those who *do* survive win big."

"Yeah. And die of heart attacks before their time." She laid her cheek against his shoulder for a moment. "Go ahead and take your shower. I'll put breakfast out."

Dick shot a grateful glance in her direction and dragged himself down the hall to their bedroom, careful not to wake the baby. Pat had thought it best for Julie to sleep with them for the first few months, before moving her to the nursery. He took a hot shower, shaved and dressed in a fresh white shirt, dark blue suit and a blue and silver striped tie. But he was still exhausted and he was filled with a sense of impending doom.

His thoughts went back to their marriage in June 1940. Since the wedding, Pat had been the one consistent thing in his life. Her sense of humor brightened each day. *If I lost her*, he thought, *life just wouldn't be the same.*

Images of the wedding flooded his mind. It had been a modest affair, just for their immediate families and a few close friends. Since Pat's family was not well off, he and Pat had paid for most of it themselves. They had rented the presidential suite at the Mission Inn over in Riverside, but only for the afternoon since it was so expensive. He had worn a dark suit. He remembered how beautiful a bride Pat had been in a light blue dress with fitted bodice and a full, gathered skirt extending to her ankles.

The newlyweds had planned to drive to Mexico City for their honeymoon. Right after the reception they jumped into his Oldsmobile and headed south, the car's trunk loaded with canned goods, since they could not afford to eat at restaurants along the way. When they stopped for their first meal, they discovered that friends had removed the labels from all the cans as a joke. They couldn't tell what they were going to eat! Every meal was a real surprise. Sometimes cold pork and beans for breakfast, grapefruit slices for dinner. They had laughed all the way to Mexico City and back two weeks later.

Gathering himself, he checked on the baby, closed the door quietly behind him and walked to the dining room. There, he stopped in surprise and let out a long whistle. The table was set as if they were entertaining dinner guests. Pat had put out their best china and silver. Tall yellow candles in silver candlestick holders brightened the scene. Orange juice in crystal goblets was set at two places on the dark blue tablecloth, and white linen napkins were folded at each place.

He threw her an appreciative glance. "What's the occasion?"

"It's a special breakfast for a wonderful, hard-working husband."

Dick took his seat and admired the setting. The food had been laid out in several covered serving dishes. He couldn't quite place the aroma. Was it bacon? Scrambled eggs?

"What did you make?"

She removed the lid from the largest serving dish. "Duck l' Orange."

"Duck what?"

"Duck l' Orange."

At a loss, he glanced at his watch. "But, it's time for breakfast?"

She smiled benignly and nodded. "I made it last night. You didn't come home for dinner. I suggest you eat it now."

His eyes roved from the dish to his wife and back again. He brought his keen legal mind to bear, analyzing the situation. Then his face broke into a wide grin. "Let's eat!" He said.

CHAPTER 11

Friday, August 20, 1948
Washington, DC
Old House Office Building
Office of Representative J. Parnell Thomas (R-NJ)
4:20 p.m. Eastern Standard Time (EST)

THE DAY HAD BEEN OPPRESSIVELY hot, the air so heavy with humidity that it felt to Parnell Thomas like the city had become a gigantic sauna.

His chronically bad health had become worse since Drew Pearson had gone public with charges against him. Sitting behind his cluttered desk, suit coat off and tie loosened, his hands began to tremble. The day before, a spasmodic tic had made its presence known in his lower lip. Unable to control it this afternoon, he was glad no one was there to see it.

In his office, tension hung in the air like an opaque fog. His staff knew he was on the way out. Finished. And they loved it. To make matters worse, the opposition party was clamoring for a House Ethics Committee investigation into whether he had improperly used his office for personal gain. Several members of his own Party had joined them. In a Congress where bipartisan effort had been woefully lacking, a bipartisan consensus was forming. Against *him*. Several of his colleagues had publicly stated that they were uniting to uphold the integrity of Congress. What he had done was perceived as threatening that integrity.

His phone rang. Reflexively, he reached for it, but changed his mind and drew his hand back as if he had touched a hot stove. It continued to ring. Gathering himself, he picked it up.

"Thomas here." His voice was barely above a whisper.

"Bob Stripling, Parnell. Didn't want to disturb you, but I just learned something from the State Department. Thought you should know right away."

He sighed. "You're not disturbing me, Bob. What is it?"

"When we questioned Whittaker Chambers back on August 3rd, he mentioned the name Noel Field. Remember?"

"Yeah, I remember. Chambers said Alger Hiss had tried to recruit Field but found out he was already working for some other apparatus. Right?"

"Nothing wrong with your *memory*, Parnell."

Thomas bristled. He was sensitive to any references to his health, no matter how subtle.

"Go ahead, Bob. Please."

"An assistant in the House Foreign Relations Committee's office called. State sent notice to Congress this afternoon that Noel Field and his wife, Herta, disappeared about ten days ago. Turned up in Budapest."

"Really?"

"Yeah. Apparently State knew he was missing, but kept it quiet for a few days while they tried to locate him. Then Budapest announced through diplomatic channels that *they* had him. He's asking for political asylum for himself, his wife, their adopted daughter and his brother."

"What do you make of that?"

"Well, we *could* infer that Chambers's information is accurate. Field and Hiss *did* know each other. Field was aware of Hiss's spying activities and vice versa. Field reads Chambers's testimony in the papers and thinks he and Hiss are about to be exposed."

"Didn't that Russian defector, General whatsisface, name Field as a Communist agent back in '39 when he testified before one of our Special Committees?"

"General Walter Krivitsky? Yeah. I wasn't around here back then but I read about it in some old minutes. Special Committee sent the information over to Justice but they never followed up on it."

Thomas dropped his eyes to his desk momentarily and then looked up. "So, Field believes he might be arrested or at least subpoenaed for questioning. He's not real thrilled about that. He knows he could probably cut a deal—his freedom in exchange for testimony against Hiss—but he doesn't want to testify against his friend; so he runs for cover."

"That sounds about right to me," Stripling answered. "Going behind the Iron Curtain means we can't reach him with a subpoena. Can't extradite him, either, because we have no extradition treaties with any of the communist countries. Smart move."

Thomas paused, thinking. Developments were breaking by the day. After Chambers made his first appearance before HUAC, the Committee had received a telegram from Hiss requesting to be allowed to answer the charges being made against him. Hiss first appeared before the Committee on August Fifth, in the company of William Marbury, a Baltimore lawyer and longtime friend. Wearing a crisp, well-tailored gray suit, Hiss denied ever meeting Whittaker Chambers. He was so convincing that HUAC decided to recall Chambers. In executive session on August 7th, they grilled that gentleman for the entire day, but were unable to shake him. It appeared that he was telling the truth.

Then Nixon and McDowell had pulled that stunt: a secret confrontation between Hiss and Chambers in New York City at the Hotel Commodore. *They arranged it behind my back,* Thomas thought. *True, at the last minute they asked me to go along. But they knew I was too exhausted to make the trip.* Bob Stripling, Lou Russell, Don Appell and Ben Mandel had all gone up there together. When they returned they had come to see him immediately, flushed with success. Hiss had admitted that he *did* recognize Chambers as a man he'd known in the 1930s under the name George Crossly. *That had been Hiss's first mistake.*

But the fast pace was taking its toll on him. This kickback problem was sapping so much of his energy that he was finding it hard to keep up with his work. And he had noticed that some of his friends seemed to be avoiding him, while at home his wife was casting long, sad glances in his direction.

Resignation as HUAC's chairman seemed the only option. He knew he was going to have to do it soon. Why not now? John Wood, Karl Mundt, and Dick Nixon could handle things. He realized that he still held the phone in his hand. His mind had wandered.

He stifled a sigh. "Bob?"

"Yeah. I'm still here, Parnell."

"Please do me a favor. Call Wood, Mundt and Nixon. Tell them to come to my office first thing tomorrow. We'll discuss ... the future. Oh. And come to the meeting yourself."

He placed the telephone down softly, his mind in turmoil. What was he to do? Where could he turn? His wife? No. They had drifted apart. He had realized a few years ago that their marriage was not what it should be, but he'd put off doing anything about it. Now it was probably too late. No, there wouldn't be any help from that quarter.

Religion? He was not a religious man. A modernist, he saw himself as essentially autonomous, independent, self-governing; a law unto himself. He had gotten along perfectly well relying on empirical data—whatever he could see, hear, feel and smell— what his senses reported to him. Nothing else existed. Wasn't Mankind improving yearly by relying on reason and science? He had never had any use for God in *his* rational world.

True, when he first entered politics he and Cheryl had joined the Episcopal Church. She liked the solemnity of high Episcopal Sunday services, so similar to a Roman Catholic Mass. But she would never consider joining the Catholic Church. Their maid and gardener were Catholics. He had gone along with her decision because the Episcopal Church seemed to be the choice of wealthy voters, and he needed to rub elbows with people who had money, to obtain financing for his campaigns. Cheryl attended services regularly. When she insisted, he'd accompany her, but only to please *her* and to be seen there by his constituents, not for any benefit of a religious or spiritual nature he might personally derive from it. On Sunday, women go to church; men go to a football game.

The silence grew heavy around him. He now recalled that his minister, a somewhat effeminate fellow whose masculinity was suspect, was fond of saying that if we prayed, God would not abandon us to deal with trials or heartaches alone. Thomas had not prayed for years, preferring to leave that sort of thing to Cheryl.

But this new problem placed things in a different light. He thought about the French scientist-philosopher, Blaise Pascal, and his famous wager about the existence of God. Pascal lived back in the Fourteenth Century. One evening, while playing cards with his buddies, he had been given a choice and had made a bet: that God existed, rather than that He did not. *Maybe the guy was right,* Thomas thought. *He very well could have been. And if he was right. Maybe I really don't have anything to lose if I believe. And if I believe, maybe I should pray.* Another thought struck him and he chuckled cynically. *Pascal was a Jansenist. And, according to Cheryl, Jansenists were considered heretics because they denied free will and believed that Christ died for the elect and not for all mankind. So, was Pascal right or wrong? No matter. Maybe I ought to make an attempt anyway.*

Wheeling his chair around, he faced the window. Afternoon rush hour traffic noises drifted up from the hot street below. A patch of almost cloudless sky was visible above a nearby building. He decided to focus his gaze there.

"I'm gonna be honest with you. Haven't talked to you in a long time because I'm ... not sure you exist. Actually, I'm not sure what I believe about that. Frankly, there are days when I'm not even sure *I* exist. But the minister said you do, so you might be able to help. Got myself in a jackpot, this time. I don't know what to do. Can you help me?" He paused and waited. For what, he didn't really know. Nothing happened. Having never taken the time to develop a relationship with God, he felt ... disconnected. He shrugged fatalistically.

Then, two emotions swept over him, threatening to drown his senses: shame and embarrassment. Shame for what he'd done to his staff. Embarrassment for having foolishly indulged himself in such a childish activity as prayer; talking to Someone who may not even exist. Still, something *was* different from a few moments ago. Emerging from deep inside, from a place he had neither explored nor touched for a very long time, was this strong wish that somewhere, there might be Someone to whom he could say he was sorry, and that he'd try to do better.

He wheeled his chair around again, his eyes drifting to the artwork on the wall directly across from his desk. Two stylized reproductions of hunt scenes by the English artist, John Frederick Herring, flanked the closed door leading to the outer office where his aides and secretary were busy. Muffled sounds of voices, the chatter of a typewriter and the jangling of a telephone easily reached him. Ordinarily comforting, these mundane sounds now seemed threatening.

A wave of anxiety seized him. Had he really thought he could get away with it? He had displayed poor judgment and even greed. A phrase from a Psalm learned as a youngster came to mind. Something like, "God will punish sinners. He will let them fall by their own devices." Surely he had destroyed himself by his own "devices." His heart was heavy, burdened by regret and pending loss.

He reached down and pulled open the lower right hand drawer of his desk. It was crammed full of various items. This was the drawer into which he tossed miscellaneous items that he didn't use. Years ago he had deposited a copy of the King James Bible in there. He rummaged through the drawer, pushing things roughly aside. Yes, there it was. Thank God! Pulling it out, he opened it at random and let his finger fall on the page. He'd seen Cheryl do this; a game she played with God, looking for a sign. *Does God play games?* he wondered. *If He exists at all, does He respond to this sort of thing?* The words were from John's Gospel, chapter fifteen, verse five:

"Apart from Me,
you can do nothing."

The palms of his hands began to sweat. He felt utterly alone. Panicky, he turned the pages to another spot, stabbed at the page with his finger and read from Psalm Twenty-seven:

"Hear, O Lord, the sound of my call;
have pity on me, and answer me."

Swallowing the lump in his throat, he turned a few more pages. Again his finger jabbed the page. It was Isaiah, chapter forty-one, verse ten:

"Do not fear, for I am with you;
Do not be afraid,
for I am your God.
I will strengthen you,
surely I will help you,
surely I will uphold you
with my righteous hand."

He looked up from the Bible. A curious sense of relief flooded his mind and body, as if a great weight had been removed from him. Moments later, he rested his heavy head on his arms and wept as he had not wept since his childhood.

CHAPTER 12

Wednesday, September 28, 1948
Washington, DC
Blackie's House of Beef Restaurant
22nd & M Streets, NW
7:45 p.m. Eastern Standard Time (EST)

"**A** SLANDER SUIT?" DICK NIXON'S eyebrows arched in surprise. He, Representatives Karl Mundt and John McDowell, and Chief Investigator Lou Russell had settled at a table in the main dining area of Blackie's, an up-scale steak house on 22nd Street in the District.

The foursome was seated under a beautifully-framed copy of *Niagara Falls*, one of the Hudson River School of American landscape artists, Frederic Edwin Church's works, painted in such detail that it seemed that water pouring over the falls would cascade onto their mahogany table at any second. A white linen tablecloth, green linen napkins and a small vase containing a fresh red rose completed the decor. The men had finished their first round of drinks; a Martini for Dick, a Rob Roy for Mundt, a Bloody Mary for McDowell and a Carling's Black Label beer for Russell. But they had not yet ordered dinner. The aroma of flame broiled beef hung heavily in the air, tantalizing the early diners.

Since their arrival, they had been discussing American foreign policy and the Washington scene, as only those who lived it daily could. Dick had been particularly vocal. He was a bit nervous because he had a secret he needed to reveal. But he wanted to wait until after his companions were fully relaxed; that meant after they had had a couple of drinks and had eaten. While killing time, he spoke of his brief career in politics, foreign policy under Roosevelt and Truman, including the Truman Doctrine, a plan for resisting communist aggression, and the Marshall Plan, a program designed to aid economic recovery in Europe. Dick had an intuitive grasp of international affairs, which others were beginning to recognize and envy. Prefacing each remark with a comment like, "This is how the *real* world works," he described the events leading up to the Berlin Airlift, which had begun in June as a result of a land and water blockade of that city by the Soviet Union.

"They were hoping we'd abandon almost two million West Berliners and pull outta there, leaving the place entirely to them." he said. "But their plan didn't work. Instead, three days later we started flying in food, water and coal for heating. "

Mundt poked the air with a finger. "Yeah. At its height, we had a flight going into West Berlin every few minutes around the clock. The commies didn't think we could do it."

As they started on their second round of drinks and began to glance at the menu, their talk had returned to Committee business.

"Yep! Fifty grand worth. He filed it yesterday," Karl Mundt responded. "I read it in the *Baltimore News-Post* this morning. Hiss retained William Marbury, an old college chum, and they went to the US District Court in Baltimore. Hiss said that Chambers's allegations were 'untrue, false and defamatory.'" They all laughed.

"Seems like a strange move to *me*," Dick remarked.

Lou Russell finished examining the menu and made his decision in favor of the New York strip. "I agree. Either the man is one hundred percent not guilty of anything or he's a real gambler, willing to shake the dice and trust his future to a jury." He glared at the others for emphasis.

"Well," John McDowell joined in, "Hiss challenged Chambers to make his charges in a public forum where he wouldn't have immunity from a libel suit. It was at the Commodore, when the one-on-one meeting we arranged was winding down. Looks like Chambers accepted the challenge. Went on that TV interview program, *Meet the Press,* and told the whole story." He shook his head. "I think Chambers doesn't have all his marbles."

"Yeah. *Meet the Press* has been on the air for about a year. I just happened to tune in that night," Karl Mundt said. "Chambers had lost his job at *Time Magazine* the previous Friday. The furor over his testimony against Hiss was just too much for the publishers over there." He drummed his fingers on the table next to his dinner plate.

"What do you think?" Russell asked.

"What do *I* think? I think he's got a big mouth," Mundt responded.

"It's possible that Chambers is a liar," Nixon said.

"He appears to be untrustworthy at first glance," McDowell affirmed.

"The dumby should've kept quiet," Dick added. "He's not showing a lotta good judgment." His eyes roamed the room, examining the gumwood paneling, the artwork, and nearby diners.

"I don't know about that," Russell said. "Look at it from another perspective. He's put himself and his family at risk doing what he's doing. I think *that* shows a certain strength of character."

"When's the trial scheduled?" Dick asked.

"Don't know," Mundt said. "But pretrial motions are set for the middle of November. Depositions will have to be finished before then."

"Who's representin' Chambers?" Russell wanted to know.

"Bill Macmillan from Semmes, Bowen and Semmes, in Baltimore," Mundt responded.

They broke off conversation as their young waiter arrived at the table.

"Go ahead and order, Dick," Mundt said.

"No! I'm not ready yet," Nixon responded peevishly. "You order."

"Somebody order, please," McDowell said. "I'm hungry." Nobody made a move. The waiter hovered expectantly.

"Isn't this just like a bunch of congressmen?" Russell said. "Can't agree on a damn thing." Loud laughter from the others. "Here," he continued, "I'll go first. I've decided."

As the waiter finished taking their orders and moved away, Dick voiced a thought. "It'd be interesting to see what comes out in the discovery process before this trial."

"You're right." Mundt sipped from his drink. "Lou? Why don't you go up to Baltimore after all the depositions and pretrial motions are concluded. See if we can get hold of any of it."

"We can subpoena all of it if we want to," McDowell said.

"Who's the trial judge gonna be?" Dick wanted to know.

"It was assigned to Judge W. Calvin Chesnut," Karl Mundt answered. "Know anything about him?" A woman's laughter drifted to them from a nearby table.

"Naw. He must be a Democrat," Russell said. "I better take a couple a subpoenas along just in case."

Finally, when they had finished dinner and started on coffee, Dick cleared his throat and looked around the table. "There's something else you guys should know."

Mundt wiped his lips with a green linen napkin. His eyes sought Dick's, a concerned look on his face. "What is it, Dick?" The others quickly became attentive.

"Last month, just before we set up that meeting between Chamber and Hiss at the Commodore? I wasn't really sure that Chambers was telling the truth," Dick began.

"You weren't alone," Mundt said. "When I left the session on the 5th, I was almost convinced that Chambers had taken us all in." Nods of agreement from everyone." He chuckled. "I even thought about draggin' him off somewhere, tyin' him to a chair, and shootin' him full of scopolamine so we'd know we were getting the truth." The others, unsure whether he was joking or serious, laughed nervously.

"Well," Dick continued, "I knew that John Foster Dulles was Chairman of the Board at the Carnegie Endowment for World Peace."

"And," McDowell, who had a quick mind and a photographic memory, chimed in, "that means Foster Dulles is Alger Hiss's boss over there." He removed his thick, horn-rimmed glasses and began polishing them with his napkin.

Nixon shot McDowell a smile and a nod. "Foster Dulles was Alger Hiss's mentor and benefactor. He actually *sponsored* Hiss for the post as Director of the Endowment."

"If Hiss became a source of embarrassment ..." McDowell let his thought hang in the air.

Mundt nodded. "I heard a rumor that if Tom Dewey wins the election, Foster Dulles will be nominated for Secretary of State. As a matter of fact, Foster Dulles has been acting as Dewey's primary advisor on foreign affairs during the campaign. If his name is linked to a possible communist spy, he can kiss any nomination goodbye ..." his voice trailed off.

"Foster Dulles's brother, Allen, is also a prominent Republican," McDowell added.

"We're all ears, Dick. What did you do?" Russell asked impatiently.

"I was worried that Chambers's information wouldn't hold up, so I wanted to show the transcript of his testimony to someone who knew Hiss well; someone I could trust to give me an objective opinion as to whether or not Chambers actually had known Hiss. I called the Dulles brothers. They agreed to see me, but they asked me to come to New York quickly, because the trustees were about to go public with a vote of confidence for Hiss. So, on August 11th, I took the train to New York City. We met that evening, at the Roosevelt Hotel. They brought Doug Dillon and Christian Herter along."

"Douglas Dillon? The New York banker?" McDowell asked.

"Yeah. He's also a Republican *and* his judgment is sound," Dick said.

"Go ahead, Dick," Mundt said, throwing an annoyed glance at McDowell.

"I showed them the transcript of Chambers's secret testimony; the one where he told us a lotta details about Hiss's life. Asked them to tell me if they believed that Chambers had, in fact, known Hiss."

"And?" McDowell demanded. Smoke from cigarettes and cigars now hung thick in the air around them.

"It took them almost an hour, but after they read the transcript they were unanimous," Dick said. "They all agreed that Chambers and Hiss knew each other."

"*Way to go!*" Mundt cried. Reaching over, he slapped Dick on the back. The others were also elated. They took turns pumping Dick's hand and congratulating him for bringing such a bold move off successfully.

When quiet was restored at the table, they ordered Armagnac, an expensive French brandy from southwestern France, and lit cigars. As Karl Mundt sipped the smooth golden liquid, a thought struck him and a furrow settled on his brow. He turned to Dick. "The Trustees at the Carnegie Endowment never *did* issue a statement of support for Hiss."

"And Hiss resigned a few weeks later," McDowell added.

"Yep," Dick said. "Foster Dulles must have lost confidence in Hiss after that. Maybe he even *asked* Hiss to resign."

"Tell me something, Dick," Mundt said. "If the Dulles brothers, Dillon and Herter had been of the opposite opinion, would you have pushed this thing the way you did?"

Dick sat back in his chair and took a long drag on his cigar. At the next table, an elderly man and a gray-haired woman raised their wineglasses in a toast to something. The clinking sound reached Mundt, McDowell and Russell as they waited for Dick's response. "Truthfully?" Dick said. "Good grief! No. Do you think I'd be that crazy?"

CHAPTER 13

Thursday, May 15, 1949
Washington, DC
Old House Office Building
Office of Representative John Wood (D-GA)
3:30 p.m. Eastern Standard Time (EST)

"JOHN? YA BUSY?" LOU RUSSELL poked his head inside Representative John Wood's office, waving away a cloud of cigarette smoke as he entered. Wood, gold-plated fountain pen hovering, sat behind his desk signing letters. A bacon, lettuce and tomato sandwich and a warm Coke were on the desk next to him, undisturbed, and a Lorillard Tobacco Company's Old Gold cigarette burned in his ashtray, neglected.

"Not at awl, Lou. Jes' sitting back heah twidlin' mah thumbs." He pushed back in his chair. "Ackchully, today's been unusually busy; dictation the entire mownin', telephone calls most a the aftanoon. The damn phone's rung so often I've hawdly had time ta breathe between cawls."

Since taking over as chairman of HUAC, Wood had been putting in long hours. A HUAC member the entire previous year, he had not attended meetings regularly because he had not considered the assignment important. But ethics problems had forced Parnell Thomas to resign, and by reason of seniority the Democrat from Georgia had been catapulted into the chairmanship. Now, he was trying to stay abreast of developments, do the administrative work the job required, and at the same time familiarize himself with recent Committee history. Under pressure, he was showing signs of stress. When that happened, he chain-smoked cigarettes and his southern drawl became very noticeable.

"I wanna talk to ya about somethin'," Russell said tentatively, moving to the chair in front of Wood's desk.

"Even Vice-President Barkley checked in," Wood muttered, ignoring Russell momentarily. "Wanted ta talk about the end of the Berlin Airlift a few days ago, and what we might wanna do wif the money we'll save now thet it's ovah. Federal debt is up to two hundred twenty-three million, an' the Administration's got all these ideas for new gov'mint spendin' programs. Truman thinks he can *buy* votes fo' the Democrats in the next election."

"You got a minute, or not?" Russell asked impatiently.

"Whut is it?" Wood was mildly annoyed. He glanced uncertainly at the toasted BLT. "Didn't get out for lunch and ain't had time ta even nibble this heah sandwich Estelle ordahd fo' me when she figured out ahh wouldn't be able to git away from mah desk t'day."

"Well, I got this friend over at State. An investigator like me. Name's Sammy Klaus. He's assigned to look into possible security leaks inside State, ya know?"

A loud snort from Wood. "He must be vurry busy." It was common knowledge that the State Department had been plagued with security problems for years. "Git own with it, Lou, please!" He picked up the stub of his cigarette, gave it a nasty glance, and snuffed it out in the ashtray.

"Yeah, yeah," Russell said. "He and I went out ta dinner last night. We got ta talkin' about the Soviet Union's espionage activities here in the United States. He knows lots a general information about that."

"Like, for instance?"

"Well, he tole me the Soviet foreign intelligence service had once been known as the OGPU. It was renamed the NKVD back before the war. Later, it came to be known as the KGB. During the last ten years some spy activities have also been carried out by the NKVD's counterparts in Soviet military intelligence."

"Yeah?"

"Yeah. They're known as the GRU. The Red army and navy had separate agents targeting areas of special interests. But most Soviet espionage is conducted by the NKVD, which replaced the old GRU in the late 1930s."

"So, wheah's all this headin', Lou?"

"We also talked about the Alger Hiss thing. You know what Sammy told me?"

"Ah have *no* idea," Wood's exasperation was showing. He reached for the toasted BLT and made ready to take a bite.

"He told me that three years ago he'd been assigned to work on a possible security leak where classified documents were bein' routed into the wrong hands within State, and then those same documents were bein' leaked to outside sources."

Wood set his sandwich back on its paper plate. "Whut's this got ta do wif us?"

"I'm gettin' to it, John," Russell said petulantly.

"Okay, okay."

"Back in September 1946, a classified US Army document was leaked ta Drew Pearson. It was a study of British military operations against the commie insurgents in Greece, called "British Garrison in Greece." British troops had been sent over there ta stop the commies from takin' over. The Soviets and some socialists and communists in this country had problems with the Brits and us over that move, but the American high command was convinced it was a good thing for British troops to be there. You remember?"

"Yeah, aah recawl some a that. Go ahead."

"Well, Pearson wrote a short piece based on this classified study and published it in his *Washington Post* column. Only he garbled the facts and misquoted the study, see. He reported that the American high command was havin' second thoughts about British troops in Greece. So the British and the Greeks read this article. They got upset and for a while there was a lot a bad feelin' between the Brits and us."

"Ahh remembah that, too," John Wood said soberly. "Theah was quite a strain on Anglo-American relations fo' the balance a '46. So *that's* what caused it. Wasn't until aftah Mistah Truman announced his get-tough policy featurin' economic aid for both Turkey and Greece that thangs finally settled down ovah theah."

"Yeah. Well, this secret document? Even though Pearson misquoted it, it was obvious that he'd seen a copy. The State Department was real concerned because it also contained classified information about the Brits order of battle against the Greek commies. So the Department assigned an investigator to look into it. My friend Sammy. He discovered that the document was missin' and he traced it to the Office of Special Political Affairs. It was there just two weeks before Pearson got it. Somebody in that office leaked it ta Pearson."

"So?"

"So! At the time, guess who was Chief of the Office of Special Political Affairs? Our friend Alger Hiss, that's who."

"Vurry interestin'," Wood stood, came out from behind his desk and paced the length of the small office and back. "Whut did Chambers tail us about the mission of the Ware group? Do y'all recawl that?"

"He said their mission was to infiltrate the government with people sympathetic to communism, have them work their way up until they were in positions to influence policy, and then mess it up wherever they could."

Wood smiled. "Eggxacly. Shore sounds like that's what happened heah don't it?" He resumed his seat. "In a few weeks Algah Heiss is due ta be tried fo' perjury, based own info'mation Whittaker Chambers supplied to the Committee."

"Yeah. And on the stuff that came out durin' Chambers's attempt to defend himself from Hiss's libel charge."

It was no secret that the Truman Justice Department had been at best a reluctant player in the legal proceedings against Hiss. A New York Grand Jury had almost arrived at the end of its term without returning an indictment. But Nixon and Stripling had driven to Chambers's farm in Westminster, Maryland, and confronted him about certain matters that had come to light in his libel trial. They returned with five rolls of microfilm that Chambers had hidden in a pumpkin patch and which he claimed Hiss had given him between '34 and '38 for transmittal to the Soviet Union. They also brought back four documents allegedly typed on a typewriter belonging to Hiss's wife, Priscilla. These and the microfilm were now being referred to as "the pumpkin papers." Dick Nixon had raced up to New York and presented this evidence to the Grand Jury, which returned an indictment against Hiss for perjury.

"Ta this point," Wood said, looking at Russell over steepled fingers, "all the evidence dealin' with Heiss's alleged spyin' activities shows that he may hev spied between 1934 and 1938. That's why he's bein' tried fo' perjury 'stead a treason. The statute a limitations is only five years and it's expired own thet crime."

"Right, John! But this is less than three years old. It *could* be enough to get Hiss indicted for treason."

"Don't the Consteetooooshun requiahh two witnesses testifyin' 'bout the same overt act, to convict someone fo' treason?"

"Yeah. But Chambers knows Hiss was headin' up that office. And he told us that passin' on secret documents was Hiss's primary role while he wuz there. He'd testify that Hiss passed a number of documents along ta him ta be sent ta the Soviet Union. If we had just one more person who had some knowledge of Hiss's activities. Sammy, maybe. Or somebody else—"

"Was anythin' done 'bout this?"

"Well, Sammy told me State tightened up its procedures for routing top-secret and secret reports. He said the OSPA had no business bein' on the routing lists for a lot of those documents. So routing to that office was stopped. But Sammy found out how they got on those lists. Alger Hiss had requested it."

"Office of Special Political Affairs? State's liaison office to the United Nations. That's *mah* undustandin', anyway," Wood remarked. "The potintial fo' security leaks seems obvious, don't it, Lou? What ahh mean is, lots a United Nations membah gov'mints hev interests not compatible with those of the good ole US of A don't they?"

Russell nodded his agreement. "One other thing. Sammy said I should specifically bring this ta your attention. He got curious about all those top-secret documents he found layin' around in Hiss's office. Wanted to see where else they might've gone. So he ran a quick check of visitor's logs at a few friendly embassies. It seems that two days after Pearson's article ran in the *Post*, Alger Hiss had an appointment at the British Embassy with one Donald Maclean, an attaché over there."

"Really?"

"Yeah. Maclean's job dealt with Anglo-American relations. And here's somethin' else. The code breakers in Virginia had been working alone for years on this stuff. But in '45, they began cooperatin' with the Brits. They also began urgin' the FBI to start usin' their encrypted information to identify spies. Bob Lamphere got together with Meredith Gardner over there, and they started identifying cover names for spies in the messages."

"Ya don't say!"

"Yeah. And they've already identified Klaus Fuchs, Harry Gold, David Greenglass, Gus Hall, William Perl, Ethel and Julius Rosenberg, Harry Dexter White, and Guy Burgess as spies."

"What about Maclean?"

"Information comin' outta the Venona Project indicates that Maclean may be a Soviet spy, too."

"Ya don't say. Venona? That's the top-secrut code breakin' project they been runnin' outta thet girl's school ovah neah Awlington, ain't it?"

"Yep. In Arlington Hall. It was a former girls' school on Route 50. Military took over the school and built lots a temporary buildings on the campus to accommodate the code breakers. The Army Signals Intelligence Agency's been workin' over there for years. They got the best code breakers in the US and the latest technology. When they come up with somethin', they feed it to the FBI so they can identify the cover names used in the Soviet messages. That's how the FBI confirmed Elizabeth Bentley's information."

"Lou, when did Algah Heiss leave the gov'mint?"

"He resigned in December of '46."

"Well, now! That's not too long aftah this happened, is it?"

"That's what I'm sayin', John. You want I should get Sammy over here ta talk to ya?"

Wood nodded. "Ahh thank we oughtta look inta this fu'ther, don't you?"

"Yeah."

Leaning back slowly, Wood picked up his neglected sandwich. "See if y'all can git him ovah heah right away. After you set it up, call mah sec'tairy back. Tell her ahh wont Nixon, Mundt, Tavenner, Mandel, Appell, an' you at the meetin'. Okay? Oh. An' Lou?"

Russell had risen and was turning to leave. "Yeah, John?"

"Thanks for bringin' this ta mah attintion. Aftah we talk to yoah frind, we'll schedule a hearin' befoah the full Committee and git the facts own record, unda oath. Then we'll send it ova ta Justice. It'll be their baby after that. If they decide ta do nothin' wif it, thet'll be jes' one moah thang we'll have to embarrass the Truman Administration wif."

CHAPTER 14

Washington, DC
Thursday, June 2, 1949
Old House Office Building
Office of Representative Richard M. Nixon (R-CA)
11:30 a. m. Eastern Standard Time (EST)

REPRESENTATIVE RICHARD NIXON STOOD AT his office window staring down at the tree-lined street below. Though early in the day, the sun beat mercilessly on the pavement. People hurried along the sidewalks, shirt collars open, ties loosened, determined to get inside to the pleasant relief of air-conditioning as quickly as possible.

At that same moment six hundred miles north, in the United States District Court for the Southern District of New York, jury selection had begun in Alger Hiss's first perjury trial. In a few days, US Attorney Thomas Murphy and his team of prosecutors would present the case before Judge Samuel Kaufman and twelve of Hiss's peers.

Worry lines creased Dick's forehead. He knew that if that jury failed to convict Hiss, HUAC's reputation would be tarnished. If Hiss somehow got off the hook, in no time at all the liberal Press, which had recently been sounding like a mouthpiece for the Democrat Party, would accuse HUAC of "witch-hunting." But, what worried him most was that he had stuck his *own* neck out and placed his reputation on the line by leading the charge against Hiss. He knew it wouldn't be long before that same accusation would be directed at him. So far, nothing had surfaced in his home district. But, politicians thrive on good publicity. He understood that. And he understood that bad publicity in his back yard could affect his re-election chances.

On the other hand, if Hiss were convicted, Dick's reputation would be enhanced. He was pondering whether there was anything he could do to assist in securing that conviction. An idea occurred to him. Spinning from the window, he leaned over his desk and buzzed his secretary on the intercom.

"Yes, sir?"

"Get me Victor Lasky, in New York. He's a writer with *The New York World-Telegram*."

Dick knew that Lasky was close to Tom Murphy. Maybe a word or two about Hiss dropped in Lasky's ear could be passed along to Murphy in time to do some good.

Monday, June 6, 1949
Washington, DC
Office of Representative Richard M. Nixon (R-CA)
Old House Office Building
1:05 p.m. EST

Back from a quick lunch in the House cafeteria, Representative Richard Nixon was alone in his office. He had given his secretary instructions to hold his calls. Two piles of newspapers were neatly stacked on his desk, one containing the past week's issues of the conservative Scripps Howard's *New York World-Telegram*, the other a dozen recent copies of the *Oakland Tribune*. His coffee carafe had been re-filled with freshly brewed coffee. A full cup was at his right elbow.

Nixon's suit coat was off, his sleeves rolled up and his tie loosened, as he scanned articles in the *New York World-Telegram*, passed up the offerings of noted writers, Heywood Broun and Westbrook Pegler, and focused instead on stories about the Hiss case. He had been following the trial carefully for several reasons. One was that he'd made a decision to run for the Senate in 1950. As he had predicted, Sheridan Downey had announced that he'd retire at the end of his present term, for health reasons. Downey wanted to spend more time with his family. Dick wanted his senate seat.

Satisfied that the first week had gone reasonably well for Murphy and his team of prosecutors, Dick turned his attention to the *Oakland Tribune*.

California's other Senator was William F. Knowland, a fellow Republican. Knowland had been named by Governor Earl Warren to replace Hiram Johnson, who died after serving twenty-seven years as a senator. Dick and Knowland were on speaking terms and Dick believed that Knowland approved of him. His support would be essential. Not only was he the Republican Senator with whom, if Dick won, he'd be working closely in the Senate, but of some importance to a California senatorial hopeful, Senator Knowland's father was Joe Knowland, publisher of the *Oakland Tribune*. An endorsement by that newspaper would be a major boost to his election campaign.

Representative Nixon had scheduled a meeting with Senator Knowland for two o'clock, believing that the Senator would be more favorably disposed to the idea after a good lunch. Out of deference to Knowland's membership in the clubby 'upper house,' Dick had offered to come to Knowland's office, but the Senator had vetoed that idea, saying he preferred to "get out and stretch my legs a bit," and would walk over to the House Office Building.

Before meeting with him, Dick wanted to learn what tack Knowland's fathers' editors were taking on the Alger Hiss matter, on HUAC's recent doings, and on himself. Satisfied that news items and the editorial pages were favorable, he stood and came around his desk, hand extended, as his secretary ushered the Senator in.

"Senator! Nice to see you," he said cordially.

"Dick. Been hearing lots of good things about you lately." Knowland was of medium height, a slightly-built, dignified man, with sparse sandy hair graying at the temples. He came forward and grasped Dick's hand confidently, a trace of a smile playing about his thin lips.

Coffee was offered and accepted, and after some small talk, Dick sketched out his idea of a run for the Senate. "This is very preliminary, you understand," he said nervously. "I wanted to discuss it with you early." He stopped speaking and waited.

Senator Knowland shifted in his chair. A Republican activist for years before arriving in the Senate, he was known as a very cautious man. He uncrossed and re-crossed his thin legs, and smiled. "I'm favorable to your possible candidacy," he said slowly, "but I won't go public with my support until I'm sure you have a good chance to win."

"Well, how can I demonstrate that possibility to you?"

The Senator from California ran his hand across his chin. "Have you considered a tour of the State this summer? To see what kind of support might be out there for you."

"I hadn't thought that far ahead," Dick replied. "But that's not a bad idea."

"Yeah. You could find out who's in your camp, how much money you can count on.

Then get back to me. Let me know what you learn and we'll go from there."

Representative Nixon relaxed. He was tempted to ask about a possible endorsement from Knowland's fathers' newspaper, but decided it was premature. Instead, as Senator Knowland made his exit, Dick picked up the phone and dialed his home number. Having heard what he was hoping to hear, he wanted to share this good news with Pat right away.

Monday, July 12, 1949
Washington, DC
Office of Representative Richard M. Nixon (R-CA)
Old House Office Building
1:10 p. m. EST

Representatives Dick Nixon and Karl Mundt were relaxing in Dick Nixon's office after returning from lunch. The topic of conversation was the news that Alger Hiss's perjury trial had ended in a mistrial, the jury unable to agree on a verdict.

"Six weeks of court time," Dick said, "and that damned Tom Murphy couldn't get a conviction." He shook his head in disgust.

"Well, from what I read, Judge Kaufman didn't permit him much latitude. His rulings were very defense oriented. He wouldn't allow Murphy to call Hede Massing as a witness. Said the issue was not whether Hiss was a communist but whether he had committed perjury. If they try Hiss again, I hope the government gets a different judge so Massing can testify."

Dick brushed that aside. "Murphy couldn't prosecute his way out of a paper bag," he scoffed. "And the guy's up for a judgeship, I hear."

The door opened and HUAC's new Chief Counsel, Frank Tavenner strode in, carrying a folded copy of *The New York Herald-Tribune* under his left arm.

"Glad you're back, Dick," he said. With a wave of his hand, Mundt rose to leave but Tavenner motioned for him to stay. "I wanted to get your opinion about something. Yours too, Karl." Tavenner pulled up the remaining empty chair and sat down. Mundt resumed his seat expectantly.

"Go ahead," Dick said. He lit a cigarette, inhaled deeply and waited.

Tavenner unfolded his newspaper and spread it on Dick's desk. "Does the name Lawrence Duggan mean anything to either of you?" Without waiting for a response, he continued. "I read an article about him in this morning's *Herald-Tribune*. The name rang a bell. Been reviewing transcripts of both Bentley's and Chambers's Committee testimony in my spare time since I took over from Stripling."

"I recall Chambers telling us something about Lawrence Duggan," Mundt responded.

"Chambers said he'd given Lawrence Duggan's name to Hiss as a possible connection. Duggan was Chief of the Latin American Division at the State Department during the time Chambers was talking about," Tavenner continued. "He said he thought Duggan was working for the NKVD through the Massing apparatus, and Hiss could use him to channel documents to the Soviets. Just like he used Chambers." He paused, lit a cigarette, put it between his lips, removed it quickly and resumed. "Duggan left the State Department and took a job with private industry in New York a while back," Tavenner continued. "Yesterday, he was killed."

"Really?" Mundt's eyebrows shot up.

"Yeah," Tavenner said. He looked down at *The Herald-Tribune*. "The paper says, *'It is believed that Mr. Duggan, despondent in recent months, jumped out of his office window on the tenth floor, falling to his death on the street below.'*"

Dick immediately thought he saw a conspiracy. "Did he jump or was he pushed?"

"We'll never know for certain," Tavenner said. "The police are treating it as a suicide."

"But why would Duggan want to commit suicide?" Nixon asked. "I haven't heard of anybody being interested in *him*. Nobody's talking about charging him with anything, or even trying to get him to testify against Hiss in a future treason case. You heard anything, Karl?"

"No. But think about it," Mundt said. "Duggan would have been following all this in the newspapers; Chambers's testimony before our Committee, Hiss's denials, the libel suit and perjury trial. He thinks both Chambers and Hiss knew about his activities while he was at State. He's concerned that they'll expose him and the government will charge him with espionage and try to get him to testify against Hiss. He doesn't want to cooperate. When Hiss's trial ends in a mistrial, he thinks maybe he's out from under. Then, two days ago Murphy announces that Hiss will be retried. Duggan can't handle the shame of possible exposure. He goes up to his office, opens the window and jumps."

Dick shook his head. "Sounds more like a Krivitsky thing to me."

Tavenner blinked. "Krivitsky?"

"General Walter Krivitsky," Karl Mundt explained. "A high ranking Soviet intelligence officer. Worked for their military intelligence unit, the GRU. He defected in '37 and went into hiding. His real name was Shmuel Ginsberg. Stalin ordered him killed along with Krivitsky's friend, Ignace Reiss, who had also defected. Krivitsky was found murdered in a hotel room here in Washington. In '41, right after he testified before our predecessor committee. Reiss had been assassinated in Paris a few months earlier."

Tavenner digested this bit of information. Then, "Noel Field took his family and ran behind the Iron Curtain. Everybody seems to think he did that so he wouldn't have to testify against Hiss. So why didn't Duggan do the same?"

"You think he was murdered?" Mundt asked.

Tavenner nodded. "I'm thinking the commies decided that another Noel Field behind the Iron Curtain wouldn't be in their best interests."

Thursday, January 26, 1950
Washington, DC
Capitol Building
House Chamber
11:05 a. m. EST

In Washington, national events always assume a greater degree of public attention than elsewhere in the country. This week, the Capital was buzzing about the audacious Brink's robbery in Boston, which had grossed almost three million dollars for its perpetrators.

The House of Representatives, waiting for Mr. Truman's pending announcement regarding development of a hydrogen bomb and the appropriations bill that would follow, was in full session. Five days had elapsed since the end of Alger Hiss's second perjury trial. The jury had considered many classified documents passed to Chambers by Hiss, weighed the testimony of both men, and returned a guilty verdict on two counts of perjury.

Success having crowned its efforts, HUAC was basking in the spotlight. Committee members believed they had brought to earth a giant in the spy business, eliminating a threat to the U.S. in the process. Even some of the socialist press had reluctantly begun to admit that HUAC had been right, and since Hiss could not have been charged with treason due to the Constitutional requirement contained in Article 3, section 3, clause 1, that in order to convict for treason, the government must produce no less than two witnesses who could testify to the same overt act, based on the evidence available, justice had now been done.

The Committee had asked to be allowed to send one of its members to address the full House about the Hiss case. Dick Nixon had been given the honor. No one on the Committee had done more or pressed harder to bring it to a successful conclusion. Several HUAC members had wanted to drop the case, but Nixon had insisted that they continue until the charges against Hiss were either proved or disproved.

Dick relished the opportunity. After a tour of California during the summer of 1949 revealed extensive support, and receiving assurance of Senator Knowland's backing, Nixon had announced his senate candidacy. Most of the major California newspapers, including the *Oakland Tribune,* had decided to publicly support him. As a result of their endorsements, he was unopposed in the Republican primary. But the Democrats, who wanted desperately to stem the tide of mounting Republican victories around the nation, felt they had to retain that Senate seat. They had nominated Helen Gahagan Douglas, a former Broadway and motion picture actress and popular liberal who had supported Mr. Truman's Fair Deal program, to oppose Nixon. The election was only a few months off and Dick was looking for any opportunity he could get to be in the spotlight.

Now, in the crowded House chamber, Dick was at the podium recounting how Whittaker Chambers had come to the Committee's attention. "... and so on August 3, 1948, a week after Bentley appeared before HUAC," he said, "the Committee called a witness who might be able to corroborate her testimony, because up to this time all we had was Miss Bentley's testimony about the espionage ring she said she worked with. No other ring members had been broken; so it was only her word against the word of some who denied the charges and others who refused to answer questions on Fifth Amendment grounds.

"Consequently we subpoenaed Chambers to appear for the purpose of seeing whether he could corroborate Miss Bentley's testimony in any respect. This was the first opportunity our Committee members had to see Mr. Chambers." He described what had happened next, finishing up with the favorable result in the recent trial. He ended to applause; thunderous from the Republican side of the aisle, polite and subdued from the Democrat side.

Dick was in no hurry to leave the House floor. As the wire service reporters scurried to the media room to send in their news leads, he dallied, soaking up accolades from colleagues while working his way out of the chamber and into the hallway. There, a circle of eager reporters from *The Washington Post, The Baltimore Sun, The Chicago Sun-Times*, and others, surrounded him. For ten minutes, he answered their questions. Returning to his office a few minutes later, he found the representative from Georgia and the representative from South Dakota waiting for him.

"What's up guys?" Smiling, Dick slipped into his seat behind the desk, extracted a pack of cigarettes from his pocket, tapped one out, lit up and looked at his visitors expectantly.

"We been havin' a discussion 'bout somethin', Dick," Wood began. "Somethin' thet became apparent ta us a few weeks ago." He turned to Mundt. "You tell him, Karl."

"Okay," Mundt said, gathering his thoughts. "Throughout this whole HissChambers mess, several names keep popping up. People who apparently know that Hiss, Chambers and others are communists involved in espionage activities. Noel Field was one. He took his wife, his kid, and his brother to Hungary to avoid prosecution and to avoid being forced to testify against Hiss." He paused, took a deep breath and continued. "Lawrence Duggan was another. He either jumped or was pushed from his office window. Same result. No prosecution. Scratch another witness against Hiss. Maxim Lieber's name has been mentioned several times."

"Chambers mentioned Max Lieber in *his* testimony," Dick interrupted. "Said they rented a house and spent a summer together. And Hiss and his wife visited them."

"Thet's raht," Wood said earnestly. "Thet piece a info'mation would've bin valuable ta the gov'mint, wouldn't it? As corroboration of a bit a Chambers's story, ahh mean. Lieber might even know 'nuff ta be thet second witness we bin lookin'foah agin' Heiss."

"You bet." Karl Mundt nodded. "But did anybody go looking for him?'

"No," Dick answered.

"Yes, as it turns out," Mundt corrected. "John and I did some digging. We confirmed Chambers's testimony about the summer in Smithton, New Jersey. Hiss visited twice while his wife was there, and Lieber was there at the same time. Then, we confirmed that Chambers also told us about Max Lieber buying a farm in Buck's County, Pennsylvania. He said he and his wife had been invited to stay there, but when Lieber married for the second time, that plan had to be scuttled. Finally, I got to wondering if either defense lawyer had interviewed Lieber during preparations for Hiss's perjury trials."

"Well, in view of what *we* know," Nixon said, "they wouldn't have wanted Lieber to testify. That would've been damaging to Hiss's defense, wouldn't it?"

"True 'nuff. But if you had been either Lloyd Stryker or Claude Cross, wouldn't you hev at least interviewed Lieber ta see whut he knew and ta suggest thet he not testify?" Wood asked. "Aah think ah'd hev wanted ta know what his plans were."

"And I'd have wanted to know if the government had interviewed him, and if so what he told them," Mundt added. "I'd need that information so I could defend against it."

"I'm following," Dick said. "Go on."

"Last week, we asked Lou Russell to do some work on this." Mundt said. "He found out that a private detective named McLean was in charge of gathering evidence for Hiss's defense. Through McLean, he learned that an investigator named Licht, from McLean's office, had talked to Lieber and Lieber said he *does* know Hiss but doesn't propose to admit it."

"I bet they were relieved to find *that* out," Dick said.

"Yeah. But that's not all. Lieber told Licht the FBI had contacted him, but he'd refused to cooperate with them. He said the FBI had been making it rough on him ever since."

"Rough? In what way?"

"He said they'd been contacting and intimidating his clients; telling them they wouldn't be able to find publishers for their books if they continued to use Lieber as an author's rep. Claimed he already lost several authors because of that."

"Interesting," Dick responded.

"Apparently the commies had been pressuring him, too," Mundt added. "They don't want him to testify against Hiss, either."

Dick thought for a moment. "If it became widely known that Lieber had been doing secret work for the communists, publishers would tend to shun him. And with Duggan dead and Field ensconced behind the Iron Curtain, getting Hiss on a charge of treason is iffy at this point. So why haven't we called this guy to testify before the Committee?"

Wood and Mundt exchanged glances. "Do y'all thank we should?" Wood asked.

Dick shrugged. "Why not? Hiss appealed his perjury conviction. It might be overturned. You never know. " He took a long drag from his cigarette and exhaled. "Lieber may be able to give us something recent on Hiss. Or, he and Chambers might have common knowledge about one of Hiss's espionage activities. Hiss can still be charged with treason even though he's been convicted of perjury. They're two separate crimes. It's worth a try, isn't it?"

CHAPTER 15

Wednesday, March 8, 1950
Washington, DC
Old House Office Building Cafeteria
9:30 a. m. Eastern Standard Time (EST)

THE CAFETERIA IN THE SUBTERRANEAN reaches of the Old House Office Building was a genuine, no-frills affair. Its kitchen was small, its appliances outdated, and its plain rectangular tables surrounded by simple folding, metal chairs. Worn linoleum with a large, black and white, square pattern covered the concrete floor.

At a corner table, Frank S. Tavenner, Jr., sat alone, finishing a late breakfast of oatmeal, buttered toast, and coffee. He looked up and waved as Benjamin Mandel, his director of Research entered. Mandel, coffee and a Danish in hand, approached his table and sat.

"How goes the battle, Ben?" Tavenner asked.

"Good, good. You?"

"Just thinking how quickly time has passed since I took over as Chief Counsel from Bob Stripling."

"Yeah? Stripling retired at the end of 1948. December, I think. Been over a year already for you. Having fun, yet?"

Tavenner laughed. "Yep. My first year on the job has flown. I am. Thoroughly enjoyed it, so far."

"I heard you were an Assistant DA somewhere, for a few years. Is that true?"

"Yeah. Right after law school. Later, I was a US District Attorney."

"Where?"

" In the Commonwealth of Virginia."

"Really? How was life in Richmond?"

"Richmond's a charming southern city with a relaxed lifestyle and easy pace. I enjoyed it there."

"So, why'd ya leave?"

"I'd have stayed longer. But in 1945, when my draft board began eying me malevolently," a pause and a smile, "instead of waiting to be inducted, I volunteered under a program set up to attract doctors and lawyers into the army as officers."

"I remember that program. Doctors and lawyers could go directly into Officer Candidate School (OCS) and get a commission if they were able to complete it."

A nod from Tavenner. "After I completed it, I applied for an appointment with the army's Judge Advocate General's Corps (JAG). A few months later, at the other end of an ocean voyage that might have been pleasant under different circumstances, I was stationed in Japan as part of the occupation army."

"Japan, huh?"

Tavenner nodded and sipped his coffee. "I served as chief counsel at the Tojo trial. Had a staff of twenty lawyers, preparing and trying that case."

"That must've been hard."

Another nod. "The work was demanding. I wasn't there to see its conclusion on November 12, 1948 with a guilty verdict. I decided to resign my commission at that time, so I left Tokyo just before Tojo and six others were hanged on December 23, 1948. My enlistment had expired earlier that year. When I left, I was tired but pleased with what I'd accomplished and the experience I'd gathered."

Mandel finished his Danish. "What did you do after you came home?"

"I returned to Richmond and entered private law practice. Then, I heard that the House UnAmerican Activities Committee was looking for an attorney to fill the vacancy created by retirement of its general counsel. The job required a lawyer with courtroom experience, capable of directing a staff, and who was a careful planner and methodical preparer of examinations for witnesses." He glanced down, then up. "The requirements seemed to fit me perfectly. So, I drove the ninety miles to Washington for an interview, was offered the job a few weeks later, and moved into the District at the beginning of February 1949, eager to begin my new career."

Frank rose, moved to the large coffee urn and re-filled his cup. He added cream and sugar, and returned to the table. "What about you, Ben? I understand you've had a ... colorful life?"

Mandel pushed his empty plate away and smiled. "That probably means you know I was a former Communist Party official."

Tavenner nodded again. "I heard."

"I joined CPUSA in 1920. Had been a school teacher in New York before that, but I quit in 1925 to work full time for the Party. Became the Organizational Secretary for the New York District, and business manager for *The Daily Worker*. But, when Lovestone and his buddies withdrew, I went with them. By then, I'd morphed from a flaming liberal into a more thinking conservative. I applied for a job as research director with the Senate Subcommittee on Internal Security, and began working closely with the Dies Committee."

"I was reading some of the minutes from that Committee's work. Saw some of your stuff. Your correspondence with Mrs. Roosevelt?"

"Well, at the time, the NKVD thought they could recruit the First Lady. Through a friend of hers; Joseph Lash's girlfriend. Totally bizarre. Eleanor was extremely naïve and she was often fooled by the Communists, but she was *never* one of them, at least that I knew of. Still, I found it necessary to make her aware of the fact that she was being used – by communist front groups like 'The First American Rescue Ship Mission," which had solicited her as a sponsor."

"What did she do about that?"

"I sent her several articles from the Socialist newspaper, *New Leader*, about the organization. She read them and withdrew her name. Did the same thing several times after that. Eventually, she wised up and stopped allowing her name to be used. " Mandel rose. "I'm still hungry. You want anything else?"

"Yeah. I'll take one of those Danish pastries over there. And another coffee, with cream and sugar, too."

Mandel returned a few minutes later. "What do you think of John Wood?" He asked.

"John Stephens Wood? He assumed the chairman's job in September 1948, when Parnell Thomas, who was under threat of indictment, chose to step down rather than bring further embarrassment to the House and to HUAC."

"I heard about that. Also heard Wood recently presented you with a thorny assignment, didn't he?"

"Yeah. To develop a procedure for us to follow when we run into witnesses that take the Fifth."

"There's no precedent for that. In prior years, witnesses seldom refused to answer questions before the Committee. But, recently witnesses who were suspected of being Communists had been doing that in large numbers, citing their right against self-incrimination." Tavenner took a huge bite from a Danish and washed it down with some coffee. "The Committee members were getting frustrated. Something had to be done. So, he asked me to give him a memorandum; could witnesses be compelled to answer questions without violating any constitutional rights?"

"Want me to research it for you?"

"Great, if you have the time."

"Where do you want to come down?"

"I'd like to recommend that the House cite several witnesses with contempt of Congress for refusing to testify. If the members agree, it would become policy in certain selected cases."

Mandel removed a pad and pencil from his coat pocket and made a note. Then, "You know, Wood gave you a lot more authority than Stripling had. Louis Russell, me, and the clerk, John Carrington, too. Free rein and all the help we need. Later, when I asked for funding for additional investigators, Wood found the money to bring Courtney Owens and Bill Wheeler aboard. I like that."

"Owens and Wheeler are experienced investigators; we were lucky to get them. They added to the expertise of the committee."

"I also liked the way he quickly settled on the Committee membership for this Congress. Before, it was always a huge chore and was up in the air until much later in the sessions. But Wood … he brought in Francis Case, from South Dakota, Burr Harrison, from Virginia, Bernard W. Kearney, from New York, Morgan M. Moulder, from Missouri, Richard M. Nixon, from California, Harold H. Velde, from Illinois, and Francis B. Walter, from Pennsylvania. Wood asked them. They respect him. They didn't turn him down.

"Nixon's acceptance was no surprise," Tavenner said. . "He'd served on the Committee since early 1947, and is now its most valuable member. His legal training makes it possible for him to see issues others can't see. He asks questions that need asking."

"And his penchant for sprinkling his speech with profanity when under pressure often livened up an executive session," Mandel said with a chuckle. He rose to leave. "When do you need that research?"

"No huge rush. Next Monday will be fine."

‡ ‡ ‡ ‡ ‡

Wednesday, March 8, 1950
Washington, DC
Old House Office Building
Office of Frank S. Tavenner, Jr., Chief Counsel
10:30 a. m. Eastern Standard Time (EST)

By staying late several evenings a week to study the minutes of prior hearings, Frank Tavenner was soon up to speed on HUAC's recent involvement with the problem of Communism in America. After the 81st Congress convened, HUAC had speedily conducted hearings, taking testimony on November 8 and December 2, 1949, from Courtney Owens, one of the committee's new investigators, setting the evidentiary stage for the upcoming hearing. Then Max Bedacht, a CPUSA member from almost the beginning of its existence, testified. Bedacht, formerly an Acting General Secretary of CPUSA, had often presided over meetings of the Political Committee, a group of seven to ten comrades that handled many of the Party's day-to-day affairs, such as manipulating a strike or planning infiltration tactics. He named numerous associates.

Dr. William G. Burtan's testimony was next. He had been involved in counterfeiting operations in the 1930s along with Nicholas Dozenberg. Dozenberg, a Latvian-born official of the American Communist Party, had been caught in the counterfeiting scheme, which had been ordered by Moscow to help finance Soviet military intelligence operations. The bogus money had also been used to finance other Party activities. Dozenberg, indicted for also obtaining passports under false pretenses, was tried and convicted for passport fraud in 1940 and sentenced to prison. Although he possessed much relevant information about the activities of the underground Communist Party, and although he agreed to cooperate fully with HUAC, he would not agree to testify in person. But, while still in prison, he *did* send a statement describing his life of service to the Communist Party, which was read into the record.

Frank rose from his desk and walked into the outer office. Snatching a clean coffee cup from a holder, he filled it with the dark brown liquid, added cream and sugar, exchanged a few remarks with his secretary, and returned to his desk.

Today, they would finish taking testimony from John Loomis Sherman, whom they had begun to question a few days before. According to Whittaker Chambers, Sherman had conducted several covert operations for the Soviets. Chambers had confided to the FBI that while a London operation involving Maxim Lieber was getting under way, he had asked Lieber to cooperate with fellow underground operator, John Loomis Sherman, under the alias "Charles Francis Chase" and himself, as "Lloyd Cantwell" in establishing the American Feature Writers Syndicate. These three had filed a registration of trade in New York City and opened a bank account at the Chemical Bank of New York. Sherman was to go to Tokyo and set up a network there. Chambers said that Sherman had gone to work in Lieber's office, had a desk there, and his name was written on the door and some stationery was printed, and deposits were made in the Chemical Bank in New York in the name of the syndicate. These deposits were to finance the operation in Japan. Then J. Peters, who was in on most of this operation, supplied a birth certificate in the name of Charles Chase [for Sherman] and, on the basis of that certificate, which was a perfectly legal document procured legally, Sherman took out a passport and on that passport he traveled to Tokyo.

Then, after we complete the hearing with Sherman, we'll finish up this round of hearings with the testimony of Max Lieber, who used the name "Paul" while he was active in CPUSA.

Tavenner thought about Lieber. He and Hiss had apparently been friends in the 1930s.

Alger Hiss was appealing his conviction. It might be overturned. Lieber could corroborate what Chambers, who used the names "Lloyd Cantwell" and "David Breen" while a member of the Communist Party underground, had told them about the Party's attempts to set up London and Tokyo operations using Lieber's literary agency as a front.

In August 1948, when Chambers began disclosing what he knew about a communist espionage apparatus in Washington called the Ware Group, the public was astounded. His testimony about Alger Hiss had exploded like a thousand-pound bomb in the middle of a sedate neighborhood, sending shock waves reverberating throughout Washington politics. He testified that Hiss had given him many classified State Department documents for transmission to the Soviet Union. But Hiss was so well thought of that many did not believe it. The former First Lady, Eleanor Roosevelt was heard to say, "I am going to believe in Alger Hiss's integrity until he is proved guilty." *Yeah. Just like Mandel said; naïve.* Even President Truman believed in Hiss. In fact, the Democrat Administration was so supportive of Hiss during '48 that the Truman Justice Department, searching for a way to prevent prosecution of Hiss, had considered indicting Chambers instead.

Hiss, Chambers, and Sherman belonged to a generation of idealists. They believed that Capitalism as an economic system had failed and democracy as a political system was unworkable. But, as with most ultra-liberals, their idealism did not extend to a basic trust of people. Absent a belief in God and the self-imposed restraints of moral principles that are derived from that belief, they felt that government control was the answer to all problems, that centralization of power in the hands of the government and removal of the means of production from private hands was necessary. To them, communism was the wave of the future and the United States stood in its way. So, some of them spied for the Soviet Union. But Hiss may have had a more personal motive.

His father, Charles Alger Hiss, had been a Baltimore businessman who had helped build a dry goods importing firm into a small fortune. But he had exhausted himself dealing with years of business problems and the burden of caring for the widow and six children of his deceased brother, as well as his own wife and five children. In the Panic of 1907, the worst financial disaster to hit America before the depression, Charles lost his job. He was forty-two. Unable to find work, he committed suicide. Alger Hiss was two and a half years old at the time. When, as a teenager, he was told how his father died, it affected him profoundly. He may never have fully recovered from the emotional impact.

A few years later, his sister, Mary Ann, also committed suicide and his brother, Bosely, died after a long illness. These events may have turned Hiss bitter about life. His view may have been that his father, a self-made man, his sister, a kind sweet woman, and his brother, a gentle man, were victims of a capitalist society viewed as excessively harsh and exploitative. A desire to avenge these deaths, perceived as at the hands of the forces of capitalism, could have been part of Alger Hiss's motive in assisting the Soviet Union.

Hiss had attended Baltimore City College High School and Johns Hopkins University. Considered one of Hopkins's most brilliant students, a sure-to-succeed type, he earned his BA degree in 1926. After college, he attended Harvard Law School. Most would agree that a law degree from that school was a ticket to financial success. Few would disagree that it did not necessarily insure either spiritual health or success with personal relationships.

In the early '30s, Hiss entered government service, first in the Department of Agriculture and later in the Justice Department. Then he moved to the Solicitor General's Office as an assistant to Stanley Reid, who was later appointed to the Supreme Court. From there, Hiss transferred to the State Department, where he became Chief of the Office of Special Political Affairs. Everyone with whom he came in contact, agreed; he had served with distinction in the Roosevelt Administration. He was a bright star.

Whittaker Chambers had also lived in Baltimore. Max Lieber met them both in that city.

Alger Hiss testified before HUAC, attempting to refute Chambers's charges. Then he sued Chambers for slander. Filing that lawsuit may not have been a wise move because it gave government investigators a chance to compare his testimony in both proceedings for any inconsistencies. They found plenty; enough to indict Hiss for perjury.

Hiss was first tried on May 31, 1949 in a federal court in New York City, before Judge Samuel H. Kaufman. Lloyd Paul Stryker, a giant of the defense trial bar, ably defended him, and two Supreme Court justices. Felix Frankfurter and Stanley Reed, testified for Hiss as character witnesses. The trial resulted in a hung jury. A mistrial was declared on July 7, 1949.

But the case was so significant that a decision to retry it was made. The second trial began on November 17, 1949. On January 21, 1950, it had ended in Hiss's conviction on two counts. One was his denial that he had given State Department documents to Chambers. The other was his denial that he ever saw Chambers after January 1, 1937. His sentence? Five years on each count, the terms to run concurrently.

Hiss had already declared that he would file an appeal. Tavenner knew that if the lower court's decision was not overturned and Hiss went to jail, the federal parole laws of the day being what they were, he would probably be out in three years. Several Committee members however, were concerned that the conviction would be reversed. If so, the Justice Department, now under fire from Congress for years of inactivity regarding communists and communist sympathizers in the government, would be forced to try him again.

Because of information obtained from Chambers, enough was now known about Hiss's spying to warrant charging him with treason. However, the Constitution required two witnesses testifying about the same overt act, in order to *convict* someone of that crime. Proving Hiss's espionage activities would be difficult without testimony from someone like Sherman or Max Lieber. If either could be sufficiently intimidated, he might become that corroborating witness. But Sherman was proving uncooperative. It had been Dick Nixon, Karl Mundt, and John Wood, who urged that they call Lieber before HUAC, to see if he could support what Chambers had said about Hiss, especially with regard to the Party's Baltimore and Washington, DC operations.

Frank thought about Marxism-Leninism as it had evolved. A "vision of Man without God," it had picked up numerous converts with its elusive promise of *the perfect society*. In England, the Fabians had beaten the drums of socialism for decades, laying the foundation for the future welfare state so convincingly that the famed British author, Graham Greene, was referring to Fabians in disapproving tones in his novelette, *Under the Garden*. In America, it was the liberal Left, "the self-appointed elite," who became its champions. Envisioning creation of a benevolent, omniscient super state, many betrayed their country.

Why? Idealism? Romanticism? In their attempt to change and re-shape the values of American society, the Left had not only rejected capitalism, but turned away from God and religion as well. It was looking for an economic system controlled by government, one that would prevent what the Left viewed as the excesses of capitalism. Economists call such a system a "hampered market system." To some, communism seemed an acceptable substitute. So, the plain truth of what Joseph Stalin had begun to do when he came to power in 1929, governing through compulsory labor, prison camps and systematic murder of his own supporters, was ignored, explained away, or shrugged off for a time. But as Stalin attempted to combine totalitarianism and communism, the suppression of religion and the loss of individual freedom inevitable under socialism and communism caused consternation among liberals of good conscience.

Because of his own belief in God and in personal accountability, Tavenner understood these concerns. In his mind, nothing could substitute for a close, personal friendship with Jesus Christ, and through him, a relationship with God. But those who had no religious belief system to sustain them thought otherwise.

What about the freedom of action and freedom of expression that a capitalist system operating on free market principles provided for individuals? In recent years, new voices – the voices of Post-Modernists, who saw everything in terms of a struggle for power – had been heard in America, claiming that because people did not have the power to influence industrial growth, stringent government controls were necessary to regulate private enterprise. They had drifted quite far from the original intent of the founding fathers, who believed in our capacity to control and govern ourselves, and that government should be limited to only those powers delegated to it by the people. Frank recalled reading a historic letter written by James Madison, a chief architect of the US Constitution, in which he said, *"We have staked the whole future of all of our political institutions ... upon the capacity of each and all of us to govern ourselves, and to control ourselves, to sustain ourselves according to the Ten Commandments of God."*

Tavenner glanced at his wristwatch, raised his coffee cup to his lips, and gulped the rest of his coffee. It was cold. He made a wry face, set the cup on the table, and reached for his jacket. Lou Russell had been assigned to do the questioning today. Frank had sat down with Russell, determined the information they wanted from this witness, and worked out the questions. He was confident that the veteran Russell knew what he had to do.

CHAPTER 16

Wednesday, March 8, 1950
Washington, DC
Capitol Building
Hearing Room 226
10:01 a.m. Eastern Standard Time (EST)

"THE COMMITTEE WILL COME TO ordahhh!" Representative John Wood's baritone voice kicked off the hearing. "Let the record show that fo' the puupose of this hearin' the chai'man has designated a subcommittee composed of Representatives Walters, Kearney and Wood – that's me - and they are awl present. Are you ready ta proceed, Mistah Counsel?"

Frank Tavenner, Jr., seated next to Lou Russell, a few chairs to Wood's left, looked crisp in a navy blue business suit, white dress shirt, and a maroon, silver and blue striped tie. "Yes, sir," he said.

Representative Wood peered at the witness seated at a table a few feet away. "Ahh assume, in view a the fact we're operatin' today undah a subcommittee, wheaas at the last hearin' we had the full committee, I will sweahh the witness agin." Receiving no challenge to his statement, he addressed the witness, a dark-complected man with a bald head and rather large ears. "Will y'all please stand an' be sworn?" His gruff tone made it sound more like an order than a request. He ran a huge paw through his thick, silvery mane and waited.

The witness, wearing a wrinkled blue blazer and gray slacks, pushed his chair back and came slowly to his feet, his right hand raised above his head.

"You solemnly sweahh the evidence you give ta this committee shall be the truth, the whole truth, an' nothin' but the truth, so he'p you Gawd?'

"I do," the witness responded.

"Hev a seat. Mistah Tavenner, who will be conductin' the questionin' today, sir?" The witness resumed his seat, placed a full pack of Old Gold King cigarettes on the table in front of him and waited.

Tavenner adjusted his microphone. "Chief Investigator Russell will do so today, Mr. Chairman."

Wood nodded. "Mistah Russell, you may proceed," he said.

Louis J. Russell was considered the Committee's most important behind-the-scenes staff member. A short, stocky man, he had been with the Committee since May 1945, directing and conducting field investigations, which consisted of following leads, developing evidence, and assembling information for use in questioning witnesses. He was an efficient, hard-working individual who believed that communists were bad people who, if they were employed in the government, should be exposed and removed before they could do any harm.

Russell, an FBI agent for ten years, had studied accounting. He had entered the FBI at a time when both lawyers and accountants were being recruited. Prior to that, he had been a professional baseball player, rising in the minor leagues to Triple-A ball before an injury forced him to hang up his spikes. He glanced over at Tavenner, nodded and began.

"Mr. Sherman, you are appearing before the Committee by virtue of a subpoena served on you on February eighth, 1950, by Deputy United States Marshall Ross of Los Angeles?"

"That is correct, sir," Sherman said shortly.

"And for the record, we are continuing to receive testimony from you which was begun on this past Monday, February twenty-seventh, 1950. What is your full name?"

"My name is John L. Sherman. By profession I am a teacher. During the previous year I was an instructor in social science and dean of men at one of the smaller universities in Los Angeles. In the current year, due to the activities of the FBI, I have been unable to obtain a teaching position. I should like at this time to make a slight correction. It has been reported in the press and elsewhere that I have been in hiding. That is incorrect. The FBI has known of my whereabouts and I think practically every detail of my life for many years."

Chairman Wood leaned into his microphone. "Jist a minute! The Committee is not innerested in goin' inta the activities of the FBI at this moment and ahh would appreciate it if you would confine yoah testimony to answers ta questions. Theah will be ample time later fo' you to express yoah views ta this Committee."

The witness made a nondescript hand gesture. "I understand, Mr. Chairman."

Lou Russell cleared his throat. He glanced at his notes, looked quickly at the Chairman, and then at Sherman. "Have you ever used the name Don?" He asked the witness.

"I decline to answer that question on the ground that the answer may incriminate me," Sherman responded.

"Are you acquainted with a man named David Whittaker Chambers?"

"I decline to answer on the same ground."

"Did you ever know an individual named Lloyd Cantwell?"

"I decline to answer on the same ground."

"Is Lloyd Cantwell the same person as Whittaker Chambers?"

"I decline to answer that question on the same ground. May I explain that all these questions and the answers I might make are, in my conviction and belief, part of a pattern or frame-up which has already destroyed the reputation of one fine American and is now being extended, as the facts will ultimately prove, to frame others. Many persons have been investigated. I have been under constant investigation; and I think facts subsequently to be developed here will indicate this is part of the frame-up of a disordered mind."

Representative Bernard Kearney had been silent up to this point. Tall and thin, he leaned his head of thick white hair forward and asked in his cultured New York accent, "Would the witness mind giving the name of that so-called fine American he speaks of?"

"I think in time I will do that," John Loomis Sherman responded.

"Would you mind doing it now?" Kearney persisted.

"I will exercise my privilege at this moment not to disclose it until further testimony is revealed which will substantiate my point of view," Sherman said.

Representative Francis (Frank) Walter (D-PA), seated at the other end of the Committee table, spoke up. "Don't you think this would be a good opportunity to clarify the atmosphere and remove whatever stigma you think has been wrongfully placed on a fine American's name?" He was short and wiry, and wore gold metal spectacles, over which he peered at Sherman expectantly.

"I'm convinced this will be done before we are through, judging by what transpired at the previous executive session," Sherman replied haughtily.

Walter was about to speak again, thought better of it and deferred to Russell. "Mr. Sherman, I would like to read to you an excerpt from the testimony given to this Committee by Whittaker Chambers as follows:

> *'One day Bill brought me in touch with Sherman again and Sherman described what he had to do. Sherman was to go to Tokyo to be the head of a Soviet underground group and he wanted me to organize for him the facade here which would make it possible for him to operate in Tokyo which as you know, is a very difficult operation.'*

"Is that statement true or false?"

Sherman focused his gaze on the wall behind Russell's head. "I decline to answer on the ground stated."

"Mr. Sherman, you have indicated that there has been untruthful testimony concerning you. You are now being given an opportunity to refute that testimony. Do you wish to refute it?" Russell adjusted his microphone and glared at the witness.

"I don't have sufficient information at the present time to do it, but I have the greatest confidence that the true facts will come out. I have not stated that there has been untruthful testimony. I have declined to answer that testimony. I think it should be understood that any statement I make, true or false, in relation to testimony such as has developed, would put me in jeopardy, and I must exercise my constitutional right not to answer."

"Mr. Sherman, you are being given the opportunity to bring those facts out now, sir," Russell said in a quiet voice.

"I am unable to do so without my answers tending to incriminate me," Sherman responded. "But I believe the true facts will come out. They are already coming out."

"Without any assistance from the witness," Kearney remarked sarcastically.

"With every assistance that I can provide this Committee while protecting my own rights," was Sherman's quick rejoinder.

"I'd like to continue reading to you from the testimony of Whittaker Chambers, as I did several times last Monday." Russell adjusted his glasses on his nose and began to read again:

> 'So I decided that since the London project was rocking along, the expedient thing was to use Maxim Lieber to front for the Tokyo operation. That was organized in the following way. Lieber and Sherman set up what was called the American Feature Writer's Syndicate whose purpose it was to secure interesting material from abroad. As I understand it, Lieber went among various feature syndicates and various newspapers and tried to get various interests or sales in this kind of stuff, and Sherman went to work in Lieber's office, had a desk there, and his name was written on the door and I think some stationery was got out and deposits were made. I think, in the Chemical Bank in New York in the name of the syndicate. These deposits were to finance the operation in Japan. Then Peters, who was in on most of this operation, supplied a birth certificate in the name of Charles Chase and, on the basis of that certificate, which was a perfectly legal document procured in the way I have described in earlier testimony, John Sherman took out a passport and on that passport he traveled to Tokyo.'"

Russell looked up from the transcript. "Do you wish to affirm or deny the extract which I have just read to you from the testimony of Whittaker Chambers?"

"I must decline to answer on the ground of self-incrimination," Sherman answered.

"Have you ever known an individual named J. Peters?"

"I must decline to answer on the same ground," came the response.

"Have you ever used the name Charles Chase?"

"I must decline to answer on the same ground."

"Have you ever been in Tokyo, Japan?"

"I must decline to answer on the same ground."

"Do you know Maxim Lieber?"

Sherman's eyes narrowed slightly but he kept his voice under control. "I must decline to answer on the same ground," he intoned again.

"Mr. Sherman, I show you a photostatic copy of an application for a passport made out in the name of Charles Francis Chase, which discloses that the Department of State issued

Passport No. 148071 to a Charles Francis Chase on September 22, 1934, which covered travel to Japan, China and Soviet Russia for business purposes. I ask if you are the individual who executed this passport application."

Reaching for the pack of Old Gold, Sherman tapped one out and lit it. He puffed on it once and exhaled "I must decline to answer on the same ground."

"I also show you the oath of allegiance executed at the same time as the passport application, and ask if you executed that oath of allegiance," Russell said.

"I decline to answer on the same ground."

"Is that your photograph, Mr. Sherman?"

"I decline to answer. There is no way by which I can determine whether that is my photograph."

"Let me see that," Representative Walter asked. The documents were handed to the clerk who took them to Walter. He examined them briefly and then looked at the witness.

"When were you born, Mr. Sherman?" Frank Walter asked innocently.

"October 19, 1895."

"Did you sign the name Charles F. Chase to this application?" Walter asked.

"I must decline to answer on the same ground."

Russell rose to his feet. "Mr. Chairman, I ask that this passport application and the oath of allegiance be introduced in the record at this point as Sherman exhibits One and Two." He retrieved the documents from Representative Walter and handed them to John Carrington, the clerk.

The Chairman nodded. "They will be admitted."

"I have asked you whether or not you have ever been to Tokyo," Russell continued. "I ask you that question again."

"I must decline to answer on the same ground," was the response once again.

"Did you ever receive a passport from the State Department in the name of Charles Francis Chase?"

"I must decline to answer on the same ground."

Russell studied his notes for a moment before asking his next question. "Isn't it true that on March 7, 1935, you executed an application for registration in Tokyo, Japan, in which you listed your address as the Bunka Apartments, Tokyo, and in which you said that your legal residence in the United States was 545 Fifth Avenue, New York City, and that in the event of death or accident, Maxim Lieber, 545 Fifth Avenue, New York, should be contacted?"

"I must decline to answer on the same ground," Sherman again responded. Slightly agitated, he reached for a nearby ashtray and placed his cigarette in it. That question had shown him that HUAC's information about his activities was more accurate than he had anticipated.

The door behind the Committee table opened and a young, female page stepped into the hearing room. She handed a note to Representative Wood, who glanced at it and tapped his microphone with a fingernail. "This heah note says we're wanted own the House floah fo' a vote," he said. "We'll take a short recess an' resume in thirty minutes." He slapped his gavel on the bench, rose and headed for the door, the other House members following on his heels.

CHAPTER 17

Wednesday, March 8, 1950
Washington, DC
Capitol Building
Room 226
11:25 a.m. Eastern Standard Time (EST)

Representative John Wood slipped into his chair, grabbed the gavel and rapped it sharply. The other subcommittee members had already returned from the House chamber and were in their places. Members of the media and the witness took their seats.

"You may resume, Mistah Russell. Do y'all need the Court Reportah ta read back the previous question an' ainsah?"

"That won't be necessary, Mr. Chairman," Russell said. Directing his attention to the witness, he began. "Have you ever been to Russia, Mr. Sherman?"

"I must decline to answer on the ground that my answer might tend to incriminate me," came back the now-familiar litany.

"While you were in the Navy, were you ever in Russia?"

"I believe that an expedition was sent to Murmansk as part of the activities of the U.S. Navy. I believe it was Murmansk, if I remember correctly."

"Mr. Sherman, you haven't answered the question. Were you a part of that expedition?"

Sherman became rattled. "I was on the ship as an enlisted man. I don't know what is meant by 'expedition.' I was on the ship and we went ashore for a short time. That was in 1918."

"Did you ever again visit Russia?"

"I decline to answer on the same ground."

"Did you ever know a man named Hideo Noda, a Japanese American portrait painter?"

"I must decline to answer on the same ground," Sherman said.

"At this point, I would like to read from the testimony of Whittaker Chambers, which refers to the trip which Chambers said you made to Japan:

> 'Before he went he gave me another task which was to find for him an American Japanese who was connected with the highest Japanese circles and who would have

easy social access to important people in Japan. I found for him Hideo Noda, who was a Japanese American, I think born in California, a painter of considerable ability who was a communist. Then of course, I introduced Sherman and Noda and, by separate routes, they traveled to Japan.'"

"Do you wish to deny or affirm that excerpt from the testimony of Whittaker Chambers, which I have just read to you?"

"I decline to answer on the same ground."

"Did you ever travel to Japan with Hideo Noda?"

"I decline to answer on the grounds stated."

"Did you ever see Hideo Noda in Tokyo, Japan?"

"I decline to answer on the same ground."

"Mr. Sherman, I would like to read further from the testimony of Whittaker Chambers:

'I was ordered suddenly to dismantle the whole American end of the Japanese apparatus because an arrest had occurred and I assumed, of course, Sherman had been arrested in Japan. I was told to do this as quickly as possible. Russians are not used to Americans; never will be. I, of course, liquidated the apparatus overnight and there was nothing left the next morning. I met Bill the next day and he said he hoped I hadn't done anything about dismantling the apparatus because it was all a mistake, but the apparatus was gone completely, so they presently recalled Sherman from Tokyo.'

"Is that statement true or false?"

"I decline to answer on the ground stated."

"I'd like to read further from Whittaker Chambers's testimony. The statement refers to you when Chambers says, 'he':

'He came back to the United States and was again put in touch with me. His orders were at that time for him to proceed to Moscow. Through Peters I again procured a birth certificate for him. I have forgotten the name. He went to Moscow. He was gone quite a while and I had the feeling he would probably never come back but some time I think in 1937 after Bykov was here or just before Bykov came, I have forgotten which, Sherman appeared unexpectedly one night in Lieber's apartment. He was extremely agitated and kept pacing the apartment and Lieber insisted that we go out at once. We went out and the minute we got outside the door he grabbed

my arm and said: "I will not work one hour longer for those murderers." He then told me he wanted me to act as his agent personally and get through a message to the proper Soviet agents that he was separating himself from the apparatus and that he would return to the open Communist Party.'

"Do you recall having had such a meeting with Whittaker Chambers and making those statements?"

"I decline to answer on the same ground."

"Were you ever in any apartment which may have been occupied by Maxim Lieber?"

"I must decline to answer on the ground stated."

"Did you ever know Colonel Boris Bykov?"

"I decline to answer on the ground stated."

"Are you a member of the Communist Party?"

"I decline to answer on the grounds stated. However, I may say, if the Committee is interested, that I have expressed my views freely, without hesitation, to my students and in my writings, and if the committee is interested I will express my feelings here."

"I asked if you are a member of the Communist Party, Mr. Sherman," Russell, ignoring Sherman's comment, responded icily.

"I decline to answer on the ground stated." Sherman was indignant.

"Have you *ever* been a member of the Communist Party?"

"I decline to answer on the ground stated," the witness answered heatedly.

"Have you ever been a member of an underground apparatus of the Communist Party?"

"I decline to answer on the ground stated."

"Have you ever engaged in espionage?"

"I decline to answer on the ground stated."

Russell then read more from the testimony of Chambers dealing with Sherman's return to the United States, his trip to Moscow, his stay there, his subsequent return to America, his attempt to break with the Russians and the underground by leaving for California, and his request that Chambers give him a twenty-four hour head start before notifying Bykov.

This excerpt drew a tirade from Sherman about a sick mind and the failure to analyze testimony, which caused Chairman Wood to stop him, after which, Russell resumed his questioning. "Were you ever associated with an enterprise known as the American Feature Writer's Syndicate?"

"I decline to answer on the ground that my answer may tend to incriminate me."

"Did that organization file with the City of New York a registration of trade name?"

"I decline to answer on the same ground."

"Did the American Feature Writer's Syndicate have a bank account in the Chemical Bank of New York City?"

"I decline to answer on the same ground."

"Did you sign the account as an officer of the American Feature Writer's Syndicate?"

"I refuse to answer on the same ground."

"Did you ever know an individual who used the name Paul?"

"I have known many individuals named Paul," Sherman said haughtily.

"Was Maxim Lieber known to you as Paul?"

"I decline to answer on the same ground."

"Did you ever request Maxim Lieber to obtain for you covering credentials which would permit you to travel from Japan into China and Russia under another name?"

"I decline to answer on the same ground."

"Did you attend a luncheon with Maxim Lieber and Whittaker Chambers in which you discussed your purpose in securing such credentials?"

"I decline to answer on the same ground."

"Did you ever meet Whittaker Chambers in Baltimore?"

"I decline to answer on the same ground."

Lou Russell nodded to Representative Wood. "Do any Committee members want to ask any questions, Mr. Chairman?" Wood leaned forward and glanced down the Committee table. "We've reached the point wheah Committee membahs may question the witness. Does anyone wish ta do so?"

"I have one or two questions, Mr. Sherman," Representative Kearney interjected. "One little thing that I think needs clearing up." He turned toward the witness. "You answered, in response to the question of counsel whether you were a member of the Communist Party, that you declined to answer on the ground it might incriminate you."

"Yes."

"Is it a crime, in your own mind, to be a member of the Communist Party?"

"I decline to answer on the ground stated."

"Would you mind answering yes or no?"

"I decline to answer on the ground stated."

"I have nothing further, Mr. Chairman," Kearney said.

Wood nodded to Russell, who had been reviewing his notes while Kearney had been questioning Sherman. "Anythin' moah, Mistah Russell?"

"Yes, Mr. Chairman. Mr. Sherman, are you acquainted with Alger Hiss?"

"I decline to answer on the ground stated. May I say, however, that I would regard it as a great privilege to have the acquaintance of Mr. Alger Hiss."

"Of course, that implies that you don't know him," Representative Walter, who had been following the testimony closely, cut in.

"I'm confident that Mr. Hiss would not know me from Adam," Sherman responded.

"Would you know him from Adam?"

"I would. His picture has been in all the papers."

"Did you ever meet him in the 1010 Saint Paul Street Apartments in Baltimore, Maryland during the winter of 1934?' Russell asked.

"I decline to answer on the ground stated."

"Why do you feel it would incriminate you to answer whether you have met him?" Frank Walter asked.

"Not answering this question directly," Sherman stated, "may I say we are dealing with a pattern or a frame-up the ends, the implications of which I have no way of understanding, and it may implicate me and others in a pattern which is now being revealed and I think will be clearly understood for what it is."

Representative Walter made an impatient hand gesture. "What do you think you might be implicated in if you would answer some of these questions?"

"I do not know for certain, but I am entirely sure that we are dealing here with the frame-up of a disordered mind." Sherman's cigarette had burned down. He reached for the pack again, tapped out a fresh one and lit it.

"No, that is *not* the fact!" Walter was now angry. "That may be your own impression of what we are dealing with. What *I'm* interested in is what you feel you may be connected with that may reflect on your loyalty as an American citizen if you should answer these questions."

"I have already explained I was under investigation, possibly still am, by a Federal grand jury. The question of the truth or falsity of my testimony is not a protection, in view of the fact that there may be counter testimony, truthful or untruthful to any degree, and my only protection, obviously, is to exercise my constitutional privilege."

There was a pause as the Committee members considered his response. Then Lou Russell continued. "Were you ever introduced to Mr. and Mrs. Alger Hiss in the 1010 St. Paul Street Apartments in Baltimore by Whittaker Chambers?"

"I decline to answer on the same ground."

Russell appeared exasperated. "Mr. Sherman, what is the bit of evidence that would implicate you, and in what?"

"I have explained that any testimony I might give here, to which there might be counter testimony which a jury would believe, would jeopardize me to a charge of perjury. Therefore, I must exercise my constitutional right not to testify," Sherman replied.

"What part of the testimony given by Mr. Whittaker Chambers about you is true and what part is false?"

"I decline to answer on the same ground."

"Don't you think this is the time to speak the truth?"

"In the long run the truth will prevail, but in the short run people have been convicted and jailed for telling the truth. I believe as a philosophical and perhaps religious conviction, that in the long run the truth will prevail."

Russell leaned back in his chair and looked over at Wood. "I have no more questions in open session. I *do* have two questions for this witness in executive session, however."

"Thank you, Mistah Sherman," Wood said. He glanced at the large Seth Thomas clock hanging above the double doors at the rear of the chamber. It was eleven fifty-five a.m. He turned toward the reporters and spectators in the room and spoke into his mike. "The Committee will stand in recess fo' fifteen minutes. Theah will be no furthah open hearin' today. The full Committee will meet heah in executive session in fifteen minutes."

CHAPTER 18

Thursday, June 15, 1950
Washington, DC
Capitol Building
Room 226
10:00 a.m. Eastern Standard Time (EST)

BECAUSE ROOM 226 ON THE House side of the stately Capital Building did not hold many people, it was used by a few committees for executive sessions and hearings when publicity was unwanted. Today, attendance was scant.

It was only mid-June, but the Nation's capital was already oppressively hot. In 1948, the federal government had begun the process of air conditioning all its office buildings in the District. After the White House, this one had been next. Finished, it was comfortable inside.

"Let the record show," Representative Francis (Frank) Walter, from Pennsylvania, began, "this hearing is being conducted by a subcommittee consisting of Representatives Harrison, Moulder and myself. Also present are Frank S. Tavenner, Jr., counsel, Donald Appell and William Wheeler, investigators." In John Wood's absence, Walter was in the chair.

The acting chairman wore a navy blue blazer, a button-down pinpoint dress shirt, a dark silk bow tie, and rimless glasses. The bow tie and glasses gave him an aura of intelligence. Walter was a well-known and respected member of the House. One of its leading Democrats, he served as chairman of the Democrat Caucus and the number two man on the Judiciary Committee, and had figured prominently in the enactment of the Administrative Procedures Act of 1946. Possessed of one of the best legal minds in the House, he was also one of the few members to experience service in both world wars. Before winning election to Congress, Frank Walter had practiced law and served as a county solicitor in Pennsylvania. A congressional hearing room was similar to a court, and he was quite at home in a courtroom.

"Raise your right hand, please," he addressed this to the witness who was standing behind the oak table reserved for witnesses and their attorneys, absorbed in conversation with his lawyer. Maxim Lieber, whose name had been mentioned by several witnesses in recent months, had been described as an important communist agent operating covertly in this country. He glanced up, frowned and raised his hand grudgingly.

"You swear the testimony you are about to give shall be the truth, the whole truth and nothing but the truth, so help you God?"

"I do," the witness responded.

"Be seated, sir. Mr. Tavenner, you may proceed."

As the hearing got under way, a tall, well-groomed woman quietly entered the room. About forty, she wore a gray rayon short-sleeved dress of a style popular since 1947. A brown leather belt accented her waist above a vertical row of five brown buttons. Her red hair was pulled back severely from her face and gathered into a bun, tightly rolled near the nape of her neck. Her shoes were gray flats, the type tall women wear when they want to minimize their height. A black leather handbag with brass fittings hung from her right shoulder. Uncertain for a moment, she hesitated just inside the door, scanned the hearing room, moved forward and slipping into a bench behind the other spectators, her chin high and thrust forward, her attention riveted on the witness.

"Are you represented by counsel?" Tavenner asked the witness.

Hearing this, the other man at the table spoke. "My name is Marvin Jesse Freedlander, Junior, 522 Fifth Avenue, New York. I am an attorney admitted to practice in the State of New York, and before the Supreme Court of the United States." He was tall, thin, and round- shouldered. His bony, stick-like arms were concealed in a three-piece, black pinstriped suit complete with vest. His attire mirrored the uniform of the successful New York City lawyer. He immediately sat down.

Tavenner glanced toward the witness again. "You are Maxim Lieber?"

"Yes," the witness said. He was of medium height, with a wiry build. His wavy brown hair was beginning to turn gray, and his thinness served to emphasize a small potbelly. He wore a brown, Harris tweed sport coat with leather elbow patches, a blue shirt, a tan and blue striped tie and gray slacks. As he spoke, he removed his horn-rimmed glasses, pulled a spotless white handkerchief from his back pocket, and began to polish them.

"When and where were you born?" Tavenner asked.

"I was born in Warsaw, Poland on October 15th, 1897."

"Will you briefly outline your educational background, Mr. Lieber?"

"I arrived here in February 1907; attended public schools in New York City; attended Townsend Harris Hall, which at that time was part of New York City College, but which has been abandoned; transferred to Morris High School in the Bronx, New York."

"Are you a naturalized citizen?"

"Yes, sir. I was naturalized in the city of Washington during the war. I was stationed at Camp Meade, Maryland in the replacement battalion in the medical service, and was brought to Washington for naturalization. I think it was June or July 1919."

"Mr. Lieber, will you briefly outline your occupational background, including the names of all writers' syndicates and publishing houses of which you have either been an officer or an employee or to whom you have been under contract for articles?"

Lieber took a deep breath and spoke into his microphone. "I am a literary agent. I have been a literary agent since May 1930. Prior to that I was with Brentano's, where I was in charge of the publishing department from 1926 until May 1930. The reason for my separation from the firm was that the firm went into involuntary bankruptcy due to expansion and the depression and so on. Prior to that I had edited a book, an anthology of short stories, which I am happy to say is in the Library of Congress. With the advance the publisher had paid me, I went abroad. I came back in March 1926 and worked for Brentano's. Prior to that I had a publishing house of my own, Lieber & Lewis. That was shortly after I came out of the army. I was a sergeant in the Medical Corps, stationed at Walter Reed Hospital prior to that."

"Beginning with the year 1930, you say you've been a literary agent?" Tavenner asked.

"Yes. I have operated as a literary agent or author's representative since May 1930 and have continued to do so ever since, and I hope I shall continue to do so."

"Will you give us the names of the writers' syndicates and publishing houses by which you may have been employed or of which you may have been an officer?"

"I do not represent any publishing houses," Max Lieber answered. "I represent authors. In fact, all literary agents represent authors, not publishing houses. Their function is to act as intermediaries in selling literary articles. If you should write a book and be good enough to send it to me, I would read it and try to exploit its sale possibilities to a magazine or publishing house. All of us agents operate on a commission basis. I do not represent any publishers."

Tavenner glanced down at his yellow pad before continuing. "Then, as I understand, the only instances in which you have been an employee of a writers' syndicate or publishing house were those prior to 1930?"

"That's true. Prior to 1930 I worked for Brentano's. Briefly before that I worked for a small publishing house, but to be honest, I can't even remember its name."

"Does that mean," Tavenner asked, "that since 1930 you have not been an officer of any publishing house or writers' syndicate organization?"

Lieber turned toward his lawyer. Their eyes met for a split second. "I decline to answer that on the grounds of self-incrimination," he responded. The hearing room became very still.

"Were you at one time an officer of the American Feature Writer's Syndicate?" Tavenner asked, his voice sounding louder than usual against the silence of the hearing room.

Marvin Freedlander suddenly became preoccupied with a yellow legal pad on the table in front of him. Lieber, wanting to ask his lawyer something, stared at him for a time, decided against it and swallowed hard. "I respectfully decline to answer on the grounds it would tend to incriminate me," he replied.

"As a literary agent since 1930, you have represented a number of writers. Is that true?"

"Well, I don't want to seem boastful," Lieber said, "but I haven't represented a great number of writers because I've been rather selective. I would say that in the course of the twenty years which have just gone by in May, I have represented only about thirty writers."

"What are the names of some of the more prominent writers?"

"I think the most distinguished writer I have on my list is Mr. Erskine Caldwell, whose books have sold over twenty million copies the last twelve years, although I have represented him since 1931. He is the author of many novels and short stories which are world famous and have made their mark. I think every department of English giving courses in American literature has been compelled to rank him as one of the three leading American writers in the last century. He will definitely go down in history in literature.

"Among some of my other writers is Carey McWilliams, who was an attorney, and although he has not practiced in some years, he wrote a book entitled, *Factories in the Field,* dealing with agricultural problems in California. I don't think he is very well liked for the book, because it was an attack on the kind of peonage that existed in California. He was in the government in California. He was, I believe, the Commissioner of Immigration in former Governor Olsen's Administration, before Governor Warren. He has written about half a dozen books. Just this week I signed a contract with Little, Brown & Company for his new book."

"Any others, sir?"

"Robert Coates, who is the Art Critic of the *New Yorker* magazine. He has written four books of considerable quality and some significance. He is published by Harcourt, Brace. He has done a good many short stories as well. His last book was a psychological thriller called *Wisteria Cottage*. That gives you an idea of some of the people I represent."

"Thank you, sir. Now will you tell the committee how the American Feature Writer's

Syndicate was formed and the purpose for that organization, if you know."

"I respectfully decline to answer that question on the grounds of self-incrimination."

"Mr. Lieber, I have some difficulty understanding how a description of the manner in which it was formed could tend to incriminate you," Tavenner remarked innocently. "I think there is an obligation on your part to at least give some information to the Committee which would indicate that there is a possibility of your answer tending to incriminate you."

"I wish to confer with counsel, Mr. Tavenner. Will you excuse us a moment?"

"Yes, of course."

His conference with Freedlander over, Max Lieber adjusted his microphone slightly and said, "By advice of counsel, I adhere to the answer."

"Do you know the name of any officer or director of the American Feature Writer's Syndicate?" Tavenner resumed.

"I am obliged to decline to answer that question on the same grounds."

"Did the American Feature Writer's Syndicate maintain a bank account in the Chemical Bank of New York City?"

"I am obliged to decline to answer that question on the grounds of self-incrimination."

At this point Frank Walter broke in. "Why would it incriminate you to answer whether or not a bank account had been maintained?"

"Well, if you please, sir, that seems to be a related question," Lieber answered.

"Related to what?" Representative Walter shot back impatiently.

Lieber turned toward him, a bland look on his face. "Related to the prior question, which I respectfully declined to answer on the grounds of self-incrimination," he explained.

"Did you have any connection with the bank account of that organization, either as an agent, employee or officer of the American Feature Writer's Syndicate?" Tavenner asked.

"I decline to answer that question on the grounds of self-incrimination."

"Did the American Feature Writer's Syndicate maintain a representative in Japan?"

"I decline to answer that question on the grounds of self-incrimination."

"Mr. Lieber, do you know Whittaker Chambers?"

"I decline to answer that question on the grounds of self-incrimination."

"Did you know him by the name of Lloyd Cantwell?"

"I decline to answer that question on the same grounds."

"Did you know an individual by the name of John Loomis Sherman?"

"I decline to answer that question on the same grounds."

"When did you last see John Loomis Sherman?"

"I decline to answer that question on the grounds of self-incrimination."

Tavenner looked over at Don Appell, whose face was a study in calmness. "How could an answer to that question tend to incriminate you?" He asked Lieber.

"Well sir, that seems to be related. If you ask me when did I see the gentleman who just walked in, and I had previously told you I did not want to tell you if I knew the gentleman, I would be giving you a half-truth and an untruth."

Lieber and Freedlander conferred briefly and Lieber nodded his head vigorously in the affirmative to something that Freedlander told him.

"Did you know John Loomis Sherman under the name of Charles Francis Chase?"

"I respectfully decline to answer that question on the grounds of self-incrimination."

"Did you, together with Whittaker Chambers and John Loomis Sherman, organize the American Feature Writer's Syndicate, Mr. Lieber?"

"I decline to answer that, sir, on the grounds of self-incrimination."

"Was John Loomis Sherman sent to Japan as a representative of the American Feature Writer's Syndicate?"

"I decline to answer, sir, on the grounds of self-incrimination."

"Mr. Lieber, Whittaker Chambers has testified before this Committee and before the United States District Court for the Southern District of New York that you and he set up, together with John Loomis Sherman, the American Feature Writer's Syndicate, and that the Syndicate's account in the Chemical Bank of New York City contained both his name and your name on its account. Do you deny this testimony?"

"I decline to answer that question, sir, on the grounds of self-incrimination."

At this point, the door behind the committee table opened. A young, male page entered and handed a note to the Acting Chairman. Glancing quickly at it, Walter leaned into his microphone. "Gentlemen, a roll call has started in the House. It seems we're wanted over there for a vote. I'll adjourn this hearing now, and we'll resume promptly in half an hour."

CHAPTER 19

Thursday, June 15, 1950
Washington, DC
Capitol Building
Room 226
11:45 a.m. Eastern Standard Time (EST)

FRANK TAVENNER LOST NO TIME getting back to business after the members returned to the hearing room. The witness did not miss a beat, either.

"Mr. Lieber," Tavenner began, "did the American Feature Writer's Syndicate register with the Board of Trade in New York City?"

"I decline to answer the question on the grounds of self-incrimination."

"Did you, along with Whittaker Chambers, using the name Lloyd Cantwell, and John Loomis Sherman, using the name of Charles Francis Chase, file a registration of trade for the American Feature Writer's Syndicate?"

"I decline to answer the question on the grounds of self-incrimination."

"On March 7, 1935, Charles Francis Chase executed an application for registration in Tokyo, Japan, on which he gave his residence in the United States as 545 Fifth Avenue, New York City, and your name at the same address as a person who should be contacted in the event of death or accident to Charles Francis Chase. Do you, in view of this evidence, deny knowledge of or acquaintance with Charles Francis Chase, either under the assumed name or under has actual name of John Loomis Sherman?"

"I decline to answer the question on the grounds of self-incrimination."

"Where was your office in New York City, Mr. Lieber?" Tavenner did not expect an answer to this question. Now, he held his breath as the answer came back.

"At one time it was 55 West Forty-Second Street; at another time it was 545 Fifth Avenue; and more recently it was 489 Fifth Avenue."

"Over what period of time did you maintain an office at 545 Fifth Avenue, New York City?" Tavenner asked. Answering that question had been a mistake. Lieber had disclosed information that corroborated more of Chambers's statements.

"From about 1931 or 1932 to 1944 or 1945. Those dates must be regarded as approximate, because without looking at leases I couldn't tell. Those are fairly close dates."

"In 1937, did you meet with John Loomis Sherman and Whittaker Chambers in your apartment in New York City following Sherman's return from Moscow?"

"I decline to answer the question, sir, on the grounds of self-incrimination."

"Did you know a man named Colonel Boris Bykov?"

Lieber would not have made a very good poker player. His eyebrows shot upward in surprise. "I decline to answer the question on the grounds of self-incrimination."

"Did you know Alexander Stevens, alias J. Peters?"

"I decline to answer the question on the grounds of self-incrimination."

"Did you ever use the name Paul as an identifying name?"

"I decline to answer the question, sir, on the same grounds."

"Did you obtain credentials for John Loomis Sherman as a reporter and writer?"

"I decline to answer the question, sir, on the same grounds."

"Did you at any time own or lease property in the State of Pennsylvania?"

Lieber's face again mirrored surprise. "Yes," he said in a strained voice.

"Will you state the time and the location of the property?"

"I had a farm in Ferndale, Bucks County. It was one hundred and three acres. It was bought through an agent by the name of Joseph or John Strand. I'm not sure of his first name; I think it was John. I had that from some time in the thirties, I am not clear whether it was 1935 or 1936, and sold the farm because it was inaccessible during the war in 1944 or 1945."

"Was Whittaker Chambers a guest at the farm which you described as having owned?"

"I decline to answer on the grounds of self-incrimination," Lieber said. "Mr. Walter, I was subpoenaed before the grand jury of New York City, as the Committee is fully aware, and I was called to testify at grand jury hearings on two occasions. Subsequent to that, there were two trials in New York City, as is also known to the Committee, and certain things have occurred. I feel I am not being capricious, because the constitutional grounds on which I claim a certain privilege are valid under the circumstances, because certain hazards are clear, are manifest."

"Do you still decline to answer the question, Mr. Lieber?" Tavenner asked.

"Yes, I certainly do."

"Mr. Lieber, were you acquainted with Alger Hiss or his wife, Priscilla Hiss?"

"I decline to answer that question on the grounds of self-incrimination."

"Were either Alger Hiss or Priscilla Hiss, or both of them, guests at your farm in Pennsylvania, or at any other property owned by you or leased by you in Pennsylvania?"

Marvin Jesse Freedlander again leaned toward Lieber. Tavenner displayed momentary impatience. He believed lawyers representing witnesses tended to slow the proceedings. Still, witnesses had a constitutional right to bring counsel with them, and Freedlander, having come all the way from New York City, was probably charging an arm and a leg for his presence.

"I decline to answer that on the grounds of self-incrimination."

"Did you know Alger Hiss to be a member of the Communist Party?"

"I decline to answer that on the grounds of self-incrimination."

"Did you know Erwin Kisch?" Tavenner asked.

"I decline to answer that question on the grounds of self-incrimination."

"In fact, did he not visit you in December 1945 when he entered the United States from Mexico en route to Czechoslovakia?"

"I decline to answer that question on the grounds of self-incrimination."

"Where were you living in New York City in December 1945?"

"At 280 – I haven't been living there for some time, so I am trying to remember – Riverside Drive, New York City."

"Where was your office at that time, in December 1945?"

Lieber thought for a moment. "I believe it was already at 489 Fifth Avenue. I say I believe it was at 489. I had been at 545 and subsequently moved to 489 Fifth Avenue."

"Mr. Lieber, Mr. Kitsch, in a transit visa application through the United States, executed in Mexico on October 23rd, 1945, listed as a New York friend whom he intended to visit en route, Maxim Lieber, 489 Fifth Avenue, New York. Did he visit you?"

"I decline to answer that question on the grounds of self-incrimination."

"Are you a member of the Citizens Committee to Defend Representative Government?"

Lieber hesitated. "I don't think so."

"I hand you an advertisement appearing in the February 19, 1948 issue of *The New York Times*, which I will have marked for identification as 'Lieber Exhibit Number One' and ask you to examine it and see if you do not find that your name is listed as author's representative of the Citizens Committee to Defend Representative Government." Tavenner left his seat at the table, walked around it and handed the document to Lieber's counsel. Freedlander studied it briefly before handing it to Lieber, who adjusted his horn-rimmed glasses and looked at it.

"I will ask you," Tavenner continued, "if that does not refresh your recollection? For the record, the advertisement contains a list of names of persons signing a petition to Mayor O'Dwyer for the seating of Simon W. Gerson, a member of the Communist Party, to succeed Peter Cacchione as councilman. Does the examination of 'Lieber Exhibit Number One' refresh your recollection, Mr. Lieber?" He took the document back and waited for the answer.

"No. I have no recollection of any membership in such an organization. The name means absolutely nothing to me."

"Did you authorize the use of your name as a member of that committee?"

"Sometimes people ask me if I want to sign a document, and sometimes people just put my name on it. I can't recall whether I was asked to sign this petition or whether I was not asked to sign this petition and my name was used nevertheless. I can't say."

"You do recall whether you supported the movement to seat Mr. Gerson, do you not?"

"I decline to answer that question on the grounds of self-incrimination."

Tavenner picked up a newspaper lying next to him on his table and walked around to Lieber. "I hand you the April 22, 1946 issue of *The Daily Worker*, which I will ask to have marked for identification as 'Lieber Exhibit Number Two,' and point out to you an article entitled *'Noted Artists, Professionals Back May Day; Parlay Spurs May Day Parade Preparations,'* in which your name appears. Will you examine this issue?" He handed it to Lieber, who scanned it.

"I would like for you to examine the list of names appearing there along with your name. Do you know any of those individuals?"

Lieber, with Marvin Jesse Freedlander looking over his shoulder, examined the newspaper article. They exchanged a few words. Then Lieber said, "I refuse to answer on the grounds of self-incrimination."

"Did you authorize the use of your name in connection with that publication and did you sponsor or in any way back the Communist Party's May Day conference?"

"I decline to answer on the grounds of self-incrimination."

"Mr. Lieber, I now hand you the May 25, 1948 issue of *The Daily Worker*, which I ask to be marked as 'Lieber Exhibit Number Three'."

"Let it be so marked," Congressman Walter intoned.

"The issue contains an article entitled *Culture Against War Makers*, and in the course of this article you are named as one of the sponsors of a mass demonstration of writers and artists against the Mandate bill and the 'war makers.' Will you examine the article and observe that your name is one of those listed, and will you examine the list of names listed along with your name and state whether or not any of those persons are known to you?"

"I decline to answer on the grounds of self-incrimination."

"Did you authorize the use of your name in connection with that article and did you sponsor the mass demonstration referred to in the article?"

"I decline to answer on the same ground."

Frank Tavenner consulted his notes. "Did you know a person named David Breen?"

"I decline to answer on the grounds of self-incrimination."

"Do you know whether Whittaker Chambers used the name David Breen?"

"I decline to answer on the same ground."

"I hand you a photostatic copy of a passport application in the name of David Breen, that name, according to the testimony of Whittaker Chambers, being an alias used by him, in which he gives the address of the person to whom the passport should be mailed as David Breen, in care of Maxim Lieber, 545 Fifth Avenue, New York City. I ask that this passport application be marked for identification as 'Lieber Exhibit Number Four.'"

"Let it be so marked," Walter intoned again.

"Will you examine the photostatic copy and state whether or not that passport was received by you at your address or by any other person at that address?"

"I decline to answer on the grounds of self-incrimination."

"Is that your address, Mr. Lieber?" Representative Walter asked.

"545 Fifth Avenue *was* my address."

"Mr. Lieber," Tavenner continued, "I asked you several questions relating to a John Loomis Sherman, who used the alias Charles F. Chase and you declined to answer questions relating to him. I now hand you a photostatic copy of an application for a passport signed by Charles F. Chase, which I ask to be marked as 'Lieber Exhibit Number Five.' Please examine the passport application and particularly the photograph appearing thereon, and state whether or not that is John Loomis Sherman."

"I decline to answer on the grounds of self-incrimination," was the familiar response.

"Are you now or have you ever been a member of the Communist Party?"

"I decline to answer on the grounds of self-incrimination."

Tavenner again consulted his notes to make sure he had not overlooked anything. "I have no further questions, Mr. Chairman."

"Does any committee member have any further questions for this witness?" Acting Chairman Walter asked. Upon receiving negative responses from the other members, he said, "Very well. Mr. Tavenner, I'd like you to stay for a moment, please. The hearing is adjourned."

Frank Tavenner collected his notes, crammed them into his briefcase, and joined Representative Walter at the door. "What do you think, Congressman?" He asked.

A few members of the press had gathered in the hall hoping for an interview or some brief, newsworthy comment from one of them, but Walter waved them away. "I think we got some remarkably good stuff, today. Several things Chambers told us were corroborated. Lieber left himself open to criminal charges for perjury, as an accomplice in obtaining passports by giving false information, and possibly espionage. Also, we could threaten him with contempt for taking the Fifth so often. If we handle it right, his lawyer will call begging for immunity. We need to talk with John Wood and the attorney general on this. I wish Dick Nixon had been here today. Where the ... he been?"

"Dick? I talked with him last week. Says he's really tied up with his campaign. We're not likely to see much of him until after the election in November."

They stopped at the door to Walter's office. Walter made as if to enter, but stopped. "The word in California is that Nixon's got a solid shot. Helen Douglas is a lousy campaigner. Doesn't seem to have her heart in it. If he wins, we won't see him at all anymore. He'll have to submit his resignation before he moves across the street."

Tavenner pulled a half empty pack of Camel cigarettes from his jacket pocket. "Nixon's one of the Committee members who's worried the Hiss conviction won't hold up on appeal. He's still pretty angry about the whole thing. Says the Truman Justice Department's been derelict in its duty. He's the one who came up with this idea of trying to set Lieber up for use as a witness against Hiss if his appeal is successful. And the Attorney General agreed with him."

Opening his office door, Walter stepped inside. "By the way. That lawyer Lieber brought with him today?"

"Marvin Freedlander?"

"Yeah. Very well-known up in New York. Represents numerous Communists. Runs some sort of seminar for them, too. Training sessions on how to testify before a grand jury. He's been making a damn good living off them for the last few years."

"Who pays his fees?"

"I think the Party does. Most of the people he's been representing don't have that kind of money. The rumor I heard is that he's also General Counsel for New York State's Communist Party." He again made as if to enter his office. "The Committee needs to have a meeting to go over this transcript. Executive Session. See if you can arrange it for some time next week."

CHAPTER 20

Thursday, June 15, 1950
Washington, DC
Union Station
12:15 p.m. Eastern Standard Time (EST)

THE HEARING CONCLUDED, MAX LIEBER and Marvin Jesse Freedlander, Jr. hailed one of the cabs that constantly trolled for fares in front of the Capitol Building and headed for Union Station and the train that would whisk Freedlander back to New York.

Freedlander settled himself in the back seat as their cab sped down Massachusetts Avenue to Union Station at the other end of Capitol Hill. "If it wasn't already obvious to you, Max, it should be now. They've dug up an awful lot about you *and* your activities."

Lieber nodded. "Yes. Their investigation seems to have been *very* thorough."

"And all those questions about Alger Hiss? Looks like the Justice Department wants to try him again, for something more serious than perjury. Treason, next time, probably. But for that they need *you*. Or someone *like* you."

Their cab pulled up in front of Union Station. Freedlander aimed a friendly punch at Lieber's arm, opened the door and stepped out. Max followed Freedlander out of the cab, paid the driver and dismissed him. "Bykov and I have already discussed that," he said.

The two men entered the station through huge ornate glass doors framed with bronze. Moving quickly, they passed the gift shop, bookstore and a bar, skirting scurrying people and luggage as they went, and arrived at the boarding area where Freedlander's train was already taking on passengers. He immediately stepped aboard. "Good to see you again, Max. Go and have a great lunch with Anna. But don't wait too long before you leave the country." He waived an arm. "A bientôt, my friend!"

Thursday, June 15, 1950
Washington, DC
The Dubliner Restaurant
12:15 p.m. EST

As the noisy mass of metal pulled out of the station, Max threaded his way through a throng of new arrivals. Ignoring people carrying suitcases and overnight bags, red caps and cab drivers, he headed for the recently opened Dubliner, a bar and grille with an Irish theme, diagonally across from the station. He and Anna had agreed to meet there for lunch.

It was a typical mid-June day in Washington. He navigated the restaurant entrance, glad to trade heat and humidity for the coolness of air conditioning. Inside, the entrance hall was adorned with photographs of celebrities who had dined there since the restaurant had opened its doors. The place smelled of charcoal beef and cigarettes. His quick glance took in a long, cherry wood bar with a brass rail, and tastefully framed and lighted portraits of stylized Irish thoroughbred racehorses mounted on the brick walls.

Anna had not yet arrived. Max picked his way through the dining room, crowded with politicians, lobbyists, local VIPs and workers from nearby office buildings. He spotted an empty booth in the back from which he could see the entrance. The sound of Nat King Cole's voice drifted to him from a jukebox near the bar as he removed his coat and slid into the booth:

> *"Unforgettable, that's what you are,*
> *Unforgettable, though near or far ... "*

Reaching for his meerschaum pipe and tobacco pouch, he carefully filled the bowl, tamped the tobacco down and lit up. Worry lines appeared on his brow. *Where did Anna go?* he wondered. *She walked out at the end of my testimony. She should have been here before me.*

A young oriental waitress clad in a white cotton blouse and short emerald green skirt, a dark green beret on her head approached the booth. Smiling, she handed him a menu.

"Would you care to order?" she asked in flawless English. His eyes roved over her appraisingly. Her short, black hair and oriental features, contrasting sharply with the Irish waitress outfit she wore, were somehow disconcerting to him.

"No. Just some coffee. My wife will be along soon."

He looked after her absently as she walked away. A woman's laughter floated to him from somewhere along the row of booths. He began to browse through a menu, but his thoughts were on Anna. She was, of course, quite angry. He conceded that she had a right to be. But it worried him. Anna and his kids had become everything to him. He could not contemplate life without her, nor did he want to see his family destroyed. More, he hated the thought of going through the pain of another divorce.

The Nat King Cole tune ended. In the relative quiet that ensued, his eyes frantically searched nearby tables and booths, hoping she would materialize at one of them, having been there all along. His scanning eyes reached the door. She was there, weaving her way among the tables and slipping quickly into the booth, out of breath. Her pale cheeks were flushed from exertion. Placing her black handbag next to her on the bench, she smoothed her skirt. They acknowledged each other with nods and just the briefest of eye contact.

After settling herself, Anna leaned forward. "Well?" she demanded.

"Well!" He repeated. "It's as I suspected. They obviously want me to testify against Alger. They're trying to set things up so I'll have no choice."

"How did they find out?" A vein throbbed at her right temple. She was making an effort but she could not conceal her smoldering anger.

Max puffed on his pipe, exhaled and watched as the smoke swirled over their heads and blended with smoke from the cigarettes and cigars of the other patrons. He tried to appear calm, but it was an act. His muscles were tense and a huge knot was forming in his stomach.

"I think it was Whittaker," he answered finally. "He probably told them about *me* as well as about the others." He puffed on the pipe again. "We were very close. When he left the Party in the late '30s, he urged me to get out, too."

Anna swallowed hard and reached for her menu. She began scanning it, but stopped immediately. "Will we have to leave the country?" Her voice was unsteady.

"It would probably be best."

The waitress returned. "Ready to order?"

Max glanced at Anna. "She needs a minute more. I'm ready. A cup of Maryland clam chowder. A small tossed salad. Vinegar and oil dressing. Some bread, dark rye, if you have it. That will do." He handed his menu to the waitress.

Closing her menu, Anna placed it on the table. "I'll have the same." She was too upset to think about food. Making a decision about what to order for lunch seemed trivial, even ludicrous, in view of the decision they needed to make regarding their future.

"Where did you go?" Max asked. "You left before me. I was worried."

"There's a synagogue a few blocks from here." She covered her face with her hands, removed them and leaned over the table. "I went inside and prayed. I asked Yahweh how I could have come to this? I've always tried to view things in the light of His will as I've been given to understand it. But *this*, I don't understand." She dug her nails into her palms. Sounds of laughter mixed with the clinking of glasses reached them from the bar. "My husband, a known spy for a foreign power. A man whose footsteps are dogged by the FBI, whose clients are approached and warned away from him." She raised her eyes to the overhead brass lamp and back to Max. "And *now* it seems the government wants your help in order to prosecute one of our best friends. How could this happen, Max? Tell me!"

The jukebox began to play again; the same song. Max reached for her arm across the table. "Anna! Don't. You *knew* this might happen. I told you everything before we married."

Anna snatched her arm away. "You told me!" She snarled. "You led me to believe you hadn't been involved since '38 or '39. Now, I find out that you had continuous involvement with the Party long after that."

Max puffed on his pipe, shrugged his shoulders and shifted in his seat. He said nothing, but it seemed to him that the cozy restaurant had grown cold. He had never seen Anna as angry as this, and it scared him. The thought occurred that his third marriage might, like the two before it, be slipping away as he sat in this trendy Washington pub waiting for his lunch to be served by an oriental waitress wearing an absurd Irish uniform.

"Maxim," she continued, her lips pursed with suppressed fury, "you came to this country from Poland with your parents when you were ten or eleven, right?"

He nodded. "In 1907. I was ten. Like many European countries, Polish society had rejected the medieval view of nature, dependent as it was on superstitions and belief in God. Before about 1830, atheism was restricted to a very few. But between 1830 and 1930, atheistic attitudes became widespread in Western Europe. The people had been heavily influenced by the modernist school of thought going all the way back to the enlightenment. They had passed through deism and into atheistic modernism. And, wherever atheism spread, communism and socialism quickly followed. Socialists dominated Poland at the time."

"Deism?"

"Yes. The belief in a cosmic, depersonalized God who may have created the universe but then disappeared, leaving it to run on its own. Practically everyone accepted the idea that the laws of nature alone now governed the universe. God had become unnecessary."

"And your parents? Did they believe that?"

"Well, they had no use for God, but my father had read Adam Smith, who taught that competition for markets appeals to a person's rational self-interest and success in the marketplace tends to maximize human creativity and personal freedom. So, since Europe was moving in a different direction, he decided to emigrate to America. By that time, I'd had almost ten years of atheist and socialist thought seeping into my virginal consciousness."

"And after you came here, your parents did rather well financially, I understand. You grew up in New York City in a middle class home?"

"Yes. My father, for all his faults, was a creative, if overly ambitious person. He enjoyed the personal freedom he found here and made the most of it. We were comfortable. Not rich, but comfortable."

"Then answer me this. How is it you became a communist?" Her eyes scoured his face. "You weren't poor or a Negro, like your friend, Richard Wright. Now there's a man who was justified, if anyone was, growing up dirt poor on a plantation in Mississippi, his father gone, his mother a simple washerwoman. *Him* I can understand. But not you. Why did you reject the system that was so good to you and your parents for so many years?"

Replacing the pipe in his mouth, Max puffed on it. The smoke swirled around his face. Removing the pipe, he spoke softly. "I've asked myself that same question often over the last twenty years."

"I'm waiting."

He squirmed in his seat. "The poor weren't the only ones in America to become communists, you know. Actually very few of them have. Most communists in this country are from the middle class or even the rich. A lot of them consider themselves to be intellectuals. Then there are the student-intellectuals. In America, atheism became respectable around 1870, but it was still somewhat restricted to intellectual and academic circles well into the 20th Century. It was in those circles that communism took hold and still thrives, even today."

"Don't give me a lecture!" Anna hissed. "I'm not some wet-behind-the-ears college kid."

He took her hand and tried an apologetic smile. "You know, Anna, even Marx didn't become a communist because of poverty. His parents were middle class. His father was a lawyer. Marx himself attended several universities; Bonn, Berlin and Jena."

But she would not let up. "Answer me, Max!" She said between clenched teeth, indignant at this apparent evasion. "What *was* it that caused you to join the Communist Party?"

Stifling a sighed, he puffed on his pipe again. At that moment, he realized how much he wanted to answer her; to fill one of the gaps that still existed between them even after all these years. "I guess, because I, like Marx, lost my faith in a personal God. If one believes in a personal God, life has obvious meaning. One generally takes seriously the issues of moral and social responsibility."

Anna, unimpressed, waived away a cloud of smoke from his pipe. Seeing this, he decided to try humor. "Remember Voltaire? He once said, 'Don't tell the servants there is no God, or they'll steal the silver.'"

She leaned forward. "Voltaire?" she said scornfully. "I read about him. A skeptic about all things religious who denied the concept of a personal God as Father." She shook her head. "He rejected his *own* father, repudiated his family name and took on that idiotic name, 'Voltaire.' Pity no one seemed to have connected those two things as reflections of the same basic need."

"There *is* something to that. It was Voltaire who wrote the play, *Oedipus*. It recounts the classic legend, only with heavy undertones of religious and political rebellion. He was in his twenties when he wrote it."

"Did *you* ever believe in God?"

Max thought a bit. "No. Since my parents didn't, they never taught me to believe."

"So?"

"So, like a good modernist, I came to think that humans are purely material machines living in a physical world where nothing exists beyond what our senses perceive. You know — if it can't be seen, heard, felt, smelled or tasted, it doesn't exist." He struck a theatrical pose. "Empiricism reigned in my innocent young heart."

"This is no time for joking," Anna said coldly. "What about things like love and hate? They can't be seen heard, felt, smelled or tasted. Yet no one would dream of denying that they exist."

Max shrugged and glanced around the restaurant before continuing. "At some point, life became meaningless to me. Without purpose or goal. I became an atheistic modernist. But I never lost hope. Albert Camus was a despairing atheistic modernist. I was a *hopeful* atheistic modernist." He smiled ruefully at his own attempt at humor. "I had passed from the worldview of the Middle Ages through deism and into that, without stopping to consider very deeply. When Communism came along with its promise of a system that might lead to peace on Earth and freedom from exploitation, I was a twenty-year-old student, ripe for the picking. I always prided myself on having an open mind."

Removing her hand from his, she leaned further forward, until her head was only inches from his across the table. Her eyes blazed. "An open mind? That's true. But you have a mind that never closes on *anything*, Max. You say you're looking for truth. But you know what? I think if you ever met truth you'd fall over dead. You're the seeker who never finds what he's seeking." Her voice rose an octave. "You want *truth*, Max? *Here's* truth. Western capitalism has created a wealthier, more numerous middle class than socialism. In every country where it exists, capitalism has spread wealth; housing, food, clothing and consumer goods among more people than any other system. And with more personal freedoms intact, too. Socialism, on the other hand, has simply produced a dependent middle class, with its hand out."

The waitress returned carrying a tray with their food. They pulled apart and sat back while she served them, neither looking at the other, Max playing absently with his pipe, Anna twisting the leather strap of her purse in her fingers.

Placing the last dish on the table, the waitress asked if there was anything else she could get them. They both shook their heads. She moved away.

"But I'm no longer a communist, Anna. I haven't been since a few years after we married. I never told Bykov. Or anyone. Oh, yes, you're right. I *was* involved after Whittaker left in '37. The relativist still rejecting truth. Or goodness. Or an absolute of some kind. But I couldn't accept those things when I was younger. You know why? It's the same reason my first two marriages failed. Because to accept that I'd found truth, goodness, an absolute, would have committed me to moral and social responsibility. And I couldn't accept either."

"Well, you've always *seemed* to be responsible. Toward the kids and me. Your clients, too. I don't understand, Max."

"It's really very simple. The explanation is *you* and the *children,* Anna. Not until you and the kids came along could I accept any responsibility. Then it became easy. When I thought life had become meaningless, my mind became the mind of a revolutionary."

Puzzled, Anna leaned back. "I'm not sure I follow you."

"Think about it. A boiler has a purpose, imposed by the will of its inventor, to hold steam at a certain temperature. When it loses its purpose it explodes. When a young man rejects the normal pattern of human life, a pattern I guess *you* would say has been set by God, he revolts—"

She held up her hand to stop him. "Yes! A pattern of behavior engraved on the human heart by God. That's a Christian theological idea called the *Natural Law*. It provides very helpful answers to some difficult questions."

"The Natural Law? I was just talking about that."

"No, you weren't." Anna said scornfully. "You were talking about the laws of nature. Scientific laws, like gravity and molecular structure. The two are very different."

Clearing his throat, Max continued, his voice cracking. "When *you* came into my life, I began to realize the meaning of existence. I'd never learned that. Not from my parents. Not from the teachers to whom I'd been exposed. Whittaker understood. He tried to tell me. I couldn't accept it then. But later I found it to be quite clear, actually. To love someone. To serve. To get out of bed every day with a goal of providing for a wife and children. At that point I stopped reacting against what I'd perceived as an irrational, unpurposeful existence."

"Never before, has someone been more unforgettable than you ... "

Max looked up. He absorbed the clamor from the bar, the diners and drinkers around them, the busy waitresses hurrying among the tables. His gaze came to rest on Anna. He realized that she was weeping silently. She had listened intently to what he had been saying and begun to cry. But through her tears she was smiling.

"That's why I love you, Max," she said, her voice constricted. "I guess I've always been able to see that you loved the kids and me." She dabbed at her eyes with a napkin. "It's a wonderful feeling to know that someone loves you." She tried to blot her running mascara, without success. "Let's eat. The soup's getting cold."

They ate in silence. After a few minutes, Anna managed a half smile. "How long do you think we have? Before we need to leave the country, I mean?"

He felt a surge of elation and relief at the same time. "Does this mean that we're okay? That you'll go with me wherever I have to go?"

"Yes."

"You won't change your mind later?"

"No, Max. For better or for worse, remember? Up to now I've had lots of the 'for better' part. I may be about to get some of the 'for worse.' But you know what? Life with you has never been dull. Now it may just get more exciting. Or at least different."

Max's heart soared. His eyes moist with joy, he reached for her hand and held it. In the middle of the table, next to the rye bread and a butter dish. "Thank you," he said softly.

Finally, Anna asked in a strained voice, "Where will we go?"

Picking up a fork, Max attacked his salad. "There's a contingency plan. It's called "'the Cuernavaca plan.' It calls for me to go to Mexico and live there until arrangements can be made to get us settled behind the Iron Curtain. Housing. Jobs. That sort of thing."

"But what country?"

"I was born in Warsaw. I'm still a Polish citizen. When the time comes, it's possible they'll arrange for us to go there."

CHAPTER 21

Friday, November 9, 1951
Branford, Connecticut
The Triple-T Diner
Main Street
11:00 a.m. Eastern Standard Time (EST)

FRIDAY MORNING ARRIVED IN THE town of Branford, Connecticut, population about seventeen thousand, with a penetrating cold and a drizzle at just above freezing temperature A raw wind off the waters of nearby Long Island Sound tore at the coats of the hardy souls who struggled on the icy sidewalks, propelling each much like tiny ships at sea under full sail.

Inside the Triple-T diner on Main Street, Max Lieber sat alone at a window booth, sipping hot coffee. Around him, the tired staff, most of whom he knew by name, had finished serving breakfasts and was preparing for the lunch crowd.

Max was nattily dressed in his brown Harris tweed jacket with leather elbow patches, a yellow dress shirt, a regimental tie of black, gold and red stripes, and charcoal gray wool trousers. He was an intelligent man, and because he was smarter than most of the people around him, that, at times, made him seem a bit arrogant or at least self-assured to a fault. A meerschaum pipe, its bowl ornamentally carved in the shape of a bulldog, was parked in an ashtray on the table, next to a leather pouch filled with fresh tobacco. Smoke from the aromatic blend he was using this year had gathered above the booth.

He liked the Triple-T. The pleasant aroma of bacon and eggs mixed with coffee reminded him of the kitchen at home when he was a boy. Now and then he'd glance behind the long diner counter where the stoves were, half expecting to see his mother standing there, smiling back at him.

But this was a different time and he was a different person. What he now liked most was the fact that he had a fine view of the sidewalk through plate glass windows that ran the length of the diner. Peering through the rain-streaked glass, his eyes sought the small library on the opposite side of the street near the end of the block. He reached for his pipe, took three nervous puffs, and glanced at his wristwatch. An audible grunt escaped from him. Puffing once more on the pipe, he tapped the bowl gently against the ashtray. A fellow pipe smoker had told him that meerschaum cracked easily, and since this pipe was his current favorite, he didn't want that to happen.

From speakers overhead, actress Deborah Kerr's voice drifted to him, singing a piece from a new musical that had just opened on Broadway, *The King and I*:

"Hello young lovers who ever you are,
I hope your troubles are few ..."

Max picked up a white paper napkin and dabbed at his shoe brush mustache. Removing his glasses, he polished them vigorously while scrutinizing the scurrying pedestrians on the windblown sidewalks, and the small shops along the street on either side of the library.

"All my good wishes go with you tonight,
I've been in love like you ..."

Satisfied, he stood, reached for his gray tweed topcoat on the hook next to his booth, and slipped it on. At the door, he paid his check and paused, noting that the rain had become a steady drizzle. He pulled a tweed driving cap from his coat pocket, settled it over his thinning gray hair and stepped outside. A gust of wind immediately threatened to knock him over. Cursing softly under his breath, head down, and chin thrust into his coat, he moved in the direction of the library, placing his feet carefully on the slippery concrete, as if walking on eggshells. He'd heard that, at his age, a fall often meant broken bones: a leg, ankle or hip. A broken hip could be deadly.

Inside the library foyer moments later, he removed his cap, tucked it into a coat pocket and passed through the double glass doors into the warm interior. Every Friday morning for the past five months Max had come here before continuing on to Riptide Cottage. After informing Colonel Bykov that he would be spending his summer and fall weekends in Branford, Bykov had insisted on setting up a way to keep in contact. They had decided on this procedure.

Max thought the man was overly cautious. Still, there was that time, a year ago when Bykov had notified him that a subpoena had been issued for him to appear before a grand jury in New York. That information was closely followed by tidings that the House Un-American Activities Committee was also going to subpoena him. Both bits of information had been communicated to him a full week before either subpoena had been served on him.

How had Bykov learned in advance of these developments? He assumed the Party had agents highly placed in the government. The early warnings had enabled Lieber to hire Marvin Freedlander, a lawyer known to be favorably disposed to Communist Party goals. Freedlander had briefed Max about how to testify before a grand jury and a congressional committee. *The lawyer's help had been invaluable. Expensive but invaluable.* And, they had become friends.

He now knew the drill by heart. Acting the part of a retired middle aged man with little to do, he would proceed to a table near the book stacks, remove his cap and coat, and walk over to the front desk. After a friendly exchange with young Miss Gaines, the Librarian, he would take a copy of *The New Haven Register* from its rack. Back at his table, he'd spend ten or fifteen minutes reading the paper, taking the opportunity to catch up on the latest local and national news. Then, he'd move into the stacks, to the section containing Russian history and literature and take down the hardbound copy of Fyodor Dostoyevsky's *Crime and Punishment*. There, on page seventeen, if Bykov wanted to communicate with him, a message would be waiting.

Seventeen was for the year of the Revolution. He snorted derisively. *It should have been one thousand nine hundred and seventeen. But, this book did not contain that many pages. Why had Bykov not picked a different book? Just one shelf above this one, there was a volume of Russian History with more than two thousand pages. That would have been perfect.*

He and Bykov used a code that the Soviet and Eastern bloc nations utilized to communicate with their agents: numbers corresponding to letters of the alphabet. His sometimes overactive mind reflected that the word *alphabet originated* from combining the Greek words *alpha*, and *beta*, the terms they used to describe the symbols representing their first and second letters. *I'll bet Bykov doesn't know that*, he mused smugly.

He studied his wristwatch: eleven thirty a.m. Carefully closing and folding the newspaper, he strolled into the stacks, trying to appear unhurried. Miss Gaines and a young blonde woman were laughing about something over at the front desk. An elderly man sat at a table skimming a copy of *Life Magazine*. No one else was in the place this morning, the weather being what it was.

Sauntering to the Russian history and literature section, he found Dostoyevsky and opened it. He caught his breath and blinked. There, in between pages seventeen and eighteen, where nothing had ever been for at least a year, was a single folded sheet of paper. The hair on the back of his thin neck rose as he picked it up. It contained lines of numbers packed tightly on the page—each number corresponding to a letter of the English alphabet—with no breaks between the numbers or between groupings of numbers, as one would expect to find at the end of a word or words. That was done so that anyone accidentally coming across the paper would think it was only a sheet used to mark someone's place and then forgotten. The code was simple to understand and easy to use.

Glancing around furtively, he considered whether to decipher it here or return to the diner to work on it. He felt a rush of heat to his face, and wondered what had happened? Quickly slipping the paper into his jacket pocket, he returned the book to its place on the shelf. His heart was pounding so hard he was sure the two women at the desk fifty feet away could hear it. Squinting toward them, he forgot that he was supposed to appear relaxed and unhurried. He was not relaxed; he was panicked.

Breathing hard, he almost ran back to the table where he had left the newspaper and his topcoat. He reached for the coat, but his curiosity got the better of him. Sitting down, he removed the message from his pocket, unfolded it, and with a pencil, began to decipher the simple code. Although it was far from hot in the building, he was sweating freely ten minutes later as he stared at a full translation of the message.

"Paul,
Hiss conviction will likely be overturned on appeal. He
will be tried yet again. Peters found out they want you
as a government witness. Without you they have little
or nothing. Sunday they will come for you there. Get out
immediately. Proceed according to Cuernavaca plan.
Do not try to contact anyone. Agents will be at Riptide
Saturday night with ambulance. You know what is
required.

Bykov."

A lump formed in Lieber's throat. The time had come. He no longer held
any illusions about Communism; had harbored none for many years. Several of
his friends had abandoned the Party altogether. Wright in Chicago, Koestler in
Germany, Silone in Italy, Gide in France, the American correspondent, Fischer,
the English poet, Spender, and, of course, Chambers. They had been attracted to
Communism because it seemed to promise an end to poverty and war. But their
eyes had soon been opened. He could have left as they had, but he had not. Finally,
he'd seen that the Soviet effort to combine totalitarianism with Communism
was a grave mistake. That was the end for him. But, although he had hidden his
disenchantment, his loyalty to Communism had been tried and found lacking.
He'd been forced to think too much, to examine his past actions and his whole
previous philosophy of life. His conscience still alive, justification would not
come.

‡ ‡ ‡ ‡ ‡

Saturday, November 10, 1951
Branford, Connecticut
Brockett's Point
Riptide Cottage
8:40 p.m. EST

Max Lieber held a lighted match to the bowl of his bulldog pipe, not knowing
if he would have enough time to finish smoking it. He was warmly dressed in
jeans, a black turtleneck sweater, heavy wool socks, and boots. In the darkness,
the match briefly illuminated his worried face. A puff or two later, tobacco scent
spread throughout the room.

He was standing quietly at the window, listening. Eventually he heard in the
distance what he was hoping to hear; the wailing siren of an ambulance. Clamping
his teeth over the stem of his pipe, he moved to the living room, picked up a well-
used leather suitcase and carried it into the entrance hall.

Headlights from the ambulance lit up the front of Riptide Cottage, the small
porch and front door behind which he stood. On its roof, revolving red and blue
lights cast shafts of light against the drizzle. Pulling open the Cottage's door, he

stepped out, but quickly stepped back inside, nearly tripping over the suitcase in his haste.

That was a mistake, he thought sheepishly. He shrugged. What did he know about this cloak and dagger stuff anyway? He had not been called upon for any of it since ... '35. He chuckled as he recalled that he'd not been very good at it back then, either. His sense of humor had continually gotten in the way because he viewed covert operations as so contrary to everyday life as to be somewhat comical.

But, even when he had been most active he had never thought it would come to this. True, he had had some misgivings when, in the early 1930s, Peters and CPUSA had turned him over to the Soviet apparatus. They wanted to use his business connections to advance their interests both here and abroad. He had agreed because he felt nothing could go wrong; that his part was so insignificant he would never come to the attention of the authorities. Events had shown otherwise. Chambers had removed himself, and that was a disaster because Whittaker knew much and had told all. When the House UnAmerican Activities Committee opened hearings in August 1948 on Communist Party activities, it became clear that the government had learned more about Max and some of the others than anyone cared for them to know.

I expected to be called before that grand jury in the Federal District Court for the Southern District of New York in 1948. I had even anticipated being summoned as a witness in Hiss's perjury trials. But neither had happened. Then in early 1950, the subpoena from the grand jury had arrived. Shortly after that, in June, I was subpoenaed to testify before HUAC.

They had subpoenaed Sherman, too, questioning him about the Tokyo operation. Marvin Freedlander had told them to simply take the Fifth to every question. And with the exception of only a few preliminary ones, they had done so. Still, it had been an ordeal.

No longer loyal to the communist cause, he didn't want to go through it again. But he wanted even less to be tried for treason and sent to prison. Still, testifying against Alger Hiss was out of the question. The note from Bykov said he should get out if he didn't want to go to jail. His friend, Noel Field, had fled behind the Iron Curtain in 1949 for precisely these reasons. With Field in mind, Max had concluded that leaving the country was the thing to do. He had discussed it with Anna almost a year ago. To his surprise, she had agreed to go with him. Together, they had prepared the children for the "wonderful adventure" ahead. That done, they waited. Now the time had come. His family had already left that morning.

The drizzle became a heavy rain, sheets driving against the door and cascading off the weathered porch floor in tiny Vs. He wondered whether to turn the outside floodlight off, but decided to leave it on. Two men clad in white intern jackets appeared at the back of the ambulance. Pulling open its doors, they dragged out a stretcher and carried it up the front steps. He held the door open for them.

"Paul?" One of them asked. His voice was low and devoid of any trace of nervousness, as if he had done this sort of thing before.

"Yes," Max answered. "What took you so damn long?"

"An accident on the highway near the exit ramp. Traffic was backed up. You ready?"

"Of course." Max glanced at his wristwatch again. "We'll go directly to the airport."

"Do you think that's wise? We should at least make it look real by driving through the hospital's emergency entrance in case anyone follows us."

"No, no!" Max hissed. "There's no time."

"But New Haven's airport is close by," the other man interjected.

"The pilot's flight plan calls for take-off at nine thirty p.m." Max shot back. "The plane can't wait out on that runway without arousing suspicion, and it's already eight forty-five."

The agents exchanged glances. With a shrug, the first man opened the stretcher and set it down. "Get on the stretcher, then," the other man said. "I'll carry this bag."

‡ ‡ ‡ ‡ ‡

Saturday, November 10, 1951
Branford, Connecticut
Brockett's Point
8:40 p.m. EST

Rhoda Loeb heard the eerie sound of an approaching ambulance, its wailing siren becoming louder as it turned off the expressway onto Brockett's Point Road, the only access road to Brockett's Point, which was out along the beach on the shore of Long Island Sound.

She had settled her weary body into her favorite leather armchair in front of a roaring fire after a solitary dinner. An avid reader, Loeb had begun the practice of relaxing before her fireplace each evening, with either the daily newspaper or a good book. She loved the mystery genre. Tonight she had dozed off, an Agatha Christie novel, *Evil Under The Sun*, open in her lap. The fire she had lit earlier had gone out, but not before it had taken the chill from the air inside. On a small end table next to her chair was a carafe on a stainless steel tray, the coffee long-since cold. A white cup with a delicate blue and orange floral design, sat in a matching saucer on the tray, empty.

Pushing herself up, she rose stiffly and walked to the bedroom. From that window, she saw the lights of the ambulance dip and cut through the drizzle as it started down the inclined lane toward Riptide Cottage. This puzzled her. Anna Lieber had packed their old Ford sedan and, with the two kids, had driven quickly away that morning without stopping to say goodbye. Rhoda's feelings had been hurt because she and Anna had become friendly during the previous several months, and Anna had not stopped in to say goodbye.

When Rhoda had first seen the ad for a Workman's Compensation Commissioner, she had immediately been drawn to it. She had never liked solo law practice with its constant need to develop clientele or perish, so the idea quickly grew on her. She thought about how it might be, working in New Haven, living at the old house in which she had spent so much time as a child. The idea appealed to her. Learning that the position had not been filled, she had driven over to New Haven for an interview. *There were only a few applicants,* she recalled. *The interview had gone well.*

Afterward, Rhoda had driven the seven miles through gently rolling farmland, with an industrial and commercial area scattered here and there, to Branford. From there, she followed Short Beach Road along the Sound to Brockett's Point Road and then to Brockett's Point. Only three homes, a narrow strip of dark sand and a sea wall separated the Loeb cottage from the water. She did not get out of her car, but parked on the steep hill and sat looking at the house, reminiscing about all the good and bad time she had experienced there. Her conclusion? That "coming home" might be rather nice.

After her father retired, he and her mother had moved here. But since graduating from law school, Rhoda had not lived with them. Instead, she had taken an apartment in Battery Park near her office in Lower Manhattan. After her father's death — he had been the last of the two to pass away — she had inherited the cottage. But she had only used it on weekends during the summer months.

The summer of 1951 was Rhoda's first back at the family cottage. It had passed quickly. The lease on her expensive Manhattan apartment had expired in May, and she moved directly into the old house. Beginning work a week later at the Commission in New Haven, she found that she didn't miss the hustle and bustle of Manhattan. Fighting traffic had always bothered her, and parking was a horrendous problem. Garage space was terribly expensive. Some people in other parts of the country did not pay in rent what she had to pay to keep her car in Manhattan. Now, the daily commute to and from New Haven was one of the few unpleasant things left in her new life. And that was not too bad.

I worked hard on the old house during my evenings and weekends, and quickly whipped the lawn and gardens into shape. Then, I began planning how to improve the interior. Nothing had been done to the kitchen or bathroom for many years.

Her thoughts returned to her first meeting with Anna Lieber. Rhoda had been out in the yard preparing a new bed for geraniums the day Anna had come home in her old Ford, thoroughly upset. She had, she told Rhoda, been driving into Branford when a car pulled out of a blind driveway and rammed her car on the right side. Since neither automobile had been moving fast, the damage was minor. Anna, alone in the car, was not seriously hurt; a bruised left shoulder and a stiff neck had been the extent of it. Rhoda explained that she was a lawyer and asked if Anna needed any help. Anna had accepted her offer.

Rhoda had handled this simple personal injury case efficiently. The insurance company had agreed to pay for repairs to Anna's car, her doctor bills, medication costs, and something for her pain and suffering. She was pleased and grateful for Rhoda's help. They had sipped coffee together on the Liebers' back yard patio several mornings each week, until September, when the Liebers had returned to their home in the City.

That morning, as she watched them drive up the lane, Rhoda assumed they were going back to New York. Anna's six-year old daughter, Ruth, had already started first grade, and the four-year old boy, Luke, was in some new preschool program in the City. So for the last six weeks the family had only been here on weekends. But why leave on Saturday? They usually stayed until Sunday evening, leaving as late as possible in order to avoid the heavy traffic that clogged the roads from the resorts into the City.

Rhoda hurried to the second bedroom, which she had converted into a den. From there she had a clear view of the Lieber cottage. The ambulance had already stopped there. What hospital? No name was visible. Just the word *Ambulance* in large, red letter on the side facing her. Its back doors were open. Through the fine mist made surreal by the revolving red and blue dome light, she watched as two white-coated attendants carried a stretcher out of the house. Someone was on it. Was it Max? *Dear God! Yes, it was!* He sat up as they rested the stretcher on the back of the ambulance and said something to one of the men. *Funny. He didn't appear injured or ill.* She could see them clearly, but the distance was too great for her to hear their voices.

In the stillness of her den, Rhoda watched as one of the men hefted a suitcase into the ambulance. Both then shoved the stretcher inside, with Max on it, and slammed the doors. The driver, a heavy man with a large belly, trotted around the ambulance and slid behind the wheel. The other hastily returned to the house. The lights went out. Jogging back, he stepped aboard on the passenger side. The ambulance backed into the turn-around and lumbered off, its dome light flashing and its siren wailing again.

CHAPTER 22

Saturday, November 10, 1951
Towson, Maryland
Hampton House Apartments
Joppa Road
8:55 p.m. Eastern Standard Time (EST)

"HI, UNCLE ALVIN!" ALVIN ZELINKA, alone on the front steps of the Hampton House Apartments, heard Ruth Ann, his pretty niece, yelling to him even before the dark green, 1946 Ford came to a stop. The evening was cool but not cold. He was wearing a long-sleeved gray sweatshirt, blue jeans and tennis shoes. Less than five feet tall, he had a full head of jet-black hair. His only other noticeable feature was the pronounced curvature of his spine.

When the old car, crammed with boxes of kitchen items and bags of clothing pulled up, Alvin saw that there was barely enough room for its human occupants. He yanked open the back door and braced himself as Ruth, red pigtails flying, sailed out and jumped into his arms.

"Hello, kids! Jeez, I sure have missed you!" Setting Ruth down, he picked up Butch, his tiny nephew, swung him around once and glanced toward the driver's seat where his sister sat, her eyes closed, her cheek resting heavily against the steering wheel.

She had called earlier and informed him that they had left Connecticut that morning, driven all day, and were in Maryland at a gas station on the east side of town, in Essex. This was their first leg of a long trip and they wanted to stop off to see him, perhaps even stay with him for a few days. "I'll explain everything when I see you," she had said, sounding subdued, not at all like herself.

Whatever had happened, it must be serious, he thought after replacing the phone. He glanced at the Seth Thomas timepiece on his mantel above the fireplace. Since a much-needed beltway around the city was still in the talking stages, he knew there was no easy way to get from Essex to Towson. It should take about an hour. But this was Anna driving. Anna, who always drove too fast. He would wait for them in the lobby a few minutes before nine.

"Max not with you?" Alvin asked as his sister swung her long legs out of the car and straightened up. She was dressed in a burgundy flannel shirt, a pair of men's khaki-colored chinos and loafers. A tall woman, she towered over her brother, whose dark hair barely reached her shoulder. As a child, Alvin had been slow to grow and had topped out at four feet ten inches, prompting his parents to say that Fate had played a cruel joke on them. Their girl grew tall and straight while their boy remained tiny and his spine had curved, creating a noticeable hump in his back.

"No," Anna answered evasively. Looking up at the tall apartment building, she mentally compared it to the last time she'd been there several years before and then glanced at the stars that dotted the chilly night sky. "He had some last minute things to tend to." She wiped her hands on her chinos. "We'll need two suitcases from the trunk. I'll get them."

Excited to see their uncle, Ruth and Luke were jumping up and down, grabbing his shirt, his trouser legs and his hands. "You kids have sprouted like weeds since I saw you last," he said, poking Butch in the chest with a finger.

"We're not weeds, Uncle Alvin," Ruth Ann squealed. "We're just kids growing up."

Alvin was glad their father was not with them. He had never liked Max. He thought of his brother-in-law as a boorish man who talked politics incessantly, a pipe, which Alvin considered an affectation, clamped between his teeth. Except for Anna, the kids, and a son from a previous marriage, nothing else seemed to interest Max. After listening to him expound his Marxist theories at their New York home, Alvin had surmised that, politically, he was far to the left; a socialist, maybe even a communist.

That kind of talk made him uneasy. He was a career employee in the Department of Defense (DOD) who prided himself on his patriotism. Having a communist for a brother-in-law would not help him one little bit if it were discovered. *The House Un-American Activities Committee's been looking into that sort of thing for several years,* he thought. *There's a hearing going on right now in Washington.*

Alvin had never been able to figure out what his sister saw in Max Lieber. But for now it didn't matter. *The two kids look worn out from their trip. The important thing is to get them fed, bathed and into bed. They can sleep in my room. They'll love the big queen-sized bed. Anna looks tired, too. She can have the guest bedroom. I'll take the long couch. There's plenty of room on it for me. I can handle it for a few nights.*

Alvin glanced at his sister again. Her face was ashen and dark hollows accented her eyes. She did, indeed, seem exhausted. But there was also something else. A wounded look occupied her face and an aura of sadness surrounded her.

Saturday, November 10, 1951
Towson, Maryland
Hampton House Apartments
Joppa Road
9:30 p.m. EST

"Good coffee!" Anna Lieber sat on Alvin Zelinka's two-seater couch, which was set at a right angle to the fireplace, her long legs pulled up beneath her, gazing into the warm fire that Alvin had built earlier. The kids had been given their baths and put to bed. She appeared completely relaxed, although downcast, and the stricken look had not yet left her drawn face.

"One of my goals in life," Alvin replied, contentedly. He was seated on the long couch in front of the fireplace, a brandy snifter in his stubby fingers and a cup of hot coffee next to him. His jeans had gotten soaked as he helped bathe the kids, so he had changed to khaki trousers before making a pot of fresh coffee and bringing out a bottle of Cognac.

"Do you remember when Daddy died?" Anna asked.

"Yeah. For a while I thought he was gonna make it back. But, in early '45 Momma got the telegram from the War Department. Just before the war in Europe ended."

"I never knew what he did in the war. Always meant to ask you. Do you know?"

"He was a civilian employee for the army. Worked as an interpreter and administrator. He was based in Munich when he died. He got sick. The letter said it was bronchopneumonia." Alvin took a sip of the delicious golden nectar and gently swished it around in his snifter.

Since her arrival, his sister's mood had been curiously subdued. With an unsteady voice, she had told him why they were leaving New York and going to Cuernavaca, in the Mexican State of Morelos. The news that Max was a communist spy had shocked Alvin, but he was trying not to show it. He wanted desperately to offer his sister emotional support during an obviously trying time for her. And of course, he was also concerned about the implications in all of this for himself. He could, possibly, lose his position with the federal government. He liked his job and didn't relish the thought of being forced to look for another line of work.

"Momma was so sad. I don't remember ever seeing her smile after that. I think she loved him a lot, don't you, Alvin?" She sipped her hot coffee.

Sensing that his sister needed re-assurance, Alvin readily agreed. "I always thought so. Never heard them speak a harsh word to each other before he joined the war effort." There was a comfortable family pause as his mind went back to his deceased parents. Then, "What about you? Do you still love Max after finding out what he's been doing all these years?"

Anna's eyebrows shot up. She focused on her brother. "Do I still love him? Yes, I do. But I also feel a sense of betrayal."

"But you're not gonna leave him?"

"No. He's already been through *two* failed marriages. If I left him *now* it would destroy him. Besides, I believe marriage vows really mean what they say: for better or for worse, for richer or poorer, in sickness and in health."

"If there ever was a situation where a wife was justified in leaving her husband, I think this is it."

"Maybe. But I *won't* do that. Max has always been good to the children and me. As a matter of fact, he treats his son by his first wife well, too. He's always made us feel loved. That we're important to him. And he's also been a good provider."

Never having been married, Alvin wasn't sure he could understand. He shrugged. "Why did Max ever get involved with the communists?"

Anna took a large sip from her brandy snifter. "For the same reasons other educated people—college professors, intellectuals and many idle rich—became involved. He fell for the basic appeal of communism; a false promise of 'the perfect society.' Max had a lot of intelligent friends. I'm not talking about men and women who were merely very smart. Maybe I should use the word 'intelligentsia'. We spent lots of time with them. These people were all educated beyond their intelligence. Andre Gide was a perfect example.

"Why do you say that?"

"Max and Gide met when Andre was looking for an agent to handle the sale of one of his books in America. He visited us in New York. Later we visited him in Paris. But they *all* had similar traits. Usually, there was disenchantment with capitalism, a lack of belief in a personal God as Father, a materialistic philosophy of life, cynicism, and a great deal of intellectual pride." She stared into the fire for a moment before continuing. "Andre's personality was complicated by another factor; inherited wealth. *That* gave him a sense of guilt that he had *more* than others but had worked *less* to get it."

Alvin nodded. "Except for the inherited wealth, Max is like that, isn't he?"

"Yes. Or rather, he was. Max became a communist as a young man. He'd been educated in liberal institutions but he wasn't the same kind of liberal as the rest of us. Most Americans are liberal in *one* sense; we believe in fundamental rights within the law. Max was the kind of person who believed in liberty without law, or to put it another way, freedom without responsibility. The type of liberal he was back then is only interested in freedom *from* something, not in freedom *for* something."

Alvin rose, went to the kitchen and brought the coffeepot into the living room along with the Cognac. He replenished their coffee and his drink. Anna handed him her snifter and he did the same for her.

"I think I understand," he said. "Most of us believe that everybody should be free to draw a triangle provided they draw it with three sides, because that's the nature of a triangle.

Everybody should be free to draw a giraffe provided they show it with a long neck. That's the nature of a giraffe. Everyone should be free to drive a car, provided they obey the traffic laws.

In that sense we're all liberal, even if we're conservative in everything else."

Anna smiled at her brother. "Yes. Freedom under the law. Black or white, rich or poor, no one is above it." She took a sip from her fresh drink. "Do you know what's really sad about all this? Max is not a communist any more. He hasn't been for quite a while. With maturity came understanding of what Communism and Socialism really are. But *now* he may have to go and live in a communist country for the rest of his life."

The doorbell rang, startling Anna. She shot her brother a concerned look. "Are you expecting someone?"

Alvin got up. Carrying his Cognac with him, he started toward the entrance hall. "That's probably Jeannette," he said over his shoulder. "On Saturday nights she always goes to Bingo at the Immaculate Conception Church and then stops by here for coffee. You'll like her."

Jeannette Sellman was an attractive brunette in her middle forties. Widowed when her husband was killed in a car accident several years before, she had not remarried. In need of people in her life, she'd returned to work for the federal government, where she had been employed before her marriage, and had met Alvin there. She liked him. Alvin Zelinka was smart and he displayed a sensitivity and depth of understanding that she found lacking in other men. With Alvin, Jeanette could talk easily about many things.

"Hi, Alvin. It's getting colder out there," she said as she removed her tan cloth coat and tartan plaid scarf, revealing a dark green cowl-neck sweater and plaid skirt. She swept past him, heading for the living room and the fire she knew he would have made. Jeannette enjoyed sitting in front of Alvin's fireplace, sipping hot tea, relaxing and talking. She pulled up short as she entered the room and saw a woman there; an attractive woman.

"Oh! I didn't know you had company, Alvin. Should I have called first?"

Placing Jeannette's coat and scarf on the Windsor chair in his small entrance hall, Alvin followed her into the living room. He noticed the appraising glance she threw in Anna's direction; a look that he thought betrayed just a touch of possessiveness. His eyes twinkled. "Jeannette, this is my sister, Anna Lieber."

Jeannette relaxed. Smiling broadly, she swooped across the few feet and extended her hand to Anna. She had not known that Alvin had a sister. She would now be able to learn something more about her friend. Her face beamed. It promised to be an interesting evening.

‡ ‡ ‡ ‡ ‡

Sunday, November 11, 1951
Branford, Connecticut
Brockett's Point
9:20 a.m. EST

Rhoda Loeb heard the musical chimes of her front doorbell as she was making toast to go along with her two eggs, sunny side up. That was the way she liked them. She glanced at the pan in which she was keeping her eggs warm. Usually she broke at least one, but neither had broken this morning. She considered that a good omen. Her eyes sparkled.

Branford had much history about it and Rhoda was looking forward to amusing herself today with a walking tour of two older homes in town, the Nathaniel Harrison House, and the Samuel Frisbie House. Then, she would go to the Blackstone Library and browse their collection of books about the Civil War, finishing her day with a delicious Sunday dinner at the Triple-T Diner.

The doorbell rang again. "Just a minute," she called out. Snatching the hot toast from her new pop-up toaster, she wiped her hands on a dishcloth. Absent-mindedly tossing it over one shoulder, she moved from her kitchen through the small dining room, to the front door. Two well-dressed men in three-piece suits were waiting on her front porch. One wore a hat; the other did not. They seemed somewhat impatient.

"Good morning, ma'am," the one with the hat said. "I'm Special Agent Alex Johnson." He gestured toward his partner. "This is Agent Wilbur Grant. We're from the Federal Bureau of Investigation." He flashed a thin, wallet-type identification card with a shield on it, too fast for her to really make out what it was.

"My goodness! What can I do for you?" Alarmed, she briefly entertained the notion of asking him to show his badge again, but one glance at his face changed her mind. Rhoda Loeb was not easily intimidated. But something about these two men intimidated her.

"We'd like to ask you a few questions about your neighbor, Max Lieber," Special Agent Johnson said, as she stepped back to let them in. "Were you at home last night?"

"Yes, I was," she answered quickly, wondering why these FBI agents were interested in Max. Short and thin, with those intelligent but timid eyes behind horn-rimmed glasses, always blowing clouds of tobacco smoke from a pipe; what could he have possibly done?

"We came out to talk to Mr. Lieber and his wife," Agent Grant said. His dark hair was short, almost crew-cut length. "But they seem to have left. Did you see them leave?"

‡ ‡ ‡ ‡ ‡

Tuesday, November 13, 1951
Towson, Maryland
Hampton House Apartments
Joppa Road
8:30 a.m. EST

"Are you sure you won't stay another day, Anna?" Alvin Zelinka, the collar of his navy blue slicker turned up against the drizzle that had begun earlier, stood beside the little Ford. His sister was at the wheel, her window open. Ruth and Luke were in back, sprawled on two thick blankets that covered boxes of household items.

"Yes. I wish … we could stay for Thanksgiving. But we really shouldn't. We've got a long drive ahead of us," Anna said, a look of panic momentarily flashing across her face.

"Well, at least stay until this rain lets up. The roads are slick."

Anna glanced at the kids behind her. "We've imposed too much already. It's best that we get going. I'd like to do at least three hundred miles before we stop tonight." She reached out and touched her brother's arm. "You've been a gracious host as usual. I hope we weren't too much for you."

"Heck, no! I enjoy seeing you and the kids." He swallowed the lump in his throat and glanced away. "Try to stay in touch, okay?"

"Okay. I love you, Alvin."

"I love you, too, little sister. Write to me as often as you can. I'll write back. I promise."

Turning the key in the ignition, Anna listened as the car's engine roared to life. "I'll try," she said. "Good bye for now."

He leaned in and kissed her cheek. "Bye. Don't drive too fast. Bye, kids!" He rapped his knuckles on the rear window. Ruth and Luke both waved. With a glance over her shoulder, Anna accelerated into the early morning commuter traffic on Joppa Road, and they were gone.

Oblivious to the drizzle, Alvin watched them go. They were his family; the only family he had in the world. His throat constricted. *Cuernavaca, Mexico is so far away. Will I ever see them again?* With a heavy heart he turned and made his way back inside.

‡ ‡ ‡ ‡ ‡

Thursday, November 15, 1951
Towson, Maryland
The DOD Baltimore Contract Management Area office
Division of Quality Control
8:30 a.m. EST

"You wanted to see me, Howard?" Alvin Zelinka worked for the federal government as a contract marketing specialist in the Department of Defense's District office in Towson. Howard Keller was his friend. He was also Alvin's boss.

"Yes, I did, Al. Come on in. Sit down."

Zelinka did as directed. As he took a seat, he noticed a copy of *The Baltimore Sun*, lying open on Keller's desk.

"A week or two ago, when we were at the Towson Diner for lunch, you mentioned you had a sister."

"Yeah."

"Was her name Lieber?"

"Yes."

"Is she married to a man named Maxim Lieber?"

Alvin's heart sank. He now understood what this was all about; why he'd been called to his boss's office. He looked away. "Yes," he responded softly.

"Been reading about these House Un-American Activities Committee hearings going on over in DC," Keller said. "They're lookin' into the activities of some Communists who may have infiltrated the government. That name has come up several times."

Alvin said nothing.

"Might that be your ... brother-in-law, Alvin?"

"Yes."

"You've never mentioned him before. Never mentioned that your sister was married to a Communist."

"Right. I never mentioned it." He mustered a weak smile. "Would you have, if you were in my position?"

Keller studied Alvin's face for a few moments before shaking his head. "Nope. Guess I wouldn't have."

Silence for a few moments. Then, "You mentioned your sister's name was Anna, and you have a niece and nephew, too. See much of them?"

"No. Hardly at all."

"Well, you realize that this is a bit ... dicey, right? I mean, we're friends and all, but I'm also the Division Chief. Got to be thinking about anything that might jeopardize the DOD in any way."

"I guess so, Howard."

"When you're with your brother-in-law, does he ever ... pump you for information about your work?"

Alvin chuckled. "Never. The guy is so opinionated, all he ever talks about is what *he* thinks about ... things."

Keller mulled that over. "Okay. Look. It goes without saying that you should never discuss your job with him. Or with your sister, either. Right?"

"Yeah."

"Okay. I'm going to need to make a note of our conversation in your file, Al. I don't know what else to do. But, if anything ever comes of it, I'll be sure to give you a heads up about it."

"I appreciate that, Howard."

"Meantime, let's try not to let this affect our friendship, okay?"

BOOK THREE

"There is nothing concealed that will not be revealed, nothing hidden that will not be made known."

Luke: 12, 2.

CHAPTER 23

Thursday, April 17, 1987
Towson, Maryland
The Home/Office of John Harris, Esquire
2:10 a.m. Eastern Standard Time (EST)

THE SHRILL SOUND OF HIS telephone cut into John Harris's sleep fogged brain. Through layers of murky subconscious, he became aware that the noise was not part of his dream. But the dream had possibilities. He didn't want it to end. There he was, on the porch of a beachfront cottage in Nag's Head with Ginny, his lovely girlfriend, silvery moonlight shimmering off the calm ocean waters of the Outer Banks barely a hundred yards away.

She was wearing a halter-top that did little to conceal her full, round breasts. Her short, white shorts revealed shapely, well-tanned legs. Long auburn hair fell loosely to her shoulders, framing her pretty face. Her head was turned toward him, her slightly parted lips tilted up to his. They were alone, on a wicker love seat. He was about to put an end to months of speculation and ask her to marry him. The timing was right; the setting perfect. But his mind was floating up to the surface of consciousness. He was losing it. Oh, damn!

Harris groped for the phone on his bedside table with one hand while pulling the pillow off his head with the other. The AM/FM digital clock next to his phone screamed two ten a.m. Reaching for the lamp, he fumbled with the switch. "Hello?"

"John Harris, please." The crisp voice carried a note of authority.

"Mm, speaking," Harris groaned. His own voice wouldn't work quite the way it should. Clearing his throat, he pulled his long legs from under the covers and swung them over the edge of the bed until his feet were resting on the shag rug below.

"Detective Sergeant Frank Spicer, Baltimore County Police. Sorry to disturb you at this late hour, but it's important."

"That's okay. What's wrong, Sergeant?"

"I understand you were a friend of Alvin Zelinka?"

John's sleep-laden brain was suddenly alert. "Were? What's happened to Al?"

"We got a call from a neighbor of his at the Hampton House apartments earlier this evening. Said she hadn't seen or heard from him for a few days and suspected he might be sick or somethin'. We sent an officer over there. The Resident Manager let him in. He found Mr. Zelinka inside."

"Dead?"

"Yes, sir. Apparently for a day or two. Fully dressed, in the entrance hall. No sign of foul play. Had his coat on. Looks like a heart attack as he was getting ready to go out. We found your name in his address book. Were you his lawyer?"

Stunned, Harris ran his fingers over the sandy stubble on his face. "His lawyer? Naw. We were friends. Al and I shared a couple of hobbies: photography and speech making. We belonged to the same photography club. Same Toastmaster's Club, too. And we got together occasionally for dinner. We're both single. Al never married. I was divorced a while back."

"Uh, huh. Mr. Harris, we sealed the apartment and took his body to the morgue. There has to be an autopsy." Spicer sounded slightly impatient. "That's all we can do tonight. But someone's gotta claim his body after the coroner finishes with it, make the funeral arrangements and so forth. I thought you might be the one to … you know, kinda take charge of all that. He *did* live alone, and as far as I can tell there aren't any relatives."

"Yeah, of course," Harris responded. "When?"

"In the morning. Can you come to Headquarters in Towson, say around eight thirty?"

"I'll be there, Sergeant. What was your name again?"

"Francis Spicer. Just ask for Frank. Kennilworth Avenue, not too far from the firehouse." Spicer hung up leaving Harris listening to a dead line.

John replaced the receiver. His brain, still sluggish from sleep, kicked in. Little Al Zelinka. What a shame. Alvin *did* live alone. But he had a sister someplace, and a niece and nephew, whom he hadn't heard from in years. He'd been a shy person who lived a quiet life. His interests were photography, speech making and travel. Those were the things on which he spent money and time.

Alvin had made his living as a contract marketing specialist with the Department of Defense, but had retired just about a year ago. His government pension was small but adequate. It had paid his rent, provided money for him to buy his photography supplies, and allowed enough for a vacation trip once or twice a year. He seemed content with the way his life had been going. *Death,* Harris thought, *tends to happen at the most inconvenient times.*

Swinging his legs back into bed, he pulled up the covers. His eyes ached. His body craved more sleep. Reaching over, he turned off the lamp. Plenty of time to deal with this in the morning. Now, he simply wanted to sleep a few more hours. He pulled the pillow over his head. Was it possible to pick up a dream from where you left off? He would try.

Thursday, April 17, 1987
Towson, Maryland
Baltimore County Police Department
Office of Detective Sergeant Frank Spicer
8:30 a.m. EST

When John Harris arrived at Police Headquarters, he was shown to Detective Sergeant Frank Spicer's office. Spicer's tall frame, at six feet four inches, looked too large for the leather chair he sat in behind a cluttered gray metal desk. Although it was eight-thirty and sunlight had banished the darkness outside, a lamp still burned, unnoticed, on the corner of his desk. Because his toes hurt, he had raised his long legs and placed his feet up on the edge of the desk. He removed them quickly, stood, and stuck out a beefy hand, as John Harris came through the office door.

"Sergeant Spicer?"

"Yeah. You must be Mr. Harris. Call me Frank." The two men shook hands. "I been with the force almost twelve years. Much smaller back when I first came aboard; a Bureau of highly trained, highly motivated people. I stayed on after it changed over to a Department. Most of those people are gone now. Got old and retired." He took a deep breath. "Want some coffee?"

Harris nodded. "Cream and sugar." He lowered his heavy frame cautiously into a chair in front of Spicer's desk, as if the chair were fragile and might collapse under his weight. He watched as Spicer move to the end of a row of file cabinets where a coffee maker, Styrofoam cups, a jar of creamer and a sugar bowl littered a small table. Paper plates, napkins and plastic spoons were scattered next to the coffee maker. Some of the plates were soiled, as were most of the spoons. He frowned. "You must like your work," he said, to be polite.

"Yeah. I do. As time went by, instead of burnout, I found myself liking it more and more."

"That's good."

"The years have flown. Made Sergeant a while back. Got a file filled with commendations for work well done and lots of arrests made," he said proudly. Filling two cups with the steaming liquid, he turned. "When *I* get a case, the suspects are identified, the crime gets solved, people are arrested and the case gets closed," he boasted. "Even the States' Attorney's office likes me. They know when *I'm* in charge, proper police procedures will be followed, and evidence will be gathered in a legal manner and preserved for trial correctly."

"That's important."

"Yeah. I pay attention to chain of custody, too. Smart defense lawyers *already* have it all in their favor, what with *Miranda, Esposito,* and the like. But they can't get one of *my* cases dismissed on grounds of procedural errors by the police."

Spicer carried two Styrofoam cups, the creamer, and two spoons back to his desk. "Don't know why I'm borin' you with all this." He nodded at the coffee. "I used to drink it black until my wife told me caffeine was bad for me. Said it was causin' my night sweats and makin' me nervous. To placate her I cut back to five cups a day and began usin' cream and sugar." He managed a sarcastic smile. "Don't know what I'd do without her, sometimes."

Harris nodded. "My *girlfriend* wants me to quit completely, but I like the stuff too damn much."

"I know what ya mean. Besides, it's a social thing; somethin' ta do while I shoot the bull with the other guys. At the beginnin' and end of each shift, the men on my squad come in here, pour themselves a cup and talk shop before they hit the streets or head for home." He glanced at Harris. "Creamer okay?" Without waiting for a reply, he added two spoons full of white powder to each cup, tore open two packets of Sweet and Low and poured one into each.

Harris made a nondescript hand gesture. "Do you know what caused Alvin's death?"

"Yeah. Doctor Hamed was Mr. Zelinka's treating physician. Lives there in the building. He signed the Death Certificate. You know him?"

"He used to play poker with us from time to time."

Handing one of the coffee cups to Harris, Spicer sat down at his desk, opened a file and consulted a printed form. "Myocardial infarction, arteriosclerotic heart disease and diabetes mellitus." He looked up and studied Harris thoughtfully. "We'll be going back to Mr. Zelinka's apartment later today." He raised the Styrofoam cup to his lips, tested it and then took a larger sip. "You need to get inside?"

"Yeah. I'll need to search for Al's Will. Then an appraiser needs to go in and inventory his personal belongings. Besides the furniture, Al owned a car and some photography equipment. The car's old. Not worth much, but it runs."

"Some kid might buy it to fix it up," Spicer volunteered.

"The equipment isn't worth much either, but all those things will have to be inventoried and sold as part of his estate." Harris hesitated. He peered at Spicer. "Alvin had a sister, you know."

Spicer's eyebrows shot up. "A sister?" He checked his notes. "Our preliminary checkin' found a name — 'Mrs. Anna Zelinka Lieber ' — might that be her?"

"Yeah, that's her."

"She had an address in Mexico somewhere," he said irritably. "We tried callin' her but the number's not a working number anymore." He looked aggrieved, as if this might become a black mark in the file he valued so highly. "I don't suppose you know where she lives?"

"No. Alvin told me he hadn't heard from her for a long time."

"They couldn't have been close. No pictures, or nothin'."

"They weren't. Alvin didn't like his brother-in-law's politics. So he and his sister drifted apart. There was a niece and nephew, too."

Sipping again from his coffee, Spicer moved some of the clutter on his desk aside with a forearm and set the cup down on his coffee-stained desk blotter. A partially eaten slice of pizza on a paper plate and a crumpled paper napkin, all that was left from his abbreviated dinner of the evening before, fell off the desk and landed on the floor. Harris moved his feet a few inches to the left, glanced down at the mess, but otherwise did not react. The carpet was threadbare and dirty. *One more spill will hardly matter,* he thought.

Spicer mumbled an apology but did not move to pick the things up. "The resident manager's name is Dolores," Spicer said. "If you want, I'll tell her you got clearance and she should give you a key. That way, you can come and go without waitin' for my people." He reached for the phone as Harris nodded his assent.

CHAPTER 24

Tuesday, May 5, 1987
Towson, Maryland
The Home/Office of John Harris, Esquire
9:00 a.m. Eastern Standard Time (EST)

PEOPLE WHO LIVE IN THE Baltimore area understand that spring comes and goes quickly, usually giving way to the heat of summer before people are quite ready. Most of them had grown accustomed to it. It was only the first week in May but temperatures had already climbed into the low nineties twice. Tall and slightly overweight, John Harris was bothered by the heat. He dreaded what was yet to come. Soaring temperatures and high humidity foreshadowed an unpleasant summer ahead.

Harris was in his home-office on Cedar Avenue in Towson, engaged in winding down his law practice. Outside, groups of teenagers trudged past on their way to another day of classes at Towson High School, a few hundred feet down the street.

In three weeks John was due to begin a new job with the State Accident Fund. He had sailed through the interview process with his usual confidence, and was not surprised when the State Office of Personnel had notified him that he'd been selected for one of three positions it was trying to fill.

John had put some time, effort and money into the task of decorating his two-room office. A waiting area and secretarial station took up what used to be the living room. His office, formerly the dining room, had double windows, which gave him a view of the lawn and garden in his rear yard. Both rooms were painted in a warm, Williamsburg gold. The ceilings were ivory. One wall in each office was covered with green, fabric type wallpaper. Towle lamps on end tables supplied light in each room.

For artwork, he had been very selective. After visiting several galleries and almost every store in Baltimore that sold quality artwork, he had seen the work of a local artist, Edward George Sacco, Jr., hanging in the living room of a friend. The friend had commissioned Sacco to do a watercolor. John had admired it and was put in touch with the artist. The result? A beautifully framed set of pen and ink drawings of four local Towson landmarks by an artist who obviously knew his medium. Sacco had also mastered watercolor and oils. Jim had asked him to do a watercolor of his home, which he then framed and placed in his own office.

Later, he had asked Sacco to do a portrait of his deceased mother. It hung on the wall across from his desk. John loved that oil painting from the moment he first set eyes on it. Working from several photographs, the artist had captured a look in his mothers' eyes, one that Jim had seen there often and had grown to love.

Leaning over, Harris pulled out the lower drawer of his desk and extracted a thick manila file. The Alvin Zelinka estate was one of the few remaining open cases in his office. Because Alvin was his friend, he wanted to conclude it, if possible. But, each time he opened the file, sadness settled on him as memories of Alvin flooded his mind. He now realized he might not be able to close it before his job change. After that, he would have no time to devote to it.

A Petition for Judicial Probate and a List of Interested Persons needed to be filed. As in all estate cases, a Personal Representatives' bond was required, to secure the State of Maryland for inheritance taxes should he abscond with the decedent's money or otherwise breach his myriad duties to the estate. These papers should have been filed within a short time after Alvin's death. So far, however, he had not filed anything with the Court because he had been unable to locate Alvin's only heirs, Anna Lieber and her kids. For all he knew, they might be dead. While going through Alvin's possessions he had found some letters from Anna to her brother, written from Cuernavaca, Mexico. That was all the information he had on her.

After completing Alvin's funeral arrangements, he had called in an appraiser, the Milton J. Dance Company, in Towson, whose work he was familiar with from hearing other lawyers talk about them. Lee and Stephen Dance had done their job quickly and efficiently. Their Inventory listed the value of all Alvin's personal property; his car, the furniture in his apartment, his photography equipment, and even his clothing.

Once the appraisers had finished, Jim had placed all of Alvin's belongings in storage where they would remain until everything was sold, and relinquished the lease to his apartment. Alvin's car, a 1978 Chevrolet Caprice 4door sedan, was nine years old, and was fully depreciated. Its book value was probably no more than fifty dollars.

There were also some US government Series EE savings bonds made out to Alvin and his sister, Anna, as joint tenants. They were nonprobate assets, so they did not have to be listed in the Inventory. These, along with everything else, now belonged to her if she were still alive. If not, then the entire estate would pass to her children, if *they* were alive.

The List of Interested Persons required by Maryland law called for the name and address of anyone who might be an heir of the deceased person. He pulled two blank forms from a folder in his file cabinet and decided to enter Anna's last known address in New York. He knew this was fruitless, but it would have been even more ridiculous to list the address in Mexico. He had sent a letter down there. It had not come back, but his attempt to telephone her in Mexico had produced the information that no one by that name was listed in Cuernavaca.

Was the Lieber family still in Mexico? Living in another city or town, or there in Cuernavaca but with an unpublished number? He knew he should try to find out. He decided to devote the entire afternoon to Alvin's estate. In one afternoon he could fill out the required forms and take care of all the preliminary telephone work.

First, he called T.J.A Ltd., a company in nearby Parkville which specialized in estate liquidation sales. He made an appointment to meet with a representative and arrange the sale of Alvin's possessions. That done, he called the Mexican Embassy in Washington, DC, and was informed that the Mexican authorities *did* attempt to keep track of Americans entering and leaving Mexico, but the information was not public. He also was told that the US government asked all its citizens traveling into Mexico to register when they arrived. The American Embassy in Mexico City could help, but he'd either have to send a letter or go to Mexico City and personally request the information.

A letter would take weeks. John didn't have weeks. He wanted to at least file the opening papers with the Orphan's Court for Baltimore County before he began his new job. He reached for the phone again and dialed Ginny's office number. She picked up on the first ring, her voice sounding efficient, and busy.

"Hi, beautiful."

"I was just thinking about you."

"Something lascivious, I hope."

"John! Someone might hear." He could tell she was blushing.

"Listen. A couple of weeks ago you mentioned taking a vacation together before I begin my new job? Well, I have an idea." He quickly filled her in.

"I've heard Cuernavaca's a nice place for tourists," Ginny said. "Know how much it would cost?"

"No. But, I think I'd be justified in spending some estate money that way. We'll combine business with pleasure. I'll pay for *our* vacation expenses. Al's estate will pay for the rest."

"When would we go?"

"We could go down there next week. We'll fly into Mexico City, rent a car, drive to Cuernavaca and personally check out the address I have for Anna."

"I thought you said the information you have on her is sketchy?"

"I *did* say that. It is. Alvin's infrequent conversations about his sister and a few old letters from Anna place her in Cuernavaca a long time ago. But, we can talk to people in the neighborhood where they lived. If it turns out that the Liebers have left Mexico, we might dig up a neighbor who knows where they went when they left."

"Sounds good to me," Ginny said. "See you tonight." She hung up.

John leaned back in his chair, convinced that he was doing the right thing. By allocating part of the cost to personal expenses and part to estate business, he could go down there and nose around. If he found nothing, he would come back, publish the usual Notice to Creditors and to Interested Persons in a local weekly newspaper, and then refer the case to an estate lawyer, someone more experienced than he was, to resolve it.

He took a deep breath and expelled it. What would happen if he could not locate any of the heirs? In that situation, Alvin's assets would be given to the State of Maryland under what was called the Doctrine of Escheat. He frowned at the idea of the State getting Alvin's assets. But if Anna and her children were not found, that's exactly what the law required.

Rising from his desk, he moved to the double windows and gazed out over the back lawn, noticing the shades of yellow-green where new blades of grass had pushed their way through, seeking the warmth of spring sunlight. He would do this much and see what happened. For Alvin's sake.

BOOK FOUR

"I can do all things through Christ
who strengthens me."

Philippians, 4:13.

CHAPTER 25

Saturday, February 17, 1990
Timonium, Maryland
Padonia Village Apartments
2312 Chetwood Circle
9:15 a.m. Eastern Standard Time (EST)

MORNING FOUND MATT DAWSON SITTING at the dining room table in his apartment, the Alvin Zelinka estate file on the table in front of him, unopened. He glanced at the file and then out the window at gray clouds under a sunless sky. Wind whistling between the buildings invaded the courtyard and created tiny funnels of leaves here and there. A pair of squirrels played just a few feet beyond the glass, unaware of his presence. Motionless, he watched them chase each other in ever widening circles until, tiring of that, they ran off.

Turning to his notes, he quickly reviewed the meager data Winkler had given him. Even before he'd finished, the thought that he might not be able to find Anna Lieber began bouncing around inside his head.

After their meeting the day before, Bob had pulled his checkbook from a desk drawer and written Matt a check as a retainer. Matt picked it up and studied the numbers. A nice check, it would relieve some of the financial pressures that were closing around him like a vise.

As he shuffled through some of the papers on the table, he realized he was having difficulty concentrating. The file was a huge magnet, at once attracting and repelling him. He sighed and pushed it aside. *Better go deposit this check and pay some of my overdue bills. Then I'll hit the supermarket and pick up some groceries. After that, it'll be easier to work.*

By noon, groceries put away, checks written and envelopes addressed, Matt's mind *was* clearer. A grin spread across his face as he slipped into a chair and again addressed the file. He felt the creative juices beginning to flow. He flashed forward to the end of the case. *Visualize success, the motivational experts say, and you'll succeed.* He pictured Bob Winkler shaking his hand after hanging up the phone from talking to Anna Lieber, and reading him an invitation to dinner at the White House. But he knew most of that was not going to happen. He also knew none of it would happen unless he dug into this file and worked it hard.

One very troubling thing was apparent about this case. A substantial length of time had elapsed since Alvin Zelinka and his sister had been in contact. Al had never married. Surely loneliness would have dictated that he maintain contact with his only sister and his niece and nephew. But he had not. Winkler had been convinced – and it looked like he was correct - that Alvin and Anna had not been in touch for years. Why? Anna was Alvin's younger sister, his "little" sister. The phrase, "little sister lost" began to play in Matt's mind.

Since he'd never done this before, he decided to begin by reading through the entire file. Some interesting things would no doubt come to light. Then, he'd map out a plan of action that would lead him to Anna Lieber. A bit more confident, he settled down to read.

‡ ‡ ‡ ‡ ‡

Saturday, February 17, 1990
Timonium, Maryland
Padonia Village Apartments
2312 Chetwood Circle
7:15 p.m. EST

By evening, Matt had perused the entire file, examined each document and separated everything into neat piles: court papers in one, bank records and estate checkbook in another, correspondence from various people to and from Alvin, Harris and Winkler in a third. In the background, his radio was tuned to a report from the Baltimore Orioles training camp in Florida, of that day's intra-squad game. It had been three long years since the Orioles had gone to the playoffs. The wait-till-next-year mantra had been replaced by "This is *our* year."

A small stack of letters from Anna Lieber to her brother, written many years ago, sat on the table next to his computer. He had read them quickly and set them aside.

On a yellow pad, Matt had made a list of Alvin's family, friends and acquaintances:

1. M. Saffron (A friend. Male or female? Probably female)
2. Mrs. Maxim (Anna) Lieber (Alvin's sister, the person he was looking for)
3. Howard Keller (Alvin's former boss)
   Chief, Quality Assurance Division
   Quality Assurance Specialist
   Defense Logistics Agency
4. Richard La Course (worked with Al)
5. Ruth Ann Lieber (Alvin's niece)
6. Luke (Butch) Lieber (Alvin's nephew)
7. Rose Zelinka (Alvin's mother)
   290 Riverside Drive
   Manhattan, New York County
   died 6/25/50 in New York. Age at death: 69
   name of father: Morris Bettelheim,

name of mother: Klava Schwersten
8. Harry Maxim Zelinka (Alvin's father)
    died 1945 in Munich. A civilian employee for the U.S. Army
9. Jennifer Walton (friend)
10. Noreen Matsunaga (friend)

That was it. Not many friends; no other known relatives. *It won't take too long, but I need to contact all of them,* Matt thought. *If I ask enough questions about Alvin's sister, eventually I'll learn something helpful.*

Alvin had lived a long life. His date of birth was July 15, 1914. He was seventy-two years old when he died. Apparently he had traveled extensively. Copies of hotel bills, receipts and travel folders from different places dotted the file. Photography, travel and his membership in a Toastmasters Club had been the high points in his life.

A review of Bob Winkler's handwritten notes revealed that Bob had received a phone call from an irate Martin Saffron, complaining about not being notified when the sale of Alvin's property had been scheduled. Was this the M. Saffron referred to on a scrap of paper with Alvin's belongings? *I'll have to talk to the man. Might be a bit unpleasant.*

He picked up a Christmas card from a woman named Jennifer Walton who lived in Acapulco, Mexico. Alvin had traveled to Acapulco and probably met her there. No other letters from her? Surely they had exchanged correspondence more than once, even if only a card or note at holidays? Bob must have disposed of the bulk of them. There was an address but no phone number. Matt made a note: call the long-distance information operator for her number.

Among Zelinka's papers was a letter from a woman named Noreen Matsunaga. Friendly, but not a love letter. A picture included inside showed an attractive native Hawaiian woman of about thirty; slender, with long black hair and dark skin.

Alvin had been a camera buff. They had probably met on his trip out there, and he had asked her to pose for pictures. Some women didn't mind doing that and were even flattered that anyone would ask. No telephone number for her, either. Matt scribbled another note: call the long distance operator to get her number.

Alvin's father, Harry Maxim Zelinka, had died during World War II while stationed in Europe. Among Alvin's personal papers was a communiqué from the War Department to his mother, notifying her of her husband's death. Matt pictured Rose Zelinka standing in her doorway clutching the unopened letter, sensing what it contained but afraid to open it. He decided to retrieve the letter and read it again. It might be important.

He would also need to find an obituary for Harry Zelinka. It would list the names of other relatives. One of them might know what had become of Anna Lieber and her children. The Zelinkas had been living in New York at the time of Harry's death. The Baltimore County Public Library in Towson had *The New York Times* on microfilm. Matt knew the date of death from a note in Winkler's file. He could find the obituary.

Rose Bettelheim Zelinka had been a New York City resident when she died. Alvin had kept a copy of her death certificate all these years. It had her date of death as June 25, 1950. *I can get her obituary, too. Also, most families have at least one genealogy buff. Even if there isn't one in the Bettelheim family, I might stumble across a relative who keeps track of the others.*

Matt jotted another note on his yellow pad and then glanced at the clock. His stomach told him it was time to eat. Anxious to begin work, he had not stopped for lunch. But he *had* absorbed an enormous amount of information. *I feel as if Alvin Zelinka had been a personal friend. Well, almost.* Stifling a yawn, he decided to quit for the day and begin again in the morning.

‡ ‡ ‡ ‡ ‡

Tuesday, February 20, 1990
Timonium, Maryland
Padonia Village Apartments
2312 Chetwood Circle
9:15 a.m. EST

Two days passed before Matt resumed work on the Zelinka case, because his black cloud of depression had returned. Not with the same intensity as in the past, but it was back, causing his mind to race over earlier events, like an out-of-control truck hurtling down a steep grade.

Before leaving, his ex-wife had said she felt stifled and didn't want to be married any longer. She also complained that he spent so much money on the farm and horse business that little was left for her and the kids. That was an exaggeration, but since it was a concern to her, he had tried to explain that his earnings as an attorney in solo practice were not going to be enough to put four children through private high schools and colleges. Another source of income was needed. To him, since they had the land, developing the horse business seemed essential. He also pointed out that the farm would appreciate in value over the years and become a substantial legacy for their kids. But, nothing he said made any difference. She simply switched to another tack; she needed room to grow. Matt had thought she was fully-grown when they married.

Because his years as a lawyer had shown him the devastating effects of divorce on families, he didn't want them to separate. It didn't take a rocket scientist to see that there were problems in their relationship. He understood that a lot of them were his fault. But with his vows in mind, he had concluded that since their marriage was not what they wanted it to be, they should try to fix it. Now, four years later, the taste of rejection was still bitter in his mouth. A home and a family had existed and six lives had been shared. From the moment Miriam left, those lives were changed and forever damaged.

After her departure, Matt had wrestled with feelings of anger, sadness, grief and loneliness. Although Miriam refused to admit it to him, he knew the children were deeply troubled as well. Despite his grief and the problems with which he was dealing, he had tried to reach out to each, to be available if they needed him for emotional support and comfort. But, in shock over the break-up of their family, they rejected his overtures. For a time, they had rejected him. He sighed. *Nobody ever said being a husband and father was easy.*

‡ ‡ ‡ ‡ ‡

Tuesday, February 20, 1990
Timonium, Maryland
Padonia Village Apartments
2312 Chetwood Circle
10:00 a.m. EST

The winter air was cold and crisp. Acknowledging the need to shake off his depressed mood, Matt drove to nearby Dulaney High School. Behind the brick classroom buildings and tennis courts lay the football field with a cinder track circling it. Because it was so cold, the school kids were inside, and the track, usually popular with local joggers, was deserted.

After some stretching exercises, he walked the first quarter mile to warm up. Then, his breath visible on the air with every stride, he ran four laps in just under ten minutes, following that by walking two more laps and jogging a final lap. This routine seemed to help him stay in shape and tended to temporarily relieve the stress that had been assaulting him for years. Finished, breathing heavily, sweat drenching the T-shirt under his woolen sweatshirt, he wiped his face with the towel he'd brought with him and smiled. *Now maybe I'll feel more like working.*

‡ ‡ ‡ ‡ ‡

Tuesday, February 20, 1990
Timonium, Maryland
Padonia Village Apartments
2312 Chetwood Circle
11:30 a.m. EST

Refreshed by the exercise and a quick shower, Matt decided to spend the day contacting Alvin Zelinka's friends. M. Saffron seemed like a good place to start.

Saffron's phone was ringing. Four, five rings. Then six. Matt was about to hang up when a sleepy male voice answered. Matt asked for M. Saffron.

"This is M. Saffron ... Martin Saffron, that is," came the response in a guarded tone.

Matt introduced himself. There was no reaction. He then explained why he was calling and asked if Martin had known Alvin Zelinka well.

"We were friends with Alvin for thirty years. My mother more so than me. Until he died a couple years ago."

"Did Alvin ever mention having a sister, a niece or a nephew?"

"Yeah. Just a few months before he died — I think it was around Christmas — he was over here for dinner. He *did* mention a sister. Told us she was livin' in Mexico. He said he thought his niece and nephew had gone back to the New York City area."

"Do you know if he was in contact with them?"

"No. Listen. My mother's name's Melissa. She lives here with me, but she ain't home now. She knew a lot more about him than I did. She won't be home until later tonight. Call her back tomorrow." His voice was not altogether friendly, but he was willing to talk.

"I'll do that," Matt said. Thanking Saffron for his time, he hung up. As he picked up the phone again, he wondered what time it was in Honolulu.

Long-distance information found a listing for Noreen Matsunaga. Same address as the one on her card. Noreen herself answered the phone. He quickly explained who he was and why he was calling and asked if she would answer a few questions.

"Oh. Sure, Mr. Dawson," she responded, her voice warm and friendly. "Wasn't he that photographer fella? Came out here around 1980. We spent a few evenings together while he was here. A nice man. Wrote me now and then after that, until a couple a years ago. I *wondered* what happened to him."

"Did he ever talk about a sister to you? Or a niece and nephew?"

Noreen Matsunaga expelled a breath as she attempted to recall anything that might be helpful. "I don't think so. We didn't talk about our families. He was only here for a week. It's so expensive, who can stay longer? And when he was in, he took his pictures. Then we'd visit. A couple of times we went to dinner afterwards. Nothing about family in his notes and cards, either."

Matt thanked her for speaking to him.

"It was a real pleasure. If you're ever out this way, please look me up. You sound like a nice guy, yourself." He recalled the pictures Alvin had taken of her; the tanned body reclining on a blanket as if at poolside. For just a moment, he toyed with the idea of flying out there to meet her. *What would life with her be like on a sun-drenched beach on one of those Pacific islands?* Although he had been living an abstinent lifestyle since his ex-wife had left, he was far from immune to the opposite sex. But, his new relationship with Jesus had led him to develop habits of discipline and self-restraint previously lacking in his life. He swallowed, thanked Noreen Matsunaga again for her time, and hung up the phone.

Nothing. She had only known Alvin for a week on one of his vacation trips. But Matt now knew enough about Alvin Zelinka to speculate that he had been a lonely person. Because of his loneliness, he had reached out to people he'd met on his trips. But the relationships that resulted were superficial, at best. Alvin had not understood that, from a distance, he could not be a part of their lives. Because, for a reason that Matt did not yet understand, Alvin had not maintained contact with his sister, at the end he had died as he'd lived; alone.

CHAPTER 26

Tuesday, February 20, 1990
Timonium, Maryland
Padonia Village Apartments
2312 Chetwood Circle
6:15 p.m. Eastern Standard Time (EST)

JENNIFER WALTON IN ACAPULCO WAS next on his list. Matt called long-distance information and was told to dial the area code 52748 for telephone service in Mexico, then 5551212 for information. He did that. An operator gave him the listing for Jennifer Walton. He dialed and a young woman answered the phone, switching immediately from Spanish to thickly accented English when she heard his voice. Speaking slowly, Matt explained who he was and what he wanted.

"My name is Marcella," she said. "Jennifer is my sister. She corresponded with Alvin Zelinka. No doubt she sent that Christmas card."

"Well, can I talk to Jennifer?"

"Jennifer and my mother are out. They will be back around eight o'clock this evening."

"Please leave word that I'll … to expect a return call from me tonight," he told her.

"I will do it," Marcella assured him. "I liked Alvin. In fact, we *all* did."

Matt hung up. The first doubts were now building, doubts that sat there grinning at him like a Cheshire cat, challenging him to prove that he could cut it as an investigator, that he had any ability to succeed in this new line of work. He was beginning to understand something: that the job of an investigator was about half information gathering and half intuition. And his intuition was letting him know that he needed more information if he expected to locate Anna Lieber.

A thought struck him. He rooted through the file looking for the police report. In a section for notes, the name ANNA ZELINKA LIEBER appeared, with a Cuernavaca address. The police must have found it in Alvin's personal telephone book. Yes! A phone number was listed. *The cops probably called the number. And John Harris had this information when he went down there. Surely he'd have checked it out. Still …* He dialed the number and listened to it ring until an operator came on the line and explained that it was not a working number. Matt told her what he was trying to do. She connected him to an operator in

Cuernavaca. "I'm looking for listings for Anna Lieber, Maxim Lieber, Ruth Lieber or Luke Lieber," he explained.

After a long pause, the operator returned. "Sorry, señior. "No listings for any of those names in either Cuernavaca or Mexico City."

He hung up. *Of course not. That definitely would have been too easy.* He decided to eat something. *A salad, some bread. Tea. That'll be enough. Then I'll call Acapulco again.*

‡ ‡ ‡ ‡ ‡

Tuesday, February 20, 1990
Timonium, Maryland
Padonia Village Apartments
2312 Chetwood Circle
9:00 p.m. EST

Matt finished the last of his late dinner and cleared away the dishes, piling them in the sink along with those from breakfast and lunch. *I really should wash those dishes soon,* he thought. *But right now I need to make a return call to Acapulco.*

His radio was on. The first spring training game between the Orioles and Phillies, played earlier that day in Fort Lauderdale, was being aired to Orioles fans by delayed broadcast. With one ear on the game, he thumbed through his notes, found the number and dialed. A woman who said she was Jennifer Walton answered. "What has happened to Alvin Zelinka?" She wanted to know. She spoke with just a trace of a Spanish accent.

"Alvin passed away in April 1987. I'm trying to locate his sister. At one time she was living in Cuernavaca."

"His sister? I did not know he *had* a sister. He never mentioned a sister to either my mother or me. I think it is strange that she was living in Mexico and he never told us about her."

"I agree. How did you meet Alvin?"

"Let me see. In Acapulco, in the summer of 1978. He was vacationing here at a hotel. We met him in the restaurant. He had a camera with him and took pictures of our baby. He was so nice! He had copies made and sent them to us. Beautiful pictures. We corresponded regularly after that. I *thought* something must have happened to him."

"Will you ask your mother if she can recall anything about Alvin's sister?"

Jennifer left the phone. Matt heard the sound of muffled voices in the background. Then, "My mother's name is Josephina. She will check all of Alvin's old letters and cards. I will write you if there is any mention. Please to give me your name again, and your address."

He gave her the information and with that, Jennifer Walton was gone.

Matt was suddenly feeling tired. And mystified. Alvin had told Martin Saffron as late as Christmas 1986, that his sister was still living in Mexico. That was just a few months before his death. He'd met Jennifer Walton in 1978, corresponded frequently with her over the years, but never mentioned a sister living in Mexico. Did this mean that the Liebers had left Mexico prior to 1978? If so, why, in 1986, was he telling people in Baltimore that she was still living there? Was it possible that they left briefly and then later returned?

It was late, and Matt had had a very taxing day. The Orioles baseball game had progressed into the late innings with the Orioles behind. As usual. But Matt was no longer listening. He decided to fix himself a drink. Never more than a light drinker, he maintained a liquor cabinet so that he could make drinks for dinner guests. Most of the liquor had been received as gifts from clients at the end of successfully concluded cases. Some had come his way as Christmas gifts from relatives and friends.

During his years as a practicing lawyer, he had become fascinated with spirits, wines, liqueurs and cordials, and had spent time delving into their history; how long each had been around, and where each was produced. He had done it because he wanted to impress when out to dinner with clients or when entertaining at home. Later, his spiritual discernment told him that it had been a vanity; harmless, perhaps, but a vanity, nevertheless.

Matt thought about the change that had occurred in him over the past four years. The Roman Catholic religion referred to it as a metanoia; a spiritual awakening coupled with a strong sense of repentance. He believed it had been a gift; that God had reached out to him, helping him to become more as He wanted Matt to be.

Smiling to himself, he selected an open bottle of Maker's Mark bourbon, dropped a few ice cubes into a glass, poured a shot, and added ginger ale. Then, he moved to his bedroom, lay on the bed and placed two pillows behind his head. Adhering to his habit of daily prayer, he picked up his rosary from the night table and began to recite it for the intention that he'd be given a clear mind to work on the Zelinka investigation. Someone had once told him, "Pray the rosary every day and watch it change your life." He believed it. He'd seen it work.

His prayer sessions had evolved over several years, and now included time for thanks and petition, Bible reading, the rosary, extemporaneous prayer and a period of meditation. Most of the time he prayed directly to God and Jesus. But when saying the rosary, grounded so solidly in Scripture, he asked Mary to intercede for him. An hour later, his prayer session concluded, he felt at peace.

His glass of unfinished bourbon rested on the bedside table, neglected. Carrying it to the kitchen, he replenished the ice and added more ginger ale, returned to the living room and sat on the couch. A lamp on a corner table was the only source of light in the room.

He'd learned a lot about Anna Lieber so far, but what he'd learned had not led to answers. It had simply produced more questions. Why had the Liebers left their home in New York City and their snug Connecticut cottage and gone to Cuernavaca, Mexico? Did it have something to do with Max Lieber's business?

Then there were those five letters post marked from Cuernavaca; newsy letters, the kind a sister would write to a brother far away. Each described what the kids were doing in school and what Anna was doing in the city. In one, a long drive or a trip they had taken, and the Thanksgiving holidays were mentioned. Little was said about Max.

Why had the letters stopped? From their tone, he could infer that Anna and Alvin got along as well as siblings generally did. Had Alvin received many more letters and thrown the others away? But why would he keep only these five? *Have I missed something here?*

It was after eleven o'clock. He was finding it hard to absorb all the information he'd been gathering. Moving to the bathroom, he washed up, brushed his teeth and chuckled as he recalled an old joke. *"First man: Where was the toothbrush invented? Second man: I dunno. Where? First man: In Arkansas. If it had been invented anywhere else, it would have been named the teethbrush."*

As he climbed into bed, he realized it was not going to be easy to find Anna Lieber. *Well, I was hoping something challenging would come along. This fills the bill.* Yawning, he turned out the lamp and was soon asleep.

He was standing in a field at the top of a hill. The kids had given names to all the pastures. They called this one Lovely Plains. Someone was with him. A tall, sturdily built figure with striking features and a disarming smile. But fear prickled Matt's spine as the man spoke:

"You really worked hard on this place. Blood, sweat and tears. Turned that old house into a comfortable home for your wife and kids, and a profitable horse breeding farm. The envy of all your neighbors." Something between a grin and a leer crossed his face. "Especially the people across the street. I devoted lots of time and energy to that. Trying to convince you people that it's okay to be envious."

Matt turned toward the other. "I wasn't the only one who worked hard around here. Miriam and the kids did, too."

"But that last year? The kids gave you fits figuring out ways to avoid their chores. Then they pulled out and left you with the entire burden."

He moved a step closer.

Matt had no response. Lowering his eyes, he thought about the new shoots of clover and orchard grass that would soon be blooming, provided by a kind, benevolent God. When he glanced up, he was staring into the dark eyes of his companion, eyes that betrayed the suppressed rage of thwarted power, and a cunning driven by intense hatred.

"It was hard after they left, that's for sure," he said.

"So, why don't you call them up and tell them how angry you are at them and how much you hate them for what they did to you?"

"But, that would cause strife and dissension between us."

"Yes! Yes!" The other said gleefully.

"And it wouldn't be true. I'm angry all right, but I don't hate them. And my anger is more at myself than at them."

"But, they were the reason you lost the farm, you know."

"No, that's not true, either!"

"Truth!" the man said scornfully. "Everybody knows truth doesn't exist; that it's only culturally constructed reality." He leaned closer, and Matt could smell his foul breath. "Objective truth does not exist!"

With considerable effort, Matt forced himself to focus. "No. They were not the reason we lost this place."

"Really? What was, then?"

"One reason was that I didn't understand that the horse market might collapse. Another was that I made some mistakes in judgment. But..."

"But what?"

"The main reason was that I didn't gather my family to pray. We should have been doing that every night, what with all the problems we faced. Praying to God and to Jesus for help and the grace to weather the storms."

The figure drew back a few steps. He seemed to shrink in stature.

"And," Matt continued, "you may deny the existence of objective truth, truth that's true for everybody and exists whether or not we believe it, but I don't."

"No one can know objective truth," the other bellowed. "Anyone who claims he knows should be ignored."

"Do you seriously claim that objective truth is unknowable? That we can't use our reason to identify it?"

"Of course!"

"But, that in itself is a statement of objective truth. So if I believe you, logically I must ignore you."

"Logic!" the other muttered. "Logic has no place in my philosophy."

Now it was Matt's turn to take a step forward. "I believe that the existence of God and the person of Jesus are two undeniable objective truths."

"Fool!" Matt's companion screamed. Turning on his heel, he began to walk away. "I'm leaving now, but I'll be back," he said over his shoulder. "Count on it."

‡ ‡ ‡ ‡ ‡

Wednesday, February 21, 1990
Timonium, Maryland
Padonia Village Apartments
2312 Chetwood Circle
9:45 a.m. EST

At his dining room table the next morning, a cup of hot coffee at his elbow and his troubling dream of the night before forgotten, Matt spread Anna Lieber's letters out in front of him, picked one at random and read it. Undated, it spoke of Thanksgiving in Mexico and a long car trip they had taken. Bob had placed it last in order. Matt set it aside.

He went to another, also dateless. Anna wrote about a cottage in Brockett's Point near Branford, informing Alvin she had placed the house up for sale; that some of their parents' things were there, and if he wanted anything from the house he should contact a realtor named Lars Fromen, at 332 Main Street, Branford, for the keys. She said that Alvin could take anything he wanted. The rest would be sold. She also mentioned a lawyer, Arthur B. Weis, at the firm of Saltman, Weis and Connors, in Bridgeport. He scribbled a note to locate these men. *Those guys dealt with Anna Lieber. They would have known where she was living at the time.*

All the others had dates. He stacked them in chronological order. They were short and newsy, but as far as he could tell, contained nothing of value to his investigation.

Matt rose, stretched, and went to the kitchen. Glancing at the dirty dishes piling up in the sink, he felt a twinge of guilt. Not enough, however, to motivate him to wash them. He rummaged through a cabinet searching for a clean cup, found one and poured some coffee. A long car trip. Thanksgiving. What had Anna said about Alvin? The kids? About … Baltimore? Returning to the dining room, he picked up that letter:

"It was nice seeing you in Baltimore, even though the time we had together was short. Ruth and Luke enjoy their 'Uncle Alvin' very much. They are still talking about you, your place, and especially the oh so very big bed'.

"As for me, I'm very tired but glad the trip is over. Max is with us now. He flew into Mexico City and drove up from there, to join me and the kids. We are preparing for Thanksgiving now. I praise God that we are together and well."

He looked up. *What if this letter's not the last one she ever wrote, but in fact, the first? Doesn't that explain some things? Could it be that Anna and the kids drove through Baltimore on their way to Cuernavaca? Would they have attempted such a long trip by car? Of course they would, if, for some reason they had had to do it.* Back then, Baltimore was a long day's drive from Long Island. It would have been reasonable for them to stop here for the night, and possibly even a few days while visiting Alvin. If the Thanksgiving mentioned was the Thanksgiving of November 1951, and not November 1952, then it would establish their arrival in Cuernavaca. *Yes! That worked.* It also shed some light on Maxim Lieber's movements.

Reaching for the phone, he dialed Bob Winkler's number.

"Hi, Matt," Bob came on the line. "What's up?"

"Wanted to let you know I've made some progress on the Zelinka matter. I've been able to establish that the Liebers left the United States in mid-November 1951, and were living in Cuernavaca by Thanksgiving of that year."

"How did you figure that out?"

"One of the letters that had no date. We'd been assuming it was the last one she ever wrote, but it was *really* the first. It talked about her trip down, their stop in Baltimore to visit Alvin, Max's arrival by plane later and their first Thanksgiving in Mexico."

Bob grunted. "Fantastic. I remember that letter. Sure … that fits all right."

"It also tells us that Max Lieber left by plane and that they didn't travel together. But it doesn't tell us *why* they left in the first place, or *why* they didn't fly or drive down together."

"That's true. What's your next move?"

"One of Anna's letters talks about Branford, Connecticut, where the Liebers had a summer home. Anna told Alvin she was putting it up for sale back in 1952."

"Branford, Connecticut is where Gene Towner's family comes from. He's working on a family tree. At Friday lunches he was always talking about his relatives up there."

"I remember," Matt said. "Is it possible for me to go up there and nose around? Maybe I can turn up somebody who can help us."

Bob thought for a few moments. "Go ahead," he said finally. "But the Orphan's Court may object to the cost. I might have a hard time justifying it."

"Don't worry. I'll keep the expenses down."

Matt hung up and reached for the phone again. Gene Towner was another friend, a lawyer, a sole practitioner and a member of the same law school fraternity. They had met at a frat party for local alumni, and Gene had joined Matt's Friday luncheon group shortly after it was formed. He was a graduate of Yale, and had the mind and education to prove it. He had also attended Johns Hopkins University in Baltimore, and for a few years, had been a practicing engineer with a local engineering firm. Apparently tiring of that, he had enrolled in law school at night and earned a law degree. A history buff, Gene often talked about his family ties to the Connecticut area and the exploits of his ancestors during the Civil War.

"Hi, Matt. Long time no see," Gene was on the line.

Matt described the Zelinka case briefly and told Gene what he needed to do in Branford.

"Brockett's Point? That's out on Long Island Sound. Lots of summer cottages out there."

"Know anyone up there that I can contact for some help? Preferably someone who knows lots of older people in the area."

"Sure. A lady named Janet Gaines is your best bet. She's a family friend. Used to be the Librarian. She's with the Historical Society now. When I want information on some of my ancestors, I talk to *her*."

"Is she smart?"

"You want smart, too?"

"Yeah. If possible."

"Yep. Janet fits the bill."

"Thanks, Gene. If this works out I'll buy you lunch."

CHAPTER 27

Wednesday, February 21, 1990
Towson, Maryland
Baltimore County Public Library
York Road
10:15 a.m. Eastern Standard Time (EST)

TOWSON, A BEDROOM COMMUNITY NOTED for its well-kept homes, good schools, parks and playgrounds, an affordable property tax, and low crime rate, is also the county seat of Baltimore County. The main branch of the public library was always a busy place. Retired men, mothers with kids, unemployed people scouring the daily papers for job leads, students from Towson University, Goucher College and several area high schools, used it for their respective purposes. This morning, Matt was there to search *The New York Times* for the obituaries of Harry Maxim Zelinka and Rose Zelinka.

In the microfilm section, he extracted Rose Zelinka's date of death from his notes — June 25, 1950 — he obtained the correct roll of microfilm and inserted it into a viewer. Moments later, he found her obit in the June 26 issue:

> *"Zelinka, Rose wife of the late Harry M., devoted mother of Alvin and Anna Lieber, and sister of Emily Mildenberg, and Mr. & Mrs. Leo Bettelheim. Service Tuesday, 9:45 a.m. at 'The Riverside,' 76th Street and Amsterdam. Please omit flowers."*

Matt knew Rose had lived at 290 Riverside Drive, in the Borough of Manhattan, New York County, New York, her father had been Morris Bettelheim and her mother's name had been Klava Schwersten. *This obituary gives me three new leads,* Matt thought. *A sister named Mildenberg, who would be an aunt of Alvin and Anna, a brother named Leo Bettelheim, who would be an uncle, and the brothers' wife, an aunt by marriage. One of them might know where Anna Lieber is living. If they're not deceased.*

Harry Maxim Zelinka had died while stationed in Munich, part of Bavaria, Germany. He'd been working as a civilian employee assigned to the Department of the Army. Rose had received the dreaded letter from the War Department dated August 25, 1945, informing her that her husband had passed away on August 11, almost three months to the day after Germany had surrendered.

Matt placed the *Times* microfilm for August 1945 in a viewer, fast-forwarded to August 11th, and scanned the obituary pages for the rest of the month. He found nothing. This puzzled him. It was unlikely that Zelinka's wife had forgotten to publish one. Possibly, since he had died overseas, she'd been in no hurry to plan a funeral service. He decided to search the obits for the remainder of the year to see if anything turned up. A few minutes later, his hunch paid off, in the issue for September 2, 1945:

> *"Zelinka Harry M., on August 11, overseas, husband of*
> *Rose, devoted father of Anna Edith Lieber, and Alvin*
> *Raymond Zelinka, and loving grandfather of Ruth A.*
> *Lieber."*

Short and to the point, printed after Rose, now a widow, had had time to recover from the shock of her husband's death, pull herself together and set about doing what the situation required, her heart no doubt heavy with grief. Matt was glad she had, because it added several bits of information to what he already knew; that as of August 1945 only Alvin's niece Ruth Lieber was living, and that her middle initial was A, probably standing for Anna, after her mother. Alvin's nephew, Luke, had not yet been born. So in 1951, when Anna and the kids came through Baltimore on their way to Cuernavaca, Ruth had been five or six years old. Luke could not have been more than five, and was probably younger.

Matt decided to break for lunch and then begin reviewing telephone books for the Boroughs of New York, searching for listings for Liebers, Mildenbergs, and Bettelheims.

‡ ‡ ‡ ‡ ‡

Wednesday, February 21, 1990
Timonium, Maryland
The Crowley residence
6:15 p.m. EST

"I'm home, Denise!" Jim Crowley yelled as the front door of their pleasant, three-bedroom home slammed behind him.

"Don't —slam the door, Jim," Denise called out, a bit too late.

Jim strolled into the large kitchen in time to watch his wife pour cold water into their coffee maker, add fresh Maxwell House coffee, and flip the switch.

"Dinner will be ready in five minutes," she said. "Baked chicken, mashed potatoes, beets and salad." She turned, examined him over her spectacles and frowned. "You've been walking around with a long face ever since the other night. Did that conversation at Matt's house get you thinking about Bobby again?"

Jim managed a weak smile. "Been thinking about nothing else since."

Pulling the chicken from the oven, Denise filled both plates. "Anything you want to share with me?" She asked hopefully.

Moving up behind her, Jim wrapped his arms around her ample body. "Don't worry. I won't shut you out." He planted an affectionate kiss on the back of her neck and took his seat at the kitchen table.

Denise spooned the mashed potatoes and beets into plates, brought the dishes to the table, placed a full gravy boat next to Jim, and sat. "Well?"

He smiled tiredly. "Well, the conversation repelled me at first; opened the old wound again, and caused all that pain to wash over me. Sort of like a huge wave rushing up on a sandy beach, covering everything in its path."

"Hmm. I knew you didn't sleep much last night." They began to eat.

"If only Bobby hadn't been killed, our lives would be so different. He'd have been married by now. We'd have a sister-in-law and maybe even a couple of nieces and nephews."

Denise ate some mashed potatoes. "I suppose," she said absently.

Jim glanced away for a moment. "If only ... If only ... That phrase ran through my head all last night, like a broken record."

"Um, coffee?" Without waiting for his response, she rose, carried their cups to the coffeemaker, which had just stopped making a bubbling sound, and filled them.

Jim nodded. "But, then I had another thought. I asked myself if I intended to remain unhappy for the rest of my life over this? My brother's dead. If Matt and Dan are right, God didn't have anything to do with Bobby's death. Yet, I've been blaming *Him* all these years."

Denise returned to the table and placed a full cup at each of their places. "Well, anyone who lost a great brother like Bobby would probably have done the same thing." She tore open a packet of Sweet and Low and added half of it and some creamer to her coffee.

Jim reached for her arm. "No! Don't you see? That's rationalizing at its worst. Like saying, 'I wanna go on suffering until Bobby comes back.' How long? Another year? Another five years?" He struck a pose. "God, I'm only gonna give you another five years to bring Bobby back," he said in his best stage voice.

Denise laughed out loud. "That's ridiculous, Jim. You can't go around giving God ultimatums. And another thing. Since you say you don't believe in God any more, why are you talking to Him at all, much less like that?"

He put down his fork and shot his wife once with a finger. "The discussion at Matt's place actually helped. It started me thinking, and I came up with this: the past can't be changed. Actually, it's not the past that has controlled me but the *decision* I made to go on being unhappy about it, to blame God for Bobby's death. I've been letting it control me, thinking of myself as a victim in a senseless tragedy masterminded by an uncaring God."

Putting down her fork, Denise rested her elbows on the table and looked directly at her husband. "You've got my full attention."

"Once I realized that it's within my power to decide how long I want to go on suffering, I understood that it's also within my power to decide whether to go on being a victim or not."

Denise's eyes sparkled. "What did you come up with?"

"I decided that I don't want to be sad about it for another minute. I don't want to be upset with God any longer, either."

"Jim! That's wonderful." Denise said, her eyes moist with joy.

Jim glanced down at his hands. "I've been upset with God for a long time. I have a lot to make up for. I need to get His graces flowing to me … to us, again. A family without God's graces is a family heading for trouble."

Denise studied her husband's face for a moment. "What are you going to do now?"

He exhaled loudly, reached for the phone and dialed a number. "Just listen," he said.

‡ ‡ ‡ ‡ ‡

Wednesday, February 21, 1990
Towson, Maryland
Padonia Village Apartments
2312 Chetwood Circle
6:45 p.m. EST

"Hi, Matt. Jim Crowley," the voice on Matt's phone said.

"Hi, Jim."

"Denise and I enjoyed dinner at your place the other night."

"Thanks. I did, too." Matt, taking a break from the Lieber case, was sitting in his living room watching the evening news on TV, anticipating a radio broadcast of an Oriole-Dodgers exhibition game to follow. An avid Oriole fan, he listened whenever he could, which was often, even though he understood that at this early stage in spring training, the games meant little, except to get the players in shape.

"Are you free for breakfast tomorrow morning after the eight o'clock Mass?"

"Tomorrow? Sure. I can do that. You going to that Mass?"

"Yes. I don't usually go during the week. To be truthful, I haven't been going much lately. Not even on Sundays. But I've been thinking maybe I'll change some things. It can't hurt."

"No," Matt agreed. "It can't hurt. We can decide on a place for breakfast after Mass."

Replacing the phone, Matt said a quick prayer of thanks. He'd been concerned about the other night's conversation. *At least that little talk didn't turn Jim further away from God than he had been. Maybe some good will actually come of it.*

The news over, Matt turned his attention to the Zelinka case again. He had run the names of Lieber, Mildenberg and Bettelheim in telephone books for the Boroughs of Manhattan, Queens and the Bronx. These three Boroughs alone had yielded dozens of listings with the Lieber name; six listings for A. Lieber and ten for Ruth Lieber. The Bettelheim name was plentiful, too. They would all have to be contacted, and since these were home numbers, the calls would have to be made in the evening, since most, if not all of them would be working during the day. If he came up empty, he'd need to tap into the Internet, the worldwide computer network that connects mass media, libraries, government agencies, corporations, universities and private users, and run the names again. *That* would probably yield hundreds of people with the same names, living in other parts of the country.

First, he decided to check with the phone company in Branford, Connecticut, to see if Maxim, Anna, Ruth or Luke Lieber might be listed there. Pulling his telephone over, he dialed the area codes for Branford and Bridgeport, Connecticut. But there were no listings in either place for any of the Liebers.

Who was that lawyer Anna had written her brother about? Arthur B. Weis, Esquire. What had he done for the Liebers? And the realtor who had handled the sale of the cottage? Lars Fromen.

Another call to directory assistance drew a blank. No listing for either of them in Branford or Bridgeport. *Well, after thirty-nine years, it's not surprising,* Matt thought.

He paused for a moment's reflection, lifted the phone again and redialed directory assistance in Branford. "Operator, I'd like the numbers for the Branford Historical Society and the Branford Public Library." He wanted to contact the woman whose name Gene Towner had given him. Janet Gaines had lived in Branford all her life and probably knew almost everybody.

Dialing the number for the Branford Public Library, he asked for the information desk and spoke with a cheerful woman who informed him that Branford was in New Haven County and New Haven was the county seat.

"Where is the county court?" Matt asked.

"The Superior Court for New Haven County? It's in New Haven. Do ya want the phone number and address?"

"Is that where the land records for New Haven County are kept?'

"Yes, sir."

"Then I want it." He wrote the information down as she gave it to him, replaced the phone, and glanced at his watch. Seven o'clock. Checking his notes, he dialed the number for the New Haven Historical Society. No answer. They must not be open in the evenings.

Dialing Branford's directory assistance number again, he asked for Janet Gaines's home listing. Then he dialed that number. No answer there, either. He would just have to try her again later. She was an older woman. He doubted she'd be out late on a weeknight.

To kill some time, Matt decided to go over to the track and run. Then he'd come back, make dinner for himself, and continue his telephone work.

Wednesday, February 21, 1990
Towson, Maryland
Padonia Village Apartments
2312 Chetwood Circle
8:45 p.m. EST

Back from his run, having taken a shower, eaten a light dinner and done a quick check on the status of the Orioles baseball game, Matt again looked at his notes; ten listings for Ruth Liebers and one for a Ruth and Arnold Lieber. He dialed the number for Ruth and Arnold first, got an answering machine and left a message for them to call back, collect. One after another, he called the listings for all the Ruth Liebers. Half an hour later, he had drawn a blank.

What about the US Embassy in Mexico City? Matt thought. He dialed the long distance operator and was connected to an information operator in Mexico City, where he asked for that number. A Spanish-speaking woman answered the phone on the fifth ring. Matt began speaking slowly and distinctly, and was relieved when the woman immediately switched to English. He asked to talk to the American Consul.

"That is Mr. Garcia. He is not in just now. Shall I connect you to Mr. Maher?"

"Who is Mr. Maher?"

"He is the General Duty Officer." Then, "Oh, dear. He is not in either."

"I'm trying to learn if a couple of Americans are still living in Mexico. Can he help me?"

"No, señior. Mr. Maurice Parker of the Consular Section can help you with that. He will find out if they are registered."

"Great. Please connect me to him."

"I cannot, señior."

"Why not?"

"He is also not here. You must call back mañana, err … tomorrow. He will help you."

"Thank you. I'll do that," he said and hung up.

Exhaling slowly, Matt consulted his notes again and dialed the number for the first of some thirty Maxim Liebers in Manhattan, the Bronx and Queens. He let it ring a long time. No answer. He jotted a note to call that number back.

Half a dozen calls later, he glanced at his wristwatch and decided to try Janet Gaines again. *Surely she'll be home by now.* He dialed. An elderly woman answered the phone on the third ring, obviously out of breath. "Yes, this is Janet Gaines."

"Mrs. Gaines, this is Matthew Dawson. Gene Towner gave me your name. He said you had been very helpful to him in the past, and I was hoping you could help me, too."

"Oh, yes. Mr. Towner is working on a family history. His father was Lester Towner. Insurance, I believe. We went to school together. The Towner family was very well thought of in this area before they moved away."

"I'm looking for a woman named Anna Lieber, who had a cottage in Brockett's Point in the 1950s," Matt said. "Her brother died and left her some money." He also gave her the names of Maxim, Ruth and Luke Lieber, Arthur Weiss, the lawyer, and Lars Fromen, the realtor.

Janet thought for a few moments. "None of them sounds familiar to me. But I'd be happy to go over to the Hall of Records and look them up. How can I reach you?"

Matt gave her his phone number. Then, "Look. I'll be coming up there the day after tomorrow. I'll call you when I get into town. Just hold onto whatever information you find until you hear from me."

CHAPTER 28

Thursday, February 22, 1990
Towson, Maryland
Immaculate Conception Church
200 Ware Avenue
8:00 a.m. Eastern Standard Time (EST)

MONSIGNOR AL FLYNN BEGAN THE Mass promptly at 8. He noticed Matt Dawson enter a couple of minutes later and take a seat half way up the center aisle. He also saw Jim Crowley slip into the pew with Dawson a few seconds later.

Since this was a weekday, Monsignor Flynn used the abbreviated Ordinary of the Mass and a lay reader then read a selection from the Old Testament. Today it was Psalm Twenty-Seven, dealing with David's efforts to revive his faith in God while being chased all over Judea by his former mentor, King Saul.

When the lay reader finished, Monsignor Flynn mounted the podium. Sixty years old, of medium height, with brown eyes and a full head of gray hair, he did not usually preach at daily Mass. But, today he had felt a pull to say a few words; someone was out there who was in need of what he would say. As for the words he should use? He paused, opening himself to God, listening. Instantly he knew what his topic should be.

"One of the hardest things for us to do is to place our full trust in God. It's hard because most of us really want to feel in control of our lives. In today's reading we hear from David, who is in big trouble. He's gone through some trying experiences. He's in the process of re-kindling his faith to a point where he can genuinely say, 'the Lord is my light and my salvation; whom shall I fear?' But things have not been going too well for David recently. He'd angered his friend and mentor, Saul, and been forced to flee to the desert and hide out in caves while Saul's troops hunted him. Because of his situation, he'd lost much of his faith, and his ability to trust in God." Monsignor Al paused again, gathering his thoughts.

"When you face doubts and fears, adversity, or an extreme sorrow, such as you feel after the loss of a loved one through death or a spouse through divorce, what do you think of? Do you turn to God and affirm your trust in Him? Do you tell God that you know He has a divine plan and that you're certain He'll work things out?"

Monsignor Flynn sipped from a glass of water placed on the podium by an altar boy before Mass. "God always answers the heartfelt cries of His people. He wants you to know that the sorrow you've been feeling will pass away, by the power of His grace. Your responsibility is simply to be willing to love God despite your sorrow, to look up at the Cross through your tears and say, along with Jesus, 'Thy will, not mine, be done!'

"If you try to manage your life apart from the Savior's wisdom, fearfulness, worry and doubt will *always* be present. In the case of loss of a loved one, sorrow over that loss is magnified, until you think you can't possibly endure it and that your broken heart will never heal. But when you can trust Jesus, who is God, the sorrow you've been feeling will pass away and you'll notice an inner peace like nothing you've ever felt before. Then you will know the goodness of God. And along with the writer of that hymn we sometimes sing on Sundays, you'll be able to say, 'Our God is an awesome God.'"

After Mass, driving to the restaurant at which he and Jim had agreed to meet for breakfast, Matt was pleased. The sermon had been just the right thing for Jim to hear. One glance at Jim's face as they left the Church and Matt knew the words had not been lost on him.

As Matt turned onto York Road, a discernment came to him, like the clear tone of a bell carried on an autumn breeze. Monsignor Flynn's words had meaning for *him* as well. He now understood that failing to put his total trust in God had affected his ability to see that his life wasn't over; that even though his family was no longer there and he was alone, his future could still be bright.

‡ ‡ ‡ ‡ ‡

Thursday, February 22, 1990
Towson, Maryland
The Towson Diner
York Road
8:35 a.m. EST

The Towson Diner was a popular spot for locals to conduct business over breakfast. That morning, it was crowded. Matt and Jim ordered their meal, drank coffee and waited. From the busy kitchen, mouth-watering aromas of pancakes, sausages and bacon drifted out to them.

"What you said the other night?" Jim began. "About the death of your sister? Do you really believe those things, Matt?"

"About God not causing evil? Yeah, I really do. That's one of the basics of Christianity. To think otherwise about God doesn't make any sense."

"What about the part where God allows evil to occur and then turns it to good?"

"Yes. I believe that, too. Look, nobody can completely understand how God works. Especially regarding the death of someone close to us. That's a troublesome problem. But God always seems to bring something good out of these things."

Jim was quiet for a moment. Then, "I've never really developed a relationship with God. My brothers' death hasn't helped any. It's been a sticky issue for me."

Matt acknowledged Jim's comment with a nod as the waitress brought their food and refilled their coffee cups. The two men ate in silence for a while, until Jim spoke again. "You and Dan? It's been a real eye-opener for me knowing the two of you. I've never hung around with guys who not only *believe* but try to *live* their faith, too." He buttered a piece of whole-wheat toast and took a bite.

"Thank you. You know, I really value our friendship. When I was down, you and Denise, Dan and Barbara were a source of emotional support for me."

"Do you pray much, Matt?"

"I didn't used to. Now I do. Every day, for about an hour."

"I stopped praying after my brother died. I'd like to start again but I'm not sure how. What do you suggest?"

Matt picked up his coffee cup and sipped from it. "What's been helpful for me is to begin with a prayer of thanks for all the good things God has done for me. Because I believe that in justice I owe Him at least that much. Then I read from the Bible. After that I might say a rosary or talk to God, or just meditate. Sometimes I do all three."

"But I don't know any prayers."

"No? Well, you probably know a few. Like the Our Father? You could start there."

"Why that one?"

"Because according to the Bible, that's the prayer Jesus personally taught his disciples. Say that. Then talk to Jesus as if He's a friend who is right there with you. Talk to God, too. You might say something like: 'God, I want you to be close to me. I acknowledge that I'm a sinner and I need your forgiveness. Thanks for sending Jesus to redeem us from sin and open the gates of Heaven. I ask Jesus to come into my heart and life as my personal savior and friend."

"Okay," Jim said. "I'll try that."

Matt sipped his coffee. Recalling the words of Monsignor Flynn's sermon that morning, another thought struck him. He gazed at Jim over the top of his cup. "And you might add this: I place my entire trust in You, and ask You to take control of my life and guide me from now on."

‡ ‡ ‡ ‡ ‡

Thursday, February 22, 1990
Timonium, Maryland
Padonia Village Apartments
2312 Chetwood Circle
10:00 a.m. EST

Back in his apartment an hour and a half later, Matt eagerly resumed work on the Lieber investigation. He was leaving for Connecticut the following day, and the thought of a trip out of town for a few days had energized him. Also, the words of the sermon he'd heard that morning had bolstered his flagging confidence. For the first time in a very long time he felt … well, hopeful.

He was calling Melissa Saffron. Martin Saffron answered the phone and he put down the receiver to call his mother. She came on quickly.

Matt got the conversation rolling. "Were you and Alvin good friends, Mrs. Saffron?"

"Yes. I knew Al for forty years. He spent every Christmas with us. Knew he had a sister, a niece and a nephew. I never really knew where she lived, though. Al told my sister she had moved to Mexico."

"He did? What's your sister's name, Melissa?"

"Mary O'Grady. Mary's in Florida just now. She'll be there for a while."

"Is there some place down there I can reach her?"

"No. She won't be available until she returns at the end of March."

Matt thought that was a bit unusual but didn't press it. Melissa didn't seem to want him to disturb her sister. He took down Mary O'Grady's home phone number. *Surely I'll be finished with this search by the time O'Grady returns from Florida.*

"Alvin had several friends in the area who used to work with him," Melissa went on.

"Jeannette Sellman was one. Al spent his Thanksgivings with her and his Christmases with us. Jeannette also met his sister."

"Sellman? I noticed her name and telephone number among his papers."

They talked for a few minutes. He tossed Melissa several questions about Alvin, trying to prime the pump of her memory, but without much success. Disappointed, he thanked her and hung up. *For someone who had been friendly with Alvin for so long, she doesn't seem to know a lot about him. Or, she doesn't want to reveal what she knows.*

Alvin Zelinka's personal telephone book contained two numbers for his former boss, Howard Keller. Matt tried the work number first but was told it was not in service, so he dialed the home number, got an answering machine and left a message.

Next, he dialed the number for another of Alvin's work friends, Richard La Course.

After several rings an elderly man answered. Matt explained who he was.

"Yeah, Al and me was friends at work and socially, since about 1955," La Course said. "We worked at the District office in Towson."

"Did Alvin ever mention his sister, Anna Lieber, to you?"

"Yes, a few times. Said she moved to Mexico a while back."

"Did he mention where she might have been living recently?"

"No. He didn't talk much about himself or his family. We mostly talked about the people at work and what was goin' on there. Stuff like that. Then after he retired, we'd talk about cameras and daily events. The only thing I remember him saying about *her* was that they hadn't had any contact for years. That was about it."

"Did you know Howard Keller?"

"Keller? Howard Keller was Division Chief, Personnel, Towson. That was the DOD's Baltimore Contract Management Area office. It's not there anymore, ya know."

"I didn't know that."

"Al and I, we went way back. I been retired for almost eighteen years. We used to go to breakfast together at the Towson Diner on York Road."

"I know where *that* is. As a matter of fact, I ate there this morning."

"Ya did?" Reassured, La Course warmed to the subject. "Al and I were members of the Baltimore Camera Club, too. Course I'm older than Al. I'm in my late 70s now."

"Well, you sound real good, Richard. Is there anyone else from that club who might have been friendly with Alvin?"

"No. Al was kind of a loner. He didn't have many friends. Another thing. That club's not active now. It was goin' great in the late seventies but folded up later on."

"Thanks for talking to me, Richard." Matt gave La Course his number and hung up.

‡ ‡ ‡ ‡ ‡

Thursday, February 22, 1990
Timonium, Maryland
Padonia Village Apartments
2312 Chetwood Circle
12:30 p.m. EST

"Embassario de Los Estados Unidos," a cheerful Spanish voice came over the line.

Matt began talking in English. As before, the woman on the other end immediately switched to fluent, though thickly-accented English. He was envious. He had studied French and Spanish in high school and continued with Spanish for a year in college. In the early seventies, he had spent two weeks working in France and had become fluent in French. But because he had not spoken either language in years, he'd lost the ability to speak them.

Matt was directed to a woman clerk named Herminia. After telling her the story, she connected him to a Consul named Ken Sachett.

"If they're registered, I can find them for you, Mr. Dawson," he said. "I'll run these names on our register this afternoon."

"I'll need an address or a telephone number or both."

"Well that's a problem. Under the Freedom of Information Act, I can't divulge that information without their permission," Sachett replied. "Actually, I can't even tell you whether they're here or not." He sounded apologetic, but he was not going to break any rules, even in this situation.

"What *can* you do, then?" Matt asked, mildly annoyed.

"I'll run the register. If they're here I can send them a letter informing them you're looking for them. That way, they can get in touch with you. It becomes their choice. Give me your address and telephone number, and I'll include it in my letter."

Matt gave him the information, explained again why he was looking for the Liebers, and hung up. Government regulations designed to protect people's privacy, while necessary, were not always helpful and could actually get in the way at times. In this case, suppose the Liebers didn't want any contact with Alvin or anyone working on his behalf? They might not get in touch with him, and if they didn't, Anna Lieber would lose her inheritance.

He decided to spend some time calling all the Bettelheim listings that he'd found in the telephone directories at the library. It occurred to him that New York City was made up of six or seven Boroughs. The County library in Towson had directories for only three: Queens, Manhattan, and the Bronx. *What if the Liebers are in the New York area but living in another Borough? Well, if nothing turns up, I might have to expand the search. For now, I have my hands full.*

His first call was to Eric B. Bettelheim's number in Manhattan. A machine answered. Frustrated, Matt left a message for him to call back, collect.

He dialed the number for Hanna Bettelheim and an elderly man with a very thick Jewish accent answered. He informed Matt that Hanna had died two years ago, but she had not been related to anyone named Rose Bettelheim; she was a Bettelheim by marriage. Her husband had passed away many years ago and had no relative named Rose. Matt thanked the man and hung up.

Next, he tried the number for Ralph W. Bettelheim on 44th Street and an operator gave Matt a working number for him in Nyack. He dialed and Ralph himself answered.

"No, I don't believe my family is related to anyone named Rose Bettelheim. I did a family tree some years back. No Rose turned up," he said. "I'm related to Professor Fred Bettelheim of Adelphi University. He gave me lots of help. Also gave me a long history. Let me get it and see if there's anything about a Rose in there." He left the phone and returned minutes later. "Sorry, Mr. Dawson," he said apologetically. "There's no Rose anywhere in my line."

CHAPTER 29

Friday, February 23, 1990
Timonium, Maryland
Padonia Village Apartments
2312 Chetwood Circle
9:30 a.m. Eastern Standard Time (EST)

"MR. HARRIS, PLEASE," MATT WAS calling John Harris at the Maryland State Accident Fund. Harris was the attorney who referred the Zelinka matter to Bob Winkler. Matt thought it would be less than thorough if he didn't touch base with him.

"He's on the other line." The secretary sounded busy. "I'll have him call you back."

Hanging up, Matt rose, went to his stereo and inserted a tape. It was a composition by Johan Sebastian Bach, *The Saint Matthew Passion*. He had first heard of this music in the British novelist, Ethel Mannin's 1948 novel, *Late Have I Loved Thee*, a book recommended to him many years ago by his sister, Rosalie, who had been five years older than him. Matt and his sister had not had much in common in their reading material. But this story, about a rich, somewhat jaded playboy-writer who underwent a spiritual conversion after the death of *his* sister whom he dearly loved and for whose demise he felt responsible, was a pleasant surprise. The protagonist converted to Roman Catholicism, entered the priesthood and began a life that led to rejection by his family and friends, who could not understand how anyone could place God at the center of his life and live only for Him. Mannin had written that Bach's *Passion* was the most beautiful music she'd ever heard.

Matt's phone rang as he was fixing a fresh pot of coffee. The voice on the line announced itself as Eric B. Bettelheim. "I got your message. Actually I may be related to Rose Bettelheim. My grandfather had several sisters and one of them *was* named Rose."

"Can you find out from him? Maybe he'll know where Rose's daughter is living now."

"Well, my grandfather's dead. But my father might know something. I'll talk to him and call you back later today."

Matt was elated. Was this the break for which he'd been waiting?

The aroma of freshly brewed Folgers coffee filled his apartment. Matt poured himself a cup, added milk and a bit of sugar, brought it to the table and sat, listening to the strains of *The Saint Matthew Passion* and thinking about the case that he'd been spending so much time on. It *had* become interesting, but it had also become tedious as he opened one avenue of inquiry after another and followed leads that went nowhere. He'd recently read that an investigator always traveled roads that terminated in dead ends, never knowing in advance which were going to pay off and which were not. Still, every lead had to be followed. *Somewhere along the line I'll get lucky*, he thought.

His phone rang again. John Harris was returning his call. "I thought Al Zelinka's estate had been wrapped up a long time ago," he said.

"No. Bob Winkler was never able to locate Alvin's sister, Anna Lieber."

"No? Her husband, Max Lieber is probably dead. I think there was an obituary in *The New York Times* about it."

This was surprising news. "Do you know when he died?"

"No. But it wasn't too long ago. Heard he died from a lung problem. I think the family returned to New York."

"I understand you went to Mexico looking for the Liebers."

"Yeah. Didn't learn anything, though. No one down there in Cuernavaca knew anything about them. Disappointing, but not unexpected. A lot of time had passed."

"What did you do while you were there?"

"Visited the Embassy in Mexico City and requested their help. Then, we drove to Cuernavaca and talked to the people living at the address I had for the Liebers. They had never heard of the Lieber family." He paused. "There were other things I could've done if I'd had more time to spend down there," he said pensively.

Matt perked up. "Like what?"

"Well, there's an American community in Cuernavaca. Some of those people have been there for a long time. Leftist types. Writers and poets. Socialists and Communists like Max Lieber. It might have been helpful to talk to a few of them."

"Did you ever find out why the Liebers left the United States?"

"No. And that bothered me. They didn't seem to have had any reason to go; at least none that I could see."

"Did you develop any leads about where they might have gone after Cuernavaca?"

"No. I drew a blank down there. Changed jobs right around that time. Went to work for the State and turned the file over to Bob because I knew he had lots of experience with estate work. Then I got married a few months later and forgot about it."

"Did Alvin ever talk about his sister or his niece and nephew?"

"That was another strange thing. He didn't talk about them much. He *did* tell me they had come to visit him for a few days way back in the fifties, on their way to Mexico. Al said *that* was the last time he ever saw his sister."

"Did he tell you why they didn't keep in touch?"

A long pause ensued. Then, "Alvin couldn't stand his brother-in-law. Max Lieber's politics were leftist. He was a radical liberal who believed in government control of everything. Always very critical of America, too. Al didn't like that. He was a federal government employee all his working life. And very patriotic, too. So he spent less and less time with his sister. When Al's mother died, he went up to New York for the funeral. There was a disagreement with Max about something. That ended it for Al with his brother-in-law."

"So, you think they might be back in this country, living in the New York area?"

"Well, if my memory isn't deceiving me about that obituary, yes."

"Thanks, John. I'll check that out. If you remember anything else, please call me, okay."

Matt hung up. Harris's admission that his trip to Mexico had not been as thorough as it could have been, worried Matt. But if Max Lieber had died, it wouldn't matter. Max's obituary might lead him directly to Anna Lieber. He allowed some excitement to show.

The telephone rang again. To his surprise, Eric B. Bettelheim was on the line. Matt hadn't expected him to call back so quickly.

"I spoke to my father about this. My grandfather's name, by the way, was Joseph. My dad said he was an only son, but he had several sisters. One of them was named Rose."

Matt's eyebrows shot up. "Terrific. Did she marry a Zelinka?" He tried to sound just the way an investigator would, although he didn't actually know how that was.

"That's the bad part. She *did* marry, but her husband's name was Baranski. Rose had only one girl. Her name was Esther, not Anna. She died early. Rose died in New York a few years ago. She also had a son named Eddie. He's dead, too."

Matt's heart sank. He remembered the elderly Bettelheim in New York, with the incredibly sad voice, to whom he'd spoken by telephone. Wife, daughter, son-in-law, niece and nephew; all dead. Eric Bettelheim went on, "My grandfather's father's name was Jacob, not Morris, so it's clear I'm not related to the Rose Bettelheim you're looking for. Dad says there's no one named Morris in our family."

"Well, thanks for taking the time to help, Eric. I really appreciate it."

"Not at all," Eric answered. "Let me know how you make out with this." He hung up. *Another promising lead that didn't pan out,* Matt thought. *Well, at least it didn't take long to find that much out.*

‡ ‡ ‡ ‡ ‡

Friday, February 23, 1990
Towson, Maryland
Baltimore County Library
York Road
12:05 p.m. EST

Matt was back at the Baltimore County library in Towson. John Harris had said he'd seen Max Lieber's obituary "not too long ago." Pulling microfilm, he ran the obituary sections for the past ten years in both *The New York Times* and *The Baltimore Sun*. Three hours later, he left the library disappointed and convinced that Harris had been mistaken.

Home soon after, he slipped into a chair in front of his computer, booted up and went on the Internet. He had recently read of the existence of a Social Security Death Index on line. *Maybe I should've started here. If one or both of the Liebers are deceased, it might've saved me a lot of time.* He surfed through the Altavista and Google search engines, found nothing in either one, and went to Lycos.com, where he discovered what he was looking for, a Social Security Death Index that could be searched without a fee. Punching in both Anna's and Max's names, he was relieved to see no record for either of them. *That's a good indication they're still alive, although it's not conclusive. If no one claimed their Social Security Death Benefits, they wouldn't be listed even if they had died.*

‡ ‡ ‡ ‡ ‡

Friday, February 23, 1990
Timonium, Maryland
Padonia Village Apartments
2312 Chetwood Circle
3:30 p.m. EST

The drudgework of a search is never fun. Of course, this being Matt's first investigation, he didn't yet know about drudgework. It was all new and, if not exciting, at least interesting to him. He spent the rest of the afternoon making phone calls to more than two dozen remaining Maxim Liebers listed in the New York area phone books, preferring to have this part of his work concluded before his trip to Branford.

Finally finished with that, he called E. Lieber, obviously a woman, listed on East 74th Street, Manhattan, but was told she was not related and had no relatives named Max or Anna.

Next came M. J. Lieber on West 21st Street, but the ringing phone went unanswered.

Then he called the number for Arnold Lieber, a doctor on West 88th Street. He was not in his office. Matt left word and made a note to retry both numbers later.

Turning to the Liebers listed in Brooklyn, he tried the number for M. Lieber on West 5th. A woman told him she was a Lieber by marriage, but her husband had died. She did not recall any Max or Anna in his family. However, as they talked she did recall that her husband had an uncle named Max, who had died before 1950, which was the year that she and her husband had married. Matt gave her his phone number, just in case.

Phone calling continued for several more hours with only a pause for a light dinner. When the Brooklyn listings were exhausted, he returned to the number for Ruth Lieber in Manhattan. She was listed as a psychotherapist. He had called yesterday and had left messages on an answering machine. Since one of the listings in the telephone book showed her name linked with Arnold Lieber, a home number no doubt, Matt realized that she was a Lieber by marriage and not the niece of Alvin Zelinka. He crossed her name from his list.

Matt was now becoming alarmed. He had applied the full sweep of his imagination to this case, but nothing at all useful had been uncovered. He decided to go over to the track to run, come back, pack a bag and go to bed early. He had a plane to catch in the morning, and flying had never been a pleasant experience. He intended to pray that the pilot scheduled to fly that plane would get a good night's sleep that night.

CHAPTER 30

Saturday, February 24, 1990
Branford, Connecticut
The Ramada Inn
Business Park Drive
4:20 p.m. Eastern Standard Time (EST)

A THICK, GRAY FOG ROLLING in off Long Island Sound threatened to bring traffic to a stop as Matt Dawson approached Exit 56, off US Route 95, near Branford.

Just what I need, he thought. *A white-out to start off my trip.* Visibility quickly became so limited that he turned his rented, red Pontiac Grand Am off at the first of Branford's two exits and began searching for a motel. If it had not been for the fog, he'd have driven around for a while, checking out the town, trying to imagine the Lieber family doing the same thing so many years ago. Soon, the dark shape of the four-story Ramada Inn on Business Park Drive loomed in the grayness. A few drops of rain began to fall as he locked his car, and by the time he'd reached the office, the rain had become a torrent, raking noisily across the asphalt parking area and sidewalk, drenching him.

His room on the fourth floor was typical Ramada. A kitchenette and bathroom flanked each other at one end. Two queen-sized beds, a dresser, and a TV were in the middle. A round table, two chairs, and a lamp filled a corner at the far end next to the window, providing a work area for those who were there on business.

Grabbing a fresh towel from the bathroom, he vigorously dried his dripping hair, tossed the wet towel aside, and examined the kitchenette with its stove, refrigerator and sink. *This Ramada has no restaurant,* he thought. *I'll either have to buy groceries or go out to eat. Maybe I'll do both.*

Matt figured he'd be staying at least two days. After unpacking his things and placing his shaving gear in the bathroom, he pulled the Zelinka file from his briefcase, found Janet Gaines's number and dialed it, catching her just as she was arriving home from work.

"Hi, Mr. Dawson. How do you like our thriving metropolis?"

"I just got in a few minutes ago, Janet. Fog's so thick I couldn't see anything."

"Too bad. It won't lift until tomorrow. I've got some information for you."

"Hold on while I get my pen and pad. By the way. Nobody ever calls me Mr. Dawson anymore. Please call me Matt."

"Okay, Matt. On my lunch break yesterday, I drove over to New Haven and looked at land records. Found out that on December 9, 1950, Maxim and Anna Lieber bought a property in Brockett's Point called Riptide Cottage. A lawyer named Archibald Marshall was involved, but it's not clear which party he represented."

Matt broke into a broad grin. "Now we're making progress. Where's Marshall's office?"

"He doesn't have one. It might've been in Branford; more likely over in Bridgeport. He retired some years back and moved away."

"Oh. What else, Janet?"

"The Liebers sold Riptide Cottage in December 1958, to Herbert H. Larch and wife. It looks like Archibald Marshall and T. Holmes Bracken were the lawyers involved, but I can't tell which one represented Lieber and which one represented Larch."

"Well, do we know where Bracken's office is?"

"He's dead."

"Hmm."

"Yeah, but a lawyer named Howard Zorski took over Bracken's practice after he died. I think he got all of Bracken's files."

Matt almost hated to ask the question again. "How can I reach this Zorski?"

"Want his number?" Janet asked brightly. Before he could answer she gave it to him.

"Okay. Larch and Zorski. Those are things I can follow up on."

"Thought you'd be pleased. Oh. That realtor, Lars Fromen? There's no record of him in Branford. He either died or moved away. Also, the lawyer Arthur Weis? No record of him, either. Probably dead, too."

"It's been a long time. That's a good bet."

"By the way. There's a notation on the deed that as of 1958 the Liebers were living in Warsaw, Poland."

Matt's mouth flew open. "Did you say Warsaw, Poland?"

"That's right. Make any sense to you?"

"No, it doesn't. Nothing about this case makes much sense to me."

"The land records don't show any other land transactions in their names."

"Janet, Gene Towner was right about you. You've been really helpful. Thanks very much. Are you free for lunch tomorrow?"

"Yes."

"Good. I'll treat you to a nice Sunday dinner. Name a good place."

"The Triple-T Diner's nice. It's just a few doors down from the Historical Society office on Main Street. Say about one fifteen?"

"Sounds good."

"And if you're looking for a great restaurant to have your dinner this evening, I've always liked the Pasti Cosi over on South Montowese. The owner of the place is also the chef. Does some interesting things with fish and meat."

"I'll check it out," Matt replied. "See you tomorrow."

Stunned, Matt sat on the bed, grabbed two pillows, propped them behind his head, and lay back. *Things sure change quickly. This information is right outta the blue. I don't know what to make of it.*

Picking up the ice bucket, he strolled down the hall to the ice machine and filled it. Back in his room, he dropped three cubes into a plastic cup, added water from the tap and took a sip. His eyes came to rest on the coffee maker in the kitchenette. He poured two glasses of cold water into it, added Folgers coffee from packets provided by the motel, and flipped the switch.

As he waited, Matt pondered what he'd learned. Janet Gaines said the records showed the Liebers buying Riptide Cottage in December 1950. Anna Lieber's mother had died that year.

Anna and Alvin would have inherited cash, furniture and everything else their mother had left, including the proceeds of any life insurance policy. Anna probably bought Riptide Cottage with the money she inherited from her mother. Speculation? Yes, but it made sense.

Then, in November 1951, the Liebers left the United States for Mexico. Matt had no explanation for that.

Later, Anna had written to Alvin that the cottage was up for sale and he could take anything he wanted from it. *Could the place have remained on the market until 1958? It was possible. If the real estate market were bad in the Branford area, or if Anna had changed her mind and decided to hold onto the cottage, it could have remained unsold, and possibly rented out.*

But, when they sold it in '58, the deed showed them living in Warsaw, Poland. *Why did they go from Cuernavaca to Warsaw? I can't explain that, either. But records don't lie.*

The comforting aroma of freshly brewed coffee filled the room. Matt fixed himself a cup, sat at the worktable, and dialed the number given him by Janet Gaines for Howard Zorski. When Zorski came on the line, Matt explained his mission yet again and finished by saying, "I'm looking for one of the files of T. Holmes Bracken, who had been involved when the Liebers sold a piece of real property in 1958."

"T. Holmes Bracken, Esquire. He was quite a character around here. We used to call him 'Speed' for reasons only another lawyer might appreciate." Zorski chuckled at his lawyer's humor. "He died back in '68. I got his files. But, they were all severely damaged in a flood a few years ago. It rains a lot around here. I'm a judge now. When I left law practice last year, I threw all that damaged stuff out so I wouldn't have to store it any longer."

Matt digested what he'd just heard. "Thank you for your time, Judge."

"Sorry I couldn't help, Mr. Dawson."

Another dead end, Matt thought. *Been a lot of them so far. But, several leads look promising. All I need is for one of them to pan out.* He did not feel the confidence his thoughts conveyed.

‡ ‡ ‡ ‡ ‡

Branford, Connecticut
Saturday, February 24, 1990
The Ramada Inn
Business Park Drive
7:00 p.m. EST

The rain had ceased, but the fog had turned cars and pick-ups in the parking lot into indistinct gray shapes as Matt left the Ramada Inn that evening. Everybody knows real men don't ask for directions. Nor did this car have one of those new Global Positioning Systems (GPS), which a guy probably invented so he wouldn't *need* to ask for directions. So it was with some difficulty that he found Montowese and followed it to the other end of town, where it turned into South Montowese. It then wound through a mile of foggy Connecticut countryside to the Pasti Cosi, the inviting Italian eatery Janet Gaines had suggested.

The restaurant's decor adhered to the popular trend of the time: low lighting, some glass, lots of dark wood paneling and brass railings. Tasteful prints of scenes in Rome, Milan, and Venice decorated the walls of the dining rooms.

"I'd like a quiet table. Somewhere out of the way," Matt said to the young hostess.

She smiled. "You're the second person to ask that tonight. Right this way, sir."

She led him to a small room off the main dining area containing only four tables. Each was decorated with white linen table clothes and red linen napkins. Red candles protruded from empty wine bottles in the center of each table. Only one other person was in the room. The hostess handed Matt a menu. "Enjoy your dinner," she said, and left him there.

Situating himself at the table, he glanced over at his fellow diner, an attractive woman with red hair, green eyes, pale skin and a nicely-formed chin. She was wearing a simple black skirt below a light green, cowl-neck cashmere sweater that matched the color of her eyes and spoke of money. Matt guessed her age at about forty-five. Over the years, his instincts about people had sharpened. He could sense when someone was hurting. *She's got the saddest eyes I've ever seen,* he thought.

The wine steward arrived, screening his view momentarily. "Buona sera signore? Io mi chiamo Carlo. May I get you something from our wine cellar?" Tall and dark, he looked very Italian in a long-sleeved, white shirt open at the collar, a red vest, and black slacks. Matt scanned the wine list. Because it was the only wine he recognized, he ordered a glass of Sangiovese, a wine of dubious distinction from a lesser wine producing province in Italy.

Ann Kelly's thoughts had been interrupted; first, as the hostess seated a male diner at the table next to hers, then by the wine steward as he took the man's drink order. She eavesdropped as the new arrival ordered wine, pondered what she'd just heard, shrugged and drained her wineglass. *He looks an interesting chap. Not the type to make the first move, though. Probably backward about coming forward. Well, here goes nothing.*

After jotting down Matt's order, the wine steward left. The redhead leaned toward him.

"Excuse me. I couldn't help overhearing. What a coincidence! I've ordered the very same wine."

"Really?" A slow smile spread across his face. Her British accent was unmistakable. Feeling somewhat mischievous and suddenly wanting to impress the lady, he decided to go all out. "A very good choice," he said, doing his best imitation of Sean Connery playing James Bond. "It's a nice ruby red wine grown in the Italian Province of Emilia." He put the best face possible on their choice. "I've had it before and enjoyed it."

Ann's eyes widened in surprise. She studied him with frank interest, and as she did, she felt her stomach flutter. *Good grief! That hasn't happened since the night I met Sean.* Flustered, she dropped her gaze momentarily, but quickly regained her composure. "Are you alone?"

"Yes. Are you?"

She nodded. "It seems a shame for us to eat by ourselves, when we're sharing such … intimate surroundings."

Intimate? Did she select that word deliberately? Matt wondered. He was not about to pick up a woman in Branford, Connecticut. Still, he was neither married nor committed to anyone, and he needed to meet local people. She had come into his life uninvited and un-introduced, but as far as Matt was concerned, a woman with a face and figure like hers could do *that* any night of the week and he would not complain.

"Would you like to join me?" He asked, tossing aside his Sean Connery voice.

"I'd be delighted." She rose, picked up her empty wineglass and came to his table. He noticed her height, and that she moved with an athleticism not generally found in women her age. Settling herself across from him, she held out a slender hand. "I'm Ann Kelly."

"Matt Dawson. Nice to meet you." Her grip was firm, her skin soft and pleasant to the touch. *My evening's looking up,* he thought.

The wine steward returned carrying a full bottle of Sangiovese in an ice bucket. He smiled approvingly at the seating change. The woman held up her glass for a refill.

"Signora? Grazie," Carlo said. Taking her glass, he set it on the table next to Matt's, and as both of them watched, he poured the wine slowly and sensually, until both glasses were a bit more than half-full. As he lifted the bottle away, Ann raised her green eyes to Matt's. For just the briefest of moments, he felt as if he might fall into them and drown.

Their waitress arrived as the wine steward departed. Ann ordered the House specialty; lobster a la vodka. Matt ordered steak Marsala, thick beef strips sautéed with green peppers and mushrooms, in a sauce of sweet, dark wine imported from Sicily.

As the waitress moved away Matt asked, "Do you live in Branford?"

"No." I'm from Chappaqua, New York. But I spent a couple of summers here when I was a little girl." She met his gaze candidly. "What about *you?*"

Matt concealed his momentary disappointment. He felt slightly uncomfortable. It had been a while since he'd been alone with a woman. Ever since his ex-wife had left, he had led a celibate life, even during the year after the divorce had become final, when he had begun dating again and had dated several women. Quickly tiring of dating, he had settled into a comfortable existence as a bachelor. He cleared his throat. "I'm from Baltimore; staying at the Ramada Inn for a few days."

Ann nodded. "This is a bit of a nostalgia thing for me. I've not been here in almost forty years. What brings *you* to Branford?"

Matt sipped from his wineglass. He saw no reason not to reveal the purpose of his visit. "I'm looking for someone. A family who used to own a cottage in Brockett's Point."

"Brockett's Point? Why, that's where *my* family used to spend summers. What's the name of the people you're looking for?"

"Lieber. Maxim and Anna Lieber."

"Signora? Signore?" The waitress had returned with their salads, an order of fresh Italian bread on a cutting board and two small bowls containing olive oil, garlic and oregano, for dipping the bread. "Your dinners will be ready in just a few minutes," she announced as she moved away again.

Matt noticed that his new companion had fallen silent, busying herself with the bread and olive oil. He reached for his water glass and caught her glaring at him with an intensity that was decidedly disconcerting. Puzzled, he tried a smile. She returned it, but with less friendliness than she'd displayed moments before. It was then that Matt saw the large, heart-shaped diamond and the gold wedding band on her left hand. *The lady's married. And she obviously comes from money.* To get over the awkwardness of the moment, he spoke without thinking. "Did your husband come along with you?"

"My husband passed away recently," she said crisply. "At Christmas."

"Oh. I'm sorry."

The waitress arrived with their meals, generous portions of sumptuous Italian cooking. She arranged the dishes decoratively in front of them, like an artist setting out objects for a still life, asked if there was anything else she could get for them, and left.

Matt began to eat. But, as he attacked his steak Marsala, he realized that Ann was staring at her lobster rather than eating. A minute later, she threw down her napkin. "Damn! I didn't think the mere *mention* of my husband would set me off like this." She managed a half smile. "I seem to have lost my appetite as well." She rose from the table. "You *must* excuse me. Another minute and I shall bawl like a baby. Good night!" She turned and hurried from the room without looking back.

Dumbstruck, Matt watched her disappear through the door. He raised his wineglass in a mock toast to her departed back, drank deeply and set the glass back on the table. A rueful grin appeared on his face. *Didn't know I could still impress the ladies like that.* He glanced at the dinners the waitress had so artfully spread on the table. *Well, at least my steak's delicious. Maybe I'll ask for a doggie bag for the lobster since it looks like I'm stuck with the check.*

CHAPTER 31

Sunday, February 25, 1990
New Haven, Connecticut
The Superior Court for New Haven County
9:30 a.m. Eastern Standard Time (EST)

RAIN WAS FALLING HEAVILY AS Matt, trying not to dwell on the fact that his misadventure of the previous evening had not been an auspicious beginning to his trip, entered the Superior Court Building at 121 Elm Street, New Haven. This was where the land records for New Haven County were kept. Because of the importance of land records to local lawyers, realtors, and title searchers, the workplace was open seven days a week.

Removing his wet coat, he draped it across a nearby chair and approached the long counter under which were housed the index volumes. Selecting the one for 1950 through 1960, he quickly found the deed Janet Gaines had been so excited about:

> "To all People to Whom these Presents shall come: Greeting: Know Ye, that We, MAXIM LIEBER and ANNA EDITH LIEBER, both of the City, County and State of New York, but presently residing at Warsaw, Poland ... "

Great! He thought. *That established conclusively where they were in November of 1958:*

> "... do give, grant, bargain, sell and confirm unto the said HERBERT H. LARCH and JEAN W. LARCH, unto the survivor of them and unto the survivor's heirs and assigns forever."

And *there* was another lead. Two people who might know more about the Liebers. He turned the page and examined the signatures of Maxim and Anna Edith Lieber, scrawled there on November 13, 1958. Arthur L. Wertzel, an American Consul, had witnessed the Liebers' affidavit at the US Embassy in Warsaw, People's Republic of Poland.

Picking up the deed book, he carried it to the copy center and wrote a note for the clerk asking for a copy to be made on Monday morning. A few minutes later, he was in his car again, window wipers pushing aside the drizzle, heading back to Branford with a feeling that things were looking up.

Sunday, February 25, 1990
Branford, Connecticut
The Ramada Inn
Business Park Drive
11:00 a.m. EST

Back in his room, his mood a bit brighter, Matt decided to clear up one loose end; Howard Keller, Alvin's former boss. He thumbed through his notes, came up with Keller's home number and dialed it.

Keller had been a division chief in Quality Control at the Department of Defense (DOD). Alvin had worked for him until caught in a reduction in force (RIF) in 1976 and transferred out of that division. But they had remained close friends. An elderly man with a voice to match came on the line and identified himself as Keller. After Matt explained the purpose of his call, the old man warmed to the task.

"Al and I were friends right up until he died a few years ago," he announced proudly.

"Did Alvin tell you where his sister and her family might be living recently?"

"Well, he spoke of Anna, his niece and nephew a lot. I think he told me they were in Guadalajara, Mexico. He never mentioned his brother-in-law though, that I can recall."

"Never told you if his brother-in-law had died?"

"Nope. A few years back, my wife and me went to Mexico for our fortieth anniversary. I told Al we were goin'. He asked me if I'd look his sister up. But, he never got around to giving me an address."

"Thanks, Mr. Keller. If you think of anything else, please give me a call back." Matt gave him the number and hung up, then reached for the phone again.

"Directory assistance. May I help you?"

"Branford, please."

"Yes, sir. What listing?"

"The number for Herbert Larch or Jean Larch." There was a pause. Then the operator's voice again: "I have no listing for a Herbert Larch. But there's one for a J. W. Larch."

Matt quickly dialed the number she gave him and waited. Five rings, six, seven. No answer. *I'll try again later,* he thought. Picking up the local telephone directory, he looked up LARCH, found the number the operator had just given him and copied down the address; "26 Orchard Lane, Branford."

What next? The United States Embassy in Warsaw. He dialed "O" and asked the operator how to dial Warsaw, Poland.

"You should dial OO for an overseas long-distance operator," she responded.

He did that and an overseas operator gave him the number for the Embassy. "I'll connect you, sir. One moment." After what seemed like two or three minutes, she was back.

"The Embassy is closed for the weekend, sir."

Frustrated , Matt hung up and slumped in his chair. Through the window, he could look down into an empty courtyard, barren of flowers, but with brown patches of grass mixed with the green. The rain had ceased but the day was bitter cold. No sun broke through the thick clouds to warm the earth. During the past few days, he had learned a lot of new things, none of which were doing him any good at the moment. He had talked to people, snooped around a bit, and racked his brain. Then, he had done it again. But he had not found Anna Lieber.

He felt the sadness welling up inside him again as he thought about how much he missed his kids. Despite all the troubles with which he'd been dealing, he had made an effort to keep in touch with them. They returned his calls and even called him occasionally. But like most young people, they were busy with their own lives. When prompted, they talked about themselves, but expressed little interest in what he was doing or how he had handled the problems he had faced; selling off the horses, winding down the farm, its eventual sale, paying off as much of the accumulated debt as he possibly could, his withdrawal from law practice, and, of course, the divorce from their mother. To go through what he had gone through had taken a great deal of courage. Looking back, he was proud of the way he had handled things: confronting and resolving each problem. But they had no idea. *If they knew, they might be proud of their old man. If they understood how much I miss them and want them close to me ...* It wasn't that they rejected the love he was freely offering. They were simply deflecting it, perhaps believing that he had been responsible for many of their problems; or, in an increasingly unhealthy society where more and more women were raising kids without fathers, that a relationship with their dad was trivial and his love unnecessary.

And they definitely did not understand his growing relationship with Jesus. They seemed embarrassed by his occasional references to God. Unconsciously or perhaps consciously embracing post-modernist thought, they were comfortable with profanity, references to sex, vulgarity and any of the bizarre subjects that were topics of conversation for some. But any reference to the deity made them uneasy. They had accepted the secular humanist view that mentioning God must be avoided. *Peculiar,* he thought. *It's the same in Communist and Socialist countries; a society without God. Is someone trying to impose that kind of a society on us here under the guise of multiculturalism and fairness?*

Matt, grappling with his black cloud of depression, forced himself to concentrate. *It doesn't do any good to dwell on the past or on what might have been,* he told himself. A brief period of prayer proved helpful. Finished and feeling better, he poured another cup of coffee, added creamer and sugar, and carried the cup back to his worktable in the corner.

By his watch, he still had over an hour before his lunch with Janet Gaines. Pocketing his note with J. W. Larch's address on it, he headed for the elevators. *Was this Jean Larch, the former co-owner of Riptide Cottage?*

In the lobby, he asked for directions to Orchard Lane, retrieved his rented Pontiac and drove the short distance to a pleasant, two story brick apartment building surrounded by tall, leafless maples. *Is this the right person?* He wondered, as he locked his car. *If it is, will she even let me in or will she slam the door in my face before I can explain what I want?*

A row of mailboxes occupied most of the wall space in the cramped vestibule. The name LARCH was printed above the box belonging to apartment 1-D. He moved along the narrow hall, found that apartment and pressed the bell.

"Who is it?" The voice of an elderly woman called out from behind the door.

Matt identified himself and told her why he was there. A few moments passed. Then the lock was turned and the door pulled back to reveal a small, round woman with snow-white hair, bright eyes, thin lips with a downward curve at the corners, and a serious face.

"Yes, Mr. Dawson, I'm Jean Larch and my husband was Herbert Larch. Please come in." She closed the door behind him and led him to a small living room decorated in the style of the '70s. Matt took the chair to which she pointed. Jean Larch sat heavily, directly across from him, on an ancient couch covered in material with a faded floral pattern. Without giving him time to ask any questions, she said, "My husband died a few years ago. I've had a mild stroke since then, and I have some trouble remembering minor things. Recent things."

"How's your memory for the 1950s?"

"Well, let's find out. You just fire away with any questions you have and I'll try to answer them."

Matt took a deep breath. "I'm looking for Anna and Maxim Lieber. According to the deed that was signed when you bought Riptide Cottage in November 1958, they were living in Warsaw, Poland."

"Yes. They didn't come to settlement. I remember *that.* The closing was delayed because the deed had to be sent to Poland for their signatures. But, I never actually met them."

"Did you ever hear anything from them or anything about them after that?"

"No. But I'd heard a rumor that Max Lieber had been a Communist spy."

"What?"

"Yes. Apparently he had to leave the country rather quickly. A fake ambulance came down the hill one night and took him to the airport. A plane flew him out. It was in all the newspapers."

Matt reached inside his blue blazer and pulled out a pencil and small pad. "Do you know where the plane took him?"

"No. The FBI was looking for him. This was in the early '50s. That's all I know."

"Was anyone living in the place when you bought it, Mrs. Larch?"

Jean Larch thought some more. "No. It had been empty for a while. Before that, a family named Dahlmeier had rented it. Lived there for several years. They had two lovely girls and both got married. They're living in Guilford, now."

"Do you know their married names?"

"I'm afraid not. That was a long time ago, and I had no reason to remember them."

"What about Mr. and Mrs. Dahlmeier?"

"They both died some time ago." She was beginning to sound a bit tired.

"Just one more question, Mrs. Larch. Do you recall the name of the lawyer who represented the Liebers?"

Jean Larch paused for a few moments, the strain of trying to resurrect things that had happened so long ago, events not thought about in many years, clearly visible on her lined forehead. Matt held his breath. This was crucial.

"I'm sorry, I don't, Mr. Dawson." She shook her head. "But my son, Richard, and his wife live in the cottage now. It was too much work for me so I deeded it over to them a few years ago. Richard has the original deed and papers. *He* might be able to tell you."

"Can you give me Richard's number?"

Mrs. Larch opened her personal address book and read off a number. "I'll call him myself and tell him to expect your call."

"Thank you. You've been very helpful." He rose from his chair.

"Not at all. Thank *you*."

"For what?"

"For coming to visit me, of course. At my age, I don't get many visitors."

He hesitated, uncertain what to say next. The silence lengthened. He just wanted to say goodbye and leave.

"Will you tell me something?" She asked finally.

"If I can."

"What will you do if you actually find them?"

He sat back down. She did the same.

"Well, I suppose I'll start by telling Mrs. Lieber that her brother died."

"And then?"

"Then, I'll tell her that he left her some money. Why do you ask?"

She shook her head. "Oh, don't mind me. When you're as old as I am and realize that time is running out, you tend to want to live vicariously, you know? Through other people. I just wondered, that's all. What *you'd* say. What *they'd* say." She stood and extended her hand.

Matt took the wrinkled hand and told her where he was staying in case she recalled anything else. Then, "After I find them, may I come back and tell you all about it?"

She tilted her head slightly to one side, and the downward curves at the corners of her mouth were suddenly transformed. "Call before you come. I'll have some coffee ready."

Clouds had settled in again as he walked to his car. He couldn't quite suppress his excitement. *Jean Larch may be a lonely old lady, but she had added some valuable information to what I already knew. Max Lieber might have been a spy. If that were so, and if this ambulance incident happened in 1951, that would explain why the Liebers had left the United States so suddenly.*

How long did they stay in Mexico? A guess would be about a year. That's when Alvin had received the last letter from his sister. Did they then go to Poland? That now seemed likely. And if they didn't want people to know it, *that* would explain their lack of further contact with Alvin, and Alvin's reluctance to talk about them. *It would also explain why it's been so difficult for me to find them,* he thought.

Sunday February 25, 1990
Branford, Connecticut
The Triple-T Diner
Main Street
1:15 p.m. EST

"This place has been here over fifty years," Janet Gaines said. "I come in frequently for breakfast. Sometimes for lunch, too. At my age, I don't cook much anymore." They were drinking coffee and waiting for their lunch orders. Janet was of average height but thin, and her hair had turned completely gray, but her eyes had the sparkle of an inquisitive person for whom life still held the promise of further adventures. Matt judged her to be in her early seventies. She wore a bulky, red sweater under a navy blue cloth coat, a gray fur hat and matching gray boots.

"I tried that restaurant you suggested. Had dinner there last night. You were right. The food's great." Matt was wearing his blue blazer with a dress shirt open at the collar, a dark green cable knit sweater, and jeans. Outside, rain began to fall again.

Janet beamed. "That's one of my favorite dinner spots; especially on a Saturday night."

The waiter returned with their food "Here's the chow, folks," he said, letting the dishes clatter onto the table. He left, leaving them to sort out the order. She had asked for a cup of clam chowder and half a tuna salad sandwich on rye bread. Matt had requested the Branford Burger on a sesame seed bun, with French fries and Cole slaw.

Janet gawked at the huge Branford Burger and passed it to Matt. "Yuck," she said.

"What?"

"All those calories. When I was as young as you, I could eat like a lumberjack, too."

Matt grinned. "Well, I'm not *that* young. Just very active." He passed her cup of clam chowder across the table. "Spoke to Jean Larch a few minutes ago."

"Was she helpful?" Janet asked as she bit eagerly into her tuna sandwich.

"Yes. Told me Max Lieber had been a spy for the Communist Party."

Janet's head snapped up. "Oh, really?"

"Yep. Look, Janet. I need your help to run down several pieces of information."

"This is beginning to get interesting. I'll be happy to do whatever I can," Janet promised.

"Larch told me an ambulance took Lieber away. Said it was written up in the newspapers. Can you check the local paper for an article about Max Lieber that might have appeared in November 1951? The Liebers disappeared around that time. I want to pin down the date."

"*The Branford Review's* been publishing since the '40s. So has *The New Haven Register*. Their back issues are on microfilm. I'll check both."

Wind drove sheets of rain against the diner windows. They listened to the sound for a moment, and watched as droplets struck the glass and careened downward, merging with other rivulets, gathering speed, forming tiny, random waterfalls until eventually disappearing at the sill outside.

Matt shivered and picked up his coffee cup. "When I was in the Land Records Office this morning, I ordered a copy of that deed. I'm curious about the witnesses. They might be people I can contact. I'll go back over there tomorrow and pick it up."

They ate for a while in silence. Then Matt thought of something else. "One more thing. It'd be helpful to find an older person who has lived at Brockett's Point for a long time. I'm looking for someone who might have known the Liebers back in the early fifties."

"I'll see what I can do. What are *you* going to do next?"

"I'm gonna try to get a line on Archibald Marshall. If he's still alive, I need to talk to him. After that, I think I'll drive out to Brockett's Point and take a look at Riptide Cottage."

CHAPTER 32

Monday, February 26, 1990
Branford, Connecticut
The Ramada Inn
Business Park Drive
9:45 a.m. Eastern Standard Time (EST)

Aᶠᵗᵉʳ ᵐᵒʳⁿⁱⁿᵍ Mᴀss ᴀᴛ ᴀ local Roman Catholic Church, and breakfast at the Triple-T Diner, Matt returned to his room and dove into his notes. *Archibald Marshall, Esquire had been a local lawyer. According to Janet Gaines, he was involved in both ends of the Riptide Cottage land transactions; when the Liebers bought it in 1950, and when they sold it in '58.*

In quick succession, he dialed numbers for directory assistance in Branford, Bridgeport and New Haven, but was told there were no listings for Archibald Marshall in those places. Nor was there a listing for a lawyer named Marshall with any other first name. But there was a lawyer named James Marshall in North Haven.

Next, Matt obtained and dialed the number for the New Haven County Bar Association. A young woman came on the line. "Do you have a current listing for a lawyer named Archibald Marshall?" He did not explain why he wanted to know.

"No, we don't," she said. "Have you tried the Chief Clerk's office in Hartford? They keep a master list of all lawyers' names, addresses and telephone numbers." She gave him a number and hung up.

He was quickly connected to the Chief Clerk in Hartford, who found that they had a listing for Marshall at 80 East Main Street, Branford. "This list was updated as of January 1, 1990," he said. "But that doesn't mean Marshall was there at that time. We're fifty miles from there. Why not call the Superior Court in New Haven? They may know the man personally."

He dialed that number and his call was routed to a woman named Grace, who spoke with a thick New England accent. "I've been heea a long time." Her voice made Matt believe her. "I knew Aachie Maashall. Went out with him a few times afta his wife died. Nice guy. Good dancah too. We hadda ball."

"Do you have his address and telephone number?"

"No, I don't. He retiyad some yeeas back. Went ta Florida or someplace. I don't know wheah. He nevah asked me ta go with him. If he had, I mighta. Ya neva know." She laughed a low, throaty laugh tinged with just a trace of regret.

"Does the court have a list of attorneys' names and addresses?"

"Yeah, but his name's not on it. Not since he retiyad. I awreddy checked."

"Do you know if he had a son who might have taken over his practice?"

"As fah as I know, he didn't have any kids. Nobody took ova his practice. He jest wound things down and one day, he left." She sounded genuinely melancholy.

"I'm sorry, Grace," Matt said, because he felt the need to say *something*. "Thanks for your help."

"No trouble at all, Mr. Dawson," she said and sighed deeply.

‡ ‡ ‡ ‡ ‡

Monday, February 26, 1990
Branford, Connecticut
East Main Street
11:30 a.m. EST

A light drizzle had begun to fall as Matt parked his car on a side street and walked around the corner to 80 East Main Street, Branford. A garish sign above the door proclaimed it to be Colbert's Hair Salon, A Unique Boutique, specializing in wigs, bangs, turbans, hats, and scarves. The door had a brass mail slot, left over from a previous tenant with better tastes. The proprietor was a small, chunky woman who wore her blonde hair, probably a wig, in a billowing beehive hairstyle reminiscent of the '60s.

"I've been at this location for seven years," she said. "I don't know who had it before that." As they talked, her eyes were fastened on Matt's head. "Your hair looks a bit thin. Can I interest you in a nice wig?"

Back in his car, Matt drove to North Haven, which was, as its name implied, north of New Haven. The rain had ceased. The law office of James Marshall, Esquire was in a bustling shopping center next to a residential area. Matt passed a bench where an elderly couple sat staring icily at several teenagers with orange hair and nose rings. He dodged a female runner circling the block and found the place.

Marshall was a tall, thin man in his middle forties. "Nope. I'm not Archibald Marshall's son. And I'm not related to that gentleman."

"Did you know him?"

"Sure. He was still practicing law when I first hung out a shingle, but he retired a number of years ago and moved away. That's the last I ever heard of him."

‡ ‡ ‡ ‡ ‡

Monday, February 26, 1990
Branford, Connecticut
The Ramada Inn
Business Park Drive
4:30 p.m. EST

Fog was again drifting in off the Sound as Matt pulled into the parking lot at his motel. The day was moving right along, but he didn't seem to be getting anywhere. He decided to call Richard Larch and see if he could add anything to the equation. Back in his room, Matt dialed, and a woman who identified herself as Richard's wife answered the phone. "I'll get him," she said.

When Larch came on the line, Matt introduced himself. "I spoke with your mother yesterday. Did she tell you about my visit?"

"My mother? No, I haven't talked with her for a couple days. What can I do for you, Mr. Dawson?" The friendly voice was that of a man perhaps fifty years old, with at least a high school education and possibly some college. Matt told him the purpose of his call and asked if he still had the original deed.

"Yeah, the old deed's in a box in the attic. It'll take me about a half-hour to dig it up."

"Well, I'm here in Branford. Suppose I drop over there tonight? Say around seven o'clock."

‡ ‡ ‡ ‡ ‡

Monday, February 26, 1990
Branford, Connecticut
Riptide Cottage
7:05 p. m. EST

A thick, wet fog had blanketed the area by the time Matt turned into the macadam lane on which Riptide Cottage was located. The narrow road ran downhill to some hardwood trees and a thin spit of sand that marked lands' end. Only one other house stood between Riptide Cottage and the murky waters of the Sound. From somewhere out on that cold body of water, an occasional muffled foghorn could be heard as ships, even though equipped with radar that enabled them to "see each other in a fog" enhanced their ability to warn each other of their presence.

There were no streetlights here to illuminate the gray night. Despite an eerie yellowish glow from a light at the front entrance, turned on by Richard Larch in anticipation of his arrival, Matt had some difficulty, because of the fog, finding the walkway leading to their door.

"My parents' attorney in this was Archibald Marshall," Larch explained in answer to Matt's question after introductions had been made. "He retired a few years ago; went down south somewhere. Myrtle Beach, South Carolina, I think."

"How many pages are there to that deed?"

Rummaging through a dusty cardboard box that he'd retrieved from his attic, Richard pulled out a brown envelope and removed a yellowing document. "One-two-three-four-five. Five pages."

"Is the name of another lawyer on any of the papers you have there?"

"Well, yes. A cover letter from Arthur P. Weiss, Esquire. He represented the Liebers. His office was in New Haven before he died. A lawyer from New York hired him to handle the transaction here. I don't know who *that* was."

"Your mother spoke of a rumor that Max Lieber was a spy. Know anything about that?"

"Oh, sure. It was common knowledge around here. What I heard was, Max Lieber was in the business of duplicating books. That's how he got into trouble. He copied some army manuals and was caught. Had to leave the country. The way I heard it, he faked a heart attack right here at Riptide Cottage and was taken to the airport."

"When did that happen?"

"Back in the early '50s, I'm pretty sure."

"Anything in those papers about the lawyer in New York City who hired Weiss?"

Richard was silent as he examined the old deed and settlement sheet, and thumbed through several letters from the lawyers. "Sorry, Matt. Nothing."

"Do you think your mother might recall his name?"

"She might. My dad knew, but he passed away a while back. I'll call my mom tonight and see. I doubt it, though. She had a slight stroke last year. Claims it hasn't affected her long-term memory, but I know it has. If she remembers anything, I'll call you back later tonight at your motel."

Matt thanked Richard and stood to leave. Richard extended an invitation to stay for dinner, but Matt declined. "That fog out there bothers me. I'd best go back to the Inn before it gets any worse."

"Oh, yeah. The fog," Larch said. "Branford's famous for them. Like pea soup. They come in off the Sound so thick that sometimes you can't see your hand in front of your face. And wet, too. Stay out in one for ten minutes without a raincoat and your clothes will be soaked clear through."

‡ ‡ ‡ ‡ ‡

Monday, February 26, 1990
Branford, Connecticut
Riptide Cottage
7:45 p.m. EST

Pea soup is right, Matt thought as he stepped off the Larch's front porch. Although his car was parked less than a hundred feet away, it was not visible in the mist. He hesitated, momentarily regretting not having paid more attention to his direction when he arrived earlier. But, he now knew more than he had a few minutes ago. *Somewhere in New York City there's a lawyer who may know where Max and Anna Lieber are. I need to talk with him.*

There was no moon. Everything was shrouded in gray-white mist. Visibility was down to less than three feet. He left the feeble circle of brightness cast by

Larch's front door light wishing that he'd brought along one of those really powerful new flashlights. The boxy, lantern type would have been perfect. Uneasy, he began feeling his way with his feet. Farther down the hill, he heard the muffled sound of thick, black water tumbling onto the beach and slapping against a nearby retaining wall.

Reaching the end of the walkway, he turned right, searching for the gravel driveway that would lead him to his car. He had taken only a few steps when he almost ran into a person standing perfectly still at the entrance to the Larch's driveway. Startled, he froze.

"Watch where you're going, will you?" The rude voice of a woman snarled. He could make out only that she was wearing a pale green raincoat, its wide collar turned up, concealing most of her face. Without another word, she turned and walked away, quickly disappearing in the mist.

Who was that? Matt wondered. Had it been one of Larch's neighbors out for a walk after dinner? No. Her voice had sounded vaguely familiar. He found his car, fumbled with his keys, and dismissed the incident from his mind. *The drive back to the Ramada in this stuff is gonna be interesting,* he thought.

‡ ‡ ‡ ‡ ‡

Monday, February 26, 1990
New York City, NY
Borough of Queens
8:00 p.m., EST

Marvin Jonathan Freedlander sipped from a can of Coke and stretched his six foot two inch frame out on the rear seat of his customized, dark green, Ford Aerostar van. The jacket to his gray pinstriped suit, designed by Oleg Cassini, lay carefully folded on the cushion beside him. Willie Preston was at the wheel. Freedlander was on his way to a Lion's Club in Queens, the largest service club in that Borough, and it would not do to appear before his constituents with alcohol on his breath. His presentation tonight, entitled, "Crime in the Big Apple," was a canned speech that he had adapted for many different audiences with a minimum of effort.

The big Aerostar was an adaptation of Freedlander's own creation. He had loaded it with fancy gadgets; a well-stocked bar, a small refrigerator, a microwave, two phones, TV, fax machine, and a laptop computer. John Foreman sat across from him, a red, felt-tipped pen in his hand, checking his boss's speech for possible gaffes and making notes about how Freedlander might field the queries that would inevitably arise during the question and answer session following his talk.

They were driving across Thirty-first Street, heading east in light traffic. As they passed the Broadway intersection, one of the phones rang. Freedlander frowned. It was his private line. Not even his wife had that number. He leaned forward and picked it up.

"Yes?"

"Marvin Jonathan, where are you?"

"Ann? My Gawd! I've been thinking about you. Where are *you?*"

"I'm in Branford, Connecticut. Congratulations. I read about the Albertson case in the New Haven newspaper. You must have had that jury eating out of your hand."

"Another case notched in the win column," Freedlander said modestly.

" Sorry I missed our post-case tête-à-tête, sweetie," Ann leered brazenly. "You *know* how much I enjoy those occasions."

"I *did* call you. Your maid told me you'd gone away for a while."

"Maybe we can re-schedule. I'll take care of you when I return. *If* I can fit you into my busy schedule, that is."

Freedlander grinned broadly. "What's on your mind, doll?"

"Something has come up. It might present a bit of a problem for both of us," she said, a trace of alarm in her voice. "I met this man in a restaurant last night. Picked him up, actually. Well, almost, and—"

Freedlander guffawed. "You're a female predator, Ann; literally and figuratively."

"Perhaps. But, if you'll just shut up for a minute and listen, I'll get to the point."

Marvin Jonathan stared out the rear window as Ann filled him in. When she finished, he expelled a deep breath. "But you don't know *why* he's looking for your parents. It may be something perfectly innocuous."

"I doubt that. I saw him again tonight, too. Outside the cottage my parents owned when we spent summers here. He's on a mission of some sort and he's persistent. It's a problem. *My* father was wanted by the FBI because he spied for the Soviet Union and had information about Alger Hiss. *Your* father was my father's lawyer and close friend for years."

"How could this be a problem for *you?*"

"Sean Cornelius put some language in the trust instrument about me being a good little girl in order to keep my share of his estate. No scandals. No embarrassment. If that case becomes a matter of publicity again, my name could come up. If it does, his mother and distasteful siblings could move to terminate my trust fund. They'd stand to gain millions. And as for you, sweetie, if your father's past becomes public knowledge, just how many votes do you think you'll get when you next run for political office?"

Marvin Jonathan grimaced. "How did you know I might run for an office, Ann?"

"I know *you*, Marvin Jonathan. That great big ego won't be content to stay in the DA's office much longer."

Freedlander paused, annoyed that Ann understood him well enough to have figured that out. *But she doesn't know that I intend to run for Mayor in the next election, or that I'm close to making the announcement. She's right as far as she went, though.* If some enterprising reporter decided to investigate, information about his father's Communist Party background could severely damage his chances. Then, there was that other matter; the one his family had buried so deeply that no one ever mentioned it. If *that* came to light, he could kiss any further political career goodbye. He'd never be elected dogcatcher. Even his job as DA might be threatened.

"Ann? Where's this guy staying?"

"At the Ramada Inn, off Exit 56. I'm there also, but he doesn't know *that* yet."

"Stay put. I'll send you some reinforcements tomorrow."

Freedlander, his brow furrowed, replaced the phone. He didn't speak.

"Problem?" Foreman asked, glancing at Freedlander over his bifocals.

"Could be." He slid the glass partition back so that Preston could hear, and quickly filled them in.

"The Liebers are ancient history," Foreman said when he'd finished. "What possible reason could anyone have for wanting to locate them?"

"I don't know, damn it!" Marvin Jonathan ran a hand over his coal black hair. "But my gut tells me it doesn't have anything to do with Alger Hiss." He took out a gold cigarette case, extracted a hand-rolled cigarette made from the leaves of the organically grown Nicotianas he cultivated in his office, and lit up.

"Do *you* know where the Liebers are?" Foreman wanted to know.

"No." Freedlander exhaled smoke toward the roof of the van. "But, Ann is their daughter. *She* knows, of course. I agree with her. Whatever's going on could pose a problem."

"You want I should go over to Branford and help her watch this guy?" Preston asked.

"Yeah," Freedlander responded, like a genial host arranging a weekend outing. "Find out what he's up to. If it's any kind of a threat, we might have to take more drastic measures."

As the van pulled into the large parking lot in front of the Lion's Club's meeting spot, another thought occurred to him. Beyond Foreman and Preston, only two other people knew of his connection to a notorious Communist Party lawyer, and the dark secret hidden in that lawyer's past. One was a nameless, faceless old man who still lived in the American community in Cuernavaca. The other was Ann Kelly. He was not concerned about the men in this van with him. He knew enough about them to insure their silence. But the other two? Either one or both might, if they were so inclined, attempt to dictate the terms of his political future. He did not want anyone to have that kind of power.

Monday, February 26, 1990
Branford, Connecticut
The Ramada Inn
Business Park Drive
8:10 p.m. EST

Alone in her room, Ann Kelly hung up the phone, lay back on the bed and stared at the ceiling, thinking about her meeting with Matt Dawson the evening before and her just-concluded conversation with Marvin Jonathan Freedlander. Her mood was dark; as dark as the room, illuminated now only by the dull light from a small bedside lamp.

What disturbed her most was that she didn't know *why* Dawson was looking for her parents. Silently, she cursed herself for not having had the presence of mind to find out before bolting from the restaurant. *The man probably thought I was daft, running off like that. I should have finished dinner and invited him back here. Lots can be learned from a man while in bed with him.*

Another thought occurred. Should she call her mother? She had not had much contact with either her parents or her brother since their return from Poland in '68. When her parents had left Cuernavaca in early 1954, she had been sent to Birmingham, England, where she attended primary and grammar schools. After that, she entered University, where she read for a degree in marine biology. Then, she had embarked upon a career of sorts, before returning to America after meeting Sean years later. By then, her parents had become strangers to her. The old adage, "absence makes the heart grow fonder" had not worked for them. Instead, during their long period of separation, love had grown cold. She moved to pick up the phone, but decided against making the call. *What will it tell them? That I almost picked up some chap in a restaurant last night who said he was looking for them? Smashing. No. I'd better wait a while to see what develops before I go alarming them with this.*

CHAPTER 33

Tuesday, February 27, 1990
Branford, Connecticut
The Ramada Inn
Business Park Drive
1:00 p.m. Eastern Standard Time (EST)

MATT HAD BEEN CAUGHT IN a freezing downpour as he walked back to his hotel after lunch. His hair was wet, his shoes were soaked and he was chilled. Grabbing a towel from the bathroom, he went to the phone and dialed the number for the American Embassy in Warsaw. A woman who spoke perfect English, but with a Polish accent answered. Matt told her who he was and what he wanted.

"If you'll wait, I can check to see if they ever registered," she said. "If they did, I can tell you something about them. If they were never registered, I'll connect you with one of the Consuls who can help you from there."

While he waited, Matt pulled off his shoes and socks, hung his wet socks over the back of a chair, and dried his hair as best he could. He was about to pull off his damp tee shirt and underpants and replace them with dry underclothes when another woman came on the line. "This is Karen Christianson. I'm a Vice Consul here, Mr. Dawson. I understand you're looking for the Maxim Lieber family?"

Shivering, Matt yanked a blanket off the nearest bed and wrapped himself in it. "That's correct, Ms. Christianson. They would have arrived there sometime after 1951."

"Well, they're not in our records. These records go back to 1948. But it's not unusual for Americans to come over and not register."

He found it difficult to conceal his disappointment. Assessing the situation quickly, he decided to be completely candid with her. "While I was looking for these people, I came across an unusual bit of information about Maxim Lieber."

"Oh? What's that?"

"That he was thought to have been a Communist spy, and had fled the United States with the FBI looking for him."

Vice Consul Christianson sucked in her breath audibly. Then, in a somewhat guarded tone, "Could you hold the line for a moment more? I can check another record."

She was gone for almost five minutes. Matt, who'd been drenched several times since his arrival in Branford, wondered if he'd catch pneumonia. What he wanted most was a hot bath and some dry clothes. He was stewing over that predicament when she returned. "Mr. Dawson, we have a record of Maxim, Anna and Luke Lieber entering Poland. We have an address for them. I can't give it out because of the Freedom of Information Act. But I *can* attempt to contact them and put them in touch with *you*, if you like."

He had expected as much. "Let's try that. But, if Max Lieber doesn't want to be found, they probably won't contact me unless you make it clear just why I'm trying to reach them."

"I understand. I'll try to be *very* clear," she said.

Frustrated, Matt gave her his contact information, thanked her for her help and hung up. The call had not been as productive as he'd hoped. It *had* established that Max, Anna, and Luke had actually arrived in Poland, but didn't tell him where they were living, and it gave him no information on their daughter, Ruth Ann. He frowned. What had happened to her? Well, if the Embassy could put the Liebers in touch with him, all his questions would be answered.

After a hot bath, Matt changed into dry clothing. Then, he decided to check in with Bob Winkler and give him a progress report. He dialed Bob's number.

"I was gonna call you, Matt. But, I didn't know where to reach you in Branford."

"I'm at the local Ramada Inn," Matt said. "Should've checked in with you before, but I haven't had a chance. Things have been moving along briskly." He gave Bob the number.

"You know," Bob said, "Alvin was a federal government employee. The Federal Employee's Group Life Insurance Company has been sitting on a small term policy on Alvin's life. Anna Lieber is the beneficiary. Been trying to get them to pay it over to the estate, but they don't want to do it until they finish their investigation. They're trying to locate Anna, too."

"What have they done so far?"

"Don't know. I spoke to a Miss Chevalier over there yesterday. Told her I had *you* working on it. She asked if maybe you guys could compare notes and coordinate efforts. Will you call her and kinda go with it from there?" He gave Matt a number in Washington, DC.

"I'll call you back later today," Matt said.

Tuesday, February 27 1990
Branford, Connecticut
The Ramada Inn
Business Park Drive
4:15 p.m., EST

"And Jean Larch told me that Max Lieber might have been a spy." On the telephone from his room, Matt was again talking to Bob Winkler. "Her son confirmed it. If that ambulance incident they described happened back in '51, *that* would explain why the Liebers left the United States and moved to Cuernavaca."

"Sounds plausible," Bob said. "But how long did they stay in Mexico?"

"Don't know yet. Maybe about a year. That's when Alvin got his last letter from Anna."

"Okay. Did they then go to Poland?" Bob asked thoughtfully.

"That seems likely. And if they didn't want people to know it, that would explain the lack of further contact between Anna and Alvin, and Alvin's reluctance to talk about them with anybody except a few of his closest friends."

"It would also explain why it's been so damn hard to find them."

"Yeah," Matt agreed. He thought for a few moments. "The Embassy in Warsaw told me they had the arrival record for Anna, Maxim and Luke, but not Ruth."

"No record for Ruth? Didn't she go to Poland with her parents?"

"She would have been five or six when they left the US. We know she was with them in Cuernavaca. It's unlikely they would have left her there when they headed for Warsaw. They must have made some other arrangements for her."

"According to my file," Bob said, "Alvin took a trip to Mexico in 1978. But as far as I know, he went to Acapulco, not Cuernavaca."

"Right. That's where he met the Waltons. But Alvin never told them he had a sister in Mexico. If she'd still been there it would have simply been normal conversation to mention her."

"So why didn't he tell them?"

" Maybe because the family had defected. He didn't want anyone to know."

"Alvin probably would have wanted to visit his sister while he was down there in '78. But there's nothing in the file one way or the other. Do you think he *did* go see her?"

"I'd put money on it. *If* she was still there."

"Well, we now know that Anna had been in Warsaw, Poland until at least 1958 when the Liebers sold Riptide Cottage to the Larches."

"Yep. They may have stayed there longer. But as of '83 Alvin was listing her on a designation of beneficiary form as next of kin with a Cuernavaca address. I learned that from Miss Chevalier this afternoon."

"Why do you think he did that?"

"Maybe to throw off the FBI or anyone who might have been searching for Max. Alvin may not have liked his brother-in-law, but he could have been an accomplice in keeping Max and Anna's whereabouts a secret."

"Or maybe he was just too embarrassed to reveal that his brother-in-law had been a spy and that they'd gone behind the Iron Curtain."

"Or was it because the Liebers went back to Cuernavaca later?"

Matt's thoughts returned to his recent conversation with John Harris. "Bob? John Harris told me there were other things he could've done if he'd had more time to spend in Mexico."

"Hah! What did I tell ya?"

Matt reached for the phone book. "I'm scheduled to fly back to Baltimore tomorrow. I think I'll book a flight to Mexico City instead."

"Keep in touch," Bob said.

CHAPTER 34

Wednesday, February 28, 1990
Providence, Rhode Island
US Interstate Route 95
10:00 a.m. Eastern Standard Time (EST)

EARLY THE NEXT MORNING, MATT checked out of the Ramada Inn and took the Interstate northeast toward Providence's T. F. Green State Airport. It wasn't until he was approaching the New London exit that he noticed the white BMW in his rear view mirror. The car had been back there for some time. He frowned and decided to keep an eye on it.

Flipping on the radio, he tuned into an FM music station and listened to Johnny Mathis singing *The Twelfth of Never* and Gloria Estefan doing *Here We Are*. A short time later, the BMW passed him on an open stretch. He couldn't see the occupants because their car windows were tinted almost black. Instead of pulling away and eventually leaving him behind, the BMW settled in three cars ahead and stayed there. *That's unusual*, he thought.

Several minutes passed. As he neared the Warwick turnoff, the BMW let him overtake and pass it, and fell in line about four cars behind him. It stayed there the rest of the way.

At the airport, Matt turned in his rented car and headed for the American Airlines ticket counter, where he bought a round trip ticket to Mexico City with brief stopovers in Atlanta and Dallas-Fort Worth. *Two stops*, Matt thought as he turned from the ticket counter. *The cheapest ticket I can get. That oughtta make Bob happy.* An hour later, he boarded a Boeing 747 for the first leg of his trip.

The plane was almost full on the flight from Providence to Atlanta. Matt was somewhat uncomfortable. So many people in so small a space made him feel cramped. Settling back, he decided to make the best of it. He revved up a wounded but healing sense of humor and laughed at his impatience to be there even though the trip had just begun.

The massive jet landed at Atlanta's Hartsfield International to refuel and take on passengers bound for DallasFort Worth. On this leg, the plane was less crowded. Matt amused himself by attempting to flirt with one of the pretty flight attendants. But there was a younger guy several rows back, a weight-room type, who had her attention, so Matt backed off, pouted a bit, and then consoled himself with the thought that she was much too young for him anyway.

A three-hour stopover awaited him in Dallas-Fort Worth before his connecting plane, an Aeromexico flight to Mexico City's Benito Juarez International Airport. To fill the time, Matt decided, since it was now almost 4:00 p.m. Baltimore time, to have an early dinner. He spotted a restaurant called The Lazy Longhorn, went inside and indulged himself in a two-inch thick sirloin steak, a jumbo baked potato and a huge salad. *No telling when I'll find time to eat again,* he thought, chuckling at the unsubtle rationalization. For desert, he ordered a rich chocolate mousse and joked with the waiter about the calories.

"It's been a long time since I've eaten a meal like that," Matt said as the waiter placed his check on the table.

The young man laughed. "Well, everything's big in Texas. Even our meals."

Boarding on the connecting flight went smoothly. He found his seat, stowed his bag and blue blazer in the overhead compartment, and settled into the ample seat, beginning to feel like a veteran traveler.

Sitting back, he glanced out the Plexiglas window. Night had fallen, but lighting on the airstrip made it easy to see. As the McDonnell Douglas MD-80, with a hundred and fifty passengers aboard, lumbered to its take-off point, Matt began to wonder what he was doing here; why, exactly, was he traveling to Mexico? He shrugged. His instinct was telling him that he just needed to work this case; to walk on the terrain that the subjects had walked on, and ask questions of people who could be expected to know something, but may or may not know anything. Soon he heard a satisfying high-pitched whine as the engines accelerated to full power. The plane rolled down the runway and was quickly airborne.

The flight from Dallas-Fort Worth to Mexico City took place in the dark. Nothing was visible outside Matt's window. He tilted his seat back, closed his eyes and dozed fitfully for the remainder of the flight, waking as the long bird began its descent into Benito Jaurez International, eight miles from the city center.

After the plane taxied to a stop in its designated area at the east end of the sprawling terminal, the passenger bridge was quickly wheeled into place. Matt was off the aircraft like a shot. Inside the bustling facility, he found himself in Lounge E, which handled all international arrivals. A fast food court and several all-night restaurants offered everything from traditional Mexican dishes and tequila drinks to pizza, charbroiled burgers and specialty ice cream. Stopping at a small bookstore, he picked up a map of Mexico City before riding an escalator down to the International Baggage claim section on the ground floor, where he retrieved his bag. That accomplished, he headed for Passport Control and Customs, and was quickly cleared. He searched for Hertz, one of seven major rental car companies that served the airport, rented a new Mercury Cougar, and walked to the parking area to find his car. Unlocking the door, he slipped behind the wheel and scanned the dashboard. *Air-conditioning! At least I'll be comfortable while I'm driving around down here.*

Matt pressed the gas pedal and swung the car out of the rental pickup area, turned onto the Boulevard Aeropuerto, increased his speed and merged into the traffic flow. He adjusted the air conditioner to his liking and relaxed. A short drive took him to Circuito Interior Oriente, where he hung a left onto Avenido

Rio Consulado. Following the signs, he was soon on Passeo De La Reforma, the road that led straight to the city.

In Mexico City, he took a room at the Aristos Hotel, a five-star inn on Passeo de la Reforma in the heart of the city's entertainment section. *It'd be great if I had the time to see a show,* he thought. *But except for eating in one or two nice restaurants, this trip will be strictly business; Alvin Zelinka's business.*

"Didn't have any trouble finding Ann after I got to Branford," Willie Preston said into the phone. He was talking to Marvin Freedlander. "But nothing's been easy since then."

"You haven't lost him have you, Willie?"

"No, boss. The first thing we had to do was find out what his car looked like. Ann took care of that. She bribed the motel's desk clerk and he gave us the description and tag number."

"So, where are you now?"

"In the Airport at Providence. We followed Dawson here this morning. Watched him book a flight on an American Airlines plane, but we didn't know where he was goin' and Ann couldn't pull the same trick on the airline clerks to find out. So, I called Ken Starling. He got us the information. Dawson's going to Mexico City. We're waitin' for our flight."

"That was good thinking. Sure. The FBI can access reservation and ticketing information with all the airlines; some kind of code-sharing procedure. All Ken had to do was request a reservation search for the name Matthew Dawson, and they'd access the information for him fairly quickly."

"Ann thinks Dawson's not gonna stop at Mexico City. She sez he's goin' to Cuernavaca. It seems her parents spent some time there after they defected."

"That's right. She was with them, too." Freedlander paused, thinking. "Willie, there's only one person left down there who could cause us any problems. I don't know what his name is. He'd be a very old man now. If Dawson makes contact with him ..."

"How will I locate the guy?"

"Dawson will probably locate him for you."

Willie Preston was not a stupid individual. Dark complected and stocky, with a nose that had been broken more than once, it wasn't his looks that had helped him make it through college and law school with a C+ average. His brain worked in labored fashion, but he generally came up with good results. He paused, thinking hard, the furrows on his brow showing his effort. Then, "Boss? If Dawson talks to this guy, *he's* gonna find out about yer father too, right?"

"Yes. I think we have to assume that he'll find out."

"Then I may have to take care of both of them."

"True. And since we've decided to make the announcement next week, it would be best if this whole problem were resolved before then. Do you understand what you need to do?"

"Yeah. Boss? One more thing."

"What?"

"Ann knows about it, doesn't she?"

"I've been thinking about that, Willie. She's a loose end. But let's hold off on *that* until later, okay?"

Thursday, March 1, 1990
Mexico City, Mexico
Aristos Hotel
Passeo de la Reforma
8:05 a.m. MCT

Matt awakened early from what had been a very good night's sleep. He showered, shaved, and dressed in dove gray slacks and a blue, oxford cloth, button-down shirt. Picking up a tie, he considered it, but changed his mind and left his shirt collar open. He grabbed his navy blue blazer, carefully locked the room door behind him and rode the elevator eleven floors to the spacious lobby filled with bougainvillea and potted palms. Pausing just long enough to admire the spectacular view of majestic mountains beyond the high valley to the north, he entered the hotel's coffee shop, ordered breakfast and studied his tourist map. It showed the American Embassy to be only a block from the hotel. His breakfast finished, he decided to walk there.

The Embassy de Los Estados Unidos was an impressive, two-story building of Italianate marble with a Spanish tile roof. Surrounded by a high iron fence, it was set back about fifty yards from the street; a bit too far for anyone to lob a grenade through its barred windows, but far enough to allow for a shady courtyard of palm trees, where strollers could relax and chat or eat lunch on benches next to shrubbery of bougainvillea and hibiscus. The usual contingent of armed US Marines served as guards; tough, clean-cut young men who gave the impression that anyone who messed with them would regret it.

After a brief delay, Matt was ushered into the office of the Citizens' Consular Services, where he sat on one of two straight-backed chairs in front of a large desk with nothing but a phone, an ashtray, a yellow pad, and two unused pencils on its surface. Behind the desk, a nicely framed picture of President George H. W. Bush presided over the small office.

From an office next door, the sound of low voices could be heard. The muffled clatter of a teletype machine, printing out information from Washington and other places, came from a room across the corridor. The smell of fresh coffee drifted to him from somewhere nearby. A telephone rang in an office down the hall. Matt settled back in his chair to wait.

A few minutes later, the door opened and a tall, dark man, dressed in a green blazer, tan slacks, and a white dress shirt with a green and white striped tie, strode quickly into the room. His blazer displayed the official seal of the United States on the left breast. The man extended a hand and introduced himself.

"Francisco J. Hernandez, a Vice-Consul here," he said, revealing a Spanish accent. They shook hands. *Is he CIA?* Matt wondered. *Sometimes they attach case officers and field agents to the embassies as staff, instead of giving them a mi*litary *cover.*

"What can I do for you, Mr. Dawson?"

Matt briefly described his business there. Hernandez frowned and thought for a moment. Turning back to the door through which he had entered, he spoke quietly in Spanish to a woman in the next room. Matt's schoolboy Spanish was inadequate to follow along.

The Vice-Consul closed the door and slid into the chair behind the desk. Moments later, the phone buzzed. Hernandez picked it up.

"Hernandez." He spoke in a soft, effortless voice, listened, and then said, "Nada? Gracias, Señora." Hanging up, he scribbled a note on his yellow pad and shook his head.

"Our computerized records go back to the beginning of World War II. Señora Escobar ran a check for the Lieber family on her computer. Apparently there is no information. But that is not unusual. So much time has passed since these people first came to Mexico."

"How likely is it that they would have registered?"

Hernandez hesitated. "Some Americans *don't* register with the Embassy when they come this way. Writers, artists, musicians; all very independent people. Some are eccentric; most very liberal. Many resent the fact that their government asks them to register upon arrival and keep us informed of their whereabouts while they're here." Pausing, he pointed his finger at Matt for emphasis. "Even though it's been *shown* time after time that it's for their own good." He picked up a pencil, held it at each end between his palms and continued. "Then there are those Americans who don't want *either* government, Mexican or American, to know when they arrive, where they go or what they do here."

"Does that happen often?"

"I understand it was very common during the war years. Less so now. But it still happens. We can do nothing to help them if they get into trouble." He smiled. "I will register you, now."

With assistance from Hernandez, Matt filled out and filed a missing persons report, using the name and address of his hotel as a contact point.

"I'll continue making inquiries, Mr. Dawson," Hernandez said. "But it's doubtful that we'll find anything." He shrugged. "I'm sorry. We will do what we can."

Thinking about what Bob Winkler would need to show the Orphan's Court, Matt requested a note on Embassy stationery stating that he had been there asking about Anna Lieber. That would justify reimbursal of the trip's expenses from estate funds. Hernandez eagerly complied, and a few minutes later Matt was back on the street heading for his hotel, with a letter in his pocket.

Thursday, March 1, 1990
Mexico City, Mexico
Aristos Hotel
Passeo de la Reforma
12:05 p.m. MCT

Back in his plush hotel room, Matt pulled off his shoes and sprawled on the bed. Except for a low humming sound from the air conditioner, the luxurious room was completely quiet. No noise reached him from the traffic-filled street below.

He considered what he'd learned. The American Embassy had no information about the Lieber family. Why? Just because the Embassy had no record of their arrival didn't prove they had never been here. *We know they came here,* he thought. *Anna's letters had described their life in Cuernavaca. They were filled with news about what she, Max and the kids were doing.*

But there had been only five letters. Since he had very few postmarks to go by, he didn't know how long the family had stayed. Then, there was that deed executed in 1958, which placed them in Warsaw at that time. He didn't know how that fit in? *Well, I'm here now. Might as well drive down to Cuernavaca in the morning and hunt around.* He had an address. If the Liebers weren't there, maybe someone in their old neighborhood or in the nearby American community might be able to help.

CHAPTER 35

Friday, March 2, 1990
Cuernavaca, Morelos, Mexico
La Casa el Siesta Motel
8:00 a.m. Mexico City Time (MCT)

CHECKING OUT OF THE ARISTOS early the next morning, Matt drove the fifty-three miles south on a well-maintained freeway, to Cuernavaca, capital of the State of Morelos. Home to several million inhabitants, Morelos was known as the cradle of the Mexican revolution of 1910 because Emiliano Zapata, the leader of that revolution, had been born in a village near Cuernavaca.

Once there, Matt registered at a motel built of adobe and wood, aptly named La Casa el Siesta, only a block from the central plaza and just behind the palace of the conqueror, Hernan Cortez, which had been built in 1526. To the south, Popocatepetl, the slumbering volcano, towered above the city, its bald, snow-covered crown shrouded in mist. As he stared, he reflected that the Lieber family had lived in the city itself, not in the nearby American community, and had begun each day by taking in that same view.

Matt tossed his bag on the bed in his second floor room, walked down the back stairway to his car, and drove immediately to the address he had for Anna Lieber in San Anton, a section of town that had known better days. After a false start, he found it; a one-story adobe structure situated on an undersized lot at the end of an unpaved street. He approached the Mexican family now living there, but they were new to the area and had only been in that hacienda a short time. Although they spoke some English, they stared at him with dark, secretive, and somewhat hostile eyes, conveying that they were not interested in the problems of a nortèamericano.

The office of La Periódico, the local daily newspaper, was not difficult to find. A thin-toned bell rang as Matt pushed open the dirty glass door and entered. No one was visible inside. He waited in front of a counter on which was displayed a travel poster proclaiming Cuernavaca as "The City of Eternal Spring," because, according to the poster, temperatures here hovered between seventy and eighty degrees year 'round. The city had been given its name in the Nineteenth Century by Alexander von Humboldt, because of its warm, stable climate and abundant vegetation.

A huge green fly dive-bombed him on its way to a collision with the grimy front window. He watched it absently, until a tall man in his late thirties with dark hair and a brown, wrinkled face, stepped from an office in the rear, wiping his ink-stained hands on a printer's apron as he came. *"Buenos Dias,"* he said distractedly.

"Hola."

"Cômo está usted?"

"Estoy muy bien, gracias," Matt answered, and immediately became apprehensive because that was the sum and substance of his Spanish vocabulary.

A comprehending smile appeared on the wrinkled face. "Americano? De dónde es usted? Where are you from?"

With some help from the man, who turned out to be the editor, Matt composed an ad asking that anyone with knowledge of the Liebers contact him at his hotel. He paid for it, thanked the editor and stepped back out onto the sun-drenched sidewalk.

Outside again, he paused in a small patch of shade and glanced along the street. At the end of the block, a tall, blonde woman who had been lounging under a palm tree turned and walked rapidly in the other direction, quickly disappearing around the corner. *The way she moves reminds me of that Kelly woman I met the other night in Branford. But that can't be her. Kelly had red hair.*

Retrieving his rental car, he drove back to the neighborhood in which the Liebers had lived and spent the rest of the day asking questions. But, he found no one who recalled these nortèamericanos from thirty-nine years ago.

That evening, Matt walked about the city, passing restaurants, cantinas, sidewalk cafes and theaters. The cafes and cantinas were filled with laughing people, vacationers from Mexico City, enjoying the first night of their weekend. Matt heard the tinkling of glasses and smelled the exotic aromas of foods being prepared for eager diners. The sights and sounds of Mexico filled the evening air. A sense of release from his humdrum existence flooded over him. *It's good to be alive, and good to be doing something useful with my time and energy,* he thought.

La Cantina Real, a restaurant a few doors down the street from his motel, had been recommended by the desk clerk at his hotel. Matt parted the leaves of two tall potted palms framing the entrance and stepped inside. A brown-skinned waitress with dark, flashing eyes showed him to a corner table. She handed him a menu, which listed the food selections in two columns; Spanish in one, English in the other. As a starter, he ordered Caldo Tlalpeño, chicken soup simmered with sliced carrots and peppercorns, chickpeas, cheddar cheese and avocado slices. For his main course, he selected Tinga de Cerdoy Ternera, a delicious pork and veal stew seasoned with garlic cloves, finely chopped onions, green peppers and chili peppers.

Moments later, a short, thickset man wearing a wrinkled suit and carrying a copy of *The New York Times* under his arm, was shown to a table across the room. *He's an American,* Matt thought. He considered going over to his table and introducing himself, but the guy glanced around briefly and buried his nose in his newspaper, an indication that he did not want company.

While waiting for his meal, Matt sipped Cafe de Olla, an intriguing Mexican coffee blended with cinnamon and topped with canella, while listening to strolling mariachis in colorful costumes, who paused at each table and sang whatever song that diner requested. He wondered if he should call one of his kids — his eldest daughter, maybe — and let her know where he was. Rejecting that idea, he gave in entirely to the occasion, letting the heady Mexican magic of the evening wash over him in waves.

As he ate, Matt's thoughts returned to Max Lieber. The man had committed treason during the years between 1933 and 1945. Then, when discovered, he had gathered his family and fled to this place. John Harris had told Matt about an American community in Cuernavaca filled with individuals exactly like Lieber; disaffected people who had been unduly influenced by Karl Marx, the somewhat deranged philosophical founder of communism. Marx's early writings had been extensively circulated in America by the socialist publisher, Horace Greeley of *The New York Times,* an unwitting communist dupe during that period in his life. A socialist ideology being the prevailing mind-set, many had belonged to the political left that had dominated European and American intellectual life at that time. *Is there anyone still living there who might have known Lieber?* Matt wondered.

‡ ‡ ‡ ‡ ‡

Saturday, March 3, 1990
Cuernavaca, Morelos, Mexico
The American Community
10:00 a.m. MCT

After an early breakfast the next morning, Matt drove his rented Mercury Cougar over to the west side, where the American community was located. It was an area several hundred acres in size, surrounded by a high, chain-link fence topped with three strands of barbed wire. A security guard, wearing a short-sleeved cotton shirt and khaki slacks, with a .45 caliber pistol in a black leather holster at his belt, admitted Matt through the entrance gate. Inside, dozens of adobe haciendas on postage stamp lots lined unpaved streets generously landscaped with palm trees, bougainvillea, and other semi-tropical vegetation.

The community center contained a large, well-stocked supermarket, a pharmacy, a bookstore, a small, storefront school where foreign students could sign up for courses in the Spanish language, and to Matt's surprise, a Starbucks coffeehouse designed to resemble a Mexican cantina. In front of each establishment, lush growths of large cactus plants, potted Spanish swords, and flowering hibiscus in hanging pots, graced every conceivable space.

Once inside the compound, Matt parked his car near the cantina and began walking, stopping people to ask if they had lived there very long. When he found one who had been there for a while, he asked about Maxim Lieber, but would then be told that the person had not been there in the '50s. An hour later, he was back in front of the Starbucks Cantina, having learned absolutely nothing.

His stomach told him it was lunchtime. The aromas of richly roasted Columbian coffee and charbroiled beef, propelled by fans on the cantina's roof, floated to him on the heavy afternoon air. The early lunch crowd had already begun to fill the place. Matt entered and selected a corner table. He rejected Mexico's Corona beer in favor of a Sprite over ice.

An old man with a bald head sat at a small, round table near a side window. He looked up from the book he'd been reading, Roger Morris's just published biography of the man Morris had once worked for as a National Security Council aide, *Richard Milhous Nixon: The Rise of an American Politician,* and smiled. He wore a striped Brooks Brothers dress shirt and a narrow tie, both perhaps twenty-five years out of date. His shirt was soiled and its cuffs were frayed. His faded black trousers barely suggested the remains of a crease. A pot of coffee and a pitcher of ice cubes were on the table in front of him. As Matt settled himself, the man placed his book face down on the table so as not to lose his place, rose and came over.

"Buenos Dias, señior. Hable Español?" Before Matt could answer, the man answered for him. "You don't, do you. Well, we shall speak English." Frowning, he pulled up a chair. "Too bad," he said almost to himself. "I don't get a chance to use my Spanish much." The man's voice was educated American, but it lacked volume, as if its owner were exhausted.

Matt studied him for a moment. "Have a seat," he said finally.

"I was wondering when you'd get here. But how impolite of me. Let me introduce myself. My name is George W. Cohan. No relation to the American vaudeville performer by that name. He was George M. Do you remember him?" He extended long knobby fingers. The back of his gnarled hand displayed large, dark, liver spots on his weathered skin.

Matt shook the hand carefully so as not to cause pain to fingers that appeared arthritic. "Matt Dawson. Yes, I do. He was one of my favorites until he died."

"Ah. Muerte. Do you know what I have learned? If you don't think about death occasionally, you cannot appreciate life." Peering at Matt over thick, silver-framed bifocals, he smiled through parted lips that exposed discolored teeth. "Yes. I wondered when you'd get here."

For a moment, Matt thought the old man had him confused with someone else. "What do you mean?"

Cohan made a slight hand gesture. "No, I'm not senile yet, young man. You've been walking around asking about Maxim and Anna Lieber. This is a very small place. Since I'm the oldest Americano left here, the elder statesman, you might say. It wasn't long this morning before someone came around to mi casa and told me about you." He leaned forward on bony elbows. "Since it was almost lunchtime, I then made the assumption that you wouldn't leave without sampling l'alimento, the food *here*. So I came over to wait for you." He smiled triumphantly.

Matt's eyes widened. He leaned back in the chair, folded his arms and stared at George W. Cohan. "How long *have* you been living here, Mr. Cohan?"

"Since Saturday, December 6, 1941." Cohan shot back. He grinned. "I settled in the day before the Japanese attacked Pearl Harbor, and I was listening to my radio five days later when Germany and Italy declared war on America. I was thirty years old. Been here ever since."

"Why did you settle here?"

Cohan considered for a moment and then gave a surprising, disconcertingly honest answer. "My father had been the American Ambassador to Israel for several years during the Roosevelt Administration. He and I both despised the Nazis. But *my* hatred knew no bounds. I allowed it to get out of control. I betrayed *him* and my country by supplying Joseph Stalin's spies with numerous Tel-Aviv to Washington cables between my father and Franklin Roosevelt. In November 1941, my father caught me. He gave me a choice. Leave or be arrested. I left and came here, as did many others: radical leftists, socialists, communists, and communist sympathizers." For a few seconds his face held a far away, wistful look. "You could find them *all* here back then. We were on a quest; for the elusive 'true Marxism.' Of course, none of us had ever *been* to the Soviet Union. We'd have been shocked to learn that Marxism had been so drastically altered there by infusions of Leninism and Stalinism that a Marxist living in Soviet Russia would have been a lonely individual, indeed. "

"Did you know Max Lieber?"

"Good heavens, yes!" Cohan said impatiently. "That's why I came over here to meet you. Max and I spent many enjoyable hours in my study talking, when he and his family were in Cuernavaca. They came here in 1951, I believe."

Matt nodded. "That would be about right."

"And every time that lawyer friend of his came to visit, we'd all get together at my place." He cackled, again displaying his decaying teeth. "We had some wild times."

"His lawyer friend?"

"Yes. Marvin Jesse Freedlander. Tall, scrawny, and very intelligent. Also very lacking in common sense, as so many intellectuals seem to be. Even though he had a lovely wife in New York, he became involved with a Mexican woman here. Wound up sticking a knife in her after a night of heavy drinking and wild sex. Had to leave rather quickly. Pánico. One step ahead of the Cuernavaca police.

The name meant nothing to Matt. He waited for the rest of the story.

"Freedlander didn't treat the matter very seriously. Adelina was only a loose peasant woman, even if she *was* beautiful. But the police didn't take kindly to a wealthy gringo coming down here and killing one of their own. Freedlander never set foot here again after that."

Matt frowned. "Didn't Mexico ask for his extradition so he could stand trial?"

Cohan leaned back in his chair. "No!" He said with annoyance. "Back in those days there was no extradition treaty between the US and Mexico." He removed his glasses and pointed them at Matt. "That's precisely why *I* came here. And precisely why the *Liebers* and all those *other* expatriates came here, too."

Matt nodded. "How long did the Liebers stay?"

"They left about two years later, I think. Why are you looking for them?"

"Anna Lieber's brother died and left her some money."

"Well, you're too late," Cohan said with a wide grin. "About ..."

"... thirty-nine years too late." Matt finished his sentence for him. They both laughed.

Cohan glanced around as if he were about to impart a huge secret. "You know something? Although Lieber had worked for the American Communist Party for years, when he came here he was no longer a communist."

"Is that true?"

"Yes!" The old man nodded emphatically. "Oh, he was still very liberal. But, he was not a communist. Max Lieber was a man of principle, whatever else he may have been. He was a liberal and a socialist of good conscience, as I was." He sighed. "We both gave up allegiance to the Party, although at different times."

"Why."

"Because for liberals of good conscience, to remain in the service of the KGB meant one had to ignore too many things; Josef Stalin's evil record: his 'Great Terror,' the Moscow trial frame-ups, the slaughter of millions of Ukrainians, the many purges just before World War II, the assassination of Leon Trotsky, and worst of all, the Hitler-Stalin Pact in August of '39."

"I heard that Trotsky's assassination was part of a Soviet attempt to squelch dissent."

"True. Arrest and exile was another. Just look at what they did to Sakharov, later on."

"Sakharov? Wasn't he a Russian scientist?"

Cohan nodded. "A physicist. His work made it possible for the Soviet Union to explode a hydrogen bomb in August 1953, less than a year after the US did it." He raised a hand, imitating a plane flying over. "La bomba!" Matt had a fleeting impression of unstable hilarity as the old man enjoyed his private joke. "They were so grateful they elected him to membership in the Soviet Academy of Sciences and made him a Hero of Labor at the age of thirty-two."

"What happened to him?"

"Well, in 1960, he published that essay called *Reflections on Progress, Peaceful Coexistence and Intellectual Freedom.* Very naïve. Although he expressed sympathy for the ideals of Communism, he lambasted the Soviet Union for its denial of basic freedoms, defended intellectual openness and called for the convergence of Communism and Capitalism by the end of the century. That started a mini-dissident movement. A moral, not a pragmatic undertaking, he called it. But in 1978, he was exiled to the closed city of Gorky. After that, he changed. He realized that he had helped put a horrible weapon into the hands of bad people. From an unsophisticated, unthinking patriotic scientist who never gave a thought to the consequences of his actions, he became someone who accepted responsibility for what he had done."

"Is that what led him to break with the Soviet authorities?"

Cohan sipped from his coffee. "It took a while for the true nature of these things to be understood. But when the memoirs of General Walter Krivitsky and Jan Valtin became public, many of us could no longer ignore how Stalin and members of the German Communist Party had helped Hitler come to power. Then, there was Stalin's role in the Spanish civil war."

Matt nodded. "An awful lot of Americans wasted their lives serving Communism."

"Oh, yes. People like Alger Hiss, Noel Field, Lawrence Duggan, Judith Coplon and Julius and Ethel Rosenberg. Dozens more. Not only did they betray their own country, but they also betrayed the socialist ideals that had inspired them. Field died in Budapest. Duggan's dead, too. Coplon was a Justice Department employee who was tried in the US for espionage, as were the Rosenbergs."

"Do you know where Max and Anna Lieber are now?"

Cohan drew back. The laughter of a young couple at the next table reached them. "Not so fast, amigo." Replacing his glasses, he folded his arms and glared at Matt over cloudy bifocals. "I knew them when they were *here*. I *didn't* say I knew where they went after they *left*."

"Let's not play games, Mr. Cohan," Matt said evenly. "I need to find them."

A loud cry from a waiter and the clinking sound of dishes drifted to them from the kitchen. Cohan studied the gnarled fingers of his arthritic hands.

"Assumptions again!" He said. "They can be correct or incorrect. You have assumed that I knew where the Liebers went when they left here. Probably, you have *also assumed* that I know where they are now. Neither assumption is correct." A crafty expression appeared on his wrinkled visage. "I have my suspicions, however." He paused again. "Curious? Yes. I can see you are. You must look for them in the land beyond the former Red Curtain. If they are no longer there, you will learn where they went after they left that place."

Cohan rose creakily to his feet. "Por favor. Come over to my table. I have a pot of Starbuck's best coffee. Served over ice, it makes a very cooling drink in this heat. I'm old and not well. The end of my life is quite near. Humor an old man with not much time left to enjoy good conversation. We will talk of other things."

Hoping to learn more about Max and Anna Lieber, Matt accepted George Cohan's invitation and sat with him for another hour. During that time, people came and went from the cantina. Matt ordered lunch, but the old man did not. He was hungry only for news about the States. As Matt ate a large American-style charbroiled burger and a chilled potato salad he willingly obliged Cohan and his need for stories about the country he'd betrayed, but he could not get the man to return to their former topic. Finally, Cohan's coffeepot exhausted, they left the cantina and Cohan walked Matt to his car.

"Are you sure you won't stay longer, Mr. Dawson? Perhaps come to my home this evening for dinner? I'm too old now to cook for myself, but I have a fine Mexican woman who comes in every evening and makes supper for me."

Matt hesitated. "Well, my plan is to continue asking questions in hopes of finding someone who can help me."

"But, don't you understand? There's no one left in the community who knew the Liebers except me. And there's so much more I could tell you about them."

"Yes, I understand. But, suppose you're not right? I'd feel remiss if I didn't at least try."

The old man's shoulders fell. He turned away. Matt put his hand on Cohan's bony arm. Cohan was clearly starved for company. He had revealed that he knew more about the Liebers. And he *was* an interesting person with whom to talk. *Besides,* Matt rationalized, *why turn down an invitation to sample real Mexican food?*

"Okay. Look. I'll stop by your house around five, if that's all right with you."

Cohan brightened. "Good! Number three Camino Real. See you then, Mr. Dawson."

As Matt drove off, he glanced in his rear view mirror and watched the old man hobbling down the street, alone, toward his adobe hacienda.

‡ ‡ ‡ ‡ ‡

Saturday, March 3, 1990
Cuernavaca, Morelos, Mexico
The American Community
4:00 p.m. MCT

Matt had parked his car over on the east side of the community, as he was now referring to it, and had continued his quest, stopping people in the streets, and asking questions about the Liebers. But, Cohan was right. No one had been there long enough to have known them. Several mentioned George W. Cohan as the person he should see.

Back in the town center hours later, Matt entered the bookstore, a seedy, dust-laden shop dispensing paperbacks and hardbound copies of fiction and nonfiction, as well as Mexican and American newspapers and magazines. An open doorway in the rear led to a small reading room. A wall-rack of sexually explicit magazines was clearly visible from where he stood, the naked male and female bodies displayed on their covers sensually entwined in revealing positions. He rejected the idea of going back there, browsed through the newspapers out front and, although he did not usually read it, he spurned a copy of *The Boston Globe and* bought a copy of *The New York Time, instead.*

In his car again, he tried to relax with the newspaper. As he turned to the Metropolitan section, the caption of an article leaped out at him:

"Marvin Freedlander rumored seeking Democrat Nomination for Mayor.

United States District Attorney, Marvin Jonathan Freedlander, 50, of Westchester County, is interested in becoming his party's candidate for Mayor of New York, a source close to him revealed yesterday. Freedlander, noted for his crusade against organized crime since taking over as District Attorney, has been seen touring the city's service clubs recently, and attending many elite social gatherings, where people with money to contribute are generally found.

"Marvin is a brilliant individual, who obviously has this city's interests at heart," said Special Agent Kenneth Starling, of the Federal Bureau of Investigation, who has worked closely with him on case preparation in the past. "He'd make a fine mayor, if he wants to run."

Closing the newspaper, Matt looked up. *Where have I heard that name recently?* He wondered. A minute later, he remembered. Cohan had said that Max Lieber had a friend from New York with a similar name, who had regularly visited the Liebers and eventually murdered a Mexican woman here in Cuernavaca. Was the man in this article related to that individual?

He shrugged, glanced at his watch and decided it was time to go over to Cohan's place.

‡ ‡ ‡ ‡ ‡

Saturday, March 3, 1990
Cuernavaca, Morelos, Mexico
The American Community
4:50 p.m. Mexico Central Time

Camino Real was a long, tree-shaded side street just off the main drag. No one was around as Matt turned into it. The Cuernavacan day was coming to an end. Like all the houses here, George W. Cohan's modest adobe hacienda was old, rambling and all on one floor. The vegetation surrounding the dwelling included thick, *dama de la noche* bushes, which partially screened the abode from its neighbors. The front yard, lacking a good *jardinero*, a gardener, to tend it, presented a neglected look to its occasional visitors. Out back, a shallow *arroyo* carrying just a trickle of water, ran behind the houses.

The home seemed deserted as Matt pulled into the driveway. He cut the ignition, and the air-conditioning shut down with a whine, like the sound WWII piston-engine fighter planes used to make. He heard a dog barking from somewhere down the street and held still for a moment to listen, before approaching Cohan's front entrance. Much of the paint on the old wooden door had long ago peeled away. Years of strong sunlight had faded the rest. A rusted wind chime of black, metal horse figures was mounted next to the door.

Matt pushed the bell but couldn't tell whether it was working. Pressing an ear against the door, he tried the bell again. The unmistakable odor of propane gas, the kind used for cooking, reached him.

"George? George!" He called loudly. No response.

Alarmed now, Matt tried the door. It opened easily, and he pushed it wide. Gas poured out, driving him back a step. *If Cohan's in there he's gonna need help,* he thought. Glancing around, he spotted a cloth in the flowerbed next to the porch, grabbed it and wrapped it so that it covered his nose and mouth.

Inside, he headed for where he believed he'd find the kitchen. Cohan was sitting on the floor in front of the stove, his arms resting on the open oven door, his head inside. Matt moved quickly to turn off the gas burners. That done, he pulled the cloth from his face, leaned over and felt the side of Cohan's neck for a pulse. Nothing. That's the position he was in when he heard the voice behind him.

"Police! Place your hands on top of your head, señior. Other than that, do not make any sudden moves, por favor." The man spoke English but with a heavy Spanish accent.

The hair on the back of Matt's neck stood up. He did as he was directed. "ID's in my wallet. Left rear pocket. You want me to take it out?"

"Sí. Very slowly."

Pulling out the wallet, Matt extended his arm back toward the voice. It was taken from his hand. A few moments passed.

"Mr. Dawson, I am Chief Inspector Ramon Gonzales, Cuernavaca Police Department. You may turn around now, but keep your hands on your head, please."

Turning slowly, Matt took in the scene. Gonzales was short, stocky, and dark-complected. He badly needed a haircut, and his suit looked like he had slept in it. Another man in civilian clothes and a uniformed officer flanked him, both with drawn guns leveled at Matt.

"What has happened here? Can you tell me?" Gonzalez said, as he placed Matt's wallet into a pocket of his jacket and holstered his short-barreled Smith & Wesson .38 caliber pistol.

Matt shrugged. "I was invited by Mr. Cohan to have dinner with him. Got here just a few minutes ago and rang the doorbell. He didn't respond. I smelled gas, opened the door and came inside. Found him here, just like you see him now."

The other man in civilian clothes holstered his gun and patted Matt down. "Put your right hand behind you, señior," he said. He put a cuff on Matt's wrist.

"Now the other one." He finished cuffing Matt. Wearing silver bracelets and deprived of his freedom of movement, Matt felt a sense of helplessness.

"Did you do this thing?" Gonzales asked, gesturing toward the body of George Cohan.

"No." Matt dropped his gaze to the level of the Chief Inspector's shoes. "I told you all I know."

Gonzales turned to the uniformed cop. "Mendoza, put him in the cruiser. We'll take him downtown."

His partner went to Cohan's body. "No vital signs," he said in Spanish. "He's been dead for a while. Body's cooling but no rigor mortis, yet. I'll call for the coroner."

$$\ddagger \ddagger \ddagger \ddagger \ddagger$$

Saturday, March 3, 1990
Cuernavaca, Morelos, Mexico
Cuernavaca Police Department
7:30 p.m. MCT

Matt Dawson was sitting in Ramon Gonzales's smoke-filled cubicle in the Homicide Division's, second floor squad room at Police Headquarters in downtown Cuernavaca. For Homicide personnel, the evening shift was less hectic than the day shift. Male and female detectives stood around conferring in small groups, or sat at metal desks typing reports. Occasionally, one would shout to another across the room.

The handcuffs had been removed, but Matt had not eaten since lunch and his empty stomach was making rumbling noises. He was not happy, but was doing everything he could to conceal that fact. In the next cubicle, Deputy Inspector Emilio Diaz sat quietly, listening to their conversation through the thin partition. At the moment, no one was speaking. *I had wanted to see something of Cuernavaca*, Matt reflected ruefully, *but this isn't exactly what I had in mind.*

Matt had given Inspector Gonzales a statement. After asking for the name of someone who could confirm the purpose of his visit to Cuernavaca, Gonzales had placed a call to Bob Winkler's office. Apparently, he was satisfied with what Winkler told him. Matt had been fingerprinted but not arrested, and his prints had been run through Mexico's automated fingerprint identification database (AFIDM), and the FBI's automated fingerprint identification database (IAFIS), to see if Matt had a criminal record or was wanted for the commission of a crime in either country.

Gonzales lit a cigarette and stuck it between his lips. He did not offer the pack to Matt.

Placing his feet up on his battleship gray metal desk, he leaned back, his eyes boring into Matt, alert, searching, appraising. There was real intelligence in those dark brown eyes. That worried Matt. Gonzales's voice interrupted his reveries.

"So. You come to Cuernavaca, visit the American community, and ask a lot of questions. You meet Mr. Cohan in the Cantina over there and talk to him. You leave. Apparently, he then goes home, closes all the doors and windows, turns on the gas jets of his kitchen stove and sticks his head inside." Gonzales seemed to find something amusing as he gazed at Matt through a cloud of cigarette smoke. "What, exactly, did you two talk about?"

"We talked about the purpose of my visit; finding the Lieber family. Then we talked a lot about the States."

"Is that all?"

"Yes."

"That seems a bit strange to me. How, then, do *you* explain what Mr. Cohan appears to have done after he left you?"

Matt shrugged. Put the way Gonzales had put it, it *was* hard to explain. He thought back and recalled something that Cohan had said. "He spoke about 'death' during lunch; even made a remark about the end of his life being near." He paused. "Suicide?" He said sheepishly.

Inspector Gonzales hesitated. "It will be classified that way initially, yes."

Matt's eyes narrowed. "Initially? Do you have doubts?"

"Well, it looks like a suicide. Except that someone contemplating suicide does not usually schedule a guest for dinner. And, there is the small lump on his skull just behind the left ear. We might not have found it had the Medical Examiner examined him less carefully. That has made me wonder if someone does not want us to *think* it was a suicide. You, perhaps, Mr. Dawson." He paused. "Did you know Mr. Cohan before you arrived in Cuernavaca?"

"No. I told you. I met him for the first time after I arrived here."

"Cuañdo? When did you arrive in Mexico?"

"Two days ago."

Gonzales leaned forward. "Tell me, señor. Were you perhaps traveling with a tall, blonde American woman while you were here?"

"No. Why do you ask?"

"Forgive my inquisitiveness," Gonzales said with a shrug. "It is an unfortunate result of the work I do. One of Mr. Cohan's neighbors claims to have seen an Americano couple entering his house earlier this afternoon. The woman was a blonde. The man, medium height, like you. We are trying to find this couple. I'd like to talk with them."

"I wasn't part of that twosome. But I *did* see a blonde American woman over near the newspaper office yesterday."

Gonzales gazed at Matt thoughtfully. Taking another long drag on his cigarette, he blew the smoke toward the yellowed ceiling, where a large, tired fan revolved slowly. "We dusted for fingerprints in Mr. Cohan's kitchen. *Yours* were the only ones found on his stove."

"I turned off all the gas jets just before you came in," Matt said, shifting nervously.

Gonzales ignored him. "It's rather interesting that no *other* prints were present on the stove. Not Cohan's. Not his cook's, either."

Inspector Gonzales took another drag on his cigarette. Behind the partition, Deputy Inspector Diaz cleared his throat. Matt didn't notice. He waited. The silence between them grew. Somewhere in the office a telephone rang. Matt heard a woman answer it. The chatter of a teletype machine could be heard, incessantly printing out bulletins from far-away places.

Another minute passed. Gonzales made a dismissive gesture with his free hand. "You are free to go, Mr. Dawson. For now. Do you plan to return to the United States soon?"

Matt breathed a sigh of relief. "Yes. Tomorrow morning."

"If I need to talk with you again, I can reach you at your hotel later tonight, I assume?"

Matt nodded.

"And if I need to talk to you mañana, I have your address and phone number in ... Baltimore, Maryland, USA. We will know where to find you."

‡ ‡ ‡ ‡ ‡

Saturday, March 3, 1990
Cuernavaca, Morelos, Mexico
La Casa el Siesta Motel
9:00 p.m. MCT

"Matt! What the ... going on down there?" He had called Bob Winkler at home because he believed that Bob would be worried about him after receiving that telephone call from Inspector Gonzales. Instead, Bob sounded peeved.

"Knew you'd be concerned," Matt said dryly. "I met an old man in the American community who was here when the Liebers were here. Guy named George W. Cohan."

"George W. Cohan? The famous song and dance guy?"

"No. That was George M."

"Oh."

"The *good* news is that *our* Cohan knew Max Lieber well. The *bad* news is he didn't know where they went when they left here. And he didn't know where they are now."

"Did you find anyone else who knew them?"

"No. He was the only one left who'd been here that long. And now he's dead."

"That Inspector wasn't a fount of information. What happened to Cohan?"

"After I left him, he appears to have gone home, turned on the gas burners of his kitchen stove and put his head inside the damn thing. Looks like a suicide, but the local cops aren't so sure."

"Why not?"

"There was a lump on his head. Like he'd been hit with something. And no fingerprints on his kitchen stove, even ones that should have been there. Apparently, someone wiped it clean. And, he'd invited *me* to dinner."

Winkler digested that information. Then, "When are you coming back?"

"I'm leaving *here* first thing in the morning. My plane leaves from Mexico City tomorrow afternoon at one-thirty."

"Good. Matt? Try not to get in any more trouble down there, will you?"

CHAPTER 36

Sunday, March 4, 1990
Cuernavaca, Morelos, Mexico
La Casa El Siesta Motel
1:30 p.m. Mexico City Time (MCT)

W ITH NOTHING PLANNED FOR THAT morning, Matt slept late. Inspector Gonzales had not tried to reach him. He thought *that* was an encouraging sign. After a room service breakfast, he checked out and retraced his path to Juarez Airport in Mexico City, arriving at the departure gate with a bit less than an hour to spare. Leaving empty-handed was disappointing. *Actually, if I were smart I'd just go home and forget the whole thing. But I won't do that. I'll see it through, at least until something happens to make me reconsider.*

Once aboard, he quickly found his seat, fastened the safety belt, relaxed and closed his eyes as the other passengers settled themselves in the long, thin MD-80. . Moments later, the aircraft trundled to the main runway, and he began hoping that the pilot had had a healthy but not too heavy lunch before coming aboard. After a brief pause, the jet engines accelerated to full power, the plane sped down the macadam airstrip and lifted off with runway to spare, a welcome event that left Matt breathing more easily.

When permission was granted, he unfastened his seatbelt and headed for the lavatories in the tail section. As he approached the doors, a striking blonde woman emerged from one of them. Tall, dressed in a white sleeveless blouse, a red A-line skirt, and red pumps, she appeared startled to see him. Recovering quickly, she glanced away, turned and speedily settled herself in a seat two rows from the lavatories, beside a stocky, dark-haired man. Matt frowned. *That was certainly the same woman I saw outside the newspaper office in Cuernavaca the other day. And that guy? Wasn't he the American I saw in La Cantina Real the other night?*

Back in his seat a few minutes later, Matt re-fastened his seatbelt. His mind was racing, thinking and feeling his own panic. According to Inspector Gonzalez, one of George Cohan's neighbors had seen a thickset man and a blonde woman entering Cohan's house just before he turned up dead. Was this the same couple? Had they killed him and tried to make it look like a suicide? If these were the same people, where were they headed? Dallas-Fort Worth? Atlanta? Or were they following *him?*

He tried to control his breathing. If he was going to continue with this line of work, he'd need to manage his emotions better. Fear running rampant was not conducive to logical thinking or careful planning. Logical thinking and careful planning were necessary for survival.

Leaning his head back, Matt closed his eyes and then opened them quickly. With those two on board, napping didn't seem like a good idea. But he *was* weary. He had diligently tried to find the Lieber family and he was now certain that Anna Lieber was not in Cuernavaca. And his instincts screamed that she was no longer in Mexico. Cohan had said, "You must look for them in the land beyond the Red Curtain." That probably meant the Iron Curtain. The Riptide Cottage deed, placing them in Poland in 1958, seemed to bear that out. But, where were they now? Were they still in Warsaw?

‡ ‡ ‡ ‡ ‡

Sunday, March 4, 1990
Texas, United States of America
Dallas-Fort Worth Airport
6:30 p.m. Central Standard Time (CST)

"Mr. Dawson?" Immediately upon landing at Dallas-Fort Worth Airport, Matt had raced to a telephone inside the terminal and dialed Ramon Gonzales's office number. It was answered on the second ring. "I had not expected to hear from you so soon."

"Listen, Inspector. I don't have much time before my connecting flight. I'm calling from the Dallas-Fort Worth Airport in the USA."

"What is it, my friend?"

"That American couple you're looking for? The blonde woman I saw in Cuernavaca and a man who fits the description you gave me were on the flight I was on, from Mexico City."

"Thank you for that information. We will check with Aeromexico Airways right away, to see if we can identify them. What was the flight number?"

Matt gave it to him. "Inspector? I think these people are following me."

He listened to Inspector Gonzales's heavy breathing on the other end of the line. Then Gonzales said, "I will try to identify them quickly. But, they may be traveling under assumed names. What's the airline and flight number that you are taking from there to Baltimore?"

"American. Flight 1419. If they follow me all the way to Baltimore, I'll let you know."

"In the meantime, Mr. Dawson, I suggest that you exercise extreme caution. Or, as they say in your American movies, 'Watch your back.'"

‡ ‡ ‡ ‡ ‡

Monday, March 5, 1990
Timonium, Maryland
Padonia Village Apartments
2312 Chetwood Circle
12:05 p.m. EST

Matt had been working on the Lieber matter all morning. A break for lunch was in order, and as he spread some mayonnaise on wheat bread and added tuna fish, he was still thinking about Max Lieber. His phone rang as he was fixing a fresh pot of coffee. Janet Gaines was on the line.

"I researched *both* local newspapers and wasn't able to find any articles about Max Lieber," she said.

"Nothing?

"No. But early this morning I talked with a very interesting lady. Her name's Rhoda Loeb. Lives two doors up from Riptide Cottage. She was once a lawyer for the Liebers and knew both of them." Janet sounded extremely pleased with herself. "She's leaving for vacation tomorrow, but she said if you call today she'd talk to you."

"Janet, you're terrific!" Matt was excited. "I'll call her right away. What's her number?"

Hanging up quickly, he immediately dialed the number Janet had given him. This was a real break. As he waited, he reflected that all the plodding might be about to produce a "Eureka!" moment to reward his efforts. On the fifth ring an elderly woman answered.

"Yes, Mr. Dawson, Janet Gaines asked if I'd known the Lieber family and when I said I had, she told me you were looking for Maxim Lieber?" Her voice ended in a question.

"Actually, I'm looking for Anna Lieber," Matt corrected. "Janet said you might have some information for me."

"I'm not sure how I can help. I'm a former practicing attorney and a Worker's Compensation Commissioner in New Haven. I live near Riptide Cottage. When I was still practicing law, I represented Anna Lieber in a minor matter and we became friends." She took an audible breath. "I told Janet this morning that a number of years ago I saw Max Lieber here in Branford. He was with a younger man who might have been his son. They were looking at Riptide Cottage. I got the impression it was a nostalgia trip for them. I was standing near them and spoke to them. But, I didn't realize until later that one of them was Max."

"Do you have any idea where the Liebers might be, Commissioner Loeb?"

"Look. I'm not saying I do or I don't. I may know someone who knows where they're living. But I really don't know who *you* are or what your purpose is in trying to find them. I'm reluctant to speak to you. You're just a voice on the other end of this line right now."

Not wanting to antagonize her, Matt stifled his impatience. "I understand. I'm working for a lawyer who's trying to settle the estate of Anna Lieber's deceased brother, Alvin Zelinka. Anna was her brother's only heir."

"What's the name of the lawyer?"

"Robert N. Winkler. He's located in Towson, Maryland. Suppose I have him send a letter of introduction. Will you cooperate then?"

"I think that would work. Have him do that. I'll be back Saturday. Then, we'll go from there."

‡ ‡ ‡ ‡ ‡

Monday, March 5, 1990
Timonium, Maryland
Padonia Village Apartments
2312 Chetwood Circle
1:20 p.m. EST

"Do you think this lady knows anything?" Bob Winkler asked. Matt had called Bob to report on his trip and to tell him about Rhoda Loeb.

"My gut feeling is that she knows something. *She* may not actually know where the Liebers are, but she may know someone who does. In any event, she wants a letter from you identifying me and telling her why we're looking for the Liebers."

"It's worth following up, I guess. What's her address."

Matt read off the address. "One other thing, Bob. While I was on the trip, I had the weirdest feeling that someone was following me."

"Really? You sure it wasn't just your imagination?"

"Well, that's just it. I'm *not* sure." Matt explained about the white BMW, the blonde in Cuernavaca, the American in the restaurant and the couple on his flight from Mexico City. "And they stayed with me all the way to Baltimore," he added.

"Come on, Matt. You've been watching too many detective shows on TV."

"Oh, great!" Matt said and hung up.

Going to his notes again, he found the number for Richard Larch and dialed it. He was pleasantly surprised when Richard himself answered the phone.

"Hi, Matt. Have any trouble getting back to your motel in that fog the other night?"

"No. I took it real slow," Matt said. "What do you know about a woman named Rhoda Loeb?"

"Rhoda? She's a neighbor. Used to be a practicing attorney. Now she's a Worker's Compensation Commissioner. Semi-retired. Lives a couple doors up the hill from here. Been there forever. But our houses are far enough apart so we're not close friends."

"Do you know how old she is, or anything else about her?"

"Well, she looks to be in her early seventies. I'm not that good at estimating ages. She's sharp mentally, if that's any help. Knows everybody around here.

Knows all their business, too." He chuckled. "Nice lady. Jewish grandmother type. My wife and I both like her."

Matt thanked Larch and was about to hang up when a thought occurred to him. "The other night when I left your house? There was a woman standing in your driveway. Tallish. Wearing a green raincoat. Almost ran right into her in that fog."

Larch thought for a moment. "Funny you should mention that. For the last several days there's been a woman hanging around. Parks her car up at the head of the lane and walks down to the water. Actually, now that I think about it, we haven't seen her since you left."

"Any idea who she is?"

"Nope. Don't have the foggiest." He laughed. "No pun intended. Let us know how you make out with this, Matt," he said and hung up.

Monday, March 5, 1990
Timonium, Maryland
Padonia Village Apartments
2312 Chetwood Circle
1:45 p.m. EST

Melissa Saffron had given Matt the name of a woman friend of Alvin's. Matt thumbed through his notes and found it; Jeannette Sellman. Maybe she could add something to the mix.

He dialed, but the operator told him it was not a working number. He went for the telephone books. To his dismay, there was no listing for anyone by that name in either of Baltimore's telephone directories.

Monday, March 5, 1990
Timonium, Maryland
Padonia Village Apartments
2312 Chetwood Circle
8:00 p.m. EST

Matt had not seen anything of the blonde and her friend since leaving BWI. The memory of the menacing couple had receded somewhat from his mind. The track at Dulaney High beckoned. Pulling on his dark blue sweat clothes and Nike running shoes, he slipped out through the sliding doors leading to his patio, vaulted the patio wall and walked through the courtyard to the street. His car was parked in its allotted space, as were cars belonging to other tenants. But one car was not in a space. An empty green Ford Taurus stood at the curb on Chetwood Circle, in a NO PARKING zone.

Dulaney High School was less than five minutes away. Treherne Road ran alongside the school grounds. The school building and parking lot lined one side of the street. Attractive ranchers and split level homes lined the opposite side. He parked in front of a rancher and locked his car. The evening was cold but clear and the joggers were out in force, taking advantage of the nice weather. Minutes later on the track, he warmed up with a walking lap and then ran four laps in succession, followed by two fast walking laps.

Back in his car, he slipped behind the wheel and drove to the end of Treherne, did a U-turn, and proceeded in the other direction. As he did so, his headlights illuminated a car that had pulled out of a parking spot nearby; a green Ford Taurus. Behind the wheel sat a tough-looking, dark complected man. A blonde woman occupied the passenger seat. *That's them! The same couple I saw on the flight back from Mexico City!* He thought.

It took a Herculean effort of will to resist pressing the gas pedal to the floor and racing off down the street. *Calm down! Take it easy!* He told himself. He turned left onto Padonia Road and drove slowly west, his eyes riveted on the rear view mirror. Seconds later, the Taurus emerged from Treherne, turned onto Padonia, and followed. When he reached Chetwood Circle, the car was about a quarter of a mile behind. The green Ford he'd seen parked at the curb earlier was gone. There was now no doubt in his mind. He *was* being followed.

As he parked, his mind raced over events of the recent past. He was now sure that the woman in the restaurant in Branford, Ann Kelly, was the same woman he'd seen in the driveway at Riptide Cottage that night in the fog. She was also the same woman he'd seen outside the newspaper office in Cuernavaca and the same one he'd seen on the plane. *She must have been wearing a wig to disguise her appearance. But why?*

Stepping out of the car, Matt locked it carefully, his peripheral vision straining to pick up any movement nearby. *Somewhere along the way, Kelly had been joined by the guy she was with on the plane. They followed me from Branford in that white BMW. Then, they followed me to Mexico City, to Cuernavaca, and to the American community.*

He took the stairs leading up to his entrance hall two at a time. *Had they seen me talking to Cohan?* Inserting his key in the lock, he stepped inside and closed the door firmly behind him. His mind combed the memory of that day in the Starbucks Cantina, over two thousand miles away. People had come and gone. Absorbed in conversation with Cohan, he had not paid attention to anyone else. One of his followers, probably the man — he would have noticed the blonde — could have come inside, watched and maybe even listened. If Inspector Gonzales's source was correct, they had been seen entering Cohan's house! Could they have had anything to do with his death?

Turning on the usual lights in his living room, Matt closed the draperies. Then he re-packed the bag he had so recently unpacked and placed it in the living room. A thought occurred to him. Inspector Gonzales had said he would try to identify the American couple, but Matt had not heard from him. He grabbed the Zelinka file, found Gonzales's number and raced to the phone.

It was ringing. Four, five, six rings. "Come ahn, come ahn!" He breathed. "Answer the phone." After ten rings he glanced at the clock. What time was it down there? In his panic, he had not considered that even people like Gonzales go home to their families now and then.

Matt hung up, returned to the living room and forced himself to watch a TV show about the week's happenings at the Baltimore Orioles spring training camp in Florida, where speculation was rampant that *this* would be a winning year for the team, and the grime and pain of long-suffering Baltimore fans would be washed away. At eleven, he turned off the TV and living room lights, went to his bedroom and turned on the light. He lay on the bed for a few minutes and then turned off the light.

An hour passed; then another, before he rose from the bed. When the digital clock on his bedside table showed one fifteen, he moved to the living room, grabbed his bag, unlocked the glass sliding doors leading to his patio and silently inched open one door just enough to slip through the gap. Then, he closed and locked it behind him.

Crouched in the shadows on the small patio, Matt's eyes strained to penetrate the darkness around him, illuminated only by a single light in an apartment window across the courtyard. He was looking for any movement; a nearby shadow darker than any other, or any shape not quite natural. Nothing stirred. The entire complex seemed asleep. Five minutes later, satisfied that no one was in the courtyard, he rose and quickly slid his bag out into the grass. Vaulting the wall, he picked up his bag and moved to the end of the building. From there, he could see the area where the green Taurus had been parked. It was gone. He scrutinized every car parked in the lot to make sure it had not simply been moved. He was not mistaken. *They must have seen the lights in my apartment go out at eleven and thought I'd gone to bed,* he reasoned. Striding rapidly to his car, he tossed his bag inside, slid behind the wheel and drove off.

At Padonia Road, Matt turned left and headed west toward Interstate 83. A surprising number of cars were on the road for so late at night. He slowed as if to stop for the light at York Road, but as it was about to change, he sped up and raced through the intersection. He held to the left lane on Padonia Road until nearing the on-ramp for I-83 North. At the last second, he swerved right, cut in front of a car and gunned it up the ramp.

Out on the Expressway, he drove like a crazy man, first doing forty, then seventy. Half way to Shawan Road, he pulled over and parked on the shoulder. No one paused behind him. He moved off at high speed, but stopped again, this time at the underpass, to watch and wait. No one duplicated his move. Again he pulled out into traffic but made a sudden exit at Shawan Road. He saw no sign of the green Ford Taurus or any other suspicious car, truck or van behind him. A few minutes later, he drove east on Shawan to York Road, and turned south. *It's probably not safe to go back to my apartment.* Minutes later, he began looking for a place to spend the night.

CHAPTER 37

Tuesday, March 6, 1990
Timonium, Maryland
Friendly's Restaurant
York Road
7:15 a.m. Eastern Standard Time (EST)

F EAR IS BAD FOR ONE's peace of mind. But, at times it can also be a great motivator. Matt's terror of the night before had led him to seek the safety of the local Econo Lodge at 10100 York Road, hoping he might stay alive a bit longer. However, instead of sleeping, he had tossed and turned on the pillow, wracking his brain for a reason for this predicament. It was not a comforting thought that somewhere out in the chill March night, a green Ford Taurus cruised the streets of Timonium, its occupants looking to kill *him* as they apparently had George W. Cohan. He had no clue as to why they wanted him dead. But, he was determined to find out.

His panic somewhat subsided in the light of day, he was ingesting a plate of bacon, eggs and home fries at a local Friendly's Restaurant, in a booth from which he could keep an eye on the door. In his hand, he held a steaming cup of coffee. The problems had not yet affected his appetite.

Finished a few minutes later, he paid his check and left the restaurant in a gloomy mood, his four kids on his mind. When his former wife left him, the life of his family as a family had ended; too soon for at least three of the four. Early on, the kids had loved growing up on the farm. But, after years of comparing notes with their suburban friends and hearing how much easier life would be sans farm chores, *that* had changed. Seeing the opportunity to get off the farm, instead of remaining neutral and keeping good relationships with both parents, they had sided with their mother. His boy Timmy, and youngest girl, Laurie, had gone with her; the eldest, Sallie, had taken an apartment of her own. Marcy had moved onto her college campus until graduation.

Four precious lives had been brought into the world and placed in his care; four children whom he loved. Now grown, they had become their own persons, capable of making their own decisions. Because of the divorce and his legal and financial problems, they no longer asked his opinion or accepted guidance from him. No doubt they thought their father a failure. There was a time in the not too distant past when he would have agreed.

Still, he could not help worrying about them. Had he given them enough love, guidance and discipline to enable them to make the sound choices that would permit them to live decent lives? He was not confident that his presence at home and his influence and love as they grew up, had been enough. He had heard many stories from parents crushed with grief, sorrowing over the destructive paths their children had chosen, so he knew that as kids grew and changed, there was no guarantee that the persons they became would reflect the values of the parents who had raised them.

There's not much a father can do when a child rejects his guidance. The growing influence of post-modernism is creating a secular society and teaching children that the family is the source of all their problems. Kids who can't see through these bits of falsehood are destined for damage.

But, Matt had learned that there *was* at least one thing he could do for his kids; pray. He now did that daily, as well as offering his reception of the Eucharist for them every time he attended Mass.

Driving north on York Road toward the motel, he reflected that his kids were not bad compared to some. Each had special talents and was showing the potential to turn out pretty well. Looking back, he saw that it had only been since the separation and divorce of their parents that, free from the restraining influence of their father, a couple of them had begun to make poor choices. *It's true that freedom includes the right to make your own mistakes,* he thought. *But it's best for kids to profit from the mistakes of others instead of repeating them.*

He felt a mixture of anger and love toward his kids that would not let go of his heart.

He had learned, as all compassionate parents do, that discipline and love are not opposites, that judgment and mercy work together, and that blind acceptance is not the most caring response a parent can make.

What would God want me to do about them? He wondered. His religion taught that God is a loving, compassionate and kind father. But, although He is a merciful God, He is also one who judges the actions of His creations. *God made us with free will and He gives us the distance we elect. Yet He doesn't abandon us. And He doesn't give up on us, either.*

With that idea turning over in his mind, he pulled into the motel parking lot. As he slipped the car into a spot between a large blue dumpster and a long Winnebago, effectively hiding it from any searching eyes on the street, he realized that he not only loved his kids, but he had been proud of each of them as they grew up. He was proud of them now. And like most fathers, his love was not based on whether they earned good grades in school or excelled in sports or other activities. It was unconditional. There for them no matter what. Yet he was only a temporal father; a poor human imitation of the Father-God. *Isn't God's love for His children also unconditional? If I can love my kids so strongly and so constantly, can't God do the same? Isn't His love also a constant, there for me no matter what, much stronger even than the love I feel for my own kids?*

As his car door snapped shut, his mind closed on this thought. *Of course! Now I understand!* And with that came the knowledge that he had climbed another of the plateaus that he had needed to climb.

‡ ‡ ‡ ‡ ‡

Tuesday, March 6, 1990
Cockeysville, Maryland
Econo Lodge Motel
York Road
11:00 a. m. EST

"Buenos Diás, Policia de Cuernavaca," an operator answered in Spanish. Back in his room, Matt had dialed the number for the Cuernavaca Police Department.

"Inspector Gonzales, please."

One moment," she said, effortlessly switching to English.

He waited, shifting his weight from one foot to the other. After several minutes, the operator returned. "I'm sorry, sir. No one is answering in the Inspector's office. May I take a message?"

Frustrated, Matt left his name and number and hung up. He'd have to try again later.

‡ ‡ ‡ ‡ ‡

Tuesday, March 6, 1990
Timonium, Maryland
Days Inn
Padonia and Deereco Roads
12:45 p.m. EST

"It was just like you said, boss. Dawson hooked up with this old coot in the local Starbucks a couple a hours after he got there." Willie Preston was on the phone in his room at the Days Inn at Padonia Road and Interstate 83, talking to Marvin Freedlander. "I went in and sat close enough to hear what they were sayin'. They never noticed me." Preston was five feet nine inches tall and weighed two hundred pounds. His weight and muscular build made him appear shorter, stockier than he was.

"Did my father's name come up?"

"Yeah. The old man tole Dawson all about it. So I took care of him. Fixed it so it looked like a suicide."

"What was Ann's reaction?" Freedlander asked.

"She wasn't there. I didn't want any witnesses, so I sent her off in the car to keep tabs on Dawson while I … handled things."

"Good, Willie. Now what about Dawson?"

"Well, that's the bad part," Preston said, running a hand nervously through his dark hair. "After I did the old man, I hooked up with Ann. We picked up Dawson's trail and followed him, waitin' for a good opportunity. He wound up back at Cohan's house and went

inside. He musta found the body. I thought I could do him right there, but while I wuz tryin' ta figure out some way ta temporarily get rid of Ann again, the local cops came and found the ole man's body. They hauled Dawson off with *them*."

"Are you telling me Dawson is still walking around?"

"Yeah. We came back to the States on the same plane. Followed him right to Timonium, Maryland where he lives. But, he made us last night and now he's on the run."

"Willie? Are you telling me he got away from you?"

"That's about the size of it. Right now, we don't know where he is."

"Damn it!" Freedlander exploded.

Preston flinched. "Don't worry, boss. We'll find him sooner or later."

"I know you will," Freedlander said icily. "And just to be sure, I'm sending Foreman down there to help out."

"What about Ann? Should I take care a her, too?"

"Wait. When John gets there, you can dispose of both problems at the same time."

A few feet away in the bathroom, her face ashen, Ann Kelly quietly closed the door that she had been holding ajar as she listened to Preston's end of his revealing conversation. Although she had not heard Freedlander's comments, she had heard enough. Badly frightened, she collapsed on the toilet seat, her arms wrapped around herself. *My God! Willie actually killed that old man!* She felt like she'd just been kicked in the stomach. *He told me he was only going to talk to him. And Marvin Jonathan knew about it; maybe even ordered it. And they're planning to kill me, too. I've never been so scared in my life!*

Gathering herself, she flushed the toilet, stepped to the sink and splashed cold water on her face. She shook a fist at her image in the mirror. *Get a grip, for heaven sake,* she told herself. *You've got to step out there and make chitchat with Preston for a few minutes. Then, you can excuse yourself and return to your own room.* She pressed the fingers of both hands against her temples for a moment. *This is going to be the hardest things I've ever done in my life. But I can't let Willie suspect that I know. My life depends on it.* She smoothed her skirt, opened the bathroom door and stepped out, feeling like a condemned woman on the way to her own execution.

CHAPTER 38

Sunday, March 11, 1990
Cockeysville, Maryland
Econo Lodge Motel
York Road
10:30 a.m. Eastern Standard Time (EST)

R HODA LOEB'S VACATION WEEK HAD ended. Anxious to hear from her, Matt had decided to call her immediately upon her return.

Her phone was ringing. After what seemed a long time, she picked up. Matt dispensed with the preliminaries. "I asked Bob Winkler to send you that letter we talked about," he said. "Have you received it yet?"

"No. I got back yesterday and went through all my mail last night."

Not expecting that response, Matt hesitated. His desire to move this investigation forward being stronger than his perceived need for caution, he took a deep breath and plunged ahead. "I also spoke to the former owner of Riptide Cottage and learned something interesting."

"Oh, really? What might *that* be?"

"That Max Lieber may have been a spy and that he and his family fled the country in the early fifties with the FBI in hot pursuit."

He could hear Rhoda Loeb catch her breath. When she spoke again, her voice, calm before, was pitched slightly higher. "You didn't know that Max Lieber had been accused of being a Communist agent?"

"No. Not until I talked to Jean Larch," he said.

"There *is* something to that. Are you familiar with the Alger Hiss case?"

"Only from what I recall hearing as a child and from a high school history course."

"Well, apparently Lieber was involved in that case. There's lots of information on him in Whittaker Chambers's book *Witness*. Alger Hiss also wrote a book about the case, but he didn't mention Lieber in that one."

Now it was Matt's turn to be surprised. "Really? I'll take a look at both of them."

"Mr. Dawson," Rhoda sounded a bit friendlier, "I'd rather not say anything more at this time. As I told you, I'm not certain who you are or why you're looking for the Liebers. After I receive Mr. Winkler's letter I'll call you. Is that okay?"

"Yes. I'm sure you'll have it soon."

Matt hung up. He could not blame Loeb for being cautious, but his patience was wearing thin. *Does she know someone who knows what became of the Liebers? Or does she herself know where they are?*

Moving to the window, Matt stood looking down at the parking area in front of the motel and York Road beyond, bustling with traffic. Apparently Bob Winkler had not sent that letter off to Loeb yet. *Guess I'll have to remind him. I'll do an interim report and bill and drop them off at Winkler's office tomorrow. That way, he'll be aware of everything I've done. And I can use the money I've already earned. My bills are piling up while I'm paying for motels to stay alive.*

He wondered why Inspector Gonzales had not returned his call. Going to the phone again, he dialed Gonzales's number, which he now knew by heart. It was not Gonzales, but another inspector on his staff who answered.

"Sorry, Señor Dawson," he said. "I am Deputy Inspector Emilio Diaz. He's not in the office this morning. Is it important?"

"Yes, it's important," Matt answered, his ire rising. "I wouldn't be calling if it weren't."

"Wait a moment, Señor." Diaz left the phone and was gone for about a minute. Then, "Lieutenant Cordova said that Inspector Gonzales has been trying to reach you at your home number. He has some information about the Cohan murder."

Matt's heart sank. *While I've been away from my apartment hiding in motels, no one's been able to reach me.* "Look. I've ... had some problems. I'll leave another number where I can be reached."

Deputy Inspector Diaz took down the number. "I'll see that the Inspector gets this as soon as he returns," he said, and hung up.

‡ ‡ ‡ ‡ ‡

Monday, March 12, 1990
Cockeysville, Maryland
Econo Lodge Motel
York Road
12:00 p.m. EST

Matt's meager resources were exhausted. That morning, he had dropped off an interim bill at Bob Winkler's office, along with a report updating him. However, he knew it might be a few days before Bob would write a check. In the meantime, Matt understood that if he didn't want to wind up dead he needed to continue to make himself scarce. But he could no longer afford motels. He'd need a place to stay. Picking up the telephone, he dialed a number.

"Matt? How are you?" Jim Crowley's voice came over the line.

"Aside from the fact that someone's following me, everything's hunky dory, Jim."

"What?" Crowley laughed. "You attracted a stalker? Male or female?"

"It's not funny, Jim. This is serious."

"You're puttin' me on."

"I wish. It's a problem. Thought maybe you and Denise might be able to help. Can I come by tonight and talk to you?"

"Sure. Come over for dinner around six. I'll let Denise know."

Wednesday, March 14, 1990
Timonium, Maryland
The Home of Jim and Denise Crowley
10:30 p.m. EST

Matt's room was dark, the Crowley house quiet. After confiding his problem to his friends and getting their okay to spend a few nights in their guest bedroom, Matt had checked out of the Econo Lodge and moved to their place. Early risers, Denise and Jim had retired for the night. Not wanting to disturb them, Matt had gone to his room, but had not turned in.

Two days had passed without further developments in the Lieber case. Night had fallen, and with it a light dusting of snow. Outside, no traffic moved on Springdale Avenue, but the streetlights were on, turning the macadam and concrete into a glistening world of white.

Sprawled on the bed, Matt's thoughts turned to Rhoda Loeb. She must have received Winkler's letter by now. Apparently, she had decided against revealing what she knew. He might not hear from her again. It's *probably useless to call her. Best not to rely on her.*

While practicing law, Matt had repeatedly located many people. Some had taken just a few hours. Others only a few days. But after five weeks of work on this case, he didn't seem to be any nearer to turning up Anna Lieber than he'd been when he started. *Is there something I've overlooked?* He asked himself. *Or something I'm not interpreting correctly?*

For perhaps the tenth time, he went back over the facts. Everything he had known at the start. Everything he had learned since. The question of why it had been so hard to find the Lieber family had been answered. Maxim Lieber had been a spy. When the Liebers left America, they had not wanted to be found.

Downstairs in the hall, the Grandfather clock struck eleven. Having drawn a blank, Matt donned his coat and gloves and silently let himself out the Crowley's front door. Wet snow was still falling. There had been very little accumulation on the street, but it was gathering, fresh, clean, and cold on the lawns and clinging tenuously to the naked trunks of trees. The neighborhood was quiet now, preparing to sleep. To the west, busy York Road seemed remote, as did the nearby Interstate. Matt, shoulders hunched, eyes alert to any sign of danger, gloved hands thrust deeply into his pockets, walked quickly around the block.

Back in his room a few minutes later, he flicked on a light. Having exhausted every lead, he could not think of another thing else to do. He decided that he'd call Bob Winkler in the morning and report failure.

His eyes roamed the quiet room, empty, except for himself. The stillness was a tangible thing that threatened to overwhelm him. He had lived his life for his family, but they were gone, and he was now alone in the guest bedroom of kind friends, hiding from an unknown menace. *Is there any hope for me?* He thought bleakly. *Do I have any future?*

He lay on the bed, hands clasped under his head. His thoughts went back to the words of a priest whom he'd never seen before. "There is a freedom that comes from being loved and accepted by another. But in order for this to take place; you must first have an understanding of just how much God loves *you.*"

Well, it had taken a while, but he *had* come to the understanding that God loved him, despite all his shortcomings and failings. He could truthfully say his re-born faith was built on that premise. From there to the point where he could trust in God was an easy jump. Examining the idea, he was conscious that he had, in fact, already arrived at that point.

So, where to next, in his spiritual journey? The hardest thing left was to understand that there was hope for him in the future; that his life was not over simply because his former wife had left him; that his lost career as a lawyer could be replaced by other, meaningful work, and that, eventually, he might even find another woman who would consider him worthy and love him as much or more than his first wife had. What was missing was hope; a belief that God had a plan for him and would help him if the choices he made were in accordance with His divine will.

While separated from his ex-wife, Matt had not dated because he had not wanted to antagonize her while there was any possibility of a reconciliation. He had also wanted to model to his kids that marriage vows were to be honored until death or divorce dissolved them. Prior to the divorce, he had adopted a celibate lifestyle. Making the necessary adjustments was one of the hardest things he'd ever had to do, because he'd been sexually active with his wife. His belief that sex outside of marriage was wrong had helped him to avoid occasions when he'd be tempted. Instead of dating or doing the bar scene, he had reached out to others; the families of his deceased sister and brother, and people he met who were hurting and in need of help. He had learned to express love in a non-physical way, and had grown comfortable with that.

After two years, his wife had filed for divorce using the no-fault law; separation of the parties for that length of time regardless of the reason. This "ground" was a direct attack on the institutions of marriage and the family by the Woman's Liberation Movement, a convenient way out for those who did not believe in the permanency of marriage, or who felt they could do better with someone else. With help from liberals in both the mainstream Protestant religions and the Catholic Church, and feminists focusing on the idea that women should not be forced to remain in an unhappy marriage, which was now referred to as "the fairness argument," the no-fault statute had sailed through the Maryland legislature and been signed by a Democrat governor who pandered to these special interests. But, little consideration had been given to the destructive effect widespread divorce would have on marriage, the family, or on Society generally, until it was too late. Lives were shattered, men, women and children were thrown into poverty, and the divorce rate soared. Recently, Matt had read somewhere, "Being a Liberal means never having to say you're sorry."

Once his divorce became final, however, Matt had begun to play the dating game. Since women considered him nice looking, he was never turned down when he asked someone out. However, after dating several women, he had tired of it and gradually stopped. By then he had come to terms with loneliness. He had arrived at the point where, thanks to his friendship with Jesus, he no longer feared being alone and felt no need to hit the bars, frantically searching for someone to sleep with, or with whom to begin a relationship. After a while, he was not lonely any more, only occasionally lonesome. Even that state of affairs had been quickly resolved as the activities he chose led him into the company of good people like Jim and Denise, Dan and Barbara. There was no longer any void in his life. The empty spaces had been filled. Now, the very thought of doing anything that would interfere with his relationship with Jesus was abhorrent to him.

And as his faith grew, he had felt a new freedom; the freedom that came from knowing that his passions were at last under control and no longer controlled *him*. He now believed that this was part of the peace promised by Jesus:

> "'Peace' is my farewell to you,
> my peace is my gift to you... ."
> John, 15: 27.

Again, the words of the elderly priest he had heard at church a couple of weeks before replayed themselves in Matt's mind. "There is a freedom that comes from being loved and accepted by another." At first Matt had thought this referred to the relationship between himself and God. But, now he saw it in a new light. Wasn't the priest saying that there is also *another* freedom; the freedom that comes from loving and being loved by another *human* person? *If that's so, am I now ready for a new relationship?* He wondered.

He ended his prayer session by asking God for the gift of hope, and for guidance as to whether, if he were able to extricate himself from this mess, he should begin dating again with the goal of eventually re-marrying. In response, he felt a firm conviction that he should pray regularly about these things and be open to any response from God.

His spirits lifted, Matt's mind focused on the Lieber case. Two things were plain; the Liebers were neither in Mexico nor in Warsaw. But the unanswered questions were there. How and why had they left Cuernavaca? Had they gone directly to Warsaw? Why did the American Embassy in Warsaw have no record of Ruth Lieber? Were the Liebers still behind the Iron Curtain? If not, where had they gone? And, oh, yeah, who was trying to kill him and why? He had obviously stepped on someone's toes and he or she didn't like it one bit.

It was late. He began his preparations for bed. *I've given it my best shot. Tomorrow I'll call Bob and report that I'm at a dead end. Then, I'll try to get some help with this threat to my life.*

CHAPTER 39

Thursday, March 15, 1990
Towson, Maryland
Immaculate Conception Church
200 Ware Avenue
9:00 a.m. Eastern Standard Time (EST)

SUNLIGHT POURING THROUGH FIVE STAINED glass windows above the altar flooded the sanctuary of the one hundred year old Gothic church with a soft blue light. Matt, trying to be inconspicuous, was tucked into a pew near the back, hoping that the people searching for him would not think to look here.

"You've probably discovered that times of pain or difficulty are the hardest times to remember basic truths about God. But those are the times when it's most helpful to focus on the light of His truth," Monsignor Al Flynn said as he began his sermon.

"When you're discouraged by life's ups and downs and having trouble seeing past your circumstances, you need the consistent hope only the Lord offers. Hope in God. That's one of the Lord's basic truths." He paused, gathering his thoughts.

"God has a master plan. The Bible makes it plain. His desire for each of us is that we fulfill our potential. He has given us the strength to overcome past mistakes and the trials and adversity of the present, so we can do that. But without hope, we cannot begin to pick ourselves up and go on.

"It's important to gain an understanding of what God's word says about the future, about the coming of His kingdom, about hope. We can't know everything about these things. There are some things He has not revealed because He wants us to live by faith, choosing Him every day. But *this* we do know: what happens in the future depends upon your response to God today."

Thursday, March 15, 1990
Timonium, Maryland
The Home of Jim and Denise Crowley
10:45 a.m. EST

At breakfast, Matt had mulled over Monsignor Flynn's words. His gut told him he ought to keep trying. So instead of reporting failure to Bob Winkler, he decided on another tack. A call to the Milton Eisenhower Library at Johns Hopkins University's Homewood Campus yielded the information that a US Government repository was located on campus, and it housed all sorts of government documents. He was given the phone number.

Anyone in his right mind would throw in the towel at this point, he thought, as he dialed the number. A young man answered.

"This library is a participant in the Federal Depository Library Program," the man said, in response to Matt's question. "We have many federal records; correspondence to and from presidents, cabinet chiefs, heads of state, prominent members of both Houses of Congress. And we have transcripts of House and Senate committee hearings going back to 1925, on microfilm. That includes the House Committee on Un-American Activities."

"How can I find out if a certain individual ever testified before the Committee?"

"Well, all HUAC witnesses are indexed on our computers with references to the particular transcript where their testimony can be found. Who's the person?"

"Maxim Lieber."

There was a pause as the young librarian consulted his computer. Then, "Yes. He testified in 1950. We have that transcript. Actually we have HUAC transcripts dating from 1946 all the way up to the Joe McCarthy days in the middle '50s."

Matt considered for a moment. *A transcript of the hearing that Max Lieber testified at might help me understand a few things. Like why they left the United States.* He asked the young man for directions and hung up.

‡ ‡ ‡ ‡ ‡

Thursday, March 15, 1990
Baltimore, Maryland
Johns Hopkins University,
Homewood Campus
Shaffer Hall
11:30 a.m. EST

The expansive campus of Johns Hopkins University, flanked on the east by Charles Street and on the west by Wyman Park, an older community of brick town homes, was in uptown Baltimore. The Hubble Space Laboratory was located on a tree-shaded lane in the heart of the campus, and the National Lacrosse Hall of Fame had recently opened its doors in an attractive building on the university grounds.

It took Matt only a few minutes to find Shaffer Hall, a gray stone building that contained the Federal Government Records repository. Inside, he spent the next two hours in the basement records room, reading testimony given to the House Un-American Activities Committee by people whose names he'd only seen in history books.

By two o'clock he had finished. Walking back to his car along a brick path through the gloom of an overcast day, he ruminated about what he'd learned. HUAC had believed that Max Lieber had been a key member of the Communist Party underground. His literary agency had been used as a front for communist activities. Lieber was named as the person to contact in case of death on passports and visas illegally obtained by people confirmed as communist agents, either by their own admission, or by irrefutable evidence, and by others suspected of being communist agents.

More importantly, Lieber *had* known Whittaker Chambers, and through him, had met Alger Hiss. There lay the explanation for why Lieber had fled the country in 1951. Not only could he corroborate much of what Chambers had revealed, but he also possessed more recent information regarding Alger Hiss's clandestine activities. The government had wanted to use him as a witness against Hiss. But Lieber did not want to play along. So he left the country.

Matt pointed the nose of his Skyhawk north on Charles Street in heavy traffic, absently listening to the flapping of the plastic bag taped over its rear window. He passed Waterford University, where as a student years before he had played baseball and soccer while working on a degree in Political Science. *Rhoda Loeb hasn't called back. Should I call her again?* He wondered. *Now that I know more about Lieber, maybe I can convince her to tell me what she knows.*

‡ ‡ ‡ ‡ ‡

Thursday, March 15, 1990
Timonium, Maryland
The Home of Jim and Denise Crowley
3:30 p.m. EST

Jim and Denise Crowley were both out; Jim at his office, Denise gone to visit a daughter. Matt was eating lunch in their kitchen; a peanut butter sandwich, an apple and a small carton of milk, purchased at a supermarket on Charles Street on the way home from Johns Hopkins.

He was on the phone, dialing the number for Mary O'Grady, sister of Melissa Saffron and long-time friend of Alvin's, who had been away in Florida for a month or more. She'd be home by now. A woman answered. Identifying himself, Matt told her what he wanted to know.

"Yes, I knew Alvin had a sister, a niece and a nephew," Mary said. "He often spoke of them, although he told me he hadn't heard from them in many years."

"Did he mention where his sister was living?"

"Yes, someplace in Mexico. He told me *that* a long time ago. He never mentioned that she'd moved, so I just assumed she was still there?"

"Did he ever say anything about his brother-in-law?"

"The only thing Alvin ever said about *him* was that he didn't have any use for him." From her answer, Matt figured she had no knowledge of the spying allegations that had swirled around Max Lieber. He decided not to tell her. Instead, he thanked her and started to hang up. But O'Grady had one more thing to say. "Mr. Dawson, have you talked to Jeannette Sellman? She was close friends with Alvin, too."

His pulse quickened. "No. I've been trying to locate her telephone number. Can you help me out?" Maybe he was about to get a much-needed break.

"Sure. She has an unpublished number. I'll get it for you. It's in my address book."

Leaving the phone, she was gone for several minutes before picking up an extension phone somewhere in her house. "I have it," she said, obviously out of breath. "It wasn't where I thought it was. I'm not as young as I used to be."

"None of us is. But look at it this way. We're not just getting older, we're getting better."

Mary laughed. "I hadn't thought about it like *that.*" She gave him a number. He wrote it down, thanked her and hung up.

No point in waiting. He dialed Sellman's number. Busy. Going to the kitchen, he selected a cup from the dirty dishes stacked in the sink, rinsed it and fixed himself a cup of instant coffee. Then, feeling somewhat guilty for imposing on the Crowleys as he was, he washed all their dishes, stacking them carefully in the drainer to dry. Returning to the phone, he dialed Sellman's number once more. Jeannette herself answered. She was friendly and obviously in the mood to talk.

"Alvin's sister? I met her once, ya know. In the early '50s. 1951, I think. She came through Baltimore on her way to Mexico. She and the kids stayed with Alvin for a few days."

"Really? Do you know where they are now, Jeannette?"

"No. I never corresponded with her. Alvin told me he hadn't heard from them in a long time. I told him he was foolish not to call or write to them, Anna being his only sister and all. I encouraged him to do it, but he kept making excuses and never did."

"Then, so as far as you know, he hadn't had any contact with them."

There was a pause as Jeannette considered. "Well, that's so far as I *know*. But Alvin traveled a lot. Took annual trips outside the country. When he came back he'd bring them up in conversations; like they were on his mind, ya know? He'd tell me things about his sister."

"What kind of things?"

"Oh, just stuff from when they were kids growing up together. That seemed kinda strange to me. I often wondered if he didn't visit them while he was on one of his trips, or meet with them somewhere. But if he did, he never actually said so to me."

They talked for a while. Jeannette was full of anecdotes about Alvin, but had nothing more to offer about Anna Lieber. Matt gave her his number in case she recalled anything else.

Hanging up the phone, he sat at the table staring off into space. *Something's got to work,* he told himself. *If I keep asking questions and checking leads, something'll pan out. It has to.*

Alvin's travels had come up several times. Theorizing that these trips had been to visit his sister, his niece and nephew, Matt slapped together a list of the dates and places; several times to Mexico, once to Ireland, twice to London. But, when he had finished, there was nothing from which he could conclude that Alvin's purpose for a trip had been to meet his sister.

‡ ‡ ‡ ‡ ‡

Thursday, March 15, 1990
New York City, New York
Ritz Carlton Hotel
59th and Central Park West
4:30 p.m. EST

"Mr. Radonowitz's office," the nasal voice of the telephone operator sang out.

"Is he available, Shelly?" Rhoda Loeb sat wearily on the edge of the bed. She was wearing a white silk blouse, a black wool skirt and black pumps. Her hair, more gray than brown, was tied back with a red ribbon.

"I'm sure he's available to you, Judge Loeb. Hold on, please."

Rhoda glanced approvingly around her. The room was a pleasant combination of Williamsburg gray and green, mixed with subtle wood tones of light oak. Tasteful prints by Impressionist artists brightened the walls, among them James McNeill Whistler's *Old Battersea Bridge,* Edouard Manet's *Peonies,* Claude Monet's *Houseboat,* and Edgar Degas' *Race Horses.* She always stayed in this hotel when she visited New York. And she came back often.

Rhoda truly loved this City, widely known as a world leader in the arts, communications, cuisine, fashion, finance and publishing. The excitement! The glamour! The nightlife! Vibrant energy pulsated in the bars, the clubs, and the theaters. And all those restaurants! So many it would take a lifetime to sample them all.

Kicking off her heels out of habit, she waited. She could still remember the first time she had come to "The Big Apple." The hotel had been at 45th and Madison back then, but later it had moved to its present location, 59th and Central Park West. She sighed. *I can't even recall the name of the man I was seeing back then. That was a long time ago.*

"Rhoda," came a man's cultured, well-modulated voice. "Are you in town?"

"Yes. At the Ritz Carlton. I'll be here tonight and tomorrow."

"You wanton woman, you. Can we get together for dinner tonight? Err... no, that won't work for me. Breakfast tomorrow morning, perhaps?"

"Yes, that'll be fine. I need to discuss something and I'd prefer to do it in person."

"Mmmm. Are you finally going to accept one of my marriage proposals, darling? Don't worry about a thing! Cindy's been threatening to divorce me for twenty years. Says I work too hard and never spend enough time with her. So, I'll simply ship her off to the Dominican Republic for a quickie divorce, and we can be married next month."

She laughed. "Now, Vernon, you can't do that. You have no grounds. If you try to divorce Cindy she'll take you for all you're worth, and you know I'd never marry a pauper no matter how handsome and charming he is."

"Ahh, Rhoda. Ever the practical one."

Rhoda laughed again. "Oh, be serious. But, that's impossible for you isn't it, dear?" She paused, marveling at the schoolgirl banter that this cosmopolitan man always brought out in her. "Can you come to my hotel in the morning? Say about eight?"

‡ ‡ ‡ ‡ ‡

Friday, March 16, 1990
New York City, New York
Ritz Carlton Hotel
59th and Central Park West
8:45 a.m. EST

"What did you say this man's name was?" Vernon Radonowitz, impeccably dressed in a gray pinstriped suit with vest, maroon and white striped tie, and wing-tipped cordovan shoes, sipped from his second cup of hot, black coffee, placed the cup back on its saucer and dabbed his snow-white mustache with a linen napkin. The concerned look on his face turned the corners of his mouth slightly downward as he spoke.

Rhoda Loeb looked up from the last of her eggs, which she'd ordered sunny side up, just the way she liked them. "Dawson. He said he was an investigator, working for a lawyer named Winkler in Towson, Maryland. The names don't mean anything to me. Do they to you?"

"No."

"I asked for a letter stating why he wanted to find the Liebers. Here's what they sent."

The elderly lawyer pulled his glasses from a pocket and glanced at the single sheet of paper Rhoda handed him. "Anna Lieber *did* have a brother," he said as he perused the letter. "In Maryland. Near Baltimore, I think."

"Well, this man said Towson is near Baltimore." She leaned closer to Radonowitz. "He said he wasn't looking for Max Lieber. He was only interested in Anna Lieber because her brother had died and left her some money."

Radonowitz wanted more coffee. He caught the eye of their waiter, and beckoned. "Hmm. That's a pretty common lie, err … story, when you're trying to find someone without revealing the *real* reason you're looking. Still, Anna *did* have a brother down there."

"Dawson said the brother's name was Alvin Zelinka. Is that name familiar to you?"

"It's been so long, I really can't remember."

"Vernon, was Maxim Lieber involved with Alger Hiss? Did they know each other? Will Alger be able to help with this? Will he, do you think?" She stopped to catch her breath.

"Whoa, darling," Radonowitz placed a hand on her arm. His eyes twinkled. Noting her intense look, he realized that she was deadly serious. "Do you believe this is a legitimate inquiry?"

Rhoda dropped her eyes to her hands and then raised them again. "Yes, I do. I surprised myself. Until just now, this very *minute*, I had not completely made up my mind."

"Well! You've always displayed good judgment when it comes to people. I trust you implicitly in these things."

As their waiter refilled their coffee cups, Radonowitz looked around the restaurant, which was decorated with lots of dark mahogany paneling, potted plants, and heavy furniture. His mind mulled over the problem. "Will Alger help? I don't know if he will or not." He raised his cup and sipped from it. "But, yes. They *did* know each other. And there's a certain sense of loyalty there. Alger has always acknowledged a debt of gratitude to Lieber for electing to leave the United States instead of telling *all* to the world. *And* to the government."

"Could something Lieber knew have been damaging to Alger?"

"Quite so, my dear. But, I can't say more about that. I represented Alger at one time and since he's still alive, the attorney-client privilege applies in his favor."

Radonowitz paused again while Rhoda considered this point. Sipping from his coffee, he watched her brow knit as her mind wrestled with what he'd said. *Her face was always very expressive. She'd make a lousy poker player.* He quickly continued. "I represented the Liebers too, you know, in a minor matter; the sale of a Connecticut property in Brockett's Point. While they were away in Poland, they sold a summer cottage that Anna had bought for them. I retained local counsel to work on it." A light dawned as he made a connection. "Isn't Brockett's Point where *you're* living?"

"Yes. And I'm only a couple of doors from the place you're talking about. I knew the Liebers when they lived there."

The waiter returned. He hovered, checked the sugar bowl, topped off their coffee cups, and poured cream in Rhoda's coffee from a delicate silver pitcher. Then he asked if there was anything else they'd like, and left to get their check.

Rhoda watched Vernon intently as she waited, knowing that he was thinking about what he might be able to do if he decided to involve himself. A busy, successful lawyer, he had specialized in civil rights law, had worked hard and become prominent in his field. Some believed him to have been the best in the entire United States when in his prime.

Vernon gazed fondly at Rhoda from beneath thick white eyebrows. She had been his life-long friend; only his wife of forty years was closer to him. It was not inaccurate to say that he loved this woman, although not in the same way he loved his wife. He would do just about *anything* for her, and *this* was not much for her to ask. He checked his Rolex wristwatch. "Tell you what. I'll make a phone call from here. That'll put some things in motion right away." He pushed his chair back and stood up.

"Thank you, Vernon," Rhoda said. Their eyes met. He reached down and touched her hand lightly. From the shelter of their fondness for each other, they silently acknowledged the long friendship they shared, and its value to each of them. Then, he turned and headed for the open double doors that led to pay phones in the lobby. He could have asked the waiter to bring a phone to their table. A phone jack and electrical outlet were wired under every table in the place. But he thought it best to make this call out of anyone else's hearing.

‡ ‡ ‡ ‡ ‡

Friday, March 16, 1990
Timonium, Maryland
The Home of Jim and Denise Crowley
10:45 a.m. EST

"I'm glad you called, señior," Ramon Gonzales said. "I tried to reach you at the number you left for me, but the desk clerk told me you had checked out earlier."

"Been moving around a bit since I last talked with you," Matt responded. He was lying on the bed in his room at the Crowley residence, telephone in hand, shoes off to avoid soiling Denise's yellow down comforter.

"*That* seems like a good idea, if you do not wish to become a statistic. After you called from Dallas, I contacted Aeromexico Airways. They took their sweet time getting back to me, but they *were* able to help. Their flight records indicate that the couple booked tickets from Mexico City to Dallas-Fort Worth. From there, they boarded an American Airlines plane to New York City. The same flight you were on. But careful checking revealed that they left the airplane at Maryland's BWI and did not return. That is also where *you* got off, is it not?"

"Yeah."

"So they *do* seem to be following you. But the *why* of it is still a mystery."

Matt filled the Inspector in on what had transpired since he had discovered them parked in front of his apartment building. Then, "Did Aeromexico come up with any names?"

"Sí. The woman's name is Ann Kelly. Her traveling companion is one William Preston. Both gave home addresses in your American state of New York." He paused. "Do either of those names mean anything to you?"

"One does. I met the Kelly woman in Branford, Connecticut, about ten days ago. That's where the Liebers spent a summer or two back in the early '50s. But the other name doesn't mean a thing."

"Señior Dawson, are you telling me that they may have followed you from this, err... Branford, Connecticut, all the way down here to Cuernavaca?"

"It sure looks that way," Matt said, and explained about the white BMW.

"We have done some more checking. Your Mr. Preston paid for their tickets with a credit card in the name of his employer. He is an Assistant US Attorney."

Matt's jaw dropped. He experienced the sensation of a man who steps onto a patch of ice and feels his feet suddenly slip from under him. "Is that so?" He said, lamely.

"Yes. And his boss is the District Attorney for the Southern District of New York, Marvin Jonathan Freedlander."

CHAPTER 40

Friday, March 16, 1990
Timonium, Maryland
The Home of Jim and Denise Crowley
10:50 a.m. Eastern Standard Time (EST)

MATT SLOWLY BROUGHT HIS BREATHING back to a reasonable level. There was that name again! Marvin Jonathan Freedlander. That these people might all be part of law enforcement was something he hadn't even considered.

"Señior Dawson? Are you still there?"

"Yes, Inspector. I'm still here."

"Obviously the name means something to you, no?" Gonzales asked.

But, Matt, struggling to make sense of what he was hearing, was not listening. Finally, "Inspector? George Cohan told me about an American lawyer who'd been involved in a murder down there a long time ago. His name was Marvin Jesse Freedlander."

"A murder? When was it supposed to have taken place?"

"Back in 1952. According to Cohan, Freedlander was a friend of Max Lieber. He visited Lieber several times. The last time, he left Mexico one step ahead of the authorities. He was never prosecuted because he couldn't be extradited."

"I will check the archives to see what *that* was all about. But, just what the connection might be between *that* incident and *this*, I cannot see."

"The other day, *The New York Times* printed an article about a guy named Marvin Jonathan Freedlander," Matt said. "It seems he's going to run for Mayor of New York City. The incumbent is a member of the same party, but he's ineligible for another term. Freedlander hasn't made it official yet. That article was really a pre-announcement leak."

Gonzales chuckled. "I know little about the intrigues of the American political scene. Just give me a good murder case to solve and I'm happy. Why are the Kelly woman and this Preston following you? And what does the District Attorney want with you? Are you involved in something he is investigating, perhaps?"

"Not that I know of." He stood and began pacing the small room.

"Well, do you have something he *wants?*"

"I don't think so," Matt said thoughtfully. Then it hit him. He stopped. "Inspector? I think I know what's going on here. It wasn't something George Cohan *had* that got him killed. It was something he *knew*. And it isn't something *I* have that set these people onto me. It's something I *know*."

"About the District Attorney in New York?"

"Yes. Something that happened a long time ago, to someone related to him."

"But, why kill Cohan?"

"Maybe it's because he was the only one still living in Cuernavaca who knew the story. Freedlander may want to make sure a nasty bit of his family's past never sees the light of day."

The sound of Gonzales's breathing, deep, measured, calm, came over the line. Then, "I suppose if I was about to run for an important political office, but there was something in my past, some dark incident that, if revealed, might damage my chances to win election ..."

"Yes."

"And let's suppose further that while in the process of ... attending to that problem, I discovered that another person had learned the secret while visiting with Cohan."

"*First* they'd need to dispose of the old man," Matt said.

"Making it look like a suicide."

"And *then* they'd have to take care of me."

"As you Americans say, 'Bingo!' *That* is why they are following you."

"You think they want to kill me?"

"Surely that thought has already occurred to you. Otherwise, why have you been hiding out for the past few days?"

"Well, I admit it *had* crossed my mind."

The line was silent as Gonzales ruminated. Then, "What are you going to do?"

Again, as in Cuernavaca, when silver bracelets had been locked around his wrists, Matt experienced that feeling of helplessness; of being caught up in something huge, but powerless to influence what was happening. Taking a deep breath, he shook off the temptation to think of himself as a victim. He was neither powerless nor helpless. "I'll think of something," he said.

‡ ‡ ‡ ‡ ‡

Friday, March 16, 1990
Timonium, Maryland
The Home of Jim and Denise Crowley
11:00 a.m. EST

It wasn't possible for a man to be more afraid than Matt had been during the last few days. So far, he had managed his emotions well, but the fear that had been incubating in him like a low-grade fever was now clearly visible in his eyes.

It had begun to snow. Large, wet flakes drifted silently against his window. He needed to think; to formulate a plan of action. But the heavy silence of the Crowley's suburban home, empty at midday, suddenly seemed oppressive. His safe haven had become an inhospitable, alien place from which he needed to briefly escape. Not surprisingly, he felt like he wanted to be around people. A nearby restaurant would do. There, he'd be temporarily surrounded by ordinary citizens who, although they had concerns of their own, weren't being chased by others who wanted them dead.

‡ ‡ ‡ ‡ ‡

Friday, March 16, 1990
Timonium, Maryland
Denny's Restaurant
Padonia and Deereco Roads
11:30 a.m. EST

Until he slipped into a booth at Denny's a few minutes later and opened a menu, Matt had not realized how ravenous he was. Outside, the wind had picked up and snow had begun to accumulate on the streets and sidewalks. The restaurant was filling with people from nearby office buildings, buzzing about whether or not they'd be let off work early because of the storm. Matt, beginning to relax, felt somewhat safer. The feeling did not last long.

Busy deciding on his lunch order, he sensed that someone had stopped at his table. Expecting a waitress, he closed the menu and looked up. It wasn't his waitress.

"Mr. Dawson? Matt?" She had entered quietly, spotted him, came over, and was standing next to his table before he even knew she was there. He rolled his eyes. *Matt Dawson, master detective.*

The blonde wig was gone and her red hair was pulled back from her face with a white plastic comb. She was wearing the same pale green raincoat she had worn that night outside Riptide Cottage in a thick, Brockett's Point fog while waiting for him to emerge. She carried a blue leather suitcase. A small matching blue travel bag and her purse hung from her shoulder. But it was her green eyes, devoid of any mascara, that drew his attention. The look Matt saw there was not triumph at having treed him. It was raw fear.

"Sit down, Mrs. Kelly," he said, recovering quickly. He could have saved his breath. Without waiting for his invitation, she did exactly that. Concerned about where her male friend might be, Matt was already scanning the room.

She noticed. "Don't worry," she said, pulling a fresh pack of Virginia Slims from her shoulder bag and pushing the bag aside. "I left them both upstairs. My room is next to theirs. They won't look for me for a while."

His eyebrows shot up. "Both?"

"Yes. At first it was just the cretin Willie Preston and me. We have reinforcements, now. Marvin sent John Foreman down from New York the day after you gave us the slip. He's positively creepy."

Matt swallowed hard. "Oh, great!" He said. "What do you people want?"

She brushed his question aside and managed a wan smile, but her mouth had a curious tightness to it and fright was still evident in those big, green orbs. Extracting a cigarette from the pack, she lit up and took a nervous drag before leaning forward and placing her slender fingers on the back of his hand. "I need help."

"*You* need help?" His voice dripped sarcasm.

"They're going to kill me," she whined. "I know they are." She looked down at the table. "I need to get away from them."

"Well, if they're gonna kill either one of us, *I'll* probably be first," he said dryly. Their eyes met, but he immediately understood that Ann didn't see any humor in his remark. "We *know* they want to kill *me*," he continued. "What makes you think they want to do you, too?"

"Because, besides that old man in Cuernavaca, you and I are the only ones left who know Marvin Freedlander's dirty little secret." She was knee-deep in self-pity.

"What exactly is this 'secret'?" He asked, though he already knew.

Kelly dropped her gaze and examined the backs of her hands. Matt had the distinct impression that she was choosing her words carefully. "Marvin's father, Marvin Jesse Freedlander, was a lawyer for the Communist Party back in the '40s and '50s. He killed a woman while down in Mexico visiting um … some friends. Then he ran like the Devil back to the United States."

Matt studied her face carefully, sensing she was withholding something. But, thankful for confirmation of what he already suspected, he let whatever it was go. Instead he asked, "Did you and Preston murder George Cohan?"

She leaned forward again and glared at him, her nostrils flaring. "No!" She said indignantly. "I had *nothing* to do with that."

"But," he said bluntly, "you were *both* seen entering Cohan's house the day he was killed."

The waitress approached to take their order. Kelly peered toward the entrance, the whites of her eyes showing as she did. Seeing that, Matt waved the waitress away.

"We *did* go there," she said defensively, "but Cohan had not returned yet. We decided that I'd take the car and keep tabs on you, while Willie waited there and talked to Cohan after he came home." Her fingers gripped Matt's forearm tightly. "Willie killed him! I was in the loo and overheard him on the telephone telling Marvin that he'd done it and made it look like a suicide." Her face twisted as if she were about to cry.

"Oh, great!" Matt said again. "Is all this because Freedlander intends to run for Mayor of New York City?"

"Bang on! To keep his father's past from ever becoming public. Marvin is a pure political animal," she said savagely.

Matt tried sarcasm again. "You don't say."

"You don't understand!" She sounded exasperated with him, as if he were very naïve. "Look here," she said, trying again. "You know how, in America, some men have been taken with Jack Kerouac?"

"The old '50s beatnik with no moral standards? Yeah."

"Well, Marvin has *his* favorite, too. He has modeled his life after Friedrich Nietzsche."

"Wasn't he the guy who came up with that 'God is dead' line?"

"Yes, there was *that,* too. But I was referring more to his emphasis on the 'superman' or 'Übermensch.' You know — the 'will to power'. Expediency? Pragmatism? He'd lie, cheat, steal and kill. Whatever it takes to get what he wants. He's a post-modernist man. He has *no* morals at all."

Matt couldn't resist. "And *you* do?" It was a low blow, spoken without thinking.

She glared at him angrily and her hand closed around a water glass. For a moment he thought she might fling it in his face. Instead, she removed her hand from the glass, lowered her eyes and studied her fingernails. "I've done a lot of stupid things in my life," she said evenly, "but I'd *never* resort to murder as a solution to *anything.*"

Matt was moved despite himself. "I'm sorry." He sat back in his seat.

Ann shrugged and leaned forward. "I could be of some help to you. I know what they're planning." She ground her cigarette out in the ashtray.

As he studied her intently, he had to admit that he found her very attractive; the serious green eyes, the tilt of her head, the way her emotions flitted across her face and quickly submerged. Masculine to the core, he suddenly felt a protective urge. "You seem a bit nervous," he said, adopting a gentler tone. "Is it your friends?"

"Yes! Please. Can we just leave now?"

‡ ‡ ‡ ‡ ‡

Friday, March 16, 1990
Timonium, Maryland
The Home of Jim and Denise Crowley
12:00 p.m. EST

"Whose house is this?" Ann Kelly was standing behind the closed door in the entrance hall of the Crowley home, looking out at the street through one of the long, narrow glass windows that flanked it. Snow was still falling, but not as heavily as before.

"It belongs to some friends of mine. Their name's Crowley."

"Have you been staying *here?*"

"For a couple of days. Ran out of money hiding in local motels. I'll ask my friends if we can stay for a day or two. Until I figure out what we're gonna do."

Suddenly, Ann sucked in her breath. Her eyes grew wide with fear and she pointed outside. "Look! It's Willie."

Without touching the shear curtain, Matt peered out in time to see the green Ford moving slowly past the house. "He must have followed us when we left the motel." Turning quickly, he headed for the stairs. "Stay there and keep watch."

"What are *you* going to do?"

"Pack my things. He'll probably be back soon. By then we need to be long gone."

"But where will we go?"

"Well, New York City might be a good place. They won't think of looking for us there."

‡ ‡ ‡ ‡ ‡

Friday, March 16, 1990
Timonium, Maryland
York Road
12:10 p.m. EST

"Matt! Have you taken leave of your senses?" This was Ann's first reaction upon hearing that they would travel to New York City. The two, having formed their unspoken alliance, were in Matt's Skyhawk, driving south in traffic, on the way to his apartment in Padonia Village.

Matt scowled. "You have a bad attitude, you know that?"

"You mean for not wanting to go anywhere near Marvin Jonathan? I was actually thinking someplace as far away from him as possible. California? Florida? I could sell my place by phone and - "

Matt held up a hand. "I just think — look, we're in a fight for our lives here. And I'm not ready to be measured for a casket yet. Besides, I read somewhere that the best defense is a good offense."

"Well, the idea has at least *one* thing going for it."

"What?" His voice had an edge to it.

"No one would believe that the hunted would move *closer* to the hunter rather than trying to put as much distance as possible between them," she answered. "After further reflection, I think I'm impressed."

"Humph! 'Impressed' I don't need. Cooperation is what's called for now."

"But just look at this car, will you?" Ann said. "A plastic trash bag taped over the rear window. The passenger door is jammed shut. It's positively unfit for such a trip. If go we must, then there's nothing to do but rent a nice little motor car to get 'round in while we're there."

"My car will have to do," Matt protested. "I can't afford to rent a car."

Ann thought for a moment. "Matt, I'm very grateful for your help in escaping from Preston and Foreman. I have plenty of money. Let me take charge of the finances."

"But ... I could never pay you back."

"Rubbish! You won't need to. My dear departed husband left me more money than I can spend in two lifetimes. Please. Let *me* handle it," she insisted.

They paid a visit to a nearby Budget Rent-a-Car location, where Ann demonstrated that her idea of a "nice little motor car" was a black Cadillac Coup De Ville with plenty of horsepower under the hood, a top of the line heater, air conditioning if it should become necessary, and a wrap-around sound system, for their "listening pleasure," as the saying goes. Ann leased the car for two weeks. A smile and a c-note were enough to arrange the clerk's silence.

At his apartment a few minutes later, Matt let them both in and turned to Ann. "Make yourself comfortable while I put some clean clothes in my bag."

Ann sat on the couch momentarily, but quickly rose and began prowling his apartment. Bookcases lined the walls in both living and dining rooms. On one, she noted photographs of kids; three beautiful girls and a handsome boy. No photos of a wife or any other woman. *Why a man as good looking as this chap doesn't have a woman companion staying with him is beyond me.*

She was examining one of the photos when Matt, finished packing, returned to the living room.

"You live here alone, don't you?" She asked in an accusatory tone as he re-entered.

"Yes. I'm divorced." He said it as if that were all the explanation necessary. Lowering his bag to the floor, he turned to her. "Ann? I have an idea about how to confuse our pursuers. But it'll be expensive, and we'll need to use your credit card."

"Let's hear it, then," Ann crossed her arms while he explained his plan for temporarily thwarting Freedlander's efforts to track them. Seeing wisdom in his idea, she dug into her purse and produced a card. "What better way to spend some of my money than to keep *me* alive?"

"Good thinking!" Matt said, shooting her once with a finger.

Following Matt's instructions and using her Visa card and his phone, Ann booked two one-way tickets on flights leaving from BWI that afternoon; to Chicago on American Airlines, to LAX on Southwest, to Phoenix on Continental, and to Boston on Delta. Finished, she slammed down the phone. "Done!" She said. "Let's go!"

Friday, March 16, 1990
Timonium, Maryland
Day's Inn
Padonia and Deereco Roads
12:15 p.m. EST

"She didn't leave too long ago, Marv," John Foreman said into the phone. His muscular frame was sprawled on one of the queen-sized beds in the motel room.

A few feet away, perched on the edge of the other bed, Willie Preston listened while chewing on a fingernail.

"I thought you were calling to tell me you *had* them," Freedlander said hotly, his voice betraying his mounting concern. "Do you know *why* she left?"

"No. Willie said she's been acting kinda strange the last few days. Told us she was going down to get lunch about eleven-thirty. Fifteen minutes later, we went down to join her. She wasn't there. We checked her room. She wasn't there, either. Her bag was gone, too. When we stepped outside to check on the car, we saw her in a white Buick Skyhawk, just pulling out of the parking lot. Dawson was driving."

"Why didn't you stop her?"

"If we'd known she was plannin' ta leave, we would have, boss," Foreman retorted acidly. He was a short, well-built man with a sallow complexion, black hair, and a heavy beard that sometimes forced him to shave twice a day in an effort to look clean-shaven. Divorced several years ago by a wife who had failed to sympathize with his driving need to succeed, Foreman found that situation compatible with his ambition. It gave him more time to work, unencumbered by obligations to wife or family. He stayed in shape by visiting a local gym daily, where he pumped iron, punched the heavy bag and sparred with live opponents. Over the years, he had put in long hours preparing cases for Freedlander to try. His efforts had made the DA look good. He was smart, intuitive and loyal to a fault, and he felt that these things entitled him to more respect from his boss.

"Do you know where they went?" Freedlander asked, calming a bit.

"Yeah. Willie followed them. They didn't know they were being tailed. Went into a house not too far from here. He watched them go inside."

"Well, that's better. Go back there this evening and … bring it to a conclusion. Am I *clear* on this, John?"

Friday, March 16, 1990
Timonium, Maryland
Padonia Village Apartments
2312 Chetwood Circle
12:45 p.m. EST

Matt and Ann climbed into the rented Coup De Ville and, with Ann behind the wheel, roared east on the Baltimore Beltway and then north on Interstate 95. Matt quickly learned that his new ally did not approve of speed limits and seldom obeyed them. As they sped through Cecil County, Maryland, he said, "Slow down! The speed limit is 65. You'll get us arrested."

"Speed limits! We don't have time just now for such niceties," was Ann's response.

Racing through Delaware, they crossed the Delaware River into New Jersey in much better style than George Washington and his ragtag Continental army had crossed it back on that bitter cold Christmas morning in the Eighteenth Century, bent on attacking the Hessian mercenaries at Trenton. Washington's tactic was a desperate gamble to win a desperately needed victory, the stake, freedom. Matt's move was also a desperate gamble, but at stake was his life, and Ann's, too.

By now, Ann had begun to see in Matt a ray of hope; a slim chance to rid herself of the threat to her life posed by Marvin Jonathan Freedlander, John Foreman and Willie Preston. *If Dawson can expose Freedlander and bring him down, and if I can be of some help to him...* A thought struck her. *What will happen when Matt finds out I'm Anna Lieber's daughter? Well, I'll need to tell him, of course, but it will just have to wait 'till later.*

CHAPTER 41

Friday, March 16, 1990
Timonium, Maryland
The Home of Jim and Denise Crowley
6:30 p.m. EST

"DAWSON'S WHITE SKYHAWK AIN'T HERE." Willie Preston and John Foreman had pulled their car up in front of the two-story brick home on Spring Lake Drive into which Preston had seen Matt Dawson and Ann Kelly disappear earlier. The snowstorm that had threatened to engulf Baltimore had fizzled and, instead of dropping, the temperature had risen. The car's tires splashed through an inch or two of slush, all that remained of the aborted storm.

Foreman edged the Taurus closer to the curb and braked to a stop directly in front of the house. "Whose car is *that*?" He gestured toward a light blue Toyota Camry in the driveway.

Preston shrugged. "Maybe it belongs to the people who own the house. Let's go find out."

Jim and Denise Crowley were relaxing at their kitchen table, having just finished a supper of meat loaf, mashed potatoes, broccoli, and a salad. Denise had made hot biscuits to go along with the meat loaf.

"Would you like some orange sherbet for dessert?" She asked.

The doorbell rang. Jim frowned and slapped his cloth napkin on the table. "Sure. But hold it until I see who this is." He pushed his chair back, walked to the front door and glanced out. Two men he didn't know, dressed in topcoats over suits and ties, were standing on the porch. Hesitating for a moment, he pulled open the door. As he did, one of the men threw his shoulder against it, driving it back hard into Jim.

" Ow!" Jim yelped. Struck by the full force of the heavy eight-panel door, his wrist was bent back at an awkward angle. The impact snapped his radius and ulna bones like dry matchsticks, doubling him over in pain. "Oh, damn. That hurts!"

"Get back inside. Quick!" Preston hissed, as he pushed through the doorway with Foreman close behind. In the entrance hall, both men drew snub-nosed Smith and Wesson .38 caliber pistols from shoulder holsters inside their coats as Foreman closed the door.

"What in heaven's name do you guys want?" Jim demanded angrily, grasping his wrist and fighting back the pain. He suddenly looked frightened, almost sick.

"Jim? What is it?" Denise came into the front hall. Taking in the scene unfolding before her, she turned and tried to run. But Preston was quicker. He caught her in three strides, grabbed her right arm and twisted it behind her.

"Don't either of you try anything funny." Foreman's voice was tinged with menace. "All we want is a little information. Tell us what we need to know and you won't get hurt."

"Get out of my house!" Jim Crowley said between clenched teeth his face pale.

Holstering his pistol, Foreman placed his right hand under Jim's chin, straightening him up. Smiling sadistically, he drove his left fist into Jim's belly. The punch did not travel a foot, but he had turned into it as he threw it and his whole body was behind it. Jim gasped, his eyes glazed and he doubled over again.

"Shut up!" Foreman said savagely. "That kind of thing will only bring you grief. We just want to know where Matt Dawson is. Tell us and we'll leave."

"We don't know where he is," Denise exclaimed indignantly. "Now get out —." She got no further. Preston brought the short barrel of his pistol down along the side of her head. Stifling a scream, she touched her head and ear with her free hand. Her fingers came away wet with blood. "No! Wait!" she said, trying to reason with them. "We haven't seen him today. Jim's been at his office all day and I was out shopping. When I got home, Matt was gone."

Foreman studied Denise for a long moment before turning to Preston. "I don't think they know anything. Let's get them into the kitchen, find some rope and tie them up. Then we'll search the house. Maybe we'll learn something helpful."

‡ ‡ ‡ ‡ ‡

Friday, March 16, 1990
Newark, New Jersey
Howard Johnson Hotel
Frontage Road
6:00 p.m. EST

At Newark, they left the New Jersey Turnpike, turned onto Frontage Road and followed it to an out-of-the-way Howard Johnson Hotel, not too far from Newark International Airport, the third major airport that served the City of New York.

"This end of the state is really quite scenic,, you know." Ann said.

"Yeah, if you close your eyes and think of someplace else."

"The hotel we're going to is on Newark Bay, just across the river from Lower Manhattan. I've used it a few times in the past when I … wanted to get away," Ann said, recalling the nights she'd spent there with Marvin Jonathan Freedlander. In England, she had not slept around with different men, but rather, had had a series of relationships, living with a man for a short time before moving on to another. She had not thought of herself as promiscuous. Looking back now, she held her breath for a moment, suddenly realizing that it was important to her that Matt not think of her that way, either. But, his mind on other matters, Matt only gazed at her for a moment and did not press for any further explanation.

The decor in the lobby of the Howard Johnson Hotel was primarily light oak, glass and brass. At the front desk, sensing that a "proper" woman would be uncomfortable sharing a room with a man she'd just met, Ann rented two adjoining rooms. "So we'll be close in case anything happens," she told Matt.

A tall, uniformed bellhop picked up their bags and placed them on a luggage dolly. Ann handed him the keys to their rooms. "Right," she said to Matt as they followed the bellhop to a nearby elevator and stepped aboard. "I'm famished! Let's freshen up and meet for dinner in half an hour, shall we?"

"You're on. There's a restaurant over there," Matt responded, jerking his thumb in the direction of the lobby. "We can try that."

Arriving at her room, Ann waited while the young bellhop opened her door, turned on the lights and made sure the heater was working. She handed him a large bill. "I say. Can you unlock that connecting door?"

"Yes, ma'am."

"Be a good sod and do it then, will you?"

Alone in his room, Matt unpacked his shaving gear and a clean shirt, removed his clothing and stepped into the shower. He had no idea what he and Ann were going to do next. He only knew that since Marvin Jonathan Freedlander was the source of their problem and Freedlander was in the "Big Apple," this was where they needed to be. Here now, there was no turning back. They could only go forward, and fight to win. To lose was unthinkable.

His thoughts turned to Ann Kelly. He acknowledged a curious attraction to her, something he'd not felt toward a woman in a long time. An interesting mixture of naïveté and sophistication, she was hard as nails in some ways, yet soft and vulnerable in others. He had no doubt that she was afraid for her life. That's why he felt she could be trusted. And *she certainly is a nice-looking woman. Smart, too, and extremely generous.*

He found himself hurrying more than usual, wanting to be with her again as soon as possible. He chuckled. *I may be divorced but I'm definitely not dead.* Finished, he slapped some Old Spice aftershave on his face, dressed in sand-colored slacks and a gray turtleneck sweater, grabbed his blue blazer and headed for the elevator.

Friday, March 16, 1990
Newark, New Jersey
Howard Johnson Hotel
Frontage Road
7:00 p.m. EST

"My room's very comfortable," Matt said. Recalling how Ann had surprised him at Denny's in Timonium earlier that day, he steered them to a corner table from which they could see the door and part of the lobby. Even though he knew it was unlikely that anyone had followed them from Baltimore, he had vowed that, from here on out, he'd be extra careful.

"Mine, too," Ann said. "It's what they call 'downtown hip.' Lots of glass, light-colored wood, and sleek furniture." She had showered and changed into a simple but expensive white blouse, a dark green A-line skirt, and green designer pumps. Her red hair was pulled back from her face with a white beret.

A waiter approached for their drink order. With a concerned look, Ann picked up the wine menu and began scanning it, but Matt stopped her with a gentle touch on her arm. He ordered two glasses of Sangiovese, the same wine each of them had ordered at the Pasti Cosi in Branford, Connecticut on the evening of their first meeting.

Recognizing the wine as the one they'd shared that night, Ann's heart melted. In her entire life, no man had ever made such a sensitive gesture toward her. Swallowing the lump in her throat, she acknowledged his act with a squeeze of his arm and a warm smile. Impulsively, he reached over and took her hand. They were silent. Conversation was unnecessary. Two people thrown together by unusual circumstances, they were afraid, running for their lives, and sharing their fear with each other.

A few minutes later, the waiter returned with two full wineglasses. "Are you ready to order?" Ann selected the roast beef entrée. Matt ordered the broiled chicken dinner.

As their waiter departed, Matt grinned and raised his glass. "Here's lookin' at *you*, kid," he said, doing his best Humphrey Bogart imitation.

Laughing, Ann raised her glass until the two touched lightly. "Casablanca. Bogart and Bergman. 1942, I think." She sipped her wine. He did the same.

Matt set his wineglass down and cleared his throat. "Earlier today you said you knew their plan?"

"Yes. Marvin Jonathan is going to hold a dinner and press conference next Friday evening. It's at The Regent Wall Street Hotel in Lower Manhattan, right in the heart of the Financial District. Willie told me Marvin reserved their huge ballroom months ago. He'll make his grand announcement at that time."

"The Regent Wall Street? Sounds expensive."

"Oh, it's pretty highbrow all right; perhaps the *most* expensive place in Lower Manhattan. It used to be the New York Merchants Exchange. Then it was the Customs House until it was turned into a luxury hotel. That man wouldn't do anything half-baked."

Matt was silent for a moment, thinking. Then, "I guess you know how to get there?"

"Quite. It's at the corner of Williams and Wall Streets." She peered at Matt. "Perhaps I should do the driving while we're here? I'm more familiar with the City than you are."

"Good idea. I've heard a lot of nightmarish things about New York City traffic. And the US Attorney's office? Where's that?"

"At Manhattan's Lower End. Not too far from the hotel. Matt, what are you thinking?"

"I was thinking I'd pay Freedlander a visit first thing Monday morning, at his office."

Ann gasped. "You're having me on!" She said incredulously. Matt did not respond.

She tried again. "My dear chap, are you stark raving mad? They'll kill you on the spot if you show up there."

"It was just a thought," he said, breaking into a broad grin.

‡ ‡ ‡ ‡ ‡

Friday, March 16, 1990
Newark, New Jersey
Howard Johnson Hotel
Frontage Road
10:30 p.m. EST

Ann had enjoyed the dinner with Matt Dawson immensely. It had given her an opportunity to learn more about him. *He has an indefinable quality of strength that makes me feel safe in spite of this beastly situation,* she thought. During dinner, she had laughed at his stories about his youth and countered with a few of her own experiences growing up in England. She also noticed how chastely he looked at her. Not like some other men she had known, whose eyes made the circuit, roving from her face to her breasts to buttocks and back again. At times, in the pubs of her hometown, she had felt like a side of beef being inspected.

They had lingered over dinner, prolonging it as long as possible, neither wanting to relinquish the safety, peace and contentment they were feeling. Finally, they left the restaurant and moved to the elevators, laughing because they both liked mashed potatoes with brown gravy. Her hand in his, for the first time in years Ann felt almost weightless, as if she might float away carrying her joy with her under her arm, like a purse or a shopping bag.

"Here's the lift, now," she said.

As they rode the elevator to the fourth floor, she became somewhat subdued. The evening was drawing to a close much too quickly to suit her. She did not want it to end. *Am I falling in love? She wondered. It does seem that way. He's so different from other chaps I've known. Most of them are all mouth and trousers. But he ... he's quite surprising, actually. He sounds a religious man; someone who actually tries to live his faith. Yet he's not at all lacking in the courage department. And, there's an air of quiet self-assurance about him.*

She wondered what he would do when they reached her door. Would he kiss her and quickly leave, or muscle his way into her room and stay the night. *I wish he'd stay,* she thought. While on many dates during her youth, when worrying about who would control the relationship, she had wanted to withhold her body from the man she was with. But, because of the unwritten rules of her "with-it" crowd, she had felt unable to do so. Tonight, however, she did not sense a need to be in control. She knew that Matt was a good man; that she did not need to be careful with him. She felt like a woman, free to love and free to decide on her own. And she had decided. She desperately wanted to go to bed with him.

At her door, there was a momentary pause before Matt took her in his arms. She came eagerly, wrapping both arms around his neck and moving as close to him as she could get, feeling the warmth of his body against hers.

Their first kiss lasted a long time. When it ended, she could see that he was somewhat flustered, perhaps hoping that he had not gone too far too soon. "Mmmm," she murmured, her eyes signaling how much she had enjoyed the kiss. The thought struck her that if she asked him to come in, the rest of the evening would go as she wanted it to. After all, in her world, the world before Sean, to go to bed with a man after a date was as normal as night following day; expected, like enjoying a nightcap at the end of a wonderful evening. But her inner sense warned her not to push things. *A truly religious man does not go to bed with the lady on their first date,* she thought. *Perhaps later? Since I've never been with one before, I don't really know. We'll see.*

"Good night, Mr. Super Sleuth," she said. Unlocking the door, she stepped inside.

In his room, Matt undressed. The day had been long, eventful and stress-filled. He was drained. His preparations for bed finished, he grabbed the remote, turned on his TV and flipped to a news channel. Quickly tiring of that, he turned it off and settled himself in bed. *I sure did enjoy that kiss,* he thought. His eyes moved to the connecting door between his room and Ann's. *If I try that door, will I find it open?* Reminding himself that he did not believe in sex outside of marriage, he made no move to get out of bed. *Living this Christian life isn't always easy,* he thought.

Several years ago, he had begun a devotion to the Blessed Mother. He considered saying a Rosary, the ancient prayer grounded in Scripture and loved by many, both saints and ordinary people, which had been around since the beginning of the second millennium. For the past two years, he had carried the beads with him, reciting them whenever possible. But, exhausted from the arduous day, he decided against it. Reaching for the lamp on the bedside table, he turned it out and soon drifted off.

He didn't know how long he'd slept. Five minutes. Maybe ten. But, something, a clicking sound, had pulled him back to consciousness. The room was dark. The only illumination came from what little light filtered around the edges of the heavy draperies covering the room's window.

In the darkness, his eyes again sought the connecting door between his room and Ann's. Was it open? Yes! That's what the noise had been. For a panicky moment he wondered if Freedlander's people had found them. Had Ann betrayed him and let them into her room? Was one of them standing over his bed with a pistol, preparing to shoot him as he slept? Now, more than ever, he regretted not having a gun. He gathered himself, ready to roll quickly to the floor on the other side of the bed. But a sixth sense told him it was unnecessary.

He smelled her perfume before he saw or heard her. "Matt? Are you awake?"

"Yes."

She leaned over the bed above him. "I'm frightened, Matt. Please?"

No! This is wrong! He thought. Another reflection came. *Just how wrong can it be? To want to give comfort to and be comforted by another?* Where had he read that a wrong or bad act always presents itself to the intellect as something good? He pushed the thought aside. *This is no place for philosophy 101,* he rationalized. *Especially in these circumstances.* Silently, he raised the covers. There was a rustling sound as she dropped her robe to the floor and slipped between the sheets with him. He always slept nude. She was naked, also. Matt gasped as he felt the warm, satiny skin of a woman against his body, something he had not felt in years. He embraced her. She moved closer, pressing herself tightly against him. The clean smell of her hair filled his nostrils, thrilling him. Seconds later, his blood seemed to catch fire and he was swept away, whirling in a vortex of desire. Then, and for some time after that, they were not afraid any more.

‡ ‡ ‡ ‡ ‡

Saturday, March 17, 1990
Newark, New Jersey
Howard Johnson Hotel
Frontage Road
9:30 a.m. EST

"I need a gun," Matt Dawson said. Having slept late, he had awakened pleasantly tired but refreshed, his tension and anxiety somewhat diminished, as if, after a long fast, his hunger and thirst had been satisfied. It had been four years since he'd been with a woman.

He and Ann had showered, dressed, and were relaxing in the hotel's restaurant over a breakfast of bacon and eggs, grits, whole-wheat toast and coffee. They had just discovered that they both liked their eggs scrambled.

"You *have* a gun, darling," Ann said dreamily, her clear green eyes sparkling.

He blushed. "That's not what I mean."

"And it's really quite adequate, you know," she continued, feeling euphoric.

"I mean a *real* gun. The kind you *shoot* people with."

"You were a wild man. I loved every minute of it. Can we do it again tonight?"

Matt, who was now beginning to feel very guilty at having given in to his passions last night, was not having any. "Ann? We may not even be alive by tonight!"

"Oh, bother!" She said, grinning lecherously. "Aren't we being a bit *grim* this morning? Why do you say that?"

"Because Freedlander and his cronies are not gonna give up looking for us. They'll chase us until they find us. And the odds are all on *their* side. Now will you be serious?"

Ann sighed. "Yes! All right. A gun for shooting people? I know where we can get you one, no questions asked. It's a shop just across the Holland Tunnel on Spring Street."

"Great!" Matt said. "After we finish eating, let's go over there."

Ann's eyes were dark and smoldering. "Right away? Couldn't we just go back to bed for an hour or so first?"

Saturday, March 10, 1990
New York City, New York
Corner of Spring Street and 6th Avenue
11:15 a.m. EST

"It was right *here*, I'm sure of it." Ann said, as she spun around on the crowded sidewalk, narrowly avoiding a collision with a walker plugged into a Walkman, a teen-ager with orange hair and a nose ring, and an elderly woman carrying a shopping bag. The two had finished breakfast, jumped into their car and driven the New Jersey Turnpike to the Holland Tunnel, emerging minutes later on the west side of Lower Manhattan. Here, the stores hid behind corrugated shutters, some because they were out of business, others for the protection the gray shutters offered. She pointed. "Right next to that Chemist's shop." Her lower lip began to quiver and her eyes filled with tears. Having bonded with Matt, she wanted terribly to help him.

"Well, it's not here *now*," Matt did nothing to conceal his disappointment. And his annoyance. "The authorities probably closed it down. Know where any *other* gun shops might be?"

"Not one that won't ask lots of questions, make you fill out forms and wait several days before picking up the gun. The laws here are among the strictest in the country."

"That's strange. I recently read that the murder rate with handguns in New York City is one of the highest in the United States."

"It *is* quite high. I can't imagine why, though. In *this* state you need a permit to own a gun *and* a permit to carry one."

"Maybe the bad guys don't obey the law," Matt said. He fell silent for a moment. Then,

"Well, I'll just have to make do with what I can get." He pointed across the street to a store selling uniforms of all types, wigs and supplies for investigators and private detectives. An idea was jelling. He took her hand. "C'mon. Let's go over there for a minute."

CHAPTER 42

Monday, March 19, 1990
New York City, New York
Office of the Federal Bureau of Investigation
26 Federal Plaza, 23ʳᵈ Floor
12:10 p.m. Eastern Standard Time (EST)

SPECIAL AGENT KENNETH ANDREW STARLING's boyish features made him look much younger than his forty-one years. Tall, with a light complexion, thick blond hair and a strong chin, he often reminded jurors of the 'boy next door' when he took the witness stand in a trial, to testify for the prosecution.

Starling had signed on with the FBI right out of law school, going directly into the Ten Most Wanted Division. He had quickly made a reputation as an agent who was at home in a courtroom; not as a lawyer but as a witness. A linear thinker, he could present evidence accurately and thoroughly, neither adding too much nor leaving anything out. A year later, when the Bureau announced the creation of a special unit comprised of agents whose sole responsibility would be to testify as expert witnesses for federal prosecutors, Starling was the first from the New York City Field Office (NYCFO) to volunteer.

He had worked with Marvin Jonathan Freedlander for almost seven years, testifying in all of Freedlander's major cases. Bank robberies, counterfeiting, drug cases, kidnapping, human trafficking, smuggling; he was there, casting his spell, presenting evidence in such a way that even a New York City jury could understand it.

Looking back, he was unable to say exactly when he first began manipulating the data, disregarding an unfavorable fact, making more of a favorable one than it deserved, but he'd been doing it for some time. It wasn't that he regularly ignored the truth exactly, but rather, like a sculptor, he molded and shaped the facts to fit the DA's theory of his case just a bit better, at times even bending the rules of evidence ever so slightly. His moral relativism, the belief that truth did not exist, or if it did, it was whatever he wanted it to be at that precise moment, had helped. Also useful was the mindset of some police officers, FBI agents and prosecutors; "Hey! We're simply trying to remove another criminal from society, to take one more bad guy off the streets."

When he found that it was *because of*, rather than *in spite of*, his special attributes that Marvin Jonathan Freedlander began to request his services, he realized that he would be a good fit with the DA in the Southern District. His practices did not cause the slightest twinge to a conscience long since stricken, though not completely dead.

Starling was on the telephone, taking a call from Freedlander. Across the room, his standard FBI issue .45 caliber, Smith & Wesson semiautomatic hung in its shoulder holster on a coat rack. Some agents, after being with the Bureau a few years, traded up to Sig Sauer 9-mm automatics with fifteen round magazines, or Kimber .45 caliber ACPs (automatic Colt pistols), a copy of the old Colt .45 with upgraded features. Not him. Given what he'd been doing, he did not have much use for a top-of-the-line weapon.

"How soon can you get over here, Ken?"

"Not 'till later this afternoon, Marv. Why?"

"Need your help. I sent Willie and John down to Baltimore. A guy named Matthew Dawson is wanted for murder in Cuernavaca, Mexico. Killed an American expatriate in the American community down there and then skipped to Baltimore."

"What's that got to do with *us*?" Starling asked, unaware that this was a lie.

"Ordinarily? Nothing. Except that he seems to have kidnapped a local woman named Ann Kelly in the process. Gave our guys the slip in Baltimore on Friday afternoon. They've been lookin' for him all weekend. We've got a situation here that may require the resources of the FBI to resolve it. I want you to go down there and take charge of Dawson's apprehension. "

"What do we know about this guy?"

"Not much. Maybe you can find out more, like if he has a family. A wife? An ex-wife he's still fond of? Kids? You never know when stuff like that'll come in handy."

"Ann Kelly? She the widow of Sean Cornelius Kelly, Esquire?"

"Yeah."

"Sean was a friend of the Bureau," Starling said thoughtfully. "Donated large chunks of change for state-of-the-art lab facilities at headquarters and set up a trust to generate income to help keep it running. He gave us a freebee on the legal fees, too." He glanced at his calendar. "I have a few things to clean up. Then I'll come over. Do you have a description of this Dawson?"

"I do."

"Give it to me. I'll authorize an all-points bulletin (APB) on him right away."

‡ ‡ ‡ ‡ ‡

Monday, March 19, 1990
Cuernavaca, Mexico
Police Headquarters
11:30 a.m. Mexico City Time (MCT)

Emilio Diaz poked his head into Chief Inspector Ramon Gonzales's cubicle and fanned away a thick cloud of cigarette smoke with one hand. In the other, he carried a long strip of paper removed from the teletype machine just moments before. He spoke in Spanish.

"Ramon? Got a minute?"

The Inspector looked up from a forensics report he had been reading. "What is it, Emilio?"

"Did we put out an APB on Matthew Dawson for the murder of George W. Cohan?"

"We most certainly did *not*," Gonzales said, waving his cigarette at his assistant.

"Well then, what is going on here? This just came over the wire."

Gonzales glanced at the teletype and frowned. "The American FBI authorized this APB." He handed it back to Diaz, who studied it intently.

"Oh. And look here," Diaz exclaimed, pointing to some wording that he had missed. "It originated in New York City."

Gonzales sprang to his feet. "New York? I know what this is all about." He strode to the door of his cubicle. "Señora Montoya!" He called. "Ahora, por favor!"

A sturdily built woman in her late twenties appeared in the doorway. Gonzales thought for a moment. "Carlotta, Inspector Diaz and I must leave for the United States right away," he said. "Arrange for dos billetos on the first flight out of Benito Juarez this afternoon. A direct flight to Baltimore-Washington International in Maryland. Tell Accounting to charge this and all our expenses while we're gone to the Cohan murder case." He handed the APB to her.

"After you get our tickets, I'd like for you to contact the FBI Field Office in Washington, DC. *Not* New York. Washington. Find out the name of the agent who authorized this APB and the reason why. When we reach Baltimore this evening, I'll call you for the information. Do not leave the office until you hear from me." He turned to Diaz. "Emilio, go home. Pack a bag. Bring your government issue pistol and a backup. Plenty of ammunition. Also, your permit to carry. Meet me back here in one hour."

"So. We are going to Baltimore, Ramon?"

"Sí. Dawson is in some trouble not of his making. Perhaps more than he can handle."

Monday, March 19, 1990
Timonium, Maryland
Padonia Village Apartments
2312 Chetwood Circle
8:05 p.m. EST

"That's his car, right there!" Willie Preston said, his voice edged with tension. He, John Foreman and Special Agent Kenneth Starling were standing in front of Matt Dawson's apartment building at 2312 Chetwood Circle. Less than an hour before, he and Foreman had picked up Starling at Baltimore's BWI.

Earlier that day, after meeting with Marvin Jonathan Freedlander at his office, Starling had hurriedly boarded a Delta Airlines flight at La Guardia, bound for Baltimore. Since breakfast, all he'd eaten was a bag of pretzels and a cup of coffee. As a result, he was irritable and impatient. Striding over to the car, his eyes took in the trash bag taped over the gaping hole that had once been the car's rear window. He paused, momentarily disconcerted. "What is *that*?" He said, pointing.

"It's a plastic trash bag," Preston said matter-of-factly.

"Oh." Starling shook his head, like a prizefighter who had just absorbed a blow to the chin. He didn't quite understand, but his brain would not come to grips with it. "Well, if that's his car there and he's *not* in his apartment, can either of you tell me where this fella is?"

"Look, Ken," John Foreman said. "Willie followed him and Ann from the motel to a house in Timonium on Friday around noon. But when we went back that evening, they were gone, and the people who live there hadn't seen Dawson all day."

Starling shrugged. "Come on. Let's get to the motel so I can check in. Then, I'll contact the local FBI field office and request their help. With any luck, we'll have a dozen agents out here by midnight, checking every hotel and motel in the area. We'll cover the airport, the train and bus terminals, and we'll check the airlines and the bus company to see if they boarded a plane or took a bus. If those two are still in Baltimore, we'll know by morning. We'll —"

"Ken?" Foreman interrupted. "Suppose they rented a car and *drove* outta here?"

"I doubt if they'd do *that*," Starling said patiently, as if talking to a child. "But if we come up empty, we can check all the car rental companies in the area first thing tomorrow."

‡ ‡ ‡ ‡ ‡

Monday, March 19, 1990
Anne Arundel County, Maryland
Baltimore-Washington International Airport (BWI)
8:40 p.m. EST

"What have you found out for me, Señora Montoya?" Chief Inspector Ramon Gonzales and Deputy Inspector Emilio Diaz, having just deplaned, were standing at a pay phone in the busy terminal at BWI. Gonzales was calling his office, as he had said he would. The phone was tucked under his chin while his hands probed his pockets for cigarettes and matches.

"I contacted the FBI's Washington Field Office and asked about the origin of that APB," Carlotta Montoya said in rapid Spanish. "Spoke with Special Agent Richard McIntyre. He is the agent in charge. He knew nothing about it, but he said he'd look into it and get back to me. He called back a few hours later and told me that Special Agent Kenneth Starling of the New York City Field Office had issued the APB. He said it was most unusual, since Agent Starling is assigned to the Court Room Unit and would have no need to do such a thing."

"No? Why not?"

"Because his only function is to testify in court for the local District Attorney."

"And in this case, who would that be?" Ramon asked.

"The DA for the Southern District of New York, Marvin Jonathan Freedlander,"

"I see."

"Special Agent McIntyre wants you to call him." She gave him the number.

"Good job, Carlotta. Thank you. You may go home now. I will call you in the morning."

"Inspector? You and Emilio must be very careful," Carlotta Montoya said earnestly. "The US can be a dangerous place. So many crazy people on the streets. They no longer hospitalize them, but instead, let them run loose, sleeping over warm grates or in abandoned buildings. Lots of druggies wandering around, too. Sometimes they shoot people to get money for their drugs. Then, there's the water. It is badly polluted. And the air can make you sick if you breathe too much of it. Eighteen thousand breaths a day! It is hardly surprising what can end up in your lungs. I have read about these things in *The New York Times*."

‡ ‡ ‡ ‡ ‡

Monday, March 19, 1990
Timonium, Maryland
Padonia Village Apartments
Outside of 2312 Chetwood Circle
9:45 p.m. EST

Just over forty-five minutes later, as the residents of quiet Padonia Village were ensconced in front of televisions or preparing for bed, a yellow cab with the words AIRPORT TAXI painted on its sides pulled into the parking area and stopped in front of building 2312. The rear doors swung open and two men stepped out.

"Wait for us, por favor," Ramon Gonzales said, showing his badge to the driver.

Followed by Diaz, Gonzales entered the building, found Matt's apartment and rang the doorbell. Receiving no response, he knocked at the apartment next door.

"Yes? Who is it?" A woman's voice responded from inside.

"Police. We are looking for your neighbor, Mr. Matthew Dawson."

An elderly woman in a faded blue bathrobe opened the door. "Matt? I haven't seen him for a while. I *heard* someone over there on Friday, but there's no one there now."

Ramon nodded. "Sorry to bother you." The two men left the entrance hall and stopped on the sidewalk in front of the building.

"What now?" Emilio Diaz asked.

"Now? I think we should talk to *these* people," Ramon said, gesturing. As they had emerged from the apartment building, a car, moving fast, had pulled into a parking space. A man and woman jumped out and headed for the door of Building 2312. The man was of medium height and slightly overweight. His right arm was in a plaster cast. The woman was middle-aged and also on the plump side. Both seemed agitated.

"Excuse me," Gonzales said. "Are you, perhaps, acquainted with Matthew Dawson?"

"Yes!" Jim Crowley answered, a look of surprise springing to his face. "Who are *you*?"

Introductions were exchanged, after which Gonzales said, "Mr. Dawson does not appear to be home. We have come from Cuernavaca, Mexico to help him."

"Are you sure nobody's home?" Denise Crowley asked. "That's his car right over there." She pointed to Matt's Buick Skyhawk.

Emilio Diaz glanced in the direction she indicated and took in the car with its plastic bag taped over the rear window. He blinked and a thoughtful expression appeared on his face, but he decided to let it go. "We have checked," he said, recovering quickly.

Gonzales smiled. "Was there a reason you decided to come here at this late hour?"

"We came over to see if Matt was here," Jim explained. "There are some things we need to tell him." Sucking in his breath, he glanced at Denise, uncertain how to proceed. Instantly, he made up his mind. "Denise and I don't live too far from here. Will you follow us over to our place? I think we need to talk."

‡ ‡ ‡ ‡ ‡

Monday, March 19, 1990
Cockeysville, Maryland
The Home of Jim and Denise Crowley
10:20 p.m. EST

"So," Emilio Diaz said, his eyes searching the faces of his companions, "how are we to help Matt if we don't even know where he is?" He and Ramon Gonzales had explained to the others everything they knew, beginning with the events in Cuernavaca, while Denise prepared a light, late dinner for them.

"That's the sixty-four thousand dollar question," Barbara Davis responded. Upon arriving home, Jim had called Dan and Barbara and asked them to come over.

"The last thing he said to me was that he'd 'think of something,' some way to resolve the trouble he was in." Gonzales stifled a yawn. It had been a long day. He was tired and hungry, and they had yet to check into a motel.

"Do you have any idea what he meant?" Jim asked.

"No," Ramon replied, "nor do I understand why he would leave without his car."

"Perhaps he took a cab," Emilio speculated.

"It's clear that Matt's in serious trouble," Jim said. "And we don't have a clue about where he is or what we can do to help."

"We need to hear from Matt," Dan said. "So there's only one thing we can do."

"What?" Barbara asked.

"Pray for him to call us," Dan said.

‡ ‡ ‡ ‡ ‡

Monday, March 19, 1990
Newark, New Jersey
Howard Johnson Hotel
Frontage Road
11:05 p.m. EST

"You're making this up as you go along, aren't you?" Ann Kelly demanded.

Matt and Ann had eaten a late dinner in a deserted corner of the hotel's restaurant, after which they had retired to Matt's room. She was lying on his bed on her stomach, propped up on her elbows, fully clothed except for her shoes. He was next to her. On TV, the eleven o'clock news had just begun, but they were only watching it with half an eye.

"No! Well … yes, I guess so." Matt grinned sheepishly. "It's my first investigation. I wasn't counting on running into anything like this."

Ann's eyebrows shot up. "Your *very* first?"

"Yeah."

Her spirit sank. "That's hardly a comforting thought," she said aloud. *What does it say for my chances of staying alive?* She wondered to herself.

"But, I'm not doing too badly so far, am I? We learned a helluva lot today." Matt had wisely postponed his visit to Freedlander's habitat until Tuesday, electing instead to use the day to surreptitiously reconnoiter the US District Courthouse and surrounding area and devise a plan for entering and leaving the building without being caught.

Ann balanced herself on one elbow and reached for a fresh pack of Virginia Slim 100s on the bedside table. "Are you really going through with it tomorrow?" She asked, staring at him.

"Yes."

"You're daft as a brush!"

"Can *you* come up with a better plan?"

She shook her head, inserted a cigarette between her lips, and watched as Matt reached for the phone. "Who are you calling, so late?" She asked petulantly.

"I'm gonna call Jim and Denise Crowley. They're probably worried about me. It's time to let them know what's going on."

She struck a match and held it to the end of her cigarette. "Wait. Have you decided what we're going to do *after* your little visit to Marvin Jonathan's office tomorrow?"

Matt's brow furrowed. "Yes."

"What? Tell me."

"Try to stay alive until Friday."

Ann nodded. "Well, I certainly agree with *that*. What now?"

He picked up the phone. "After I make this call we're going to bed."

"Mhmmm! I like *that* idea."

"No," Matt said. "You're going to bed in *there*." He gestured with a thumb toward the connecting door. Against his better judgment, they had slept together again on both Saturday and Sunday nights. Guilt had overtaken desire, as it frequently does with someone whose conscience is alive and well. Feeling like a farmer who locks the barn door after the horses have gotten loose, he was trying to gather his resolve. "*I'm* going to bed in *here*."

Ann sighed. "I don't like *that* idea." Sliding over until she was lying on top of him, she took the phone from his hand, replaced it on the nightstand, and ran her fingers through his hair. "These last few nights have *really* been wonderful, Matt. Couldn't you reconsider?" He started to protest, but found it hard to talk with her full, warm lips covering his.

Tuesday, March 20, 1990
Timonium, Maryland
Days Inn
Padonia and Deereco Roads
7:45 a.m. EST

Special Agent Ken Starling was pacing. He had probably walked two miles around his motel room on the fourth floor of the Days Inn since checking in late Friday night. In a chair nearby, Special Agent Walter Anderson of the FBI's Baltimore Field Office (BFO) was poring over a Baltimore County map. Special Agent Dominic Vitale, phone in hand, sat across from him. Anderson and Vitale were dressed exactly alike; blue sport coats off but nearby, gray slacks, button-down shirts, striped ties, black shoes with rubber soles, and .45 caliber pistols in clip-on holsters on their belts. Nearby, John Foreman, his tie off, was sprawled on one of the beds. Willie Preston sat on the end of the other, biting his nails.

"Keep looking," Agent Vitale said into the phone. "Rock 'n roll, fellas! When you've finished along York Road, come on in." he hung up.

"Well?" Anderson asked.

"That was Siragusa. Him 'n Harris are doing a hard location search of the motels on York Road from Towson north to Cockeysville. Found out Dawson had been staying at an Econo Lodge, but he left there a few days ago. They only have one more place to check."

The phone rang. Anderson picked it up. "Anderson." There was a long pause. Then, "Tell Johnson to go back to Amtrac. You stay there and watch for them. When your shift is over, I'll send someone to relieve you." He replaced the receiver.

Anderson glanced at Starling "Porter and Johnson checking in," he said. "They drew a blank at the Amtrac station and the Trailways bus terminal."

"Who's been checking motels in Hunt Valley?" Foreman asked.

"Driscoll and Indrisano," Vitale said. "There are only four. They didn't find anything."

The phone rang again. Anderson grabbed it. "Yeah?" He listened, smiled and pointed at Starling. "Got something!" He listened some more and the look on his face changed from smugness to anger. "American, Southwest, Continental and Delta? Well, which plane did they actually get *on*?" He breathed deeply into the phone and listened again. "Oh," he said. "Okay. Stay there. If you spot them, take 'em into custody and call me ASAP." He hung up and rose from his chair. "I can't believe this!" He said to no one in particular.

"What?" Vitale asked. The others were all ears.

"That was Grafton at BWI," Anderson announced. "He's been checking the airline offices. It took him and Chambers over three hours to cover all of them. Found four airlines that recorded tickets purchased Friday afternoon in the names of Ruth Ann Kelly and Matthew J. Dawson. *She* booked them by phone and used *her* credit card to pay.

"*She* booked 'em? That's strange," Starling said.

"Well, yes and no," Anderson responded, unaware that he and the other FBI agents were being used. "In kidnapping cases, the victims often cooperate with their kidnappers. It's called *The Stockholm Syndrome*. Some kind of bonding process takes place."

"So where did they *go*?" Starling moved a step closer to Anderson.

"We still don't know," Anderson responded glumly. "It seems they didn't board any of the flights they booked on. They didn't use the tickets."

"They think they're clever!" Starling muttered, turning away. Then a thought occurred to him. "Let's get someone tracking down Dawson's family, ASAP."

"I put an agent on that before we came over here," Anderson said. "We should know something later today." He grabbed his sport coat. "Let's go downstairs and eat breakfast. I'm hungry and I could use some *real* coffee instead of the bilge in these in-room packets. After we eat, I'll roll a couple a men to the car rental locations in this area."

Foreman caught Starling's eye and shot him once with a finger. Starling glared at him venomously before reaching for his jacket and following Anderson from the room.

CHAPTER 43

Tuesday, March 20, 1990
New York City, New York
Daniel Patrick Moynihan US Courthouse
500 Pearl Street, Lower Manhattan
US District Attorney's Office
10:15 a.m. Eastern Standard Time (EST)

Alone in his private office on the second floor of the US District Courthouse, Marvin Jonathan Freedlander, pruning shears in hand, leaned over a window box filled with Nicotianas. There were plants in five window boxes, and a few others in individual terra cotta pots scattered throughout the office, but he was especially proud of the group in this box. Their brilliant colors would shame a rainbow.

He had lovingly nursed them from the time they were seedlings, pruning and shaping until they looked exactly the way he wanted them to look. Examining their blossoms, leaves and stems, he frowned as he spotted a brownish growth. "Oh! Poor baby," he said out loud. He gently snipped the offending shoot and began looking for other brown growths. Suddenly, the loud clang of the building's fire alarm reverberated throughout the office, startling him. Placing the shears on his desk, he joined his secretary and two law clerks in the outer office.

"What's going on?" He asked gruffly.

"Don't know, sir," Daphne, his secretary responded. "But, I think we'd better go outside, like everyone else, just in case."

Out in the hall, a line of people was heading for the stairs. Orderly, trading greetings and jokes, no one paid any attention to a maintenance man standing near the stairwell. Clad in navy blue pants, a gray, white and blue vertically striped shirt and a navy blue baseball cap, he carried a bucket and mop. The left breast pocket of the man's shirt held a plastic pencil holder in which was a number two pencil and what appeared to be an ordinary ball point pen. On the wall behind him was a small red fire alarm box. If anyone had examined it, they would have seen that its glass had been broken out and its lever had been pulled.

The office workers began to descend the stairs. The maintenance man did not join them. Instead, as the last of them disappeared down the stairwell, he moved in the opposite direction. Pausing at the double glass doors of the US Attorney's office, he threw a quick glance over his shoulder, pushed open the door and stepped inside.

‡ ‡ ‡ ‡ ‡

Tuesday, March 20, 1990
New York City, New York
Daniel Patrick Moynihan US Courthouse
500 Pearl Street, Lower Manhattan
US District Attorney's Office
10:50 a.m. EST

Marvin Jonathan Freedlander slammed his office door behind him, irritated that the false alarm had taken more than half an hour from his busy workday. The sight of a motionless figure standing in the rear of his office next to the emergency exit troubled him.

"What are *you* doing in here?" He said sharply. "Why weren't you outside the building like the rest of us?"

"I was waiting for *you*," the figure said. His hand fingered the pen in his shirt pocket.

Freedlander moved toward him. The man was not tall, but his shoulders were broad and solid enough to make a cautious person stop and think before starting anything with him.

Something about the man's clear brown eyes and level gaze caused the DA to stop in his tracks.

Despite the maintenance uniform, mop and bucket, Freedlander knew instinctively that this was no janitor. Was he about to be robbed? His hand sought the wallet in his back pocket while his eyes searched the intruder for any sign of a gun. Seeing none, he cleared his throat. "Who are you and what do you want?" He asked meekly.

"My name is Matthew Dawson," Matt said. "I came to talk to you."

"Dawson?" Freedlander was incredulous. "How did you get up here?" An icy tingle of dread prickled down his spine. "Did you have anything to do with that false alarm?"

"Questions, questions." Matt said, moving a step closer to Freedlander. "I'd like to ask you some, too."

The tall DA's jaw tightened. "I have nothing to say to you, Dawson."

"I thought you might feel that way, so I'll come straight to the point. I know your man killed George Cohan. I know you're trying to kill me and you also want to kill Ann Kelly. And I know why. "

Freedlander scowled. "Maybe so. But you can't prove any of it. And I'd be foolish to allow either you or Ann to … continue as before, since you know what you know."

Matt, wanting to keep Freedlander talking, played what seemed to be a bargaining card. "If you call off your dogs, we might let you keep your job as DA. If you don't? Well, I think the police will be very interested in what we have to tell them."

"You're not in any position to tell *me* what to do," Freedlander snarled. He tried to raise his voice to call for help, but his lungs felt like they had frozen to the walls of his chest. He moved toward his desk, intending to summon help by hitting the intercom. Anticipating that, Matt leaned over, scooped up a terra cotta pot containing one of the Nicotiana plants, and heaved it in Freedlander's direction. Taken by surprise, Freedlander tried to dodge, but lost his footing and sprawled full-length on the plush carpet. When he regained his feet, he was alone in the room. Matt had opened the emergency door and slipped out into the back hall, closing the door silently behind him.

‡ ‡ ‡ ‡ ‡

Tuesday, March 20, 1990
New York City, New York
US District Attorney's Office
Daniel Patrick Moynihan US Courthouse
500 Pearl Street, Lower Manhattan
10:55 a.m. EST

Once in the narrow back corridor, Matt raced to the service elevator, the sound of his running feet muffled by thick gray carpeting. Earlier, he had summoned the elevator to this floor and jammed its door open with a broom handle. Pausing, he quickly pulled the makeshift prop aside, reached in and pressed the button for the sixth floor, four floors above. As the elevator doors snapped shut, he sprinted down the hall, rounded the corner and dived into a stair well. Taking the steps two at a time, he was soon on the first floor. From there, he made his way outside to an alley that ran along the east side of the building.

The alleyway held several illegally parked cars and five large green dumpsters, each with a half-dozen smaller trashcans clustered around it. Behind one of the dumpsters, a used up old man sat, eyes closed, a whiskey bottle clutched between his knees.

No pursuit so far. Matt's wind having returned, he approached one of the smaller cans, lifted its lid and extracted a plastic bag containing his blue blazer. The old guy turned his head toward Matt and opened unseeing eyes, but otherwise did not react. Working feverishly, Matt threw off the maintenance uniform revealing a dazzling white dress shirt, an Italian silk diamond-and-shield tie, and sharply pressed tan slacks. He donned the blazer and stuffed the now useless janitor's clothing into the bag. He was about to chuck it over the side of a dumpster when a thought occurred. A few quick strides brought him to the old man's side. Unshaven, hair matted and clothing torn and filthy, he smelled of booze and sweat. "Welcome to New York City," Matt said under his breath. Setting the bag down beside the sleeping man, he strode briskly away.

Tuesday, March 20, 1990
New York City, New York
Daniel Patrick Moynihan US Courthouse
500 Pearl Street, Lower Manhattan
US District Attorney's Office
10:59 a.m. EST

Freedlander surveyed the now empty back end of the office as his secretary, Daphne, and his two law clerks, Pete and Sam, rushed in from the front office.

"What on earth happened, Mr. Freedlander?" Daphne asked.

"We heard a noise," Pete said. A burley former Cornell University football player, he was working as a law clerk while attending law school. He took in the broken pottery shards and flattened Nicotiana plant near his boss's desk.

Freedlander, his face ashen, gestured feebly toward the emergency door. "A man! He was waiting in here when I came back. Don't just *stand* there. Go after him, damn it!"

The two law clerks ran to the emergency door, threw it open and stepped into the narrow hallway. It was empty. The sound of the elevator reached them. With a fleeting look over his shoulder in the direction of his boss, Pete raced to the elevator in time to see that it had come to a stop on the sixth floor. Quickly returning to the office, he exchanged glances with Sam before closing the door firmly and making certain it was locked. Out of breath, he studied his boss carefully. "There's no one out there," he said. "But I think he took the elevator to the sixth floor."

"I'll call Security," Daphne said. "Maybe they can catch the guy before he gets out of the building."

‡ ‡ ‡ ‡ ‡

Tuesday, March 20, 1990
New York City, New York
La Borsa Di Roma Restaurant
215 Pearl Street
11:30 a.m. EST

"Your hair is mussed," Ann Kelly said possessively. She reached into her purse and pulled out a small brush. "Here." They were seated at a cozy table all the way in the back of La Borsa Di Roma, an elegant Italian restaurant on Pearl Street, just off Maiden Lane, in the Financial District. The dimly lit eatery was beginning to fill with its usual luncheon patrons, office workers from nearby buildings. It was just a few blocks north of the Courthouse from which Matt had beaten a hasty retreat only moments ago.

The day before, while Matt had been examining the inside of the Courthouse, Ann had spotted this restaurant, and had immediately seen its value as a meeting place. She had also found an underground parking garage on nearby Maiden Lane, where the Caddy could be hidden away until they needed it. Then, at Matt's suggestion, she had rented another car, a dark blue Chevy Monte Carlo, at a local car rental agency, insisting upon two sets of keys, one for him and one for her. She had paid the fee for a week in advance, and had then stowed it in a garage on Gold Street, south of the federal courts building. They now had vehicles located at two points; one north, the other south of the courthouse, in case a quick escape became necessary.

Today, after dropping Matt off in front of the courthouse, she had parked their Cadillac in the Maiden Lane garage and picked up *The New York Times* at a newsstand on her way to the restaurant. Once inside, she ordered a whisky sour to calm her nerves, and forced herself to scan her copy of the *Times*. Half an hour later, having skimmed the newspaper, she set it aside, ordered another whiskey sour and took stock of her situation. *I really didn't need to fall in love again. Well really, one can never predict this sort of thing, can one? But we're so different. How will it ever work?* Another thought struck her. *And what's he going to think when he finds out I'm Ruth Ann Lieber and I didn't let him know right off? That should be a jolly good scene!* She sipped her drink. *Maybe they'll kill him in Freedlander's office. Beard the lion in his den, all right. But don't be a bit surprised if the lion turns on you. What a barmy idea! I should never have let him do it. Whatever would I do, then? No! God wouldn't allow such a thing. You wouldn't, would you, God?*

She took a deep swig of her drink. *How odd! I just spoke to God.* She tossed her head. *But I've spent my entire life denying that He exists. Why should I be talking to Him now? And if He does exist, why would He be interested in helping someone like me?*

Before she could do much with that thought, Matt materialized, slipping quickly through the front door, smiling and nodding at the hostess, gesturing amicably toward her table in the back, as if he were simply meeting a female friend for a casual lunch. Throwing himself into the chair opposite her, he breathed a sigh of relief, took the offered hairbrush from her hand and passed it over his hair. "Better?"

"Yes. How did it go?"

"It all happened pretty fast," Matt said. The proximity to death had pumped his adrenaline high. He quickly recounted his recent escapade in a low but excited voice. Only his accelerated heartbeat betrayed how keyed up he was.

"Really, Matt. I *wish* I could have seen his face when you told him who you were."

Matt grinned from ear to ear. "After I delivered my message, I hauled it out of there without waiting around for his response."

Ann made a nondescript hand gesture. "While you were gone, I've been busy. Just look here." Opening her copy of the *Times* to the Metropolitan section, she pointed. "This is an article about Marvin Jonathan's party. It's scheduled for Friday evening at the Regent Wall Street. Eight o'clock. Lots of very important people will be there."

"Oh, great! Now all we have to do is stay alive until then."

"Bang on," Ann said. "What's next, Mr. Super Sleuth?"

"Next?" Matt turned and glanced around the restaurant. "You picked a pretty nice place to meet. I suggest we have lunch." He removed the pen from his shirt pocket and held it up for Ann to see. "After that, you may just get your wish. Seeing Freedlander's face, I mean. We'll find a local film lab and get the film in this thing developed."

Ann squinted at the object in Matt's hand. "What is *that*?"

"It looks just like a fountain pen, but it's actually a color wireless Pencam."

She squealed with delight. "A camera! You filmed the whole thing?"

"Yeah." He pointed to a tiny pinhole near one end. "See? Here's the lens. And this," he said, pointing to another spot, "is the recorder. The film is ASA 400 and the ISO speed is 1600. It doesn't need much light, and it'll film and record sounds from anything in front of whoever wears it, up to twenty feet away. I picked it up at that store where we bought the janitor's uniform the other day." He leaned forward. "I think the FBI will be interested in what we've got here."

Speechless, Ann sat back in her chair, a half-smile playing around the edges of her mouth. The waiter stopped at their table and took their lunch order. When he had gone, she licked a finger and swiped it vertically in the air. "Another point for our side!" She said.

‡ ‡ ‡ ‡ ‡

Tuesday, March 20, 1990
New York City, New York
Daniel Patrick Moynihan US Courthouse
500 Pearl Street, Lower Manhattan
US District Attorney's Office
11:45 a.m. EST

"He's *here*, in New York City!" Marvin Jonathan Freedlander hissed. He was on the sidewalk in front of the Federal Courthouse, pacing back and forth, a portable phone tucked under his chin as he spoke to Ken Starling, who was still in Baltimore. Freedlander's face was pale and he kept scratching his head as he talked.

"How do you *know*?" Starling asked. He was still under the impression that the man he'd been sent to Baltimore to apprehend was a serious lawbreaker, a fugitive from justice.

"Because he just left my office, *that's* how I know," Freedlander snarled.

"Well, didn't you detain him?" Starling demanded.

"No, I didn't," Freedlander said shortly. "It happened too quickly. We were taken by surprise. Security searched the whole damn building after he left; every office, hallway and storage area. He got away."

There was a long pause as Starling digested this bit of news. Then, "Dawson's got an ex-wife and four grown kids. Three of them still live in the Baltimore area."

"Good! We can use that to … negotiate, if necessary, to force Dawson to come in."

"Is the Kelly woman with him?"

"I don't know. When he showed up *here* he was alone."

"There seems to be some doubt as to whether he actually kidnapped her, Marv," Starling said. "She apparently used her own credit card to charge a bunch of their expenses."

"We'll worry about that later," Freedlander said evasively. "You and the others may as well shut it down and come back. Right away. By later tonight I'd like to roll all available FBI agents in the NYFO and every NYPD blue in the City to hunt for them."

‡ ‡ ‡ ‡ ‡

Tuesday, March 20, 1990
Newark, New Jersey
Howard Johnson Hotel
Frontage Road
3:45 p.m. EST

"I figured you might need some help," Ramon Gonzales said, "as soon as Emilio spotted that APB on you." When Matt and Ann had returned to their hotel from New York City, Matt had immediately called Jim Crowley's residence. He was surprised that both Ramon Gonzales and Emilio Diaz were there. "You were on the local television twice this weekend."

Matt glanced over at Ann who was reclining seductively on one of the beds, listening. "We haven't been watching much TV since we arrived," he said sheepishly.

"Is the woman you are with the blonde woman we were looking for in Cuernavaca?"

"Yes, but she didn't have anything to do with Cohan's death. The guy she was with apparently did it while she was following me around the American community that afternoon. Now these people are trying to kill her, too. For the same reason. So we've teamed up." His eyes narrowed. "Should we be concerned about walking around on the street up here?"

"I'm surprised you have not seen anything in the newspapers there."

Matt pointed to Ann to get her attention. "Haven't looked at a paper since I left Mexico. I'll send Ann down to the lobby to see if she can find a few back issues of the local newspapers."

Ann nodded, quickly slipped her heels on, grabbed her purse, and left the room. Matt then filled Inspector Gonzales in on events that had transpired since they had last talked.

When he finished, Gonzales was quiet for a few moments. Then, "Your friends have told us that it takes about three hours to drive from here to New York City. Emilio and I rented a car this afternoon. If we leave soon, we can be there in time for a late dinner."

CHAPTER 44

Tuesday, March 20, 1990
Newark, New Jersey
Howard Johnson Hotel
Frontage Road
4:30 p.m. Eastern Standard Time EST

"JUST LOOK AT THESE, WOULD you?" Ann started talking before she was fully in the room. Dumping several newspapers on the work table, she threw herself on the nearest bed. "Those are Monday's newspapers. Our faces are in all of them, along with information about each of us. The story says you supposedly killed that old man in Cuernavaca and, when I tried to stop you, you kidnapped me."

Matt picked up a copy of *The New York Times* from the stack. "Not a half-bad picture of you," he said. "Lousy one of me, though."

"Matt! Be serious! We were wandering around the streets of Manhattan all morning. It's a wonder we weren't stopped by the police."

He tossed the newspaper back on the pile and turned to Ann. "We need to arrange for some newspaper coverage of our own."

"I'm not following you. Of what, for heaven sakes?" She asked petulantly.

"Of Freedlander's big event this Friday evening."

"Oh, that. Don't worry. The press will be there."

"Yes. But I mean *informed* press. Armed with the story of what's *really* going on and primed to ask some serious questions."

Ann thought for a minute. "I don't know *anyone* at any newspapers but I *do* know someone who may be able to help. He's a junior partner at my dear departed husband's law firm." She kicked off her heels and began massaging a foot. A gold anklet on her left ankle glittered in the soft light. "Curtis Wright worshipped the ground Sean walked on."

"Do you think he'll help?" While she had been downstairs gathering newspapers, Matt had concluded that Freedlander's party would provide them with their best opportunity to bring this matter to a head. Bringing it to a head was what he most wanted.

"Yes, for two reasons. The first is that *The New York Times* is one of the firm's most important clients. The other is that he's handling my trust as trustee. His annual commission is enormous. He'll be only too happy to do anything I ask."

"Hmm. Tell him we need at least one reporter to meet us at Freedlander's party. Two would be better. Each should bring a photographer. We'll brief them when they arrive."

Ann reached for the phone, dialed a number and waited. "Mr. Wright, please," she said when it was answered.

A few moments passed while the call was routed. Then, "This is Curtis Wright."

"Curtis? Ann Kelly. How are you, darling?"

"Ann? I'm well, dear. But how are *you?* We heard you'd been kidnapped."

"Kidnapped? Not at all! Who told you that?

"It's been on TV and in the newspapers. The DA for the Southern District released a story about it on Monday. We've all been very concerned."

"Well you needn't be. It's simply not true. Those beastly newspapers will print almost anything these days." Glancing over at Matt for reassurance, she continued. "Curtis, I need a large favor. Just listen for a minute, would you, while I explain."

‡ ‡ ‡ ‡ ‡

Tuesday, March 20, 1990
Timonium, Maryland
Office of the Crowley Insurance Agency
4:00 p.m. EST

"So when they leave in the morning, I think I should be with them," Dan Davis said. He had walked into Jim Crowley's office unannounced, as he often did since the two had become close friends. Having just finished explaining why he felt he should go to New York City with the detectives, he looked over at Jim and waited expectantly.

"Dan, these fellas are trained professionals," Jim said thoughtfully. "What makes you think you can be of any help to them? That you won't just get in their way?"

"I'm *sure* I can do something. Even if it's running errands or making telephone calls. Besides, in the Corps I got plenty of experience with a .45 caliber pistol. I still have one, along with a permit. And I practice with it regularly at the Carroll County firing range."

Jim rose, stepped to the window behind his desk and stared out at the gray March day. A low sky, heavy with clouds, threatened rain at any moment. Under the plaster cast on his right wrist, his skin felt hot and itchy. He was taking a painkiller every eight hours, but even so, he was still uncomfortable. "Did you run the idea by Barbara?" He asked skeptically.

"Yeah. She didn't say 'no.' Didn't say 'yes,' either. There are some things a guy just has to do. Matt's my friend. She knows enough not to butt in. It's really up to me."

"Matt's *my* friend, too," Jim remarked. "He helped me to ... resolve a problem that had been eating away at me for a long time." Turning from the window, he held up his right arm, displaying the cast. "Besides, those bastards forced their way into my house, roughed up my wife and broke my wrist. I'd like to be there when this Freedlander fella crashes and burns. What time are we leaving?"

Dan stood, a broad grin spreading across his face. "You goin', too?"

"Of course! You don't think I'm gonna let you and Matt have all the fun, do ya?"

‡ ‡ ‡ ‡ ‡

Wednesday, March 21, 1990
New York City, New York
Daniel Patrick Moynihan US Courthouse
500 Pearl Street, Lower Manhattan
US District Attorney's Office
10:00 a.m. EST

When Marvin Jonathan Freedlander walked into his office on the second floor of the federal courthouse, Starling, Foreman and Preston were already waiting for him, Starling pacing up and down on the oriental carpet, Foreman staring out one of the office windows, and Preston perched on the edge of Freedlander's desk, chewing his nails. Together, they gave the appearance of three scared children expecting a tongue lashing from an irate parent.

"He gave you the slip in Baltimore, huh?" Freedlander said, waiving the preliminaries. He had decided against his usual screaming and cursing, and was taking intense pride in remaining cool in this pressure situation. Moving to a credenza across from his desk, he opened it and extracted a bottle of bourbon, some ginger ale and an ice bucket. "Then, he comes up here and just drops in on *me* like he doesn't have a care in the world."

"He's a gutsy bastard," Starling said. The three men had heard the details, moments earlier, from Freedlander's secretary. "Just waltzed in here and waltzed right out again, huh?"

"When he left Baltimore, his car was still in the parking lot in front of his apartment building. Do we know how he got to New York?" Foreman asked.

"Cripes!" Freedlander said, disgustedly. "That's not too hard to figure out. Probably rented a car and *drove* up here. Anybody wanna bet Ann's not with him?" There were no takers. He poured two shots of bourbon into a glass, added some ice and turned. "Anybody want one of these?"

Starling frowned. "What time is it?"

"Time enough for a stiff drink," Freedlander responded huffily.

Foreman shook his head. "Too early. I just finished breakfast."

Starling glanced at the others. "I'll call the office. We'll put roadblocks on all major arteries leading out of the City. If they got here in a rental, they won't get out without being spotted. We can also put agents in the concourses of both Kennedy *and* La Guardia, at Grand Central and Union Stations, and the bus terminals, armed with their pictures, just in case they try to leave by one of those routes."

"What about checkin' hotels, too? They gotta be stayin' somewhere," Preston said thoughtfully. "They're *not* gonna stay at her place in Chappaqua."

Foreman looked up. "Hotels! You're right. They know we'd be watching her house."

"Chappaqua?" Starling said, embarrassed that he had not already thought of it. "I'll see if I can get a couple of agents assigned there right away."

Freedlander paused. "In the meantime," he said, partially turning his body away, "there's a hotel just across the river near the Newark airport. Ann liked to, um … use it now and then. I think I'll take a ride over there tonight and look around."

‡ ‡ ‡ ‡ ‡

Wednesday, March 21, 1990
New York City, New York
Offices of *The New York Times*
1:30 p.m. EST

Aaron Greenbaum was a big man, literally and figuratively. Six feet four inches tall, he weighed two hundred seventy pounds, fifty more than he knew he should be carrying, even for *his* lofty frame. The sedentary lifestyle he had led for the past ten years had caused him to gain weight and his blood pressure to go through the roof, which gave his pudgy face a florid look, belying his mostly sunny disposition. At times, he wished for a return to the days when he'd been an investigative reporter. Life was simpler then. His office walls were lined with journalistic awards garnered during those days for his hard-hitting articles about the sordid way the real world sometimes worked.

Pushing fifty harder than he cared to, he had hoped that by this time he'd have been able to slow down some. But, in order to do his job as Chief of the Metro Section of the paper with the largest circulation in the country's most important financial center, he was forced to work longer hours than either he or his wife were happy with.

A stubby Corona cigar clenched between his teeth, Greenbaum was on the phone with Curtis Wright, a junior partner in the firm of Blanding, Kelly, Keating, Rowe and Shapiro, the attorneys who defended the *Times* against thin-skinned public figures, movie stars, local politicians and others who thought they'd been libeled or slandered in its pages. He was irate. "The DA *himself* gave us the story, Curt." He tossed a pencil down on the desk with such force that it bounced off the hard surface and onto the carpet. His face was the color of fresh hamburger. "I really didn't think we needed to check it out all that thoroughly."

"Well, you should have," Curtis Wright said dryly. "I spoke to her myself yesterday. Sounded fine. Said she had *not* been kidnapped and that the story was a crock,"

Greenbaum balled his hand into a fist and was about to slam it into the front of his desk. Catching himself, he changed his mind and smacked it lightly on the surface, instead. Ann Kelly being who she was, a lawsuit was a distinct possibility. And if she sued, she would use a lawyer from one of the City's other major law firms, one that *The Times* could neither control nor influence.

A thought occurred to him. Taking a quick, nervous drag on his cigar, he removed it from his mouth and blew the smoke toward the ceiling. "You know, in a lotta kidnapping situations, the victim bonds with her kidnapper, and when that happens he or she'll often say and do almost anything to please him. Remember the Patty Hearst thing back in '74?"

"That's not the case here, Aaron," Wright shot back. "And the fact that the DA *himself* gave you the story tends to bear out what they're saying. Will you do it?"

Greenbaum chomped on the wet cigar, as he always did in moments of anger or stress. His newspaperman's sense for news told him this was something meaty. But his businessman's instinct urged caution. "The guy rented the Grand Hall at the Regent Wall Street. Place holds two thousand people. We *know* he's gonna announce something. Probably for mayor. Well. A story like that? We'd cover it anyway. But with the twist you just described? You couldn't keep us away. *If* it's true, that is." He removed the Corona from his mouth.

Now it was Wright's turn to be annoyed. "You want true, too? How should I know if it's true. I'm just passing it on to you for *them* and asking you to do what they want."

"Because you got a phone call from somebody claimin' to be Ann Kelly?"

"Right."

"And you know Ann Kelly to be a person whose word you can generally trust?"

"Yeah."

"But that's exactly what *we* did on the front end of this thing," Greenbaum took another drag from his cigar, inhaling deeply, savoring the taste while his agile mind explored the problem. "We took the word of the DA, someone we thought we could trust, and put out a story that now appears may have been false."

Wright sucked in his breath. "I see what you mean."

"I don't know, Curt. Before *The Times* commits to this thing, maybe I should meet with Dawson and Mrs. Kelly, and kinda get a feel for what's going on here."

"That seems reasonable," Wright responded. "I'll try to arrange it."

"Do you know how to get in touch with her?"

"Yeah. All our lines have caller ID on them. When Ann called in, I wrote down the number she called from, just in case I needed to get back to her. Didn't check to see whose it was, though. In case the police or FBI ask me if I know *where* she is. That way, I won't have to lie to them."

Greenbaum chuckled. "Cute. A pretty fine distinction, if I ever heard one."

"Who are *you* to complain about 'fine distinctions'", Wright's voice rose an octave. "Every page of your newspaper has at least half a dozen 'fine distinctions' on it, done for political or financial reasons, or to further some agenda or other."

"What's this I hear? Dissatisfaction? And from our very own firm of barristers, too."

Wright grunted. "I'll set up a meeting here at my office. That way, you can get the poop yourself and go from there."

"Sounds okay. When?"

"Possibly tomorrow afternoon? I'll get back to you after I've spoken to Ann."

Greenbaum took a last drag and ground the cigar out in the ashtray on his desk. "Curt? If she's thinkin' about filin' suit, try to talk her out of it. Another lawsuit we can do without."

Wednesday, March 21, 1990
Newark, New Jersey
Howard Johnson Hotel
Frontage Road
1:45 p.m. EST

"He wants what?" Matt had gone for a walk to ease some of the stress he was feeling. Arriving back at his room, he had found Ann waiting for him.

"A meeting. He wants us to come to his office at one o'clock tomorrow afternoon to meet some bigwig named Greenbaum from *The Times*. It seems *that* worthy gentleman isn't sure he believes what Curtis told him. Wants to hear it from the horse's mouth, so to speak."

"What did you tell Wright?"

"I told him 'yes.' What else could I say?"

Matt sat on the edge of the other bed, removed his shoes and lay back. Ann came over to his bed and curled up beside him. "What d'ya think?"

"Well, just *getting* there is gonna present us with some problems. By now, NYPD blues are probably rolling everywhere. But, we need the press at Freedlander's bash Friday night. If this is what will get them there, I guess we'll have to take the chance." Another thought occurred to him. "And we need to scout the Regent Wall Street Hotel before Friday. Just how we're gonna do *that* without being picked up by the cops is beyond me."

Ann frowned. "No way! You're *not* going to leave this hotel, Matt," she said firmly.

"Ann! Be realistic. We've got to know the lay of the land in and around that hotel before we set foot in there Friday evening. Today's a good time to do it."

Wednesday, March 14, 1990
New York City, New York
The Regent Wall Street Hotel
55 Wall Street
3:00 p.m. EST

"I should have come alone," Matt said. He and Ann were standing in the main lobby of the Regent Wall Street Hotel, just inside the double doors leading to the street.

Furnished in the elegant style of a turn-of-the century private club, the lobby walls were painted comfortable shades of deep green, relaxing burgundy and warm gold. Of concern to Matt at the moment was a police cruiser out on Wall Street, that famous symbol of Capitalism, drifting slowly past the brass and glass doors beneath massive columns that framed the entrance to this lofty Greek Revivalist landmark hotel. "They're probably looking for *us*."

"Do you think they saw us?" Ann asked, fidgeting with the strap of her purse.

"Hard to tell. With that beautiful red mop, you certainly stand out in a crowd." He stared through the glass doors, watching the police cruiser, NYPD MANHATTAN SOUTH painted on its side, until it disappeared from view. Then he visibly relaxed. "Good. They went on by."

"Whew!"

"Let's take a look at the ballroom and the restaurant first. Then, I wanna map the location of every door leading into and out of the place from this floor."

Ann's smile did nothing to conceal her concern. "The Great Hall is this way," she said, pointing. "Sean and I came here last summer for the Mayor's Charity Ball." She grimaced. "Sean was always getting invitations to events like that."

As they hurried to the twelve thousand square foot ballroom, Matt's mind tried to process everything; the flight of carpeted stairs leading to the mezzanine level, which housed the restaurants known as 55 Wall, and 55 Wall Terrace, the outdoor dining area overlooking Wall Street, where guests could sit, weather permitting, and enjoy an after dinner cigar and cocktail. Near the elevators, a sign directed visitors to the Regent Spa, where they would find a health club featuring the latest in electronic cardiovascular machines, resistance equipment, free weights, a steam room and a masseuse.

They stepped inside the Italian Renaissance style ballroom. "Big!" Matt breathed as he took in the Corinthian columns dominating the room and the large elliptical dome towering above them. He pointed to the Wedgwood panels around the circumference of the dome. "Look up there. The signs of the zodiac and the four points of the compass are there, on those panels."

"Oh. And isn't *that* lovely!" Ann said, nodding at two rows of tables set in a semicircle, partially enclosing a raised platform on which stood the head table. The guest tables were covered with pastel pink tablecloths and silver place settings for ten. In the center of each was a huge bowl of freshly cut gardenias, placed there for an event that evening.

Matt hurried behind the platform. "There's a door back here." A few strides took him to it. He turned the knob and opened it.

Ann followed. "Two, actually." She pointed to another, about fifty feet away.

"Both of them lead to the same interior hallway."

Stepping into the hall, Ann glanced around. "Kitchen down at that end. Stairway at the other end probably leads to the lower floors. Are we done in here?"

They crossed the huge ballroom's Botticini marble floor, exited the way they had entered, and rapidly re-traced their steps toward the stairs leading down to the lobby. Suddenly Ann's eyes widened in alarm. She stopped in her tracks, grabbed Matt's arm and pointed.

Matt's gaze followed her finger. He froze. Two burly New York City cops were standing at the front desk talking to the clerks. One was showing pictures taken from a local newspaper. As they watched, a clerk nodded vigorously and pointed in the direction of the Great Hall.

"They must've seen us come in after all," Matt said, the blood draining from his face. "But they don't know exactly where we are. Quick! Let's use one of those other doors and make ourselves scarce."

CHAPTER 45

Wednesday, March 21, 1990
Newark, New Jersey
Howard Johnson Hotel
Frontage Road
7:30 p.m. Eastern Standard Time (EST)

"IT WOULD PROBABLY BE BEST," Ramon Gonzales said, "except for the meeting tomorrow afternoon, that neither you nor Ann go into New York between now and Friday evening. Every police officer in the City probably has your description."

Matt shot a quick glance at Ann, who had tied her red hair in a bun at the nape of her neck to make it less conspicuous, and nodded. "You're probably right. After today's fun and games ... " The group of six had just finished dinner in the hotel's restaurant, during which, Matt had sketched out his ideas for bringing this sordid affair to an end. Ramon and Emilio had pronounced the plan workable, with a few modifications.

During dinner, Ann listened intently. The tiny ray of hope kindled in her when she had teamed up with Matt was now a beam of bright light. *This nightmare may soon be over. And perhaps, just perhaps, Matt and I can begin to enjoy our lives again. Together.* As the waiter left to bring their coffee, she rose from the table. "Excuse me, gents. Time to powder my nose."

The rest rooms were in the lobby next to a small gift shop just to the right of the front desk and directly across from the main entrance. Entering the ladies room, she sat at a dressing table and quickly repaired the damage done to her lipstick at dinner. Finished, she left and stepped inside the gift shop, where a bored shop girl was immersed in *Wildly My Love*, a recently published historical romance novel by Katharine Kincaid. Ann enjoyed the historical romance genre. She decided to buy a copy. Purchase in hand, she turned and took several steps in the direction of the restaurant. Suddenly, she froze and her eyes became like saucers.

"Oh, my God!" She gasped. The bag tumbled from her hand and she quickly stepped back into the little shop. She was staring at the broad back of Marvin Jonathan Freedlander.

From their table in the restaurant, Matt could not see the front of the lobby, but he had a view of most of the rear portion. He watched absently as Ann entered the ladies room and again a few minutes later, as she came out and stepped into the gift shop. "I wish there were some way to get the NYPD off our backs. It wouldn't do for Ann or me to be picked up Friday evening on our way to the main event."

Ramon's brow furrowed. "You are right. In the morning, I will call Mr. McIntyre at the FBI's Washington Field Office. Perhaps he can help us with that."

"Uh, oh!" Matt had been watching as Ann left the gift shop, then backed into it again, surprise and terror on her face. Then he saw her begin waving frantically to get their attention. "What's happening?" Concerned, he rose and started toward the door, but quickly put on the brakes as Ann gestured for him to stop. Ramon joined him.

"What is it?" Gonzales asked.

"Don't know." Matt responded, pointing toward Ann. "We'll have to wait."

Moments later, as the two men watched, Ann peeked into the lobby, relaxed noticeably, retrieved her fallen package and walked quickly toward them.

"It was Marvin Jonathan!" She pointed toward the front entrance. "He was just leaving as I came out of the gift shop."

"Freedlander?" Matt was surprised. "What was he doing *here*?"

Ann fidgeted with the strap of her handbag. "I, um … I don't know."

"Did he *see* you?" Ramon asked.

"He probably did," Ann said. "I was clearly visible from where he was standing."

They returned to their table and Matt hurriedly informed the others, finishing by saying, "We've got to assume that he saw Ann. If so, he'll be back with Foreman and Preston, so they can try to finish the job they started."

"I think we'd better find another hotel," Ramon said, a worried look on his face.

"Pronto! Let's get our things and meet in the lobby in ten minutes."

Wednesday, March 21, 1990
Newark, New Jersey
The Hilton Gateway Hotel
Raymond Boulevard
10:30 p.m. EST

Matt Dawson, his hands thrust deeply into his pockets, trudged the sidewalk on busy Raymond Boulevard, a block from The Hilton Gateway Hotel. Overhead, huge civilian jet airplanes, landing gears down, flew their relentless glide paths into Newark Airport less than a mile away. The night was pleasant and street traffic was heavy, but he was oblivious to his surroundings, his mind churning over events of the past week.

When the little group had re-gathered in the Howard Johnson Hotel's lobby, Dan had suggested they drive into New York and check into The Regent Wall Street, reasoning that no one would expect to find them there. But, Gonzales had vetoed that idea, saying that the NYPD would probably be conducting daily routine checks of all the Manhattan hotels. "Besides," he said, "the prices there being what they are, it would take half the annual travel budget of the Cuernavaca Police Department to finance our stay." They had found the Hilton Gateway in a tour guide before leaving the lobby, and decided to stay on in Newark.

He was relieved that his friends had arrived. When the group had transferred hotels, Ann, wanting to avoid any raised eyebrows, had again rented separate rooms for herself and Matt, just as she had done before. Although they adjoined each other and she had again made sure that the connecting doors were unlocked, she had, as Matt slipped out into the March night, been in her own room, leaving him to sleep alone for the first time since they had left Baltimore.

His thoughts turned to their brief but torrid relationship. It was now obvious to him that Ann believed she was in love with him. It was also clear that, although he liked her a lot, he was not in love with her. At least not yet. Was he moving in that direction? They had bonded emotionally because of what they were being forced to endure together, and their intellectual compatibility had become apparent as they planned each move. Their physical bonding had been born of mutual fear and loneliness. From that first night, as they had turned to each other for solace, it had been intense and pleasurable. Still, because Matt did not believe in sex outside of marriage, he knew that as enjoyable as it was, it was wrong. He had promised the Savior, four years ago, not to engage in that kind of conduct. He had broken his promise.

He turned and started back toward the Hotel. *It's not wise to be so damn sure you can keep a resolution like that. It's not very humble, either. That's false pride, not strength. I've let Jesus down and allowed something to come between us.*

He had tried to fight off the temptation, but he'd been caught off guard and had been an easy victim. And having given in, he'd temporarily forfeited some of the strength of character and numerous graces that come by reason of a successful fight. Now, he was feeling the beginning of that slow, steady deterioration of character that inevitably follows occasions of sin for a man with a healthy conscience. *I really can't blame Ann. She's a post-modernist woman. To her, having regular sex is just a part of life. She doesn't know Jesus and has never even believed in God. She calls herself an Atheist. But, maybe she's not totally. G.K. Chesterton once said, 'If there were no God, there would be no Atheists.' True or not, Ann simply doesn't think the same way I do about these things.*

Back in his room a few minutes later, he removed his shirt and headed for the bathroom. How had Freedlander found them? From Ann's obvious discomfort, he thought he knew. She had confided that she'd had a brief affair with Freedlander in the past. They had evidently used the place for a few of their nocturnal trysts. Was she feeling guilty? Of course. That was the reason why she had not come through the connecting door to join him tonight. Otherwise, she would have already been in his room, wearing only her sheer nightgown, ready to climb between the sheets.

Continuing his preparations for bed, his mind took him down another path. *What can I do about restoring my relationship with Jesus?* He asked himself as he hung his shirt and slacks on the clothing rack. A moment later, he recalled passing a Roman Catholic Church on Raymond Boulevard as they had approached the hotel earlier. A Catholic church meant a priest. A priest meant the sacrament of Confession or Reconciliation, as it was now called. *It's a no-brainer. I'll drive over there tomorrow morning, maybe catch Mass and find the priest afterwards.*

‡ ‡ ‡ ‡ ‡

Wednesday, March 21, 1990
Newark, New Jersey
The Hilton Gateway Hotel
Raymond Boulevard
Room 410
10:40 p.m. EST

In the next room, Ann lay on one of the queen-sized beds, face down, and her forehead resting on an arm. Across from the beds, a TV sat on a dresser, its blank screen staring into the room, like the eye of some unseeing giant. On the bedside table, a split of Sangiovese, its contents greatly diminished, sat beside a half-full wineglass, now neglected.

She raised her head displaying cheeks wet with tears. For perhaps the tenth time that evening she glanced longingly toward the connecting door leading to Matt's room. She had wanted to go through that door and confess to Matt that Freedlander had found them because she had used the Howard Johnson Hotel for their post-case dates. *I was a fool to bring Matt there. I just didn't think! And it could have gotten us killed. If I hadn't seen him leaving, Marvin Jonathan would have called for reinforcements and done his dirty work without us suspecting a thing. As it was, we had to run for our bleeding lives.*

Reaching for her wineglass, she recalled the first night she and Matt had met at the Pasti Cosi in Branford. She stroked the bottle, as if doing so might miraculously transport her back in time and place, to that magical night and a new beginning. Picking up the glass, she drained it and set it back on the table. *Matt knows! I'm sure he does. How will I ever be able to face him?*

Her thoughts turned to those past episodes with Marvin Jonathan Freedlander, and then, to her experiences with other men, many other men before meeting Sean, and long before meeting Matt. As she mentally clicked them off, she realized that she and Matt Dawson were very different in their views about sex. For a moment, she allowed herself a fantasy: that the connecting door to their rooms would open and Matt would come in, take her in his arms and console her, telling her that he understood and that it didn't matter to him. But, she knew in her heart of hearts that the gap between them was so wide that it might never be closed. She would have given anything, then, to have been a child again, back in the cozy little room next to her mother's, safely tucked into her bed, under a bedspread with fuzzy cotton tufts sticking up everywhere, her entire life before her, ready to be relived, while just down the hall from the nursery her little brother slept, peacefully. *It certainly hasn't been all beer and skittles,* she thought.

Eyes filling with tears again, she began to worry about the meeting ahead of them on the following day at Curtis Wright's office. *How will I get through it?* She wondered. *But I've got to go with him. Perhaps, on the ride there, I could explain about tonight, level with Matt, tell him I'm Anna Lieber's daughter, apologize for not telling him sooner and let him know where my parents are.*

Unsteadily, she rose and began to prepare for bed. *Please, Matt! Please come to me. Forgive me and tell me everything's all right between us.* She wanted desperately to see him now. But she knew it was not going to happen. Moments later, she slipped into bed and turned out the light.

✠ ✠ ✠ ✠ ✠

Thursday, March 22, 1990
Newark, New Jersey
The Hilton Gateway Hotel
Raymond Boulevard
Room 412
6:00 a.m. EST

The following morning, Matt slipped out of the hotel and drove out Raymond Boulevard to the local Roman Catholic Church. After Mass, he caught the priest and asked if he would hear his confession. Settled in a small room just inside the rectory, the priest, after gently questioning him regarding events leading up to the first night he'd slept with Ann, had told him not to be too hard on himself. "Evil always presents itself to the intellect as a good," he said. "That's why you had the thought that you were comforting this woman. This was an extraordinary time for both of you."

Matt breathed a sigh of relief. "But, I'm not sure I'm really sorry, father. I actually enjoyed the last few nights."

The priest thought a minute. He knew that sometimes, people do the wrong thing for the right reason. And he also knew that sometimes people do the right thing for the wrong reason. Making decisions in situations like these people found themselves in, could be complicated,

"Well, the fact that you're here shows how much you value your relationship with Jesus. You know, the desire to restore your closeness to the Son comes directly from the Father. We *do* have free will, although it's been greatly diminished by the fall from grace. You could have continued as you were, but you chose to come to Mass and confession this morning. That's a very good sign. I'll give you absolution, now."

‡ ‡ ‡ ‡ ‡

Thursday, March 22, 1990
Newark, New Jersey
The Hilton Gateway Hotel
Raymond Boulevard
Room 512
9:30 a.m. EST

"I thought it would be best to discuss this matter with you, Señior McIntyre," Ramon Gonzales said into his telephone. He was in his hotel room, wearing only his briefs and a tee shirt, his hair still wet from the shower, a towel draped loosely over his shoulders. Emilio Diaz, jacket off, pistol grip protruding from the holster at his belt, sat on the edge of a double bed and listened as Gonzales talked with the chief of the FBI's Washington, DC field office.

"The fact that your New York office is searching for Mr. Dawson and Mrs. Kelly is," Gonzales said, "as you Americans say, 'cramping our style' a bit."

"But, if this guy, Dawson, is involved in a murder in Cuernavaca, why should we interfere? Why don't we simply nab him in New York and sort it all out later?"

"That's a very good question. The answer is … that he was *not* involved." Gonzales paused. "But, something *else* is going on here and we're working on trying to find out what it is. And Dawson is helping us."

"You're telling me that this Dawson was cut loose because of insufficient evidence?"

"No, Señior," Ramon said patiently. "We turned him loose because there was *no* evidence. There was nothing to connect *him* to Mr. Cohan's murder, but several pieces of evidence connecting an American couple to it." Gonzales reached into his jacket pocket and removed a pack of Marlboro cigarettes. "But we were wrong about that. The woman, Mrs. Kelly, was not involved. When she found out, she went to Dawson about it. Now she is working with us."

"I see. And you learned that an APB had been put out on Dawson?"

"Sí. Apparently issued in your New York City field office …"

"… by Special Agent Starling, who has no business issuing one," McIntyre finished.

"That is right." Ramon picked up his trousers and searched the pockets for matches, without success.

"Okay. I'll call the New York City FO and talk with Tom O'Toole. He's the day Chief up there. I'll ask him to look into it right away. Give me a number where I can reach you."

‡ ‡ ‡ ‡ ‡

Thursday, March 22, 1990
Newark, New Jersey
The Hilton Gateway Hotel
Raymond Boulevard
Room 412
10:00 a.m. EST

"But, why don't I just wear the *blonde* wig?" Ann said, massaging her temples with the tips of her fingers and glaring defiantly at Matt. "I still have it, you know." The group of six had gathered in Matt's room for a planning session. She had tossed and turned in her bed most of the night. Morning had found her haggard and wallowing in self-pity, her eyes red from crying. The certainty that Freedlander had located them because she had not realized that he would check out the place where they had slept together, had left her strangely subdued. Worse, she felt that everyone in the little group knew and was judging her harshly.

"Because," said Matt patiently, "Preston has seen you wearing that blonde mop. He'd spot you in a heartbeat Friday night, even in that crowded ballroom. It'd be better if you wore a different hairpiece and carried the blonde one in your handbag."

Ann shrugged, reached into her purse and pulled out a credit card. "All right then," she breathed meekly, and handed the card to Jim.

It had been decided that Jim Crowley would go to the uniform shop at which Matt had bought janitor's clothing and the Pen cam, to buy wigs and companion latex skullcaps, a false mustache and clothing, to be fashioned into disguises for Matt and Ann on Friday evening.

Matt handed Jim a list of some other items he wanted. "These things, too."

Jim studied the list briefly, glanced at Matt and smiled. "Super." Waving his cast at the others, he quickly left the room.

Matt then turned to Dan. "I'm thinking it would be great if we knew something about this fella Aaron Greenbaum before the meeting."

"Like what?" Dan asked.

"Both personal and business information. As much as we can get on him."

Dan's brow furrowed. "Where will I find it?"

"Start with *The Times* office. These big newspapers often prepare obituaries on their employees long before they're needed. The Archives Section will probably have something. Then, ask a few people in the building about him. Ann can give you directions."

"Yes." Ann was eager to redeem herself. "And there's a stack of City maps at the front desk down in the lobby. I saw them when we checked in last night. You might want to take one with you so you won't get lost."

Another thought occurred to Matt. "Try to follow Greenbaum when he leaves for the meeting. Make sure he goes straight to Wright's office without any other stops."

"Okay," Dan said. He brandished his cell phone. "Let me have your cell phone number. If I find out anything interesting, I'll call you."

Ramon Gonzales and Emilio Diaz had been observing in silence until now. "Emilio and I will take a cab over to the Empire State Building. Better that we get a good look at the area around the lawyers' office *before* your meeting. We will brief you when we get back."

CHAPTER 46

Thursday, March 22, 1990
Newark, New Jersey
The Hilton Gateway Hotel
Raymond Boulevard
Room 412
12:15 p.m. EST

"WHERE ARE YOU NOW, DAN?" Matt was on his cell phone talking to Dan Davis. Gonzales and Diaz had returned from their scouting trip of Curtis Wright's office in the needle-thin skyscraper on 5th Avenue, briefed Matt and gone upstairs to their room. Ann stood nearby, waiting. They had been about to leave for the meeting.

"I'm in the lobby of the Empire State Building. Sheesh! This place is somethin' else! I followed Greenbaum, like you said. He left *The Times* offices and jumped in a cab. I hopped in one right behind him and told my driver, 'follow that cab.' Just like in the movies. He did."

Matt rolled his eyes skyward. "What did you find out," he wanted to know.

"I ran some microfilm first and talked to several people. It seems our man's pretty well liked. He's been in the newspaper business a long time. He started out writing obituaries.

Later, he moved to covering City Hall. Become an investigative reporter some years back, but opted against that after a year or so and went into covering local news. Worked his way up. Now he's head of the Metropolitan section and pulls down six figures annually."

Matt heaved a sigh. "That's it? Did you find anything we can use?"

"Well, people think he's a straight shooter. Got lots of integrity. When he was writing, his articles always rang true. He dug deep for the facts, then wove some pretty good color pieces. He doesn't write much anymore, though. His duties as Chief keep him too busy. The consensus is that he's become quite a skeptic."

"A straight shooter and a skeptic, huh?" Matt said thoughtfully. "Great, Dan! Wait there for us. We'll meet you in about half an hour." He hung up the phone, then picked it up again and dialed a room number.

"Ramon? Matt. I Just heard from Dan. I think it'd be a good idea if you and Emilio come with us to the meeting. Can you be ready in five minutes?"

‡ ‡ ‡ ‡ ‡

Thursday, March 22, 1990
New York City, New York
Empire State Building
Offices of Blanding, Kelly, Keating, Rowe & Shapiro
1:00 p.m. EST

"I'd like to thank you both for agreeing to meet with me on such short notice," Aaron Greenbaum said apologetically, his usual Corona cigar clenched between his teeth. Curtis Wright had just finished introducing him to Ann and Matt.

"No problem, Mr. Greenbaum," Matt responded. He introduced Ramon Gonzales and Emilio Diaz, who showed their Cuernavacan Police Department ID. That done, they all took seats around a large oak conference table, inlaid with green felt and covered with glass.

Settled, Greenbaum lit his cigar, took two short puffs and turned to Matt. "Curtis tells me you'd like a couple of our reporters and photographers to be on hand at Mr. Freedlander's announcement party tomorrow night."

"Yes."

"Well, we'll probably cover it anyway. It's the *rest* of what you want that concerns me. So, before I commit *The Times* – resources and people - to helping you, I need more information. I've been told that you whacked an elderly American expatriate in Cuernavaca and then high-tailed it outta there, taking Mrs. Kelly along as a hostage. You're telling me there's no truth to that?"

"May we ask how your newspaper came by that story?" Ramon Gonzales interjected. He extracted a pack of Marlboros from the pocket of his sport coat and placed it on the table in front of him, while his hands explored his pockets for matches.

Greenbaum removed the cigar from his mouth and frowned. "Marvin Freedlander *himself* called one of my reporters on Monday morning. Him being who he is, we had no reason to doubt what he was saying."

Ann bristled. "Well, *I* think you should have doubted it. Since it was simply untrue."

"Mrs. Kelly, I don't mean any offense," Greenbaum shot back, "but we *did* call your home in Chappaqua. You weren't there and your maid said she didn't know where you were or when you'd be back." He clamped the soggy cigar between his teeth again.

Unimpressed, Ann's face flushed with indignation. She was ready with a retort, but Curtis Wright held up a restraining hand. "It's not productive to get into all that just now," he said. "Let's talk about Friday night, shall we? Aaron? You said you have some reservations?"

"Yeah. I wanted to hear the story from these two, before deciding whether or not to let my people cooperate in their ... little scheme."

Matt nodded. "Mr. Greenbaum, you don't know me. Anything I tell you may not satisfy you. And, I don't know how much credibility you'd attach to what Ann might say because you don't know her very well, either. That's why I asked Inspector Gonzales and Inspector Diaz to come here with us. They speak with the authority of the Mexican Police. They can fill you in on the entire matter."

Greenbaum struck a theatrical pose. "I'm listening," he said.

With all eyes on him, Ramon Gonzales proceeded to do just that for the next five minutes. He finished by saying, "When we saw that an APB had been issued for Mr. Dawson's arrest, and that it had originated in the NYCFO, we decided to come up here to see if we could put an end to what seemed to be some … confusion, to say the least."

Aaron Greenbaum let out his breath. "Dirty cops in the Big Apple are a dime a dozen. Our investigative reporters are all over stuff like that. The Times runs stories about them regularly. Good for circulation. But a dirty DA? This would be the first one in maybe … twenty years."

Wright looked over at Matt. "So, Freedlander's man killed Cohan to keep him from going public with the story about his father's exploits down there some … forty years ago?"

"That's about the size of it," Matt said. "And they want to kill me because I stumbled onto the secret."

"And," Ann added, "I know they want to kill me. I overheard a telephone conversation between Willie Preston and Marvin Jonathan Freedlander about that very thing."

Greenbaum sat back in his chair. He was almost satisfied. But his newspaperman's sense screamed that there was still an unexplained detail. He glanced from Ann to Matt. "Mr. Dawson, how did you happen to be in Cuernavaca at the time this Preston killed Mr. Cohan?"

"That's a fair question," Matt said. "I'm an investigator. I'm trying to locate the sister of a Baltimore man who died and left her some money. She was married to a communist spy. They had defected. I tracked them to Cuernavaca and although I didn't believe they were there any longer, I went down there to see if I could kinda pick up their trail."

Matt looked across the table at Ann as he finished, and noted that she had become agitated, just as she had that night in Branford when he'd mentioned her husband. Only no one had mentioned her husband this time. He stared hard at her. What was it that had upset her? He willed her to look at him, but she had dropped her gaze and was studying her fingernails.

Wright and Greenbaum exchanged meaningful glances. "I'm satisfied!" Greenbaum said. Leaning down, he reached into the leather briefcase at his feet, extracted some papers and turned to Ann. "Mrs. Kelly, in view of the way this episode has unfolded, my newspaper is concerned about possible legal action against it by you. If you'd be willing to sign a paper releasing The Times from liability for any damage to your reputation as a result of Monday's story, I think we can work something out for tomorrow night."

A spasm of irritation crossed Ann's face. She glared at Greenbaum, resentful at being put on the spot in this way. On the other hand, she had no intention of suing *The New York Times*. Just now, she was more concerned about the look that Matt had given her as he mentioned the case he was working on. Had he guessed her identity? She had been trying to work up the courage to tell him, but she had not. Now she regretted it deeply. She'd even planned to do it on the way here, but circumstances had dictated that Ramon and Emilio come to the meeting with them, making a private conversation with Matt impossible. She shrugged. It was important to have Greenbaum's cooperation. Otherwise, their plan would fall apart.

"I suppose you really can't be blamed for believing Marvin Jonathan's pack of lies, Mr. Greenbaum. It seems even the FBI has done that." With a quick glance at Matt, she reached for the paper. "Where do I sign?"

‡ ‡ ‡ ‡ ‡

Thursday, March 22, 1990
New York City, New York
The Regent Wall Street Hotel
Health Spa Steam Room
2:00 p.m. EST

Marvin Jonathan Freedlander, clad only in a huge green bath towel, sat on one of several wooden benches in the Steam Room, provided for members of this exclusive Spa, enveloped in clouds of thick, white vapor. A cell phone was tucked under his chin as he waited, eyes closed, for his call to John Foreman to go through.

Something troubling had occurred. Ken Starling, although assigned to the FBI's New York City Field Office, generally spent most of his time in the DA's office. However, earlier that afternoon his boss, Tom O'Toole, had summoned him. That worried Marvin Jonathan. If Starling or anyone else over there contacted the Mexican authorities, they'd quickly learn that the Cuernavacan police had cut Dawson loose without filing charges. Marvin Jonathan didn't want them to find that out because they'd begin asking questions that he could not answer, and would probably withdraw their support. He still needed the FBI to give an aura of legitimacy to the hit, since he had instructed Willie and John to make it look like Dawson and Kelly were killed while resisting arrest.

He fingered the butt of a 9-mm Beretta on the bench beside him, concealed by the oversized towel wrapped around his waist. He had begun to carry the pistol after Dawson's unwelcome visit on Tuesday. Since then, he had not gone anywhere without it.

"It was sheer luck that I saw Ann coming from the ladies' room as I was about to leave," he said, after Foreman had picked up and he had described his venture of the evening before. "Take Willie over there with you. The desk clerks will cooperate if you show your ID. You'll be able to confirm that they're registered and get their room number. Then, do whatever you need to do to wrap this thing up."

"Okay," said Foreman. "I'll call you after ... we're finished."

‡ ‡ ‡ ‡ ‡

Thursday, March 22, 1990
New York City, New York
Federal Bureau of Investigation
26 Federal Building, 23rd Floor
Office of Thomas J. O'Toole, Assistant Director
2:30 p.m. EST

Tom O'Toole leaned over his desk and hit the switch on his intercom. His suit coat was off exposing the .45 caliber automatic he carried in the shoulder rig under his left arm. His gold and burgundy paisley print tie was loose. Although it was not a warm day, the white shirt he wore was badly wrinkled. Behind him on a credenza, framed pictures of his wife and children, taken on one of their infrequent vacations together, looked out over the eclectic flotsam of his warmly decorated office, the accumulation of a five-year tenure as Chief of the NYCFO.

"Yes, sir," his secretary said.

"Hold my calls, Hillary. And tell Agent Starling I want to see him now, all right?"

Leaning back, he placed his feet up on the desk and scratched his chin. What he'd heard that morning in a phone call from his friend, Dick McIntyre, the assistant Director down in Washington, DC weighed heavily on his mind; that the DA of the Southern District may have ordered the murder of an old man in Cuernavaca, Mexico, that one of the DA's men may have done it, and that one of his *own* agents may have been involved in a scheme to pin the rap on an innocent civilian while heading up an unauthorized manhunt down in Baltimore. Having been a field agent who worked his way up through the ranks, the possibility that an agent had been corrupted was something he took very seriously.

O'Toole's thinning silver hair lent him a distinguished air. Intelligence shone from his deep-set blue eyes. He was fifty-nine years old, nearing mandatory retirement age, and he had never encountered a situation like this. So, he'd taken some time to confirm what he'd been told. A few minutes going over phone logs, followed by a couple of telephone calls was sufficient. He now had the facts in a folder in front of him. He knew that Starling had issued an APB late last week without going through proper channels, that he'd embarked on a fictitious assignment, looking for an alleged suspected murderer and kidnapper in Baltimore, made false statements to Baltimore field office personnel in order to obtain their help, charged travel expenses while there, and been absent from his court-room duties this week while snatching upwards of eight agents from the office to scour New York searching for two innocent people.

O'Toole removed his feet from the desk. He knew what the regulations said he should do; take this to the Office of Professional Responsibility (OPR). That department investigated all allegations of misconduct against agents. Investigators over there were street-wise, thorough and tough. The mere mention of OPR could scare the living daylights out of an erring agent.

All the things Starling had done were serious infractions for which he could be suspended, transferred to some FO in the boonies, or fired outright. O'Toole frowned. *At some point, I'll have to report this, but not now.*

His intercom buzzed. "Agent Starling is here, sir," his secretary said.

"Send him in."

A moment later, Starling, his boyish face a study in concern, entered. "You wanted to see me, Chief?" He managed a worried smile.

O'Toole stood and pointed to the empty chair in front of his desk. He knew what Starling had done. What he didn't know was *why* he had done it. "Have a seat, Ken," he said, his deep voice resonating concern. "Yeah, I did, son. Are you carrying your .45?"

"Yes, sir."

"Let me have it, please. And your badge, too."

Puzzled, Starling slipped the pistol from its holster and handed it, butt first, to his chief, followed by the badge. "I don't understand," he said.

"Everything will become clear in a few minutes." O'Toole took the automatic and badge, and placed them in the top drawer of his desk. He handed Starling a copy of the unauthorized APB, his face mirroring the disappointment he felt in his young agent. "Can you tell me what *this* is all about? And why you went to Baltimore last Friday, allegedly on FBI business and stayed until Tuesday afternoon? And what you've been doing all week since you got back?"

CHAPTER 47

Friday, March 23, 1990
Newark, New Jersey
The Hilton Gateway Hotel
Raymond Boulevard
5:30 p.m. Eastern Standard Time (ST)

WHEN DARKNESS FELL IN THE Newark area, it brought with it a heavy rain. The Hilton Gateway Hotel's parking lot was busy, as travelers, escaping driving conditions on the nearby Interstate rapidly becoming hazardous, began searching for overnight accommodations.

Two people exited the o hotel and walked quickly through the downpour toward a Cadillac with Maryland plates. They appeared to be elderly, but the pace at which they moved said otherwise. Creams, latex, wigs, spirit gum and putty applied correctly can work miracles. Matt Dawson, his hair covered by a wig of gray locks above a skullcap, was dressed in an out-of-style suit, a white shirt, and a narrow tie, giving him the appearance of a retired doctor or investment banker. Under his nose was a gray mustache applied with spirit gum.

"I can't believe we're doing this," Ann Kelly said as Matt, transferring a cane from his right hand to his left, unlocked the front passenger door for her.

"Well, we are. We can't run forever. Maybe we can end this thing tonight." He knew what they were doing was risky, and the possibility of death so close had released adrenalin in his brain and made him feel more alive.

A gray wig covered Ann's red hair and her face displayed shadows and highlights mimicking the age lines of an elderly woman. "This makeup is *very* uncomfortable," she remarked irritably, as she settled into the passenger seat and fingered the putty that had changed her pretty nose significantly.

"I don't like this Kevlar vest, either. But it's only for a few hours."

With Matt driving, the Cadillac moved quickly over the Interstate, sped through the Holland Tunnel and emerged a few minutes later in midtown Manhattan. Lost in thought, he did not speak. He listened to the sound of the rain beating a tattoo on the roof and marveled at how calm he felt. Next to him, Ann sat silent, playing with the shoulder strap of her purse and rehearsing in her mind the words she'd use to confess her secret. She was eager to unburden herself. She was also apprehensive about how Matt would react.

Matt repeatedly glanced into his rear-view mirror, watching for any signs of police pursuit. Gusts of wind drove heavy raindrops against the windshield, forcing the wipers to work harder to keep up. He wondered if they'd reach the Regent Wall Street Hotel without being stopped. *Is this the right move?* He second-guessed himself. *Once inside, will the plan go smoothly? Will the reporters and their photographer-assistants play their parts well? What about Freedlander and his cronies? How will they react?*

They were moving south in the curb lane on Broadway, the heavy traffic slower, more cautious than usual because of the rain. On their left, two rivers of vehicles flowed with them. Ann sucked in her breath. *Well, here goes everything!* "Matt?"

"Uh, huh?"

"I've something to tell you; something important."

"Okay. Shoot."

"I've been trying … that is, I've certainly wanted to tell you before …" she began. But her voice trailed off as the wail of a police siren split the night air and the interior of the car was filled with the glow of red and blue flashing lights from a police cruiser that had pulled in behind them.

Matt edged the car toward the curb. "I think we got trouble," he breathed. "How did they get the tag number of this car?"

Whipping around in her seat, Ann saw the black and white cruiser just a few feet away and collapsed against the passenger door. "Oh, God!" She said.

‡ ‡ ‡ ‡ ‡

Friday, March 23, 1990
New York City, New York
The Regent Wall Street Hotel
Mezzanine Level
6:10 p.m. EST

But even as Matt began braking to a stop, he realized that the police car, its siren wailing and its rooftop lights flashing, was trying to go around them. Incredulous, he and Ann watched as the cruiser edged past them and continued on.

"They're not after us!" Ann cried jubilantly.

"Oh, thank God! They're going after that dark van up ahead!"

Visibly shaken, Matt eased the Caddy into the traffic lane again. Moments later, he pulled directly into the Regent Wall Street Hotel's underground parking garage and expelled a deep breath. "We made it!" He said.

After finding a parking space, they rode an elevator up to the lobby of the historic structure designed in 1852 by architect Isaiah Rogers, and took the stairs to the mezzanine.

"Mr. Dawson? Mrs. Kelly! Wow! I'd have never recognized you." Aaron Greenbaum greeted them warmly. In their disguises, they had been able to enter 55 Wall and walk right up to him unrecognized, as he stood talking to his cohorts from *The New York Times*. "These gentlemen are reporters, Ken Dixon and John Lucas. And these two are photographers, Richard Greene and Max Blumenthal."

Introductions accomplished, the group was shown to a corner table. A few feet away, French doors led to 55 Wall, the outdoor dining terrace overlooking busy Wall Street.

As their waiter scurried to tend their drink order, Ramon Gonzales and Emilio Diaz entered, spotted Greenbaum and approached, followed closely by FBI Chief Tom O'Toole and his Deputy Chief, Bob Gunning. Bringing up the rear was a much chastened Agent Kenneth Starling.

After introductions were repeated, Greenbaum, the ever present cigar clamped between his teeth, turned. "You've got the floor, Dawson. Tell the boys what you'd like them to do."

For the next few minutes, in the inviting atmosphere of the restaurant, surrounded by walls of deep green and soft gold shades, Matt briefed his "troops." Then, he fielded inquiries from Dixon and Lucas regarding the timing and number of questions they were to fire at Freedlander, and from Greene and Blumenthal about what *they* were to do with their cameras.

"We'll position ourselves as close to Foreman and Preston as possible," O'Toole said when Matt had finished. "As soon as the fireworks start, we'll take them into custody."

Ann placed a hand on O'Toole's arm. "I say. D'ya think it might get … sticky?"

O'Toole turned. "You mean, do I think there might be some shooting?"

"If you must put it so bluntly, yes," Ann responded.

"It's hard to say, Mrs. Kelly. We certainly try to avoid any shooting. That can be bad for one's health." He glanced at Gunning. "Everything ready in the ballroom?"

"We're good to go, Chief," his Deputy said.

Their preparations made, Matt extracted a thin canister of developed Pen cam film from his jacket pocket and handed it to O'Toole. "Tuesday morning, I visited Freedlander at his office. Filmed and recorded the meeting with a Pen cam. You'll want to look at this."

O'Toole stared blankly at Matt for a moment. Then comprehension dawned. "Seems like you've been a busy man, Mr. Dawson." He slipped the canister into a pocket and turned to the others. "Show time, folks!"

Friday, March 23, 1990
New York City, New York

The Regent Wall Street Hotel
The Grand Ballroom
8:05 p.m. EST

A twenty piece band, consisting of saxes, trombones, trumpets, a rhythm section, and a female vocalist, had been booked by Freedlander for the occasion. It had just begun to play in the twelve thousand square foot Grand Ballroom, loosening up the crowd, as Matt, with Ann on his arm entered. They moved slowly, imitating the way an elderly couple might walk.

"Looks like the Brie and Perrier set is here in force," Ann remarked, gesturing toward the crowded tables. The huge hall was packed with New York City's finest; all the Assistant District Attorneys on Freedlander's staff were there, most with spouses or dates in tow. Many high ranking City department heads had responded. Law enforcement was well represented, what with the Chiefs of Police and Deputy Chiefs of Manhattan North and Manhattan South clustered at tables in one corner. The Presidents of the Boroughs of Manhattan, The Bronx, Brooklyn, Queens, and Staten Island and their staffs had arrived, as had the County leaders of New York, Richmond, Kings, Queens and Bronx Counties. The incumbent Mayor, a member of the same political party but ineligible to run again, and members of the City Council, all the State Senators and Assemblymen who represented that area, and many politicians, most from Freedlander's party, but a few from the opposition party, had also turned out. Finally, a dozen tables had been reserved for the heavy hitters, party members who contributed large amounts of cash to the party's candidates.

Although five rows of twenty tables each had been set for the occasion, the dinner was buffet style, with food and drink stations arranged between the Corinthian columns along the wall farthest from the head table. Ann had been right. Freedlander had not spared any expense on either food or drink. The hors d'oeuvre trays spilled over with caviar, red salmon eggs, expensive cheeses, broccoli sprouts, cauliflower, baby carrots and several dips. For the main course, guests could choose from prime rib, carved glazed ham, broiled chicken or salmon cooked in white wine.

"Should we eat something?" Ann asked, ignoring a small group of TV and newspaper reporters armed with tape recorders and microphones.

Matt nodded. "Shame to let all this great food go to waste." His eyes roved the head table on the beautifully decorated platform across the hall, where Freedlander and his entourage were seated. He guided Ann toward a hot food table. "Try to look inconspicuous," he said.

"And just how am I supposed to manage that?"

"I don't know. You'll think of something."

An hour later, signaling that the business of the evening was about to begin, the band struck up *Happy Days are Here Again*, a song written in the early '30s for the musical, *Chasing Rainbows*, but appropriated by Franklin Delano Roosevelt as his theme song during his 1932 presidential campaign. As if on cue, the noisy throng rose from the tables and moved forward, filling the open expanse between the line of dinner tables and the raised platform. Seeing that, Matt grinned. "This'll make it easier for us."

Moments later, Alec Poole, New York City Democrat Party Chairman, beaming from ear to ear, strode to the podium and adjusted the microphone. "Hello, out there! Are we having fun, yet?" The boisterous crowd loved it. He introduced himself and began to acknowledge the many VIP's present.

"... and I'd like to introduce the Mayor of our fine City ..." As the guests applauded, Matt watched Ramon and Emilio move around the platform, to take up positions at the doors behind it, effectively cutting off escape for anyone who might try to leave the hall by that route.

"... did I get everyone? All the members of the Manhattan Borough Council?" Poole asked rhetorically. "Don't wanna leave anybody out." The good-natured crowd laughed. Ann gestured toward Dan Davis, off to their right, who, in the company of O'Toole and an FBI agent, had moved next to Willie Preston.

"... a man who has dedicated his life to the service of the City of New York ..."

As Poole began his introduction of Freedlander, Deputy Chief Gunning, Jim Crowley and another FBI agent sidled up to an unsuspecting John Foreman and stopped, one on each side and one immediately behind him.

" ... he has confronted crime and criminals courageously as US District Attorney for the Southern District of this great City and ..."

Matt nodded toward one of the reporters, who with his photographer was standing in the crowd to the left of the podium as they faced it. "Dixon and Greene."

"Yes. And Lucas and Blumenthal are just over there." Ann pointed in the opposite direction, her heart in her throat.

"... has given lavishly of his time, energy and money, to philanthropic causes around the City, including such institutions as the New York City Public Library, of which he is a Board member ..."

Poole droned on, citing Freedlander's impressive achievements and listing the honors bestowed upon him by local media, civic groups and others. But Matt's eyes were glued to Freedlander, seated a few feet away from Poole, flanked by Poole's wife on one side and his own on the other. Relaxed, grinning from ear to ear, he was thoroughly enjoying the well-orchestrated moment; *his* moment.

"... Marvin Jonathan Freedlanderrrrrr," Poole finished with a flourish. The band did a quick drum roll and once more struck up *"Happy Days are Here Again,"* as Freedlander, flushed with excitement, rose from his chair and moved to the microphone amid wild applause, shaking hands with Poole as they sidestepped past each other.

With Ann close to him in the crowded ballroom, Matt stood quietly, conscious of his own breathing and the light scent of perfume worn by the woman at his side. There was simply no way to prepare himself for what would take place in the next few moments. So he said a quick prayer and cleared his mind as best he could. Then he touched Ann's arm lightly.

"It's time to move. Everybody's in place."

"Good evening, ladies and gents," Freedlander began. "Thank you, Alec, for that wonderful introduction." Pausing, basking in the limelight, he gazed out over the heads of the guests below him. "I just want to take a minute to thank a few very special people …"

Matt and Ann inched forward until they were standing in the first row of listeners, directly in front of the podium from which Freedlander was speaking. They were as close to him as they could get.

" … thank Marta, my lovely wife, for …" Freedlander ended his introductory remarks and settled into the topic for which they had all come; the announcement of his candidacy.

"'New York, New York! It's a wonderful town.' All of us here tonight are familiar with the words to that dear old tune. Well, I … " Ten minutes later, he was done. " … and I will endeavor to run a good, clean campaign. And if elected, I will try not to let you, the members of our fine party, down as I lead this wonderful metropolis as its mayor."

Finished, Freedlander raised both hands over his head in a victory salute, and the guests applauded vigorously. Alec Poole, beaming from ear to ear, again took the microphone. "Thank you, Marvin. Let's hear it, folks, for the next mayor of New York City!"

When the invited applause had subsided, Poole gestured toward Freedlander. "I know you'd love to take a few questions, right?" He backed away as Freedlander again slipped behind the podium.

"I'd be delighted." Totally confident, he oozed charm and effusiveness. The guests murmured their approval and paused, waiting for the first person to toss Freedlander a cream puff. This was it. Matt sucked in his breath, raised his hand, and was acknowledged. A wireless microphone was thrust under his chin.

"Mr. Freedlander, what can you tell us about the murder of a man named George W. Cohan in Cuernavaca, Mexico a few days ago?" The Hall grew quiet. Freedlander, taken by surprise, peered over his glasses at the man who had asked the question, but did not respond.

"Mr. Freedlander, Ken Dixon, *The New York Times*." Dixon and his photographer assistant, Richard Greene, were standing about twenty feet to Matt's left. "There's been a report that you recently ordered the death of an elderly American expatriate in Cuernavaca, Mexico, to protect a secret from your past. Would you comment on that?" A collective gasp went up from those present, and the hall became deathly still as the flash of Greene's camera erupted twice.

Freedlander, his face ashen, started to speak. But he was interrupted by a voice from thirty feet to Matt's right. "Mr. Freedlander? John Lucas, *The New York Times*. Is it true that a member of your staff, one William Preston, murdered Mr. Cohan, acting on your orders?"

Astonished murmurings began to spread through the crowd. Stunned, Marvin Jonathan Freedlander shook his head from side to side, like a punch-drunk fighter who had just absorbed a punch to the jaw. This time, Max Blumenthal's camera recorded his reaction.

"Mr. Freedlander," Matt yelled over the crowd noise, "is it true that your father was accused of stabbing to death a Mexican peasant woman forty years ago in Cuernavaca?" This question exploded in the crowd like a grenade bursting in a busy mall.

Freedlander emerged from his dazed state. Terrified that his long-held secret would be exposed, he fought the panic that flooded his mind. Then recognition dawned. "You!" He screamed, leveling a finger at Matt. "I know who you are!"

"And is it true that your father ran from the Mexican authorities so he wouldn't have to stand trial for murder?" Matt continued, loudly, above the babble.

A cunning smile spread across Freedlander's pale face. "Ladies and Gentlemen, I'm terribly sorry for this interruption." He again pointed at Matt. "*That* man is a wanted criminal; a murderer and kidnapper who has been loose in our City all week. The police and FBI are hunting for him." He turned and glanced along the row of guests at the head table. "Agent Starling? Where is Agent Starling? Arrest that man and take him into custody!"

But Agent Starling was no longer at the head table. Having left his seat earlier, he was now standing in the crowd next to FBI Chief Tom O'Toole. "I'm right here, Marvin," he said loudly. The humiliating experience in O'Toole's office the day before was still fresh in his mind. He considered himself lucky not to have been exiled to some District in the boonies, or worse yet, fired outright. *All for having tried to help Marvin Jonathan Freedlander.* "No, I won't do that. It's over. Give it up. We know the truth."

Willie Preston, standing in the audience, understood that something was amiss, but his brain, processing events slowly, as usual, did not yet know exactly what it was. Looking toward the man in the crowd at whom his boss had pointed, he drew his pistol and took a step in that direction.

Dan Davis, nervously fingering the butt of his pistol beneath his sport coat, saw Preston begin to move before the others did. *Here we go!* He thought, as he pulled his gun from under his coat. He knew he should say something to Preston, but he was suddenly tongue-tied. The only thing that came to mind was what Tom Mix, an old Western radio hero used to say when confronting the bad guys. "Drop it and reach for the sky, Preston!" He yelled , and poked the barrel of his .45 into Preston's side.

Preston half-turned. "Who in blazes are *you*?" He began. But O'Toole, Starling, and another agent, all with drawn guns, immediately stopped him, while Starling reached out and snatched the gun from his hand.

Freedlander, beads of sweat visible on his brow, continued standing at the podium. His heavy breathing, picked up by the hot mike, echoed through the crowded Hall as he rocked back and forth on his heels. "Ah, ah ..." he said.

Nearby, Ramon Gonzales, who had stationed himself at one of the doors behind the raised platform on which the long head tables were situated, decided to make his move. He mounted the stairs behind the platform and closed in.

"Mr. Freedlander, I am Chief Inspector Ramon Gonzales, Cuernavaca Police. You are under arrest for the murder of George W. Cohan." Again, the open mike picked up his accented words and broadcast them throughout the hall. Gasps erupted from Alec Poole, others on the platform and many in the stunned crowd. Seated at the table a few feet away, Freedlander's wife looked on, stunned. .

John Foreman, thumbs looped inside his belt, had been enjoying the evening. Until now. He took in the scene unfolding before him and realized this was not at all what had been expected. His boss's triumphant evening was quickly turning into a disaster of major proportions. People knew about the murder of Cohan. They'd soon know he had a part in it. He looked around for a way out of the hall and spotted one of the closed doors behind the platform. But before he could move, a man whose wrist was in a cast and whose face was all too familiar blocked his path.

"Good evening, Mr. Foreman," Jim Crowley said. "Remember me?"

"What are *you* doing here?" Foreman sputtered. That was as far as he got.

"FBI, Foreman. "Put your hands up!" Deputy Chief Gunning said, as he jammed a pistol into Foreman's back, and another agent stepped in front of him.

At the podium, Marvin Jonathan Freedlander emerged from his stupor. Again, he pointed a finger at Matt. "I'll kill you for this!" He screamed, his lips twisting with anger. Before the nearest startled observers could react, he pulled the Beretta from under his suit coat and aimed it at Matt. Less than thirty feet separated him from his target.

Ann Kelly, standing a few feet to Matt's right, adrenaline pumping, watched, horrified, as the pistol came out. She saw the barrel pointed at Matt. "Noooo!" She cried, and flung herself headlong in front of Matt, as Freedlander squeezed off two shots.

‡ ‡ ‡ ‡ ‡

March 23, 1990
New York City, New York
The Regent Wall Street Hotel
The Grand Ballroom
9:35 p.m. EST

The first bullet caught Ann in the upper arm, spinning her around and knocking her to the floor. The second hit Matt squarely in the stomach. He staggered back and went down, the breath knocked from him by the impact of the 9-mm round. He tried to stand, but his legs buckled and he fell to his knees. His body felt heavy, his limbs unworkable. Dimly, he saw the legs and feet of numerous people milling about, and heard a woman scream as if from far off. Then, he felt nothing.

On the platform, Freedlander stood, pistol in hand, momentarily shocked by what he'd done. Before he could move again, Ramon Gonzales and Emilio Diaz reached him. As men yelled and women screamed, they wrestled Freedlander to the floor.

"I have him, Ramon!" Diaz cried.

"The cuffs! Get the cuffs on him," Ramon cried, as he jarred the gun from Freedlander's grip.

But Marvin Jonathan Freedlander was a big man, and his membership in the Regent Wall Street's Health Club had not been a complete waste of time. Getting his legs under him, he lunged to his feet, tossing the shorter, lighter Diaz aside like a rag doll. With a sweep of his arm he broke loose from Gonzales, reached down and retrieved the Beretta. Moving quickly for such a big man, he shoved the stunned Alec Poole aside, took the stairs leading from the platform two at a time and raced for the closer of the doors behind it.

"Marvin! Stop or I'll shoot!" Ken Starling, gun in hand, came around the platform in time to see what had happened. Sensing that Freedlander was getting away and eager to redeem himself in the eyes of his Chief and perhaps save his job, he leveled his .45 caliber pistol, returned to him by O'Toole that morning, and hesitated.

With the look of a hunted animal, Freedlander glanced over his shoulder. "You can go straight to…!" He snarled. Gun still in hand, he was almost to the door when Starling fired.

CHAPTER 48

Friday, March 30, 1990
Chappaqua, New York
The Home of Ann Kelly
11:00 a.m. Eastern Standard Time (EST)

MATT DAWSON PULLED HIS RENTED car into a wide cobblestone driveway lined with birch trees in front of Ann Kelly's Georgian Colonial home, and stopped in a gravel-covered parking area under a grove of tall pines that partially screened the Kelly house from those on either side. Cutting the ignition, he paused, listening to the soft sounds of almost spring; the chirping of sparrows nearby, and the warning caw of crows in the pines. He approached the front door, but before he could press the bell, a woman dressed in the crisp blue and white uniform of a maid opened it.

"Missus Kelly is expecting you, Mr. Dawson. She's in the garden. I'll take you to her," she said, with a look that warned him something was not quite right.

Concerned, he followed her through the house, onto a glassed-in sun porch, and then out into the back yard. They made their way along a winding brick path of rhododendrons and lilacs, leading to a magnificent garden of blooming red and white azaleas, banks of pink peonies and carefully pruned rose bushes just beginning to bud. To his right was a large, kidney-shaped swimming pool, its placement set to maximize the meager sunlight that filtered through the thick pines. The pool was, at the moment, being cleaned and painted by a crew of three noisy maintenance men. Beyond the pool, an orchard of apple, pear, and peach trees occupied an acre or more of Kelly land. A flagstone patio occupied the far-left corner of this Eden, and it was there that the maid led him. Ann, reclining on a high-backed lounge chair, eyes closed, held her face to the pale March sun.

"Wow!" He said.

"It *is* beautiful, isn't it?" The maid responded.

Matt had been saved from serious injury or even death by the Kevlar vest he'd been wearing the night of Freedlander's disastrous announcement party. Knocked unconscious, he had come around just in time to watch two emergency medical technicians (EMTs), medical professionals used to dealing daily with life-and-death situations, removing Ann from the packed hall on a stretcher. They had taken her to the nearest hospital, where she had remained for four days before being released. The bullet had severed an artery in her arm, causing her to lose a great deal of blood. Although he had called daily to see how she was doing, this was his first opportunity to visit.

"Mr. Dawson, Madam," the maid said.

Ann turned and a warm smile lit up her face. "Matt!" She said simply, and extended her hand as her maid turned and left them.

He took the offered hand, but leaned down and kissed her, noting the dark circles under her eyes and the fact that she appeared thinner than she had been. "You look beautiful, as usual." His voice betrayed his emotion. "It's good to see you." Releasing her hand, he pulled another lounge chair over as close to hers as possible and sat.

"I'm glad you're okay," she said, her tone like a restrained caress.

He nodded. "It was nothing serious. But, that Beretta Freedlander used packed a kick like a mule. It hurt pretty badly for a few days, and I have a huge black and blue mark down here." He ran a hand across his stomach. "*You* got the worst of it. Did you forget which one of us was wearing the Kevlar?"

They both laughed. "I guess so. But I'd do it again, if the need arose."

Their eyes locked. Matt took her hand again. "Thank you."

Silence. Then Ann cleared her throat. "Terrible about Marvin Jonathan."

"Yeah. He was dead before the EMT arrived."

"Will Agent Starling get into trouble over it?"

"No. Ramon had already placed Freedlander under arrest. Freedlander had a gun. He was shot while trying to escape. O'Toole already knew Starling's part in this. He'd received a reprimand, been given his badge and service pistol back and ordered to assist in Freedlander's apprehension."

"What about Willie?"

"He's been arrested and charged with George Cohan's murder. He's facing an extradition hearing next week. Mexico wants to try him down there."

Ann made a wry face. "I hear Mexican prisons are not much fun. And Foreman?"

"He's in custody, too. He's charged with being an accomplice to attempted murder of you and me, and aggravated assault on Jim Crowley. I heard he's thinking about copping a plea. The prosecution wants to use his testimony against Preston."

"And Ramon and Emilio?"

"Gone back to Cuernavaca. Said to give you their love."

Ann nodded and turned away. A pair of robins landed on the patio and began foraging. Nearby, someone had planted an herb garden; mint, ginger, thyme, basil, marjoram, fennel and dill. Matt's eyes skipped through the bed, recognizing and counting each. Ann's garden was a small Paradise, so peaceful that it was an effort to concentrate on the present.

"Ann? What were you about to tell me?"

"What? When?"

"In the car on the way to the Regent Wall Street. Before the cop car interrupted you."

She took a deep breath. "I was about to tell you that Ann is my middle name. My full name is Ruth Ann. And my maiden name was Lieber."

"I know."

She blinked and turned toward him. "How did you figure it out?"

"From your reactions. First at the Pasti Cosi and later in New York at Wright's office."

"I wanted to tell you before, you know. Really. I didn't mean to keep it from you. I was overly concerned that you might be unhappy with me."

Matt touched her hand. "I *know* you weren't deliberately trying to keep it from me."

"You're very understanding. For a man, I mean. Thank you."

Another pause. Then, "Have you told your parents I'm looking for them?"

"Yes. But mother asked me *not* to tell you where they're living. She said she would contact you herself, soon."

They were silent again, their thoughts, for a time, their own. The smell of blooming lilacs was heavy in the air. Ann broke the stillness. "It won't work, you know."

He raised his eyebrows and nodded. "When did you decide that?"

"This past week. Since I've been out of hospital and home, I've had lots of time to think about it. About us."

He gently caressed her hand. "Are you okay with that?"

She glanced toward the row of tall pines at the rear of the land that was now hers alone, and sighed. Looking back, she met his eyes with a wan smile. "I suppose. You?"

"Yes. But ... I'll never forget. And I want us to be friends."

"I was hoping you'd feel that way. I'd love to be your friend. Always. I have no regrets about our relationship, you know. And I'm very thankful."

"Thankful?" Matt half turned in his chair. "To whom?"

Sounds of laughter reached them from the workers in the pool area.

"I know where you're going with that, Matt. You'd like me to say 'to God.' But really, it's just a figure of speech. Part of the secular culture I was brought up in."

"Oh."

Removing her hand from his, she rested it on his arm. "No. I'm *not* thankful to God. I'm just not there yet. Although I *did* talk to him once during all this. At the Borsa Di Roma that day, while I was waiting for you to come back from your little visit to Marvin Jonathan's lair." She paused, thinking. "Mostly I'm thankful to *you* for saving my life and helping me extricate myself from a deadening and deadly experience. Still ..."

"What?"

"Well, I envy you people who *do* believe in God. Because you have someone to thank when something good happens to you."

Matt leaned over and kissed her cheek. "Sounds like you've been thinking about this."

Ann made a dismissive hand gesture. "Will you stay for lunch?"

He grinned broadly. "Of course. I want to hear all about your conversation with God."

Now it was Ann's turn to smile. "You'll have to admit that it *was* a very nice place to hold ones first conversation with Him, don't you agree?"

CHAPTER 49

Sunday, April 9, 1990
Phoenix, Baltimore County, Maryland
The Home of Roy and Jenny Benson
2:30 p.m. Eastern Standard Time (EST)

THE BENSON HOME ON CARROLL Mill Road in Baltimore County was a roomy Victorian style house, built in the late 1890s. A grove of tall maples screened it from the road and acted as a sound barrier. Roy and Jenny had thoroughly refurbished it, down to new shutters and a sparkling coat of fresh white paint.

Matt Dawson pulled open a screen door and found himself on a porch elegantly decorated with white wicker furniture and green potted plants. Inside, the house was crowded with pro-life workers from around the state, relaxing together after a busy winter of pro-life activities. A waiter, clad in a long-sleeved green shirt and black slacks, passed, carrying a tray of both cabernet sauvignon and merlot. Matt helped himself to a merlot and moved into the living room, where a fire in the big stone fireplace warmed the chilled guests as they arrived, and tasty hors d'oeuvres trays enticed them to expand their waistlines.

Matt tried small talk with people he knew, but quickly realized he was not in a party mood. Wine in hand, he strolled into the kitchen and out the back door. The Benson's yard contained an in-ground swimming pool surrounded by a patio, nicely landscaped with azaleas and rhododendrons. The weather being still a bit too cold, the pool had not yet been filled. Only a few guests were outside doing as he was, getting some air, standing in groups of twos and threes, talking quietly.

Drifting over to the post and rail fence at the rear of the yard, Matt paused. Beyond the fence, an open pasture stretched two hundred yards to a distant line of hardwood trees. He watched as a gaggle of geese in flight overhead circled and began calling to each other with that peculiar sound that only geese make. Nearby, a dozen brown and white cows, Herefords, he surmised, stood quietly beneath a lone maple tree growing next to a small pond.

His thoughts turned to the farm in Freeland and a wave of nostalgia swept over him. Having to sell it had been a bitter pill. Although he'd concealed his emotions throughout the ordeal, the day he had gone to settlement accompanied by his lawyer and his then separated wife, had been one of the worst in his life. Later, he had returned to his apartment and cried unashamedly, though conscious that men were not expected to do that sort of thing.

"Are you staring at those cows?" A woman's voice interrupted his musings. Turning, he saw a tall, slender brunette approaching, dressed in a dark cloth coat with large black buttons. A pink French beret was perched on her head and a soft matching pink scarf framed her pretty face and neck.

"Yes. They don't seem to mind. I'm also admiring the view. It's beautiful."

Advancing to the fence, she stopped and surveyed the scene, her dark eyes sparkling with appreciation. Taking a deep breath, she removed a slender hand from her coat pocket and extended it toward him. "It really is. My name's Karen Farley. I'm a volunteer at Pregnancy Center North." She pointed at the cows. "Are you sure they don't mind?"

Matt took the offered hand. "Matt Dawson. I write pro-life letters and also go to an occasional rescue at abortion clinics." His face crinkled in a smile as he realized that their conversation was progressing on two levels. "The cows? They'll let us know if they do."

Turning toward him, her warm brown eyes failed to conceal her interest. "Really? Have you been arrested?" She chuckled. "How?"

"No. I'm one of the people who act as prayer support while the others are carried off to the paddy wagons." He nodded toward the bovines in the field. "Maybe they'll elect a spokesman and he'll come over and tell us to stop."

She laughed a nice throaty laugh. "I've been to several rescues but I haven't been arrested, either. That takes more courage than I've got."

Matt shrugged "What you do at the Pregnancy Center is probably the most important job of all. You're a crisis counselor, right?"

She nodded, her face suddenly serious. "I enjoy it. Especially when I find that something I've said to a pregnant girl has saved the life of an unborn baby." She turned toward the cows. "You know what? I think they're staring at *us*."

Now it was Matt's turn to laugh. "It sure looks that way." He turned toward the house. "Let's go inside. There's a big fireplace in the living room with a nice warm fire in it."

The gaggle of geese had circled back and was now overhead again. Silently and in turn, tiny webbed feet extended, feeling for the glass surface of the pond, they glided to effortless landings, as if, exhausted by their long flight, they were content to find a place to rest.

CHAPTER 50

Monday, April 10, 1990
Timonium, Maryland
Padonia Village Apartments
2312 Chetwood Circle
9:45 a.m. Eastern Standard Time (EST)

Matt Dawson's telephone was ringing. Returning from morning Mass, he could just make out the sound through the door as he descended the stairs to the lower level. Quickly, he pulled a fat, leather key case from his pocket. In his haste, he dropped it at his feet, retrieved it and fumbled with it, looking for the right key.

Inside, he raced to the phone and picked it up. A dial tone greeted him. He held the receiver to his ear for a moment before hanging up.

Walking into the kitchen, Matt filled the coffee maker with cold water from the tap, added fresh Columbian coffee and flipped the switch.

A few minutes later, settled at the dining room table with a coffee cup next to his left elbow and the phone next to his right, stillness all around him, he looked out at a bright April morning. In the courtyard, new grass was pushing its way to the surface, daffodils were blooming beneath the lone tree, and the lilac bushes that lined the wall of the building opposite were in full bloom. The phone rang again, startling him.

"Matt Dawson."

"Hello, Mr. Dawson?" The voice belonged to an elderly woman. Matt could hear her breathing. "My name is Anna Lieber. I understand you've been looking for me."

Matt jumped to his feet so quickly that the chair he'd been sitting in toppled over backwards. "All right!" He exclaimed.

"What?"

"Nothing. Don't mind me. I'm just very pleased to get your call. Yes, I've been looking for you for over a month." He reached for the chair, set it upright and sat down again.

"A woman named Rhoda Loeb called and gave me your number. She told me it was about the death of my brother, Alvin. I didn't know he had died until she told me." She paused for breath. "I wasn't going to call you until my daughter mentioned you to me. She said she had met you recently, in Branford."

"That's right. I'm an investigator working for the attorney who represents your brother's estate. When Alvin died, some efforts were made to notify you, but without success."

"When did he die, Mr. Dawson?"

"April 15, 1987." Matt was thinking quickly. In order to be certain that this woman was Anna Lieber, he needed to make a positive identification. Bob Winkler would want him to be sure they were dealing with the right person. The Orphan's Court would require it.

"Mrs. Lieber, before we go any further I need to confirm that you're really Anna Lieber. Would you mind answering a few questions?"

"I understand. No, I don't mind."

"What's your middle name?"

"Edith," came the prompt response.

"What was your brother's middle name and date of birth?"

"His middle name? Raymond. His date of birth was July 15, 1914."

"What was your mother's maiden name?"

"Bettelheim," was the reply.

"Who was Leo Bettelheim?"

"My uncle. My mother's older brother. He and his family once lived in Chicago. They moved to Auburn, New York, and he later died there."

Matt relaxed. These were bits of information only she would know. "You say Rhoda Loeb told you about me?"

"Yes. I had no idea who she was. But she reminded me that we had been neighbors in Brockett's Point some years ago. She told me she had contacted Vernon Radonowitz in New York and he contacted Maxim's son, Edward, and explained about your inquiry. Edward's wife, Elizabeth, called Rhoda Loeb and told her where to contact me."

"How did Vernon Radonowitz contact Edward?" Matt wanted to know.

"I don't know for certain. Perhaps through Alger Hiss. Alger keeps up with lots of people, even though he's quite elderly now."

"Is your son Butch still living?"

Anna laughed. "Nobody has called him that in years. Yes. He lives in Canada now."

"How long did you live in Mexico before you left there?"

"We left Mexico in early 1954."

"Where did you go after that?"

"To Warsaw, Poland. Max was born there and he still held citizenship. A friend got me a teaching job at Warsaw University where he was a professor. We stayed until 1968. Ruth had been sent to England to school and when Luke was ready for college we thought it best to return to this country."

"What did you do for a living after you came back?"

"I worked as an English teacher until I retired in 1972."

"How old are you now, Anna?"

"Oh, I'm eighty years old and still going strong."

"What about your husband?"

"Max is alive, but he's feeble and senile. He's ... not far from here." She did not volunteer his whereabouts. Matt noticed, but not needing to know and concerned that she might become frightened and hang up, he did not ask her anything more about Max.

"Anna, you haven't asked me what your brother left you."

"Well, I figured you'd tell me when you were ready, Mr. Dawson."

Matt chuckled. "I don't really know all the specifics," he said apologetically. "I think the best thing is for me to report to Mr. Winkler that you've been found, and let him call you with the details. But there *are* some old letters, papers and documents that belonged to Alvin. Would you want to have any of those things?

"Yes, I would."

"Fine. Give me a phone number. I'll call Mr. Winkler right away, and you can expect a call from him later today."

‡ ‡ ‡ ‡ ‡

Monday, April 10, 1990
A Small East Coast State
The Apartment of Anna and Maxim Lieber
9:55 a.m. EST

Anna Lieber replaced the receiver, made her way to the sofa and sat heavily. An open scrapbook was on the coffee table, its faded newspaper clippings and old snapshots, bathed in the soft light from a small table lamp, looked up at her, unseen. There was a faded photograph of herself as a little girl, sitting on the stoop in front of her house with two long-forgotten friends; another of the same three girls, taken after a game of hopscotch.

With some effort, she held herself still, gathering her thoughts. Her eyes were wide with alarm. *He said his name is Dawson. But who is he, really? Some sort of government agent? Are they looking for Max again?*

Clearing her throat, she tried to control the unwieldy pounding of her heart. As a child, she had prided herself on being in control, but life had taught her that she could not always be in charge. There were times when events overwhelmed and panic got the upper hand.

She pressed both fists against her thin, gray cheeks to silence the fear welling up in her.

Rising moments later, she shuffled unsteadily to the small apartment kitchen. She was not certain what this contact meant for Max, herself and the kids. She shrugged. *Too late now. I gave him our address and telephone number.* She realized that once agents had their address it might not be long before she would hear a knock on the door.

Removing a small stainless steel pan from the dish drainer on the sink, Anna rinsed it and ran cold water into it from the faucet. She placed it on the stove.

Her mind began to re-play the phone conversation she had just had with Dawson. He had asked nothing about Max. Well, not exactly true. He'd asked one question. Either the man was extremely clever or he *was* who he said he was, doing what he said he was doing.

Opening a cupboard, she reached for the red, white and green box of Lipton tea bags. From the dish drainer she removed two cups and two saucers, placed them on the counter and dropped a tea bag into each cup. The water came to a boil; she came to a decision at the same time. Mr. Dawson was legitimate. And even if he wasn't, there was nothing she could do about it now. He had told her to expect a call later this afternoon from the lawyer for whom he was working. Okay. She'd try not to be alarmed. She'd simply wait to see what happened next.

Moments later, her wildly beating heart slowed and the rushing sound in her ears subsided. Her confidence began to return. Humming to herself, she poured hot water into both cups, added sugar and milk to each and placed both on a small silver tray. Rummaging in a drawer, she found two clean teaspoons and added them to the tray. Then, the tray firmly in hand, she left the small kitchen and made her way slowly down a long hall to a closed door at the other end. Opening it, she entered a small bedroom.

The room was brightly lit. Faded drapes on the single window were open, allowing the warm April sunlight to stream in. A frail, white-haired man sat in a chair in front of the window. His back was to the door, and a faded quilt covered his thin legs. A victim of Alzheimer's, he made no movement as Anna entered. She placed the tea tray on a metal party tray next to his chair. The bed springs creaked as she sat on the edge of the old double bed.

"We had a call just now," she said, turning toward her husband. "From Baltimore. A man has been looking for us. My brother Alvin died a while back." She paused as if waiting for a response, but having watched the subtle progression of the disease in Max, she did not expect one. It was simply that old conversational habits die hard.

Standing, she reached for her teacup and sat down again. "You remember Alvin, don't you? He lived down in Baltimore. Oh, yes. I know you didn't like him very much. You and he were so *different*. You could never get along. And that always bothered me. How much more pleasant life would have been if my husband and my only brother could have been friends."

Picking up one of the teaspoons, Anna stirred her tea briefly. She glanced at the figure in the chair, recalling when he'd first begun to exhibit symptoms: an abrupt decline in memory accompanied by the inability to express himself verbally. *I'm very fortunate. He hasn't yet shown any signs of the worst symptoms: agitation, combativeness toward me, or delusions. And he shows no interest in leaving that chair to wander. Don't know how I'd cope if he did those things.*

"I was thinking about Alvin just the other day. Recalling how much fun we used to have together when we were little; running through the sprinkler on hot summer evenings, going off with Daddy for an ice cream. That was before he went off to war. And those pillow fights in my bedroom some nights!" She smiled wistfully. "We'd laugh so hard our stomachs would hurt."

Anna sipped her tea and waited. Except for a slight shifting of the man's head, there was no response. *What are you thinking, dear, locked away forever inside that handsome head. You were always such a garrulous person, never at a loss for words. You had had an opinion about everything. There were times when even I couldn't get a word in edgewise. Not so any more. I have the stage all to myself.* "She smiled. *Is that a little reward for me? After all those years when I simply listened? Oh, no. I never really minded. You were always so interesting. Never dull.* "At first I was suspicious," she continued. "I actually thought it might be the government trying to locate us again. But, then I thought, that's crazy. Why would they be looking for us after so long?"

She cast a slow, appraising glance around the room, letting her eyes pause here and there on familiar objects; the pale green walls, the scratched maple dresser with five drawers, the faded print drapes on the window. Her thin body shivered, as if from a slight chill. "No. I don't think we have anything to worry about."

Anna sipped her tea again. The silence became heavy. She smiled. "Remember our talk the other night about how we'd manage for the next few years, dear? Well, it seems Alvin left me some money. I don't know how much yet. I'll learn more this afternoon from the lawyer. He's going to call us." Leaning over, she placed her hand on the old man's thin, bony wrist. "See? I told you God would take care of us, didn't I?"

‡ ‡ ‡ ‡ ‡

Wednesday, April 12, 1990
Towson, Maryland
Immaculate Conception Church
9:10 a.m. EST

Matt Dawson was not sitting in his usual spot at church on this cold, overcast April day that looked and felt suspiciously like it might snow. He had arrived late and had taken a seat only a quarter of the way up the main aisle so he would not interrupt the readings. That's when he noticed the tall, slender woman ten rows in front of him. *She has to be the same one I met at the pro-life picnic,* he thought. *She's wearing the same dark cloth coat, the same pink beret and matching pink scarf.*

Matt thought she was pretty. What was her name? Oh, yes. Karen Farley. They had spent a while together at the Benson's pro-life party and he had enjoyed their conversation. She seemed nice. It had not taken long for him to notice that, although there was a sadness in her eyes that spoke of life experiences not altogether kind, there was also a peacefulness about her; the peace of Christ that surpasses all understanding. Before they had parted that day, he guessed that she, like him, had had a conversion experience that had changed her life.

Matt tried to concentrate on the lector as he read the second selection. But soon his eyes drifted back to Karen. The lector's voice began to recede. Matt gradually understood that, in his mind there was another sound, a strong kindly sound, filling his head. Not a voice actually, but for lack of a better word, he thought of it that way. "YES. YOU COULD BE MARRIED TO HER."

What a silly thing to be thinking, he reflected. Although the pain of his divorce had receded, the loss of his recent relationship with Ann Kelly was still fresh. *I'm not the least bit interested in marriage just now.*

The reading continued but Matt was no longer listening. Instead, he heard the words of a priest, uttered in this same church a few weeks ago. "What happens to you in the future depends on your response to God today," Father Flynn had said.

Matt sat up straight. He had been praying about his future, asking God to send the gift of hope, and wondering if that future involved a new marriage. Was he receiving an answer to his prayers? An answer to which he was expected to respond?

"What happens to you in the future depends upon your response to God today."

But there's no way I can respond! He thought. His mind ran over the terrible financial state he was in. He had no money in the bank and little income. Bills were piling up again. Then, there was his car. The passenger door lock was jammed so that the door wouldn't open. The engine frequently overheated and the transmission was making unfriendly noises. The broken back window was still unrepaired, the clear plastic trash bag taped over the gaping hole flapped obscenely in the wind as he drove.

How can I respond? I can't see how I'd be able to afford dating. Besides, most women are concerned about security. They want the assurance that a man is financially stable and can offer them stability. What would this woman think?

Another thought occurred. *Okay! All those things are true. But it isn't like only bad things are going on in my life. Good things are happening, too. My fee in the Lieber case helped me to catch up a bit. Thanks to some of my lawyer friends, word is spreading and both investigative work and process serving work is now coming in. The business is viable. If I'm faithful to God and work hard, I'll soon be making enough to meet my needs. Then I'll be able to pay off some of my debts.*

He glanced at Karen Farley again. *And besides, what'll it cost to take Karen out for breakfast? Today. I could go up to her after Mass and ask her out to the local diner.* He stood with the others for the Gospel reading.

Can I make a good impression? He chuckled, thinking about the Skyhawk. *Yeah. She'll be impressed. But the impression might be so unfavorable that there'll be no second date.*

"Trust in God, and lean not to thine own understanding," said Father Flynn as he began his homily.

Matt rolled his eyes and gave in. Oh, all right, I'll do it. He had arrived at a point where he trusted God. If this were meant to be, it would work out. The Holy Spirit would help.

He smiled. In the last four years he had taken several positive steps in his spiritual development. Like a mountain climber scaling the heights, he had driven himself upward despite the pain of all the losses he'd experienced. He had reached and passed several plateaus.

The first was the knowledge that God loved him unconditionally. The second was the ability to trust God completely. The third and most recent plateau was something that had happened as the result of having scaled the other two heights; hope for his future. He could now see that there was hope for him. And he felt the liberating glow of the mountain climber who reaches the peak, scrambles onto a level space and discovers he can see great distances in all directions.

Matt took a deep breath, his mood suddenly brighter. *Yes. I'll assume this is God's answer; that this is the direction He wants me to move in. And I'll ask Karen out for breakfast this morning.* That decision made, a sense of peace permeated his mind and body. He felt whole again.

On the podium, Father Flynn was speaking quietly, leaning slightly forward, his left elbow resting on the rail. "We know this world is a rich, wonderful, and fascinating place.

After all, it *is* God's creation and God didn't create anything evil.

"The world sets in front of us many experiences. It attracts both our reason and our will. But in the end, it doesn't satisfy our spirit. What does? Living a good Christian life. The Christian life is part of a natural human pilgrimage, the pursuit of meaning and ultimately, the search for God. God and God alone will satisfy our spirit."

‡ ‡ ‡ ‡ ‡

Monday, August 27, 1990
Towson, Maryland
The 606 Baltimore Avenue Building
10:00 a.m. EST

Bob Winkler sat in his office, an unlit cigarette dangling from his lips. Outside, the Baltimore air was hot and humid, the temperature threatening to pass ninety-five degrees for a third straight day. He was reading a letter from Anna Lieber, which had arrived in that morning's mail.

After Matt Dawson had reported finding Anna, Bob had speedily closed out Alvin Zelinka's estate. An exchange of correspondence with the Federal Employee's Group Life Insurance Company had produced their agreement to pay over Alvin's small life insurance policy to the estate. Satisfied with the amount, Bob had collected the proceeds of that policy. Then, he'd gathered all the cash remaining in the estate bank account and the U.S. Savings bonds and sent the entire sum to Anna Lieber. In the process, he'd spoken to her several times and had gotten to know and like her, having come to think of her as a very interesting lady:

August 25, 1990

Dear Mr. Winkler:

Thank you very much for sending me the letter from the Office of Federal Employee's Group Life Insurance. You certainly have been very generous with your time and your courtesy has been absolutely limitless. If all Alvin's friends were thus, he certainly was a very lucky man indeed.

As long as you are satisfied with the letter, that is fine with me. For the honest truth is that I simply cannot follow all those statements and the, to me, involved figures.

In college I got a D for a final mark in trig and when I thanked the prof because I knew very well that he had been generous, he patted me on the back and said, 'My dear, there was no point in your taking it over again.' I haven't improved with time.

    Again, thank you!

Sincerely,
Anna E. Lieber.

    Bob grabbed matches from his desk lit his cigarette, took a deep drag and reached for the telephone. Sunlight streamed through the windows behind him. *I'll call Matt Dawson and treat him to a two-manhattan lunch. Oh, that's right. Matt doesn't drink manhattans. Well, we'll go to lunch anyway and I'll drink the manhattans. I'll take along this letter from Anna Lieber. He'll get a kick out of it. He should write a book about this case. I'll have to remember to suggest it.*
    Dawson's phone was ringing. "Hello, Matt? Robert Winkler. How the … are ya?"

Author's Note:

O N THAT BLEAK NIGHT IN November 1951 referred to in Chapter 21, when an unmarked ambulance whisked Max Lieber away from Riptide Cottage, a pivotal event in the story related in this book occurred.

Lieber had been active in the US Communist Party (CPUSA) and the Soviet Communist Party during the 1930s and early 1940s. That evening, he severed his ties with the United States and began an odyssey that took him, his wife "Anna," and their two young children, "Ruth" and "Luke" (not their real names) to Mexico, then behind the Iron Curtain, and years later, back to the United States.

"Anna" Lieber was Max's third wife. She and Max had not been married when his alleged espionage activity was at its height, but she was probably aware of her husband's unsavory past by the time she became his bride. No doubt she knew that the time might come when he'd be forced to either cooperate with the U.S. government or defect to avoid prosecution. Faced with that momentous decision in late 1951, the Liebers gathered their children and quietly slipped out of the country.

For two years, they lived in Cuernavaca, in the Mexican State of Morelos, a city which, during the late '30s and early '40s had attracted Americans of leftist orientation, dissenters from the political, military and economic policies of their country.

In 1954, Max and "Anna" relocated behind the Iron Curtain to Warsaw, Poland, where Max had been born. They were provided with housing and jobs, and resided there until 1968, when they returned to the United States and took up residence in a state on the East Coast. By then, there was no further interest in Max, either as a defendant or a witness. They had outlived the events that had made him an uncomfortably public figure.

Nineteen years later, in 1987, "Anna" Lieber's brother, Alvin Raymond Zelinka, a quiet, former federal government clerk, passed away. He died intestate, that is, without a Will. "Anna" was his closest living relative and his sole heir. He would have been shocked had he known that his death would set in motion a three-nation search to settle his estate. How ironic that Alvin, a government employee all his working life, and an avid Republican, should have had such a notorious brother-in-law.

With the exception of a few minor characters, most of the people in this novel are real. I created dialogue for the fictional characters and added appropriate dialogue for the real ones, in order to make the story more understandable for the reader. In doing so, I attempted to portray the characters as they might have sounded had the reader been present when they played their roles. For example, the events involving Richard Nixon and the House Un-American Activities Committee actually occurred, but descriptions of setting, and some dialogue were developed for the scenes which took place inside and outside the hearing rooms involving Nixon, his wife, Pat, HUAC representatives and committee staff.

The scenes of House Un-American Activities Committee hearings are based on transcripts of witness testimony before the Committee. The lines spoken in those scenes were lifted directly from the transcripts without any changes in what was said, although certain connecting words and phrases have been added. The transcripts make fascinating reading and are extremely revealing if one is searching for facts.

The chapters dealing with "John Harris" are based on Jim Haynes, an attorney and friend of Alvin Zelinka. "John's" friend, "Ginny," is purely fictional, but Jim *did* actually travel to Mexico in search of "Anna" Lieber.

The scenes in which Rhoda Loeb checks into the Ritz Carlton, an upscale New York City hotel, and meets "Vernon Radonowitz" (not his real name) for breakfast in its cozy, off-lobby restaurant, are fictional. Rhoda and "Vernon" may not have been life-long friends, but I have no doubt that they talked briefly and that their conversation was extremely important to this investigation.

I created the scene in The Dubliner Restaurant dealing with "Anna" and Max Lieber, although one can see that something along those lines very likely took place.

The steps of my investigation were based on notes made during the course of my work.

In writing this book it was not my intention to become involved in the controversy surrounding Alger Hiss and Whittaker Chambers. Many meticulously researched books have already been written on that subject. At the back of this book, the reader will find a bibliography of books and documents that provided me with background information. Also included is an appendix of newspaper articles revealing new information about the Hiss case. Anyone interested in learning more will find these references useful.

- Alger Hiss died on December 15, 1996, at the age of ninety-two, still denying his complicity in espionage activities, although there now seems to be no doubt that he was a communist agent. Maxim Lieber's part in the Hiss case is documented by historians. Much is written about him in Whittaker Chambers's book, *Witness,* and Allen Weinstein's *Perjury.* More is revealed in transcripts of proceedings of the *House of Representatives Committee on UnAmerican Activities, U.S. Congress,* in 1948, 1950 and 1951. Further, the book *The Venona Secrets: Exposing Soviet Espionage and America's Traitors, written by Herbert Romerstein and Eric Breindel, published by Regnery Publishing, Inc., in 2000, was also consulted."* The reason Max, "Anna" Lieber and their children left the country was known only to a few, back at the time. When Whittaker Chambers's information became public, Lieber knew he would soon be exposed and presented with the choice of either doing hard time or cooperating with the authorities. He could not see himself as a material witness against the communist cause. Nor did he like the idea of providing evidence against his long-time friend, Alger Hiss. He liked even less the thought of being measured for a striped suit and breaking rocks for the rest of his life. Because these bits of information became apparent to me during my investigation, I believe this book will add a further small piece to the puzzle of Alger Hiss's double life.

- Testimony of Whittaker Chambers and several other witnesses before the Un-American Activities Committee, in fact, did expose Lieber as a communist agent. When he was subpoenaed, Lieber repeatedly took the Fifth. But he *did* answer a few questions. The information he provided sealed his fate.

Prior to the start of my hunt for "Anna" Lieber, the Iron Curtain had fallen and Soviet Communism met its demise at the hands of a world full of people seeking freedom from oppression. As part of a new climate of openness between former adversaries, historians, researchers and writers were given access to records previously kept secret. New facts about Hiss were reported in newspaper articles from 1992 through 1997. I've included them in a bibliography, without comment. But I will discuss one here, because, in my opinion, the information it contains clearly reveals the reason that the Liebers fled to Mexico.

In June 1987, President Ronald Reagan made his now famous speech at the Brandenburg Gate, then a symbol of division, in which the famous line, "Mr. Gorbachev, tear down this wall!" appeared. Later, the huge wall that separated East Germany from West Germany came down. Shortly thereafter, Maria Schmidt, a Hungarian researcher, began studying previously restricted files of the Interior Ministry in Budapest, her country's secret police. Professor Schmidt released her findings in October 1993, in a paper delivered at NYU's Center for European Studies. While searching transcripts of statements made to Hungarian authorities in 1954 by an American defector, Noel Haviland Field, she discovered that Field had stated that Hiss was a Soviet spy who, in the late 1930s, tried to recruit him only to find that he was already working for another Soviet apparatus. Word of Field's spying activities had been made public by Whittaker Chambers and another confessed spy, Hede Massing. In 1949, afraid he'd be charged with espionage and that his testimony might be sought by the U.S. government in the Hiss matter, Field fled to Hungary. His motives? Fear of exposure and jail, a misguided devotion to the communist cause and loyalty to his friend Alger Hiss.

In 1948, it was clear to investigators for the House Committee on UnAmerican Activities (HUAC) that Whittaker Chambers's information about the espionage activities of Alger Hiss was stale. Hiss could not be prosecuted for treason because, in addition to the constitutional requirement of two witnesses with knowledge of the same facts, back at the time there was a statute of limitations in force regarding that crime, and it had expired. But in view of what had been brought to light by HUAC, and under the prodding of Richard Nixon, a reluctant Justice Department concluded that it had no choice but to expose Alger Hiss. That's why Hiss was tried twice for perjury. Had Noel Field not defected, it's possible that his more recent information might have enabled government prosecutors to build a case of treason against Hiss. At worst, if they had been able to convince Field to testify voluntarily, or failing that, if they had been able to coerce his testimony, the Justice Department's case might have been strong enough to convict Hiss in his first perjury trial. It *is* certain that Field's evidence would have corroborated what Chambers and Hede Massing had been saying about Hiss under oath in different settings.

It's unlikely that Max Lieber was still an active communist agent as late as 1950. Therefore, he could not have been charged with treason. As with Noel Field, Lieber's importance to the government lay, not just in his spying, but in his knowledge of Alger Hiss's recent activities. His testimony would have been "the smoking gun" of which every prosecutor dreams. But partly out of fear of prison and partly out of a sense of loyalty to Hiss, Lieber elected to defect. In Noel Field's actions, Lieber had precedent.

And that explains why, in 1990, Alger Hiss could tell the New York lawyer whom I call "Vernon Radonowitz" the whereabouts of Lieber's son by his first wife, and perhaps of Lieber and his wife. Did Hiss feel a debt to Lieber, one that he could never fully repay? "Anna" Lieber told me that Hiss had "kept up" with them for quite a while. Is that why he maintained contact with them as time passed?

The Alger Hiss-Whittaker Chambers case, like the SaccoVanzetti case, the Lindberg case and the Sheppard case, seems to have a life of its own. Contrary to postmodernist thinking, which holds that objectivity and rationality are naive illusions, objectivity and open mindedness are still desirable qualities most of us strive to attain. But they have been casualties in the Chambers case. Opinions hardened as time has passed. But, the discovery of new information may change the minds of intellectually honest people. Others will live and die with their belief as to the alleged innocence of Hiss, the alleged illicit motives of Chambers and Nixon, and the so-called abuse of power by the UnAmerican Activities Committee.

Max Lieber was born on October 15, 1897 in Warsaw. Because the purpose of my investigation was to locate "Anna," not Maxim, it was necessary to let "Anna" know that I posed no threat to her husband and family, so that she would come forward in answer to my inquiries. Accordingly, I did not ask about Max or his whereabouts.

The names "Anna," "Ruth" and "Luke" are not the real names of the wife and children of Maxim Lieber. As the book was nearing completion, I wrote Mrs. Lieber to inform her that it was being written and to request that she answer several questions about the family's activities during their years in Mexico and later in Warsaw. She responded with a polite but firm refusal, stating, "we as a family do not wish any further newsworthiness." Out of respect for her wishes

I've given them fictitious first names. But for historical reasons, I did not feel that I could change their last name. In view of the fact that they neither sought nor gained fame or celebrity status since their return from Poland, it seems that "Anna" and the children were unwilling recipients of the notoriety thrust upon husband and father, Max Lieber, so many years before.

A substantial amount of time has passed since this investigation took place. One reason for waiting so long to write the story was to protect the privacy of the Lieber family. "Anna" Lieber was eighty years old in 1990. At the time this book was first published I wrote this: "As far as I know , she still resides in the same city in which I located her, although she could be deceased." Further research at the time of this re-writing reveals that "Anna," alias Minna Edith Lieber, who was born on Saturday, October 16, 1909, died on Thursday, September 22, 2011. She was 101 years, 11 months, 6 days old.

Also at the time this book was first published I wrote: "In 1990, Maxim Lieber's daughter was a married woman, living in the New York City area. His son was a resident of Canada. I have made no further attempts to locate or keep track of these individuals since my correspondence with 'Anna.'" Since then (I think it was in 2010), I was contacted by Lieber's son, who had seen my published article, *A Most Reluctant Witness, and simply called from Canada to apprise me of that fact.*

Max Lieber died quietly in East Hartford's Forbes Village, on Saturday, April 10, 1993. He was 95 years, 5 months, 26 days old. His death went unacknowledged by the literary community to which he belonged. The media made a great hue and cry at Alger Hiss's demise, but, as far as I can tell, it took no notice of Lieber's death. I examined *The New York Times* obituary pages for the period from April 10th through April 15th, 1993 and found nothing. Apparently his wife opened no estate for him, nor did she probate any Will, if one existed. If an obituary was published it was placed only in a local newspaper. For me, this was convincing evidence that "Anna" and the children, indeed, "want no further newsworthiness," and therefore, notified few people and published nothing.

When both probate and non-probate assets are considered, the Zelinka estate amounted to approximately $30,000. To many, that's not a large sum of money. But to an elderly couple in the winter of their journey through life, it probably meant the difference between a comfortable or an uncomfortable end to their final days. Anyone interested in the details of the probate of Alvin Zelinka's estate may review the file in the office of the Register of Wills for Baltimore County, New Courts Building, 401 Bosley Avenue, Towson, Maryland 21204.

Matt Dawson is a fictional character, loosely based on the author. For more of Dawson's thrilling adventures, see *The China Connection*, Lincoln, NE: Writers Club Press, 2003. That's right. As mentioned in my Author's Note at the beginning of this book, *The China Connection* was published before *Little Sister Lost*, although the events described there happened later. It's okay. They're both exciting stories.

"Karen Farley," who is introduced at the end of this book, is based on Carol Fenchak, a real person, a jewel later plucked from the ranks of the wonderful people who for whatever reason, marry late, to become the author's wife. Carol, an accomplished portrait artist and professional photographer, operated a studio specializing in wedding photography before teaching Art for four years at Mt. De Sales Academy, a highly regarded Roman Catholic high school for girls in Catonsville, Maryland. She continues to teach those subjects at Burns Junior/ Senior High School in Burns, Wyoming. "Karen" appears much earlier in *The China Connection,* providing a wholesome female presence.

The character of "Ann Kelly" is almost entirely fictitious. Maxim and "Anna" Lieber *did* have a daughter. She *did* spend a summer or two at their cottage in Brockett's Point, Connecticut as a child, and grew up in England while her parents lived in Warsaw. Everything else written about "Ann" in this novel, her life in Birmingham, England, her relationship with surrogate parents, her marriage to "Sean Cornelius Kelly," the affair "Ann" had with Marvin Freedlander, and her relationship with Matt, are products of the author's fertile imagination.

"Sean Cornelius Kelly," "Ann's" deceased husband in the novel, is totally fictitious, as are all the FBI agents who make brief appearances.

"Marvin Jonathan Freedlander," the scheming, overly ambitious District Attorney for the Southern District of New York is also entirely fictitious. Many men of good character and integrity have occupied that post. An Assistant in that office, Thomas Francis Murphy, who served from 1942 to 1950, was the prosecutor in both Hiss trials. Mr. Murphy, after a two-year stint as New York's police commissioner, was nominated to the US District Court for the Southern District of New York by President Harry S. Truman in 1951, and served as a federal trial judge until his death on October 26, 1995.

Maxim Lieber, although not a writer himself, co-edited two books, one in 1925, and the other in 1933. They are both collections of short stories from many countries. Copies are still available at college and university research libraries in some cities. They have no connection to this matter or to any spying activities. I'm listing them here for History buffs and members of the literary world, who might find them of some interest:

1.   Clark, Barrett H. and Lieber, Maxim, *Great Short Stories of the World: A Collection of Complete Short Stories Chosen from the Literature of All Periods and Countries.* The World Publishing Company, Cleveland, Ohio, 1925. (Copyright 1925 by Robert M. McBride and Company).

2.   Lieber, Maxim, and Williams, Blanche Colton, Ph.D., *Great Stories of All Nations.* New York: Tudor Publishing Company, 1933. (Copyright 1927 by Brentano's Inc. Blanche Williams was the head of the English Department at Hunter College, New York, N.Y., at the time.

In 1970, Lieber also co-authored a short, technical manual with Nathaniel Perlmutter, titled, *Dispersal of Plating Wastes and Sewage Contaminants in Ground Water and Surface Water, South Farmingdale – Massapequa Area, Nassau County, New York.*

The character of Monsignor Al Flynn is a purely fictitious creation of mine. Although during this period of time, Monsignor Edward Lynch was the pastor at the Immaculate Conception Church in Towson, MD, and I did, in fact, know this wonderful priest reasonably well, I did not base the character on him.

Anthony Joseph Sacco, Sr.
Towson, Maryland, September 2004
Cheyenne, Wyoming
December 2012

TEXTS OF ARTICLES REGARDING ALGER HISS AND WHITTAKER CHAMBERS:

Here follows the complete texts of articles published in various newspapers regarding the Alger Hiss case from 1992 through 1997. They've been reprinted without comment, beginning with articles that burst upon the national scene in 1992, which appeared to clear Hiss of the charges of spying. But as responsible historians studied the new data, the reader can see the inexorable progression of thought leading to the inescapable conclusion that Hiss was, indeed, guilty as charged, despite his denials, the blind loyalty of family and his hopelessly misguided elderly friends.

TEXTS OF ARTICLES APPEARING DURING 1992:

1. RUSSIAN CLEARS HISS OF SPYING. Claim called "groundless" after review. (*New York Times* News Service *The Baltimore Sun,* Thursday, October 29. New York In the latest chapter of a case that catapulted Richard M. Nixon to national prominence and has divided Americans for more than 40 years, a highranking Russian official says a review of the newly opened archives clears Alger Hiss of accusations that he ever spied for the Soviet Union.

"Not a single document — and a great amount of materials have been studied — substantiates the allegation that Mr. A. Hiss collaborated with the intelligence services of the Soviet Union," declared Gen. Dmitri A. Volkogonov, chairman of the Russian Government's military intelligence archives. He called the espionage accusations against Mr. Hiss "completely groundless."

Scholars of Soviet affairs said they were struck by the categorical, almost passionate nature of the Russian official's statement. As a respected historian and key advisor to President Boris Yeltsin, they said, General Volkogonov's views should be taken seriously. But some warned that given the labyrinthine nature of the Soviet bureaucracy and the sensitivity of military and foreign intelligence operations, Volkogonov might have overstated his findings.

General Volkogonov delivered the statement this month in Moscow to John Lowenthal, a historian and filmmaker who has long studied the Hiss case. In May, Mr. Hiss, (who had been) a high ranking State Department official who was convicted of perjury in 1950, asked General Volkogonov to inspect Soviet files pertaining to him, his case, and his accuser, Whittaker Chambers. It was Mr. Chambers, a member of the Communist Party in the 1930s and later an editor at *Time Magazine*, who charged both that Mr. Hiss born and raised in Baltimore and a graduate of the Johns Hopkins University belonged to the Communist Party in the 1930s and that he had provided Mr. Chambers with classified State Department documents for transmission to the Soviet Union. Mr. Chambers called Mr. Hiss "the closest friend I ever had in the Communist Party." Mr. Hiss has always denied the charges.

"It's what I've been fighting for 44 years," Mr. Hiss, now 87, said this week. "It won't settle things for people I've regarded as prejudiced from the beginning, but I think this is a final verdict. I can't imagine a more authoritative source than the files of the old Soviet Union.

"Rationally, I realized time was running out, and that the correction of Chambers' charges might not come about in my lifetime. But inside, I was sure somehow that I would be vindicated."

Mr. Hiss said his detractors would accept Soviet documents only if they were incriminating. "I assume someone will say the real documents were shredded," he said. "They're so committed to their point of view that it's psychologically impossible for them to be open minded."

As for Mr. Chambers, the Russian official said that files confirmed his membership in the U.S. Communist Party, but not that he had any contact with Soviet Intelligence.

Mr. Chambers died in 1961. In 1984, President Ronald Reagan awarded him the Medal of Freedom.

General Volkogonov issued his opinion Oct. 14. In a separate videotaped statement made the next day, he elaborated on his findings. He said that, as a State Department official in the 1940s, Mr. Hiss had "normal official contacts" with Soviet officials and was "never a spy for the Soviet Union." Instead, he called him a victim of the Cold War. "The fact that he was convicted in the 1950s was the result of either false information or judicial error," he continued. "You can tell Alger Hiss that the heavy weight should be lifted from his heart."

"I don't doubt that he's given an honest report on what he saw, but there are a lot of things he might not have seen," said Richard Pipes, a Soviet scholar at Harvard University. "There are archives within archives within archives. To say there is no evidence in any of the archives is not very responsible on his part."

Alexander Dallin, a professor of history and political science at Stanford, said it was beyond the powers of even the most highly placed Russian official to reach into every nook and cranny of Soviet intelligence. "Disclosures of this sort gradually fill in the picture, but don't remove the question marks." he said.

But Mr. Lowenthal insisted that General Volkogonov's search was comprehensive so much so that he was apparently willing to stake his reputation as a general, historian and politician on it. "This man is a professional historian who has spent decades in the archives," Mr. Lowenthal said. "He would not lightly render an official opinion without being sure of his research. He was not born yesterday."

Alan Weinstein, author of *"Perjury: The HissChambers Case,"* said Volkogonov's statement "reopened the case. It means that every serious scholar has to take a fresh look," said Mr. Weinstein, president of the Center for Democracy in Washington. "But we can't take Volkogonov's word alone. We really have to see all the documents on Soviet espionage."

Mr. Hiss was never charged with espionage. But he was tried and convicted of lying to a grand jury. He spent nearly four years in prison, then emerged to find his legal career and marriage in shambles. For many years he sought vindication through the courts. The Supreme Court refused three times to hear his case.

Whether through headlines, newsreels or early television broadcasts of the hearings of the House UnAmerican Activities Committee, millions of citizens developed indelible images of the principal players in the drama: Mr. Hiss, who once clerked for Justice Oliver Wendell Holmes and accompanied President Franklin D. Roosevelt to Yalta; Mr. Chambers, a contrite former Communist who asserted he was sacrificing himself for the sake of his country, and Richard M. Nixon, a young congressman from California who vigilantly pursued the case when others faltered.

The public also became versed in the accoutrements of the controversy: the typewriter with which Mr. Hiss' wife purportedly retyped the purloined documents; the pumpkin in which Mr. Chambers hid on his Carroll County farm the microfilm he said Mr. Hiss had given him, and even the prothonotary warbler that Mr. Hiss, an amateur ornithologist, spotted in the early 1930s. Mr. Chambers' claim to remember a conversation with Hiss about the bird strengthened his argument that he knew Hiss at the time.

In August, Mr. Hiss wrote to a number of Russian officials including General Volkogonov, seeking his records. He informed them that Mr. Lowenthal would seek appointments with them when he visited Moscow. Working under the auspices of the Nation Institute, Mr. Lowenthal, a former professor at Rutgers Law School and the City University of New York Law School at Queens College, went to Moscow at the end of August, where he encountered researchers investigating a host of other Cold Warera personalities, including Ethel and Julius Rosenberg and Klaus Fuchs. He met for more than 30 minutes with General Volkogonov, who peppered him with questions about the Hiss case.

The Russian official pledged to search for and inspect the Hiss files personally. He said he also asked Yevgeny Primakov, director of the foreign intelligence service, to instruct his staff to find all materials on the case.

On September 25, General Volkogonov notified Mr. Lowenthal in New York that his investigation was complete. In midOctober Mr. Lowenthal returned to Moscow where the Russian official handed him a onepage opinion, typed on Russian federation letterhead.

The polarization Mr. Weinstein said, is unlikely to end. "Given the role of Nixon and the passions the case aroused, which led to an unyielding ichnography of guilt or innocence on both sides, the hardest thing that anyone can do is remain open to new evidence," he said. "There ought to be a statute of limitations on historical anger in this case, whether at Nixon or at Hiss."

2. VINDICATION FROM RUSSIA WELCOME NEWS TO HISS. By: Ian Johnson, New York Bureau. *The Baltimore Sun,* Thursday, October 29, 1992. New York - - Shaking, leaning on a cane but speaking with rocksolid conviction, 87 year old Alger Hiss presented evidence yesterday that he claims exonerates him from charges he was a soviet spy.

Unable to stand to address the throng of reporters who had come back to see him after years of absence, Mr. Hiss spoke in a wavering voice of the 44 years he spent trying to prove his innocence and overturn his 1950 conviction for perjury: "I believed that eventually the matter would be cleared up, but I must admit that in recent years I had a sense of my mortality ... and I have to say that I feared that it would not be in my lifetime."

A Baltimore native and Johns Hopkins University graduate, Mr. Hiss was a key government official in the 1930s and 1940s, holding a top U.S. State Department post during World War II and helping at the founding of the United Nations.

During the Cold War, belief in his innocence or guilt became a litmus test of political views, but he said that people should now objectively study the new material and put the hates of the past behind them. At the news conference, he released a videotaped interview with Gen. Dmitri A. Volkogonov, a respected Soviet historian who said that a thorough search of Soviet intelligence archives showed that Mr. Hiss was no spy.

"I have prepared an opinion on the basis of a careful study of the documents, archive materials, in the light of which I can make a firm conclusion that Alger Hiss was not ever or anywhere recruited as an agent of the intelligence services of the Soviet Union," General Volkogonov, chairman of Russia's military intelligence archives, said in the interview.

Mr. Hiss remained absolutely firm about his innocence despite the consensus that grew over the past decades that he had contacts with the Soviet Union in the 1930s and that he probably had committed perjury in 1948 when he refuted these assertions, which were leveled by Whittaker Chambers, a onetime Communist Party member. The charges and his sensational trial helped catapult former President Richard M. Nixon, then a young congressman, to national prominence.

Mr. Hiss presided calmly over the news conference and beamed as he watched the fiveminute film, in which General Volkogonov said, "You can tell Mr. Alger Hiss that the heavy weight should be lifted from his heart."

Later, when asked if he bore a grudge against Mr. Chambers or Mr. Nixon, Mr. Hiss acknowledged that his case is still so controversial that his innocence may never be accepted: "It may be that some people who have emotionally invested so much in it will have a contrary point of view. I can hardly expect them to change now." Mr. Hiss said that he did not blame Mr. Nixon for attacking him, putting it down to "political opportunism."

He described Mr. Chambers, the former *Time Magazine* editor who named Mr. Hiss a Soviet spy in 1948 before the House UnAmerican Activities Committee, as being psychologically unstable. Like Mr. Chambers, who died of a heart attack in 1961, most of the principals in the drama are dead.

Organized by political allies at The Nation Institute, an arm of the liberal Nation magazine, the news conference had an aura of beatification. Mr. Hiss spoke, friends nodded, and politeness reigned.

Many historians, however, remain skeptical if fascinated by the latest turn of events in the battle over Mr. Hiss' role. "Of course this does reopen the Alger Hiss case, but no one can really say for sure what the verdict will be until Western scholars gain access to the files," said Allen Weinstein, whose 1978 book, *"Perjury,"* basically supported Mr. Chambers.

Mr. Weinstein said that although he greatly respects General Volkogonov as a historian, he cannot believe that he was able to comb the labyrinth of Soviet archives in the two months that he devoted to the project. Mr. Weinstein also questioned the archival staff's openness, saying that he had been denied access to the archives just months before General Volkogonov gained entry. Officials had argued that because some of those involved are still living, they did not want to release the information.

Another problem is the number of archives involved. Soviet military intelligence (GRU), the general intelligence service (KGB), and the Communist Party all had archives. Besides the fact that the Party has no successor organization, putting their files in limbo, the KGB and GRU bureaucracies are extremely competitive, Mr. Weinstein said, and so may well not have cooperated fully with General Volkogonov.

But Leon Botstein, president of Bard College and a friend of Mr. Hiss, said that the agencies in the former Soviet Union have no interest in hushing up the case. If the Russians could admit that the Soviet Union massacred thousands of Polish officers in World War II near the town of Katyn, they can say if they received information from Mr. Hiss.

Unable to charge Mr. Hiss with treason because the alleged acts had taken place too many years earlier, U.S. authorities accused Mr. Hiss of perjury when he maintained to a grand jury that he had had no contacts with Mr. Chambers in the 1930s. The government produced witnesses who said they knew the men and Chambers produced papers, including some in Mr. Hiss' hand writing.

Convicted in 1951, Mr. Hiss served 3 and 1/2 years. He later pressed for his full rehabilitation, becoming a speaker on college campuses and author of books on his experiences. His legal appeals, however, were always turned down, which he attributes to political meddling and "the influence of the Cold War." He said he may now try again to win exoneration.

3.   BALTIMOREANS HELD HOPE THE BRILLIANT YOUTH THEY KNEW WOULD BE CLEARED. By: James Bock and Melody Simmons. *The Baltimore Sun,* Thursday, October 29, 1992. - - Edward M. Passano is an Alpha Delta Phi, as is Alger Hiss, and Mr. Passano gloried in his fraternity brother's good news yesterday.

"I think Alger was railroaded pretty much," said Mr. Passano, 87, a member of the Johns Hopkins University Class of 1927, a year behind Mr. Hiss. "I think the bulk of my friends felt pretty much as I did. I think the majority felt real loyal to him, and I was certainly one."

A Russian General's declaration that Alger Hiss was not a Communist spy is the latest evidence in a case that first polarized Baltimore in 1948. The HissChambers case particularly pained the city because Mr. Hiss was a Baltimore native and a standout alumnus of the Johns Hopkins University.

Mr. Passano, former president of the Waverly Press, is among the few Baltimoreans old enough to remember Mr. Hiss before his career was destroyed by a 1950-perjury conviction following Whittaker Chambers' accusation that Mr. Hiss was a spy. The word that almost all of Mr. Hiss' contemporaries use to describe him is 'brilliant.'

The son of a welltodo dry goods merchant who committed suicide, Alger Hiss grew up on Linden Avenue in Bolton Hill, played in Druid Hill Park, worshiped at Memorial Episcopal Church. attended City College and was a star at Hopkins.

Mr. Hiss made Phi Beta Kappa and was editor of the college newspaper, president of the student council and head of the dramatic society. The late William Marbury, who grew up with Mr. Hiss and later represented him in a libel suit against Mr. Chambers, wrote in the Maryland Historical Magazine that Hopkins undergraduates claimed that the "college administration all treated Alger as if he had a mortgage on Gilman Hall."

"Alger was a brilliant guy," Mr. Passano said. "He was so smart that wherever we went he stood out as the leader. He was smart as ..., a very personable guy who could have had almost any woman in Baltimore."

After Harvard Law School, Mr. Hiss plunged into the brilliant career that everyone expected of him key positions at the State Department and, in 1946, presidency of the Carnegie Endowment for International Peace in Washington.

The accusations Mr. Chambers made against him in 1948 that Mr. Hiss was an underground Communist who passed Mr. Chambers documents in the late 1930s for delivery to the Soviet Union shocked Baltimore.

"Baltimore was aghast," said James H. Bready, a former editorial writer for The Evening Sun. "Here was Hiss, he … was a big man on campus at Johns Hopkins, a member of the right fraternity at Hopkins and had social standing. Nobody could understand why he would do anything against the system because he was part of it. . "

Mr. Hiss proclaimed his innocence from the outset, but he was convicted of perjury in 1950 after two trials that cost $75,000 in legal fees. He served more than 31/2 years at the Lewisburg (Pa.) penitentiary. "It is safe to say that most Baltimoreans hoped to the very end that Alger Hiss would somehow prove his innocence," The Sun editorialized on Jan. 22, 1950. "Hiss … is a Baltimorean of such attainments and of such high promise that, however indirectly, the selfesteem of the community is somehow affected by his downfall."

Tony Hiss, Mr. Hiss' son and a writer for the *New Yorker* who profiled Baltimore last year for the magazine, said catharsis has come 42 years later with the Russian general's declaration.

"Certainly in the dramatic fashion it happened, it had that kind of cathartic feeling," Mr. Hiss said. "To me what's important is that a lot more people can look at him the way I do as a person with extraordinary qualities who had to go through something not of his making."

Yet the debate over the HissChambers case may never end. "I question whether too many minds are going to be changed," said Luke Marbury, a son of William Marbury. "Alger himself said a lot of people aren't going to believe anything told to them by the Russians. It's very difficult to prove a negative."

State Sen. George W. Della Jr., whose family owns the Carroll County farm where Mr. Chambers said he hid film that Mr. Hiss allegedly passed to him, said curiosity seekers continue to visit the "pumpkin patch."

"They just want to see what the place looks like. They're just fascinated by the whole series of events," Mr. Della said. "They always ask, 'Do you still grow pumpkins?'"

4. RUSSIAN ISN'T SURE OF HISS' INNOCENCE. *New York Times* News Service, December 17, 1992. Moscow - The Russian official who was reported to have cleared Hiss of spying for the Soviet Union says that he was "not properly understood," and that he meant to say only that he had found no evidence of the charges in the KGB documents to which he had access.

The official, Gen. Dmitry A. Volkogonov, a historian, said that at Mr. Hiss' request he had searched through KGB files for the 1930s and 1940s and found only one mention of Mr. Hiss, in a list of diplomats at the United Nations.

On October 14, answering a query from Mr. Hiss, General Volkogonov wrote: "Not a single document, and a great amount of materials have been studied, substantiates the allegation that Hiss was a spy."

General Volkogonov's acknowledgement that he was in no position to clear Hiss and that perhaps no one ever can, confirmed the caution of many U. S. historians who had warned that a vindication was dubious given the volume, complexity and incompleteness of archives.

John Lowenthal, a historian who was an intermediary, indicated surprise at the General's remarks. He produced a fax from General Volkogonov, dated September 25, saying that he had studied information from the intelligence services, and that "on the basis of a most careful analysis of the data, I can report to you that Alger Hiss was never an agent of the intelligence services of the Soviet Union."

Mr. Lowenthal said the general repeated this during a visit to Washington last month.

5.   RUSSIAN OFFICIAL BACKS AWAY FROM STATEMENT CLEARING HISS. *New York Times* News Service, *The Baltimore Sun*, December 17, 1992 - - The Russian official who was reported to have cleared Alger Hiss of spying for the Soviet Union has backed off the statement, saying that he was "not properly understood."

The official, Gen. Dmitry A. Volkogonov, a military historian who has been closely involved in studying various Sovietera archives, said that at Mr. Hiss' request he had searched through KGB files for the 1930s and 1940s and in them he found only one mention of Mr. Hiss, in a list of diplomats at the United Nations.

"I was not properly understood," he said in a recent interview. "The Ministry of Defense also has an intelligence office, which is different, and many documents have been destroyed. I only looked through what the KGB had. All I said was that I saw no evidence."

Responding to General Volkogonov's latest remarks, Mr. Hiss said yesterday, "If he and his associates haven't examined all the files, I hope they will examine the others, and they will show the same thing."

On Oct. 14, answering a query from Mr. Hiss, General Volkogonov wrote: "Mr. A. Hiss had never and nowhere been recruited as an agent of the intelligence services of the U.S.S.R. Not a single document, and a great amount of materials have been studied, substantiates the allegation." That letter was taken by Mr. Hiss and his supporters as an exoneration.

In a celebrated case, a former communist named Whittaker Chambers asserted that Mr. Hiss had spied for the Soviet Union as a State Department official in the 1930s. Mr. Hiss was eventually convicted of perjury.

Now 88, Mr. Hiss has insisted ever since his conviction in 1950 that he had never spied for the Soviet Union and that he was the victim of an anticommunist witch hunt.

`General Volkogonov acknowledged that he was in no position to fully clear Mr. Hiss and that perhaps no one ever can. "Hiss wrote that he was 88 and would like to die peacefully, that he wanted to prove that he was never a paid, contracted spy," General Volkogonov said. "What I saw gives no basis to claim a full clarification. There's no guarantee that it was not destroyed, that it was not in other channels.

"This was only my personal opinion as a historian," he said. "I never met him, and honestly I was a bit taken aback. His attorney, Lowenthal, pushed me hard to say things of which I was not fully convinced."

General Volkogonov evidently meant John Lowenthal, a historian and filmmaker who has long studied the Hiss case. It was Mr. Lowenthal who traveled to Moscow to meet with General Volkogonov and receive the letter.

"But I did spend two days swallowing dust," General Volkogonov said, referring to the old KGB archives.

Mr. Lowenthal, who met with General Volkogonov several times on Mr. Hiss' behalf, indicated surprise at the General's remarks. He produced a fax from General Volkogonov, dated Sept. 25, saying that he had information from the intelligence services, and that "on the basis of a most careful analysis of the data, I can report to you that Alger Hiss was never an agent of the intelligence services of the Soviet Union."

Mr. Lowenthal said that during the general's visit in Washington last month, he told Mr. Lowenthal that he had also examined archives of the Military Intelligence and "there, too, no traces of Alger Hiss have been found."

The general said he had also looked through the presidential archives, and while that work was not complete, "I have found no mention of Alger Hiss."

TEXTS OF ARTICLES APPEARING DURING 1993:

1. HISS CASE "SMOKING GUN"? By: Sam Tanenhaus. *The New York Times*, Friday, October 15, 1993. Tarrytown, N.Y. - - The Alger Hiss case, born in the first years of the cold war, has outlived it and now occupies the lofty zone where history merges into myth.

   Just last year, a Russian general, Dmitri A. Volkogonov, said he had examined a mountain of K.G.B. files and declared Mr. Hiss innocent of spying charges first raised by his accuser, Whittaker Chambers, in 1948. Under pressure from Sovietologists and experts on the Hiss case, the general then beat a hasty retreat, admitting he had consulted only selected archives and that key files had probably been destroyed during the Stalinist era.

   Meanwhile, scholars have been chipping away at the immense block of archives slowly coming to light in Russia and Eastern Europe.

   One such scholar is Maria Schmidt, a Hungarian historian at work on a study of her nation's secret police. In restricted files in Budapest's Interior Ministry, she happened upon documents so fascinating that for two years she has been examining and interpreting them. The result of her research, made available this week to a handful of scholars in New York, indicates a major breakthrough in the case.

The centerpiece of Mrs. Schmidt's discovery is a thick dossier of statements made to Hungarian interrogators by the American diplomat Noel Field, a self-confessed spy who with his wife slipped behind the Iron Curtain in 1949, seeking asylum, only to find himself embroiled in the purges convulsing the Stalinist regimes of Eastern Europe.

Field, released from a Budapest jail in 1954, applied for Hungarian citizenship and lived there until his death at the age of 60 in 1970. Before leaving prison, he sat for interviews in which he furnished authorities with a detailed resume of his career as a Soviet agent.

In the interrogations, and in the written testimony made during the same period, Noel Field categorically states that one of his most trusted accomplices in the Soviet underground was his close friend Alger Hiss. The two had met in the mid1930s when both were idealistic young public servants drawn into the Communist underworld, the political nighttown of New Deal Washington.

Noel Field's remarks about his dealings with Mr. Hiss emerge as the first documented testimony by someone still loyal to Mr. Hiss and the Communist cause.

Mr. Field recalls that while he was living Geneva in 1948, when the House UnAmerican Activities Committee began its investigations of Mr. Hiss, he "became hysterical" at the prospect that he would be summoned and that his testimony "might harm others, primarily my friend Alger Hiss." Mr. Field was sure "I would be convicted of espionage."

Unlike Mr. Hiss, Mr. Field was nervous, high strung and irrepressible. His indiscretions had already gotten him in trouble. He knew he would crumble under the questioning of Representative Richard Nixon and his colleagues: "Alger defended himself ... with great intelligence. He had been trained as a lawyer and knew all the phrases and tricks. I, on the other hand, had no such experience ... I did not trust myself to stand before my accusers and shout 'innocent' in their faces ... I also understood the same from a short letter from Hiss, who obviously could not write openly."

And so Noel Field fled to Prague and the presumed safety of a Communist regime. This was not Mr. Field's first close encounter with the committee. In 1939, Gen. Walter Kravitski, a defector from the highest echelon of Soviet intelligence, testified before the committee after having written articles for the *Saturday Evening Post* that named Noel Field, among others, as disloyal.

Since Mr. Field happened then to be traveling in the United States, "I made a detour of a few days to meet Hiss," who promised to 'send me a warning' in the event General Kravitski further damaged Mr. Field.

The warning never came. In 1941, General Kravitski was found dead in a Washington, D.C. hotel with a bullet in his temple. The coroner ruled it a suicide, but those close to the victim saw the hand of K.G.B. assassins.

Mrs. Schmidt's findings also corroborate a key point of testimony in Mr. Hiss's trial made by a witness for the prosecution, Hede Massing, a former Soviet agent. She identified herself as being, with her husband, Paul, Noel Field's superior in the Washington spy ring. Under oath, Mrs. Massing said she and Mr. Hiss had once bantered after she learned from her contact, Mr. Field, that Mr. Hiss had tried to recruit him into his own "apparatus." In his statement to Hungarian authorities, Mr. Field corroborates this story and ruefully blames himself for a typical indiscretion. When Alger Hiss "wanted to recruit me," he recalls, "I carelessly told him I was already working for Soviet intelligence."

This admission may be the most important of all because it contradicts the contents of a letter Mr. Field sent Mr. Hiss in 1957 in which he offered to make a public repudiation of Mrs. Massing's testimony. This letter, well known to students of the Hiss case, is often cited by defenders of Mr. Hiss as proof that Mrs. Massing lied.

Mrs. Schmidt's research discredits this argument. She has found several drafts of the letter, some of them as early as 1955, each doctored by Field's superiors in Budapest. This means that what has been long presented as an innocent offer of help was in fact a tool in the disinformation campaign created by the Communist Party as a means of aiding Hiss's defense.

Faced with such sensational findings, we must ask: how reliable are they? After all, in his five years behind bars Noel Field was brutalized by his captors and kept in solitary confinement. But there is no reason to believe Mr. Field's statements in 1954 were made under duress. On the contrary, at that time he was being "rehabilitated" and soon was treated as a distinguished personage, given a villa, a soft job and a salary greater than that of the Prime Minister of Hungary.

It's possible that these interrogators conspired with Mr. Field to fabricate allegations against Alger Hiss. Why? Hungarian Communists had nothing to gain from such testimony, least of all at a time when the party's propaganda machine was trumpeting Hiss's innocence. Anyone familiar with Noel Field's sad story, marked by chronic naïveté and puppyish enthusiasm, will recognize his authentic voice in the testimony introduced by Mrs. Schmidt.

There is Mr. Field's bemusement at learning he had been released by his captors from prison on the same day that Mr. Hiss was let go from his prison cell in Pennsylvania.

There is his frank admiration of the superb skills Mr. Hiss showed in manipulating the House UnAmerican Activities Committee.

And there is the added voice of Herta Field, who had assisted her husband in espionage, had been jailed in Budapest, and was herself interrogated by the Hungarian police. Recalling her surprise at the volume of State Department documents Mr. Hiss had transmitted to his contact, Mr. Chambers, Mrs. Field said she had turned to her husband and asked "You didn't give that much to Paul (Massing), did you?" Mrs. Field remembered: "Noel's reply was 'I gave a lot to him.'"

In sum, this is testimony whose truth both documentary and human seems unimpeachable.

Until such time as Alger Hiss comes forward with a confession of his secret career or Russian officials see fit to release their files on him, Mrs. Schmidt's findings will remain in the annals as the "smoking gun" in the most hotly debated spy story in American history.

2.   THE UNENDING TRIAL OF ALGER HISS. By: Jeffrey A. Frank, Staff Writer. *The Washington Post*, October 29, 1993 - - Whether or not Alger Hiss was guilty of spying for the Russians was one of the longest running arguments of the Cold War era and perhaps the only one still on the table. For those who've come late, it is difficult to explain the passionate intensity that surrounds the episode. But the Hiss case has divided and mystified Americans for nearly 50 years, enlisting new generations in a debate that has become almost purely historical.

In recent years, it has also become something of a Halloween play, a cloak-and-dagger story rising from its Cold War grave. Just a year ago, Gen. Dmitri Volkogonov, the Russian historian and archivist, asserted that Soviet intelligence archives revealed no proof that Hiss had ever spied for the Soviet Union. Volkogonov later conceded that his conclusion was based on incomplete evidence, but the caldron was stirred again and Hiss and his supporters declared that he'd been exonerated.

The latest round began earlier this month, in a paper delivered at New York University by the Hungarian historian Maria Schmidt. Schmidt reported that an American defector, Noel Haviland Field, had incriminated Hiss in various statements made to Hungarian secret police. Field had gone to Eastern Europe in 1949, only to find himself suspected of being a double agent and jailed. After his release, Budapest officials questioned him; in one interrogation transcript found in newly public files, Field reportedly said that he'd realized in 1935 that Hiss was a spy:

"Hiss … wanted to recruit me for espionage for the Soviet Union. I did not find the right answer and carelessly told him that I was already working for the Soviet intelligence … I knew, from what Hiss told me, that he was working for the Soviet secret service."

The testimony is persuasive to many because the Fields and Hisses were social friends in the 1930s and Field had no obvious motive for making up such things. Hiss himself says that he and Field were drawn together by common world policy concerns and attended meetings of the Foreign Policy Association. "Both he and I were naturally aware of the Nazi threat," Hiss, who is 88, said in a telephone interview from his New York home. But Hiss says he rejects what Field said: "He was still under duress, he was not a free man. If he didn't please his captors well, there's a quotation from Noel Field's adopted daughter, who says, 'After torture you'll say anything.'"

Others, however, point out that there is not much new in the Field statements that a lot of it had come to light in Flora Lewis's 1965 book about

Field, *"Red Pawn,"* as well as in Allen Weinstein's *"Perjury: The Hiss Chambers Case,"* published in 1978. What is new is the sudden availability of detail from the Hungarian records which has prompted historians such as Weinstein to call for their quick release.

But whether the material is revelatory or familiar depends very much on one's original stance. Thus, one researcher believes that what Field said is a "smoking gun" while lawyer Ethan Kingsberg, writing in the current *Nation Magazine* suggests that it was coerced testimony and warns about the "file fever" stemming from release of more and more Communist era archives. In other words, as is so often the case in the Hiss affair, one tends to believe what one wants.

Standing By His Story

For connoisseurs of American political drama, the Hiss case was always boffo. For starters, its casting was impeccable; Hiss, the New Dealer friend of John Foster Dulles, State Department official and president of the Carnegie Endowment for International Peace, was accused of being a spy. Not only that, he was accused by Whittaker Chambers, who was in many ways the mirror image of Hiss; a lapsed Communist, a confessed liar, a man with bad teeth and a disreputable appearance. He was also a Time senior editor and the translator of *"Bambi."*

But if Chambers was an unappealing witness in contrast to the dapper Hiss, his testimony was supported by a great deal of tangible and circumstantial evidence: documents he'd kept in a pumpkin patch (the pumpkin papers) that he said he'd received from Hiss for transmission to the Soviets; documents that appeared to be typed on Hiss's typewriter; the gift to Chambers of a Ford "with a sassy little trunk" from Hiss, a man who'd sworn that he barely knew Chambers.

Chambers's testimony was given to the House Committee on UnAmerican Activities whose members included Rep. Richard M. Nixon and whose career was launched by the case. For researchers, the Hiss matter became an obsession rivaling the SaccoVanzetti affair or, for a later generation, The Kennedy assassination. Eventually, Chambers's accusation led to two trials, one of which resulted in 1950 in Hiss's conviction for perjury lying about receiving secret documents from Chambers. His served four years in prison.

Among the witnesses at Hiss's trial was Hede Massing, who had once been married to a Soviet operative in the United States. Massing said that she'd met Hiss through the Fields. Allen Weinstein reported that Massing told the FBI that she'd bantered with Hiss about trying to lure Noel Field into spying. In one of the Hungarian transcripts, Field recalls that Massing was angry at him for loose lips. "I received a stern rebuke from her," he recalls, according to Maria Schmidt.

For his part, Hiss for 40 years has publicly and consistently proclaimed his innocence. He conceded that he had known Chambers under the name "George Crosley," but he denied all wrongdoing: He had never been a Communist, never committed espionage, hadn't a clue as to why Chambers was saying these things. He said he had been framed by McCarthyite ? or J. Edgar Hooverite ? forces and insisted that his political enemies concocted the evidence against him. Even the typewriter, he said, was forged.

Hiss still stands by this account and says: "It all goes back to the story that Hede Massing told at my trial, and that she told to a lot of people before. I don't think anybody who knows anything about Hede Massing would lend credibility to her story."

He argues that Field was simply trying to impress his Hungarian captors with names of American contacts.

Flora Lewis, the columnist and Field biographer, disagrees. "The first account of the connection with Hiss came from Hede Massing, and I had every reason to believe her. It fit with everything else."

Writing in *The New York Times*, Chambers's biographer, Sam Tanenhaus, also argues that what Schmidt found in Hungary corroborates the Massing testimony. It might, he said, be the "most important of all because it contradicts the contents of a letter Mr. Field sent to Mr. Hiss in 1957 in which he offered to make a public repudiation of Mrs. Massing's testimony." Schmidt, he writes, "found several drafts of the letter, some of them dating as early as 1955, each doctored by Mr. Field's superiors in Budapest."

Lewis says that Hiss once showed her letters from Field and, like Tanenhaus, she has her doubts. Were they written in sincerity to assert Hiss's innocence? "I don't believe that for a minute."

Field was released from a Hungarian prison in 1954. Lewis, who tried without success to interview him in Budapest, recalls going to his residence and finding that "it was quite a good house, with a gate and he sent his maid out but refused to see me. We exchanged notes."

Field died in 1970 at age 60, and in a brief autobiographical fragment (quoted by Weinstein), recalled his leftward drift in the New Deal era: "I watched and sometimes took part in radical meetings and demonstrations, sought contact with leftwingers of different shade [while working for the State Department] ... A duel life, reflecting a duel personality struggling to overcome the conflict between old and new loyalties."

The Battle Goes On

In the case of Alger Hiss, no one ever changes sides. For decades, the rightward *New Republic* has called Hiss guilty, while the leftist *Nation* has argued his innocence. When Weinstein's *"Perjury"* was published, it was assailed *by Nation's* Editor Victor Navasky. When Volkogonov's testimony was first published, it was assailed by Chambers biographer Tanenhaus, who this month applauded the Maria Schmidt findings.

Hiss's son, Tony, a writer for the *New Yorker*, wrote a loving piece about his father last year when the Volkogonov statement was issued. This week he said, "I've never met anyone who has a harder time trying to hide anything than Alger Hiss. He is proud of the fact that he was a loyal New Dealer and a believer in the founding principles of the U.N.... . I once met Lawrence Olivier, who I thought was the greatest actor in the world. Alger would have to be 100 times better."

Alger Hiss is also loyally supported by John Lowenthal, a former law professor who campaigned to have Volkogonov issue his declaration last year. Lowenthal, too, found nothing new in the Noel Field statements reported by Schmidt. The testimony, he said, "did not contain any fact or explicit statement which would indicate that Alger Hiss was delivering U.S. documents to the Soviet Union … "

Allen Weinstein, who now runs the Center for Democracy, sounds as if he has heard it all, as perhaps he has. "They stumbled right into a controversy that is only of historical interest, I am happy to say at this point."

A smoking gun? "I think it's a piece of evidence that has to be corroborated by seeing the actual documents. It's another bit of cumulative evidence to add to what we already know."

Tony Hiss says: "What astonishes me, it's like a curse in a fairy tale. It just won't go away."

3. NEW EVIDENCE OR NEW DISINFORMATION IN HISS CASE. By: Antero Pietila. *The Baltimore Sun,* November 14, 1993 - - Forty-five years have elapsed since Whittaker Chambers accused Alger Hiss of having been a Communist and a spy for the Soviet Union.

Hiss, a former State Department official, denied the charges and was eventually convicted of lying in making that denial. As the U.S. wartime alliance with the Soviet Union was turning into anti-Communist hostility, the case became a harbinger of a change in the nation's political mood from New Deal idealism to Cold War ideological combat.

The publicity that the Hiss case garnered brought a little-known congressman from California, Richard M. Nixon, to national consciousness. It also persuaded a Wisconsin senator, Joseph McCarthy, that a coordinated Communist hunt promised a path to political prominence.

McCarthy and Chambers have long been dead; the Soviet Union expired two years ago. But Alger Hiss lives on, and the controversy about his guilt or innocence goes on.

The latest rounds in this dispute started a year ago, when Gen. Dmitri Volkogonov, Moscow's leading military historian, was quoted as asserting that Soviet archives revealed no proof that Hiss had been a spy while serving in Washington as an ascending aide in Franklin Delano Roosevelt's administration.

Hiss hailed the remark as complete vindication and "the end of an ordeal." Those believing in his guilt belittled the general's conclusion, which the Russian himself later said was based on incomplete evidence.

Round two came in April with the publication in *Commentary* of an article, *"Hiss: Guilty as charged."* The material, recently recycled in *The New York Times* (Oct. 15) and *New Republic* (Nov. 8), reported that Maria Schmidt, a Hungarian historian, had proved that Hiss was a member of a Soviet Spy cell.

The supposed "smoking gun" was a yellowing confession an American had made to the Communist secret police after being imprisoned on spy charges in Budapest. Depending on whom one believes, Noel Field, who later asked political asylum in Communist Hungary and died there, was either a Soviet or CIA spy, or both.

The *Nation*, which has consistently proclaimed Hiss' innocence, quickly produced its own review of the evidence. Its conclusion was that Field was trying to save his skin and telling his captors whatever he believed they wanted to hear.

"Statements made in such a setting are neither 'unimpeachable' nor even 'testimony,' as those terms are used in our legal tradition," the *Nation's* investigator, Ethan Klingsberg, wrote in the Nov. 8 issue.

Over the years, the Hiss case has assumed a watershed quality that was not readily apparent in 1948 when Whittaker Chambers made his initial charges in an open session of the House UnAmerican Activities Committee.

Up to that point, HUAC had been a stridently Republican panel bent on discrediting Roosevelt's New Deal. Hiss' friends and counsel urged him to disregard charges from Chambers, a *Time* editor who was a repentant Communist and selfacknowledged perjurer.

Hiss, who had recently received an honorary doctorate from the Johns Hopkins University and moved from the government to head the Carnegie Endowment for International Peace, rejected that advice. He testified before HUAC and sued Chambers for libel. This turned out to be a major legal blunder because inconsistencies in his testimonies could then be submitted to a grand jury.

For a while, the grand jury seemed to go nowhere. But just days before its term was to end, Representative Nixon produced microfilms and documents incriminating Hiss that had been found hidden inside a pumpkin on Whitaker (sic) Chambers' farm near Westminster in Carroll County.

What had started as something of a crank accusation suddenly was daily frontpage news. Hiss was soon convicted of lying. Chambers became a professional antiCommunist crusader. By then, the Cold War was raging overseas, and a McCarthyite witch-hunt was starting at home.

To a British journalist, Alistair Cooke, the change of political climate from reason to hysteria was so stark that he came to call the spectacle "a generation on trial."

Until his conviction, Hiss had seemingly lived a charmed life: a year as a secretary to Justice Oliver Wendell Holmes, acquaintance with Justice Felix Frankfurter and other leading legal lights. He had worked on sensitive New Deal assignments, culminating with important roles at Dumbarton Oaks and Yalta, two conferences that shaped the postwar world. When the United Nations was established in 1945, Hiss was the secretary general of the founding conference. There was talk he might be the secretary of state one day.

By contrast, Whittaker Chambers, while unquestionably talented, had been a loser for much of his life. He had done some translations but seemingly had difficulty keeping jobs. The dozen aliases he had used suggested a man who was adrift. He and Hiss seemed to have little in common, and that was Hiss' contention. Chambers claimed the two had been very close.

There was wild speculation. Unwilling to accept Alger Hiss' guilt which he has always denied his supporters came up with all kinds of explanations for his downfall.

In his 1977 book, "Laughing Last," Tony Hiss wrote about his father and family: "I have heard as 'true stories' about Al that President Roosevelt wanted to help the Russians and secretly ordered dad to spy for them; that mom was a Russian spy and dad was covering up for her (this was Mrs. Roosevelt's own explanation); that Whittaker Chambers ... was under Kremlin orders to frame dad and thereby discredit President Truman; that dad and Chambers were lovers (this is Dick Nixon's explanation); that Chambers and mom were lovers; that Chambers and my brother Tim were lovers; that dad allowed himself to be jailed so that no one would ever know that mom had an abortion back in the 1920s or that Tim had been kicked out of the Navy for a gay episode as a teen-ager in the 1940s."

If any of this is true, we still don't know.

The American right believes Alger Hiss got what he deserved: three years and eight months at Lewisburg, Pa., as inmate No. 19137. An article of faith among leftists is that the whole case was the first in a series of frame-ups and that the FBI forged a key piece of evidence, Woodstock typewriter N230099.

Richard Nixon's subsequent 'dirty tricks' make this self-evident to them. "Watergate devastatingly ended Nixon's career. A fuller investigation of all the Russian files could expose the fraud that launched that career," The Nation's Victor Navasky wrote earlier this year.

Alger Hiss was born and raised in Baltimore, Whitaker Chambers resided here. After the accusations were first aired, the whole city became divided. Old friendships were broken in arguments.

Alger Hiss now lives in Manhattan and celebrated his birthday Thursday. He is 89. He is hard of hearing, but his mind works.

The famous Whittaker Chambers farm is still in Westminster. His son lives nearby. The original house burned years ago but pumpkins still occasionally are grown on the land. No new films have been discovered but the 10yearold son of Baltimore State Sen. George W. Della, Jr. whose deceased mother owned the farm loves to go through the fields with his metal detector.

"I used to be captivated by this case as a time capsule of Cold War Americana and thought I could solve its many puzzling questions. Long ago, I gave up. With so much suspicion of skullduggery and evidence produced by recanting informers, there were simply too many unprovables.

Whenever I see an old Woodstock typewriter, I still check the serial number, though, just in case."

4. NEW REASON TO DOUBT HISS. By: Sam Tanenhaus. *The Wall Street Journal*, November 18, 1993 - - Now that the Cold War is over, there is hope that one of its most enduring controversies, the Alger Hiss case, can finally be settled. Yet until Russian officials unlock their vast intelligence archives, we will lack a fully documented record of the services Mr. Hiss and other Americans performed for Moscow as members of the Soviet espionage underground. And without such a record, Mr. Hiss and his partisans will persist in their claim that he was unjustly convicted of perjury in the 1950s, a victim of anticommunist hysteria.

In the meantime, however, the truth is emerging from other sources. Just last month, the contents of a thick dossier in Budapest were made public, and we learned from them that Noel Field, an American diplomat and Soviet spy who defected behind the Iron Curtain in 1949, had given Hungarian Communists a vivid account of his illicit dealings with Mr. Hiss in the 1930s.

And now, thanks to recently declassified U.S. State Department files, a new witness has surfaced. He is Samuel Klaus, a State Department official who died in 1963 and whose confidential papers, kept secret for many years, illuminated a vital phase of Mr. Hiss's activities in the 1940s.

The contents of the Klaus files, revealed here for the first time, establish that as early as 1946 two years before Whittaker Chambers's celebrated testimony before the House Committee on UnAmerican Activities Mr. Hiss was directly confronted about specific security violations he was committing as a senior officer in the State Department, and about a pattern of misconduct that permeated the departments he supervised. The documents also tell an intriguing story all their own.

A Leaked Report

It is set in the first, tense months of the Cold War. And it begins with a mysterious leak. On Sept. 12, 1946, Drew Pearson, the *Washington Post* columnist known for his fertile inside contacts, published an item, only a few lines long, that had international repercussions.

The topic was Greece, which faced a possible communist takeover. This fate had been forestalled by the presence of British troops. But now, Mr. Pearson wrote, the situation might suddenly change. American military intelligence was convinced that British forces should be evacuated lest the beleaguered nation erupt in civil war. A Greek newspaper, citing Mr. Pearson, repeated the rumor and warned of a widening rift between Britain and the U.S.

The *Post* article "deeply disturbed" State Department officials, according to a memorandum in the newly declassified files. For one thing, Mr. Pearson had echoed a remark contained in a secret report, "British Garrison in Greece," which had circulated two weeks before in the Office of Special

Political Affairs, the department's liaison to the United Nations. Obviously the report had been leaked to the columnist by someone at OSPA.

Worse, Mr. Pearson had bungled the facts. The views he attributed to the American high command were a "direct inversion" of current intelligence opinion; whoever had passed along the confidential remarks had also "twisted" their meaning evidently for the purpose of disrupting an already frayed Anglo-American alliance. This was a serious breach of security: investigation was called for.

Enter Sam Klaus, special assistant to the State Department's legal adviser. Mr. Klaus traced the leak to an assistant at OSPA who had since destroyed or "otherwise disposed" of the original document, a criminal violation that for some reason had been sanctioned by two of the assistant's immediate superiors and perhaps by the office's director, Alger Hiss.

On October 4, Mr. Klaus confronted Mr. Hiss. The transcript of their exchange is included among the newly declassified papers. Mr. Hiss, while annoyed that some in his department were "trying to say that I am responsible" for the incident, was strangely unruffled by the violation itself. More than three weeks had passed since the document was leaked and the original destroyed, more than a week since he had been instructed to help in the investigation, yet he had not even examined the papers in question.

Mr. Hiss now assured Mr. Klaus he would like to see them. This should be easy enough to do, Mr. Klaus tartly replied, since "so many" copies of the report were floating around the office. Here he was referring to another disturbing development. An initial request to the document room for 25 copies of the secret report, when it first reached OSPA on Sept. 3 had magically resulted in 60 copies, and 13 had disappeared. At least one had been taken out of the office.

All this flagrantly violated security procedures but amounted to business as usual in Mr. Hiss's office. A second investigator, whose memorandum is in the Klaus files, discovered that "over ordering is a common practice in OSPA with respect to reproduction of classified documents." And given OSPA's close connection with the U.N. and its foreign delegations, "the security dangers are obvious."

The report on Greece was low grade compared with other papers flooding into OSPA. Some were among the most sensitive being created by the government's foreign policy experts and dealt with matters far outside the normal scope of the OSPA director. Indeed, they were not designated for Alger Hiss's examination.

Mr. Klaus turned up secret reports on the postwar trusteeship of Japan prepared exclusively for an elite Subcommittee of the State, War and Navy Coordinating Committee (SWNCC), which included no members of OSPA. He also found top secret documents outlining U.S. policy in China, "especially with regard to military aid to the Central government."

And OSPA received a steady flow of material, classified "top secret," on the gravest issue of national security in the postwar era, the atomic bomb. A document on the subject marked "Special Limited Distribution" had landed on Mr. Hiss's desk but bore no routing instructions indicating it belonged there. He had also seen a report, classified as top secret, on the "Disposition of Uranium." As far as Mr. Klaus could determine, it was Alger Hiss himself who "made the original arrangement" for OSPA to get copies of these papers.

Within OSPA, documents were handled in a curious manner. The secret report on Greece, supposed to be locked in a file cabinet, had sat for "a number of days" on an open bookcase. A top-secret memorandum on the China report, required to be placed in a safe, wound up "in a file otherwise containing no other material of a classification higher than 'secret.'" Mr. Hiss also neglected to classify memos he himself wrote on confidential subjects.

At the Office of Political Affairs, transformed by Mr. Hiss into a clearinghouse of toplevel intelligence materials, "security laxness" was so pronounced, Mr. Klaus concluded, as to make the department vulnerable to "penetration in the interests of other governments."

The Klaus files raise tantalizing questions. Why did contacts at SWNCC, and other offices forward topsecret papers to Alger Hiss and his staff at OSPA? What of the staff members themselves, who had proved so helpful to Mr. Hiss? Were they witting accomplices or were they misled by their director? And what became of the extra copies of documents copied in bulk?

"Mess Up Policy"

As yet we don't know. We do know that in 1946 Whittaker Chambers, when interviewed by a State Department investigator, said Alger Hiss's primary role in the Soviet underground was to "mess up policy" as the leak to Drew Pearson threatened to do. And we know too that on Sept. 14, 1946, two days after Mr. Pearson's item ran, Mr. Hiss had an appointment with an official in the British Embassy who had an abiding interest in Greece and in "messing up" Anglo-American relations. He was Donald Maclean, later identified as one of the "Cambridge Spies" who defected to Moscow in 1951.

Finally, we know that on Dec. 10, soon after Sam Klaus's inquiry ended, Alger Hiss resigned from the State Department and left the government.

The files of Sam Klaus and their record of widespread and concerted misconduct are not closely guarded in Budapest or buried in the archival tombs of Moscow. They are open to any and all who wish to study them, including Mr. Hiss's defenders. How will they explain this troubling chapter in the career of a public servant they still portray as a victim of a Cold War "witch-hunt"?

TEXTS OF ARTICLES APPEARING DURING 1994:

1.   JUST TOO FINE FOR THIS LOUSY COUNTRY. By: George F. Will, *The Baltimore Sun,* April 1995. Washington - - One of the long running lies of modern American history, that of the innocence of Alger Hiss, would long ago have suffered the death of a thousand cuts if mere evidence could kill a fiction so useful to the consoling myth of the American left.

That myth is today constantly nurtured and embroidered by historians on America's campuses, where the left has gone to earth. The myth is that the left's political futility testifies to the fact that it was just too idealistic for a nation as vicious, reactionary and paranoid as America.

However, the left's sentimentality about itself and nastiness about this nation suffered another wound last week, when the Yale University Press published *"The Secret World of American Communism,"* a selection of documents from the archives of the former Soviet Union pertaining to the Communist Party of the United States. Annotated by Harvey Klehr of Emory University, John Earl Haynes of the Library of Congress and Fridrikh Igorevich Firsov, a Russian archivist, the documents demolish the romantic notion that the party was just a manifestation of political idealism, perhaps naively and imprudently extreme, but still an institution of populist protest:

> "The documents in this book demonstrate with unmistakable clarity that the common perception That 'American communism was a Soviet weapon in the Cold War' was indeed well founded, and they reveal the process through which CPUSA became an instrument of Soviet espionage...{The CPUSA was} a conspiracy financed by a hostile foreign power that recruited members for clandestine work, developed an elaborate under-ground apparatus, and used that apparatus to collaborate with espionage services of that power."

Highly pertinent to the Hiss case is the fact that some of the documents confirm the story of clandestine activities in Washington in the 1930s as told by Whittaker Chambers, the former Soviet agent who became Hiss' accuser.

The documents, say the authors of this book, demonstrate something that Hiss's defenders scoffed at, the fact that "a thriving underground was in place in the 1930s." For example, documents 32 and 33, found in CPUSA files that had been sent to Moscow for safekeeping, demonstrate the theft of confidential information from the State Department, including a letter to President Roosevelt from the Ambassador to Germany.

Chambers supported his accusations against Hiss by producing similar documents ? memoranda that had crossed Hiss's State Department desk, documents in Hiss's handwriting and copies of confidential documents that had been typed on Hiss's typewriter. And documents in the new book further support Chambers's credibility as a witness by showing that Soviet intelligence agencies were interested in some of the people that Chambers later named as participants in clandestine Communist activities.

The evidence against Hiss was sufficient to convict him of perjury, and since then additional evidence (see Allen Weinstein's definitive history of the case) has forced his embattled defenders to adopt what is now known as an "Oliver Stone defense."

The premise of Stone's movie "JFK" was that a vast conspiracy produced the Kennedy assassination, and proof of the vastness is that the conspirators left not a shred of evidence of their conspiracy. Hiss's defenders say many individuals and government agencies conspired to frame him, even producing a flawlessly forged copy of his typewriter. (O. J. Simpson's lawyers are mounting a "Stone" defense, arguing that the night of the murders the Los Angeles police instantly organized an elaborate conspiracy to frame Simpson, but bungled it.)

The KlehrHaynesFirsov volume is important, not because the U.S. Communist Party ever was politically important, but because of the relentless romanticizing of it. That romanticizing serves the vilification of American anticommunism as a symptom of a constant "paranoia." The American left's dislike of America is not news, but it still strongly colors the teaching of history, so discrediting the left is still important.

It has been said that a paranoiac can be right about many things but is wrong about everything. That is, paranoiacs can have real problems and enemies, but not for the reasons suggested by their weird view of how the world works.

Postwar anticommunism committed excesses and occasionally partook of paranoia. However, that did not vindicate the anticommunism of many intellectuals. The people who portrayed the American Communists darkly got it essentially right, although they rarely portrayed it darkly enough.

And the deepest paranoia was and is among those who continue to consider America paranoid because they cannot face the fact that the left was on the losing side of history, and deserved to be.

2.   CULLING HISTORY FROM PROPAGANDA. By: Richard Bernstein. *The New York Times, Sunday,* April 24, 1994 - - Few people probably remember the brief stir caused a few years ago when a historian named David Irving published a book, "Hitler's War," in which he made the extraordinary assertion that the Nazi extermination of the Jews was carried out without the Fuhrer's knowledge. Mr. Irving, as Mark Kramer, a foreign policy specialist at Brown University has argued, was able to make this claim because Hitler used code words to refer to the destruction of Europe's Jews, and he never committed to writing orders to implement the Final Solution. In the absence of proof that he did know, Mr. Irving concluded that he did not.

Mr. Irving's Hitler thesis served as a reminder that even the most tendentious historical views can gain credibility in part because the sources of history can be interpreted in different ways or sensationalized or falsified or used dishonestly or ignored. And too, the frustrating and difficult search for the truth remains just that; frustrating and difficult. This is especially true when it comes to plumbing the shadowy depths of the cold war.

There is probably no better comfort that can be offered for what must be a disappointment to those who hoped that the collapse of the Soviet Union would pave the way to irrefutable resolution of the many remaining mysteries and controversies. When the empire dissolved, some parts of the largest and previously most impenetrable archives in the world were suddenly opened to researchers. And voices that had long been silent began to speak.

To be sure, some important information has resulted. The truth is, however, that some of the headline making revelations by former Soviet officials, memoirists and researchers have at best added to the continuing debate, or, in some cases, made the record even murkier and more confusing than it was before.

Last week, for example, *Time Magazine* published excerpts of a new book, *"Special Tasks: The Memoirs of an Unwanted Witness A Soviet Spymaster"* (Little, Brown), by Pavel Sudoplatov, who during the early years of World War II was the Soviet deputy director of foreign intelligence and, from 1944 to 1946, the head of atomic intelligence. Judging from his titles, he was in a position to know the Soviet Union's secrets, which is why his most sensational disclosures attracted lots of attention.

Most sensational of all, Mr. Sudoplatov says that several of the most important scientists in the Manhattan Project, the wartime program to build an atomic bomb, intentionally passed information to the Soviet Union, or knowingly allowed secrets to be passed on.

The men named by Mr. Sudoplatov include J. Robert Oppenheimer, the head of the Los Alamos laboratory where the bomb was made, as well as the Danish physicist Neils Bohr, Enrico Fermi, the brilliant Italian who supervised the creation of the world's first chain reaction, and Leo Szilard, the erratic Hungarian genius who first thought a chain reaction was possible.

The reaction of historians and researchers to Mr. Sudoplatov's claims demonstrated that the opening of the Soviet Union, rather than clearing up cold war mysteries, has often served to deepen them, to make for more argument rather than less.

"Sudoplatov makes these charges that people spied, but he produces minimal evidence," said David J. Holloway, a Stanford political scientist whose book *"Stalin and the Bomb"* will be published this year by Yale University Press.

3.   FRATERNITY HONORS HISS FOR "OUTSTANDING" PUBLIC SERVICE. By: Peter Hermann, *The Baltimore Sun*, Sunday, August 14, 1994 - - Not many people are still alive who remember Alger Hiss as a brilliant lawyer voted

the most popular man in his graduating class at Johns Hopkins University in 1926.

Most have heard of Mr. Hiss as a suspected spy who was imprisoned for perjury after he was accused of being a Communist in a case that polarized Baltimore in 1948 and helped Richard M. Nixon who served on the House UnAmerican Activities Committee rise to political prominence.

Last night at Hopkins, the Alpha Delta Phi Fraternity honored Mr. Hiss, 89, at its 62nd international convention with its annual Samuel Eells distinguished public service award. "I am not here tonight to debate the issue surrounding Alger Hiss's trials or whether or not he was a Communist spy," Mark E. Larson, the awards chairman, told the 300 guests. "His accomplishments as a young man through 1945 are nothing short of outstanding."

Mr. Hiss, who has suffered three strokes and is bedridden in New York, could not attend the ceremony. But the Baltimore native sent a handwritten two-page letter that was read at the banquet.

"As the oldest alumnus of the host chapter I send my warm greetings to the gathering of my fellow Alpha Delts," he wrote. "My years as an active member of the fraternity are among my happiest memories."

Ed Donahue, the alumni adviser to the undergraduate fraternity chapter at Hopkins and past national president who lives in Annapolis, said the national board decided to give Mr. Hiss the award "not to stir up old controversies, but to honor him for the things he did that have never been disputed."

It is another colorful episode in the storied history of the fraternity, which started at Hopkins in 1889 and boasts among its alumni former Supreme Court Justice Oliver Wendell Holmes, John D. Rockefeller, former President Franklin D. Roosevelt and author Robert Ludlum. The raucous movie, "Animal House" was based on the Alpha Delta Phi chapter at Dartmouth in New Hampshire.

Mr. Hiss is the son of a welltodo dry goods merchant who committed suicide. He grew up on Linden Avenue in Bolton Hill, played in Druid Hill Park, worshiped at Memorial Episcopal Church and attended City College.

After graduating from Hopkins, he attended Harvard Law School, was a pupil of the future Supreme Court Justice Felix Frankfurter, served as law secretary to Justice Holmes and worked in the Agriculture Administration. He later became a distinguished State Department official who worked on the Yalta Conference and was secretary general of the United Nations Conference in San Francisco, where the charter of the new organization was drafted.

But in 1948, Whittaker Chambers, a Communist secret agent and spy, accused Mr. Hiss of passing him secret documents in the late 1930s for delivery to the Soviet Union. Years of congressional committee hearings and two trials ended in his perjury conviction in 1950. He served 3 and 1/2 years in prison.

Mr. Hiss has proclaimed his innocence for 46 years. In 1992, he released a videotaped interview with Gen. Dmitri A. Volgokonov, a respected Soviet historian who said a search of Soviet intelligence archives showed Mr. Hiss was no spy.

He still has his supporters today. Edward M. Passano of Baltimore, who has known Alger Hiss for 70 years and went to Hopkins with him, has defended him for decades. "I'm sure there are some old (people) around Hopkins who think he's a crook," said Mr. Passano, who himself was honored for his contributions to libraries. "There will be some who resent it and others who think 'It's about time he gets the award.'"

TEXTS OF ARTICLES APPEARING DURING 1997:

1. THE BENIGN VIEW OF AMERICAN REDS - FLAT OUT LIES. By: John E. Haynes.

The Baltimore Sun, March 2, 1997. (Book Review) - - Truth: The record proves Hiss, the Rosenbergs, Harry Dexter White, Larry Duggan et al. were active Soviet espionage agents.

Reading Sam Tanenhaus' *"Whittaker Chambers: A Biography"* (Random House, 610 pages, and $35.00) left me with questions: How long can the American intelligentsia maintain a lie? How long before our academics and intellectuals begin to accept the truth about American communism and anticommunism in the 1930s, 1940s, and 1950s?

Throughout the more than 40 years of the Cold War a public consensus supported a foreign policy opposing the expansion of Communist rule, while within American academic and intellectual circles a dramatic shift in attitude occurred.

Since the late 1960s the dominant academic view has been that anticommunism met the one-time-legal definition of obscenity: something utterly without redeeming social value.

Similarly, in the wider circles of opinion leaders, elite magazines and the higher media, a view developed that in the era 1945 to 1960 "the statute books groaned under several seasons of legislation designed to outlaw dissent." There "stalking their prey across the land, two-by-two, prowled the FBI, J. Edgar Hoover's G-men, hunters of radicalism" in a land that was "sweat-drenched in fear" of its own paranoid fantasies, to quote from one of the most influential books of this view, David Caute's *"The Great Fear: The Anti-Communist Purge under Truman and Eisenhower,"* (Simon & Schuster, 1978).

This sinister portrait of America in the 1940s and 1950s rests on a series of widely accepted facts of what happened in that time: an idealistic New Dealer (Alger Hiss) thrown into prison on the perjured testimony of a sick anti-Communist fanatic (Whittaker Chambers); innocent progressives (the Rosenbergs) railroaded into the gas chamber on trumped-up charges of espionage; and dozens of blameless civil servants having their careers smashed by the smears of a "professional anti-Communist" (Elizabeth Bentley) with one (Harry Dexter White) killed by a heart attack brought on by Bentley's lies and another (Laurence Duggan, a senior diplomat) driven to suicide by more of Chambers' malignant falsehoods.

To these individual injustices it is asserted that the witch hunters added unjustified legal harassment and suspicion of American Communists based on false beliefs that the Soviet Union secretly funded the American Communist Party and controlled its leadership.

The reigning intellectual consensus further holds that the idea that the American Communist Party had any significant link with Soviet espionage was false. To quote Caute again, he drove home the message that concern about Communist spying was a paranoid fantasy by placing in emphasized type the unequivocal statement "there is no documentation in the public record of a direct connection between the American Communist Party and espionage during the entire postwar period."

In one variation or another, these premises of the nature of the "McCarthy" era remain embedded in contemporary history texts, are taught in classrooms, and treated as fact in films and television documentaries. Without exception, each one is false. And false not merely as a difference of judgment about murky and confused events, but flat-out unambiguously, documentedly false.

Since 1991, many Soviet-bloc archives as well as long-classified American records have been opened for research, releasing a stream of long-hidden documents. Encrypted cables between KGB officers in the United States and Moscow confirm the participation in Soviet espionage of Hiss, the Rosenbergs, White, Duggan, and scores of American Communists. The KGB cables offer nearly as complete a vindication of Elizabeth Bentley's charges as one could ever expect to see.

These records also show the American Communist Party was an auxiliary to Soviet espionage, recruiting concealed members inside the government for spying, furnishing safe houses, providing couriers for conveying orders to Soviet sources and transporting stolen documents, and running background investigations on targets of KGB interest.

The records of the Communist International in Moscow show that Soviet funding of the CPUSA was extraordinarily heavy, stretching over 69 years from payments in 1919 of more than $1 million to a 1988 payment of $3 million delivered in cash by a KGB agent to the head of the American Communist Party.

CONFIRMING GUILT.

Despite the strong desire of many in the academic world to see their nightmarish view of America confirmed by vindicating Alger Hiss and Julius Rosenberg, the only comprehensive studies that have appeared have actually confirmed their guilt. With the publication of *"Whittaker Chambers"* there are now two thorough scholarly books on the Hiss-Chambers case. Tanenhaus' massive biography joins Allen Weinstein's earlier *"Perjury: The Hiss-Chambers Case"* (Alfred A. Knopf, 1978).

Both books review the evidence in detail and conclude that Hiss was guilty and confirm Chambers' story of Soviet espionage and a communist underground. Similarly, the only comprehensive scholarly book on the Rosenberg case is Ronald Radosh and Joyce Milton's *"The Rosenberg File: A Search for Truth"* (Holt, Rinehart and Winston, 1983). This book unambiguously concluded that the Rosenbergs were spies.

While *"The Rosenberg File"* and *"Perjury"* have often been attacked, the assaults are notable more for their viciousness than for their intellectual seriousness. Both books have been subjected to sniping in academic publications, and many textbooks are written as if they did not exist. Where are the challengers, the alternatives, historical narratives that make sense of the totality of the evidence? There are none.

Any full-scale book on the Rosenberg or Hiss case that would find either innocent would be received with vast applause in the academic world, thunderous celebration in the elite media, and be a sure bet for a Pulitzer Prize. The number of scholars who have considered undertaking such a project is surely in the hundreds. Yet despite the incentives, such books have not appeared and are not even on the horizon.

Scholars who have contemplated writing the intellectual alternative *to "Perjury"* and *"The Rosenberg File"* finding Hiss and Rosenberg innocent have taken a look at the evidence and turned away. In similar fashion, too many scholars are averting their eyes from the new evidence from Moscow's archives and KGB files.

CRAFTED LANGUAGE.

Others seek to save the view of the 1940s and 1950s as a "nightmare in red" by resorting to agnosticism and evasive phrases. Recent texts often use language that implies the innocence of Hiss and the Rosenbergs without actually saying so and accepting responsibility for such a view.

Take, for example, the *"National Standards for United States History"* (National Center for History in the Schools, 1994) which has received the backing of the leaders of the historical profession and is being promoted as a guide for history teachers. The *"National Standards for United States History"* forthrightly and repeatedly condemns McCarthyism as an unmitigated evil. No equivocation there. Nor should there be; McCarthy did have an overwhelmingly negative impact on public life. But on the Hiss-Chambers case and the Rosenberg case, the two dominant public controversies of the anti-Communist era? The cases are described with language crafted not to imply guilt while not being so foolhardy as to actually assert innocence.

And of the active participation of the American Communist Party in Soviet espionage? Silence.

Of the dozens of concealed Communists in the State Department, Treasury Department, War Department, the Office of Strategic Services, and other agencies who spied for the Soviets? Silence. Of Soviet funding and control of the American Communist Party? Silence.

These silences about key facts of the postwar era demonstrate an unwillingness to face the truth. Historical scholarship, however, is only of value if it is a search for the truth. Anything else is a fraud.

NOTE: John E. Haynes is 20th century political historian at the U.S. Library of Congress. His fifth book, *"Red Scare or Red Menace? American Communism and Anti-Communism in the Cold War Era"* was published by Ivan Dee. His next book, written with two other authors, will be published by Yale University Press.

Bibliography:

Barron, John, *KGB - The Secret World of Soviet Secret Agents*. New York: Reader's Digest Press, 1974.

Buckley, William F., *The Committee and Its Critics*. New York: G.P. Putnam's Sons, 1962.

Chambers, Whittaker, *Witness*. New York: Random House, 1952.

Cook, Fred J., *The Unfinished Story of Alger Hiss*. New York: William Morrow Company, 1958.

Crossman, Richard, Editor, *The God That Failed*. New York, N.Y.: Bantam Books, Inc., 1952. Crowley, Monica, *Nixon, Off The Record*. Random House, New York City, N.Y., 1996.

Hiss, Alger, *Recollections of a Life*. New York: Seaver Books, H. Holt, 1988.

Hoover, J. Edgar, *Masters of Deceit*. New York: Henry Holt & Company, 1958.

Katcher, Leo, *Earl Warren; A political biography*. New York: McGraw-Hill Book Company, 1967.

Klehr, Haynes, Firsov, *The Secret World of American Communism*. Yale University Press, 1995.

Kreeft, Peter, *A Refutation of Moral Relativism*. San Francisco, CA: Ignatius Press, 1999.

McCallum, Dennis, *The Death of Truth*. Minneapolis, MN: Bethany House Publishers, 1996.

Romerstein, Herbert & Breindel, Eric, *The Venona Secrets: Exposing Soviet Espionage and America's Traitors*. Washington, DC: Regnery Publishing, Inc.

Sheen, Fulton J., *The Church, Communism and Democracy*. New York, N.Y., Dell Publishing Co.   Inc. 1964.

Schwarz, Dr. Fred, *You Can Trust The Communists To Be Communists:* Englewood Cliffs, N.J., Prentice-Hall, Inc. 1960.

Tanenhaus, Sam, *Whittaker Chambers: A Biography*. New York, 1997.

Vitz, Paul C., *Faith of the Fatherless: A Psychology of Atheism*. Dallas, TX: Spence Publishing Company, 1999.

Weinstein, Allen, *Perjury; The Hiss-Chambers Case*. New York, Alfred A. Knopf, 1978.

Transcript, Hearings on H. R. 4422 and H. R. 4581, Proposed legislation to curb and control the Communist Party of the United States, February 5, 6, 9-11,

19, 20. 1948 - 80th Congress, Second Session. Includes hearings pursuant to those of 1947 on H.R. 1884 and H.R. 2122 with testimony from John Foster Dulles and Hon. Karl E. Mundt.

Transcript, Hearings Regarding Communist Espionage in the United States Government, July 31; August 3-5, 7, 9-13, 16-18, 20, 24-27, 30; September 8, 9, 1948 - 80th Congress, Second Session. Includes testimony by Whittaker Chambers, Alger Hiss, Elizabeth Bentley and others regarding the influence of Josef Peters in the CPUS. Peters was thought to have been Chambers's main controller in the communist underground. This session also included testimony about the activities of Alger Hiss; also testimony from Victor Perlo, who worked for a while as chief of the Aviation Section of the War Production Board, Solomon Adler, Lee Pressman, who was the Assistant General Counsel for the Agricultural Adjustment Administration (AAA), and Lauchlin Currie, regarding the extent of communist infiltration within the federal government.

Transcript, Hearings Regarding Communist Espionage, November 8, December 2, 1949; February 27, March 1, 1950; Includes testimony from Max Bedacht, who had belonged to the CPUS from its earliest days, concerning his experiences as a party member, and by William Gregory Burton, John Loomis Sherman, and Maxim Lieber